Nashville - Books 1 - 5

Nashville - Books 1 - 5

INGLATH COOPER

Contents

Dedication

For all the songwriters whose songs have provided the soundtrack to my life.

Copyright

Book One - Ready to Reach

THE NASHVILLE SERIES
BOOK ONE

ready *to* reach

RITA® AWARD WINNING AUTHOR

INGLATH COOPER

*

Nashville – Book One – Ready to Reach

Inglath Cooper

*

Ever thought a dream might pass you by?

Nineteen-year old CeCe Mackenzie is determined to make her dreams come true. She heads for Nashville with not much more to her name than a guitar, a Walker Hound named Hank Junior and an old car she'd inherited from her grandma called Gertrude. But when Gertrude ends up on the side of I-40 in flames, Nashville has never seemed farther away. Help arrives in the form of two Georgia football players headed for the Nashville dream as well. When Holden Ashford and Thomas Franklin stop to offer CeCe and Hank Junior a ride, fate may just give a nod to serendipity and meant to be. Because while CeCe is chasing after her dream, she might find love as well.

CeCe

I've been praying since before I can ever actually remember learning how. Mama says I took to praying like baby ducks to their first dip in a pond, my "please" and "thank you" delivered in a voice so sweet that she didn't see how God would ever be able to say no to me.

Mama says my praying voice is my singing voice, and that anybody listening would know right off that the Father himself gave that voice to me. Two human beings, especially not her and one so flawed as the man who was supposedly my Daddy, would ever be able to create anything that reminiscent of Heaven.

I'm praying now. Hard as I ever have. "Dear Lord, please let this old rattletrap, I mean, faithful car Gertrude, last another hundred miles. Please don't let her break down before I get there. Please, dear Lord. Please."

A now familiar melody strings the plea together. I've been offering up the prayer for the past several hours at fifteen-minute intervals, and I'm hoping God's not tired of my interruptions. I've got no doubt He has way more important things on His plate today. I wonder now if I was a fool not to take the bus and leave the car behind altogether. It had been a sentimental decision, based on Granny's hope that her beloved Gertrude would help get me where I wanted to go in this life.

And leaving it behind would have been like leaving behind Hank Junior. I reach across the wide bench seat and rub his velvety-soft Walker Hound ear. Even above the rattle-wheeze-cough of the old car's engine, Hank Junior snores the baritone snore of his deepest sleep. He's wound up in a tight ball, his long legs tucked under him, his head curled back onto his shoulder. He reminds me of a duck in this position, and I can't for the life of me understand how it could be comfortable. I guess it must be, though, since with the exception of pee and water breaks, it's been his posture of choice since we left Virginia this morning.

Outside of Knoxville, I-40 begins to dip and rise, until the stretch of road is one long climb after the other. I cut into the right hand lane, tractor-trailer trucks and an annoyed BMW whipping by me. Gertrude sounds like she may be gasping her last breath, and I actually feel sorry for her. The most Granny ever asked of her was a Saturday trip to Winn-Dixie and the post office and church on Sundays. I guess that was why she'd lasted so long.

Granny bought Gertrude, brand-spanking new, right off the lot, in 1960. She named her after an aunt of hers who lived to be a hundred and five. Granny thought there was no reason to expect anything less from her car if she changed the oil regularly and parked her in the woodshed next to her house to keep the elements from taking their toll on the blue-green exterior. It turned out Granny was right. It wasn't until she died last year and left Gertrude to me that the car started showing her age.

What with me driving all over the state of Virginia in the past year, one dive gig to another, weekend after weekend, I guess I've pretty much erased any benefits of Granny's pampering.

We top the steep grade at thirty-five. I let loose a sigh of relief along with a heartfelt prayer of thanks. The speedometer hits fifty-five, then sixty and seventy as we cruise down the long stretch of respite, and I see the highway open out nearly flat for as far ahead as I can see. Hank Junior is awake now, sitting up with his nose stuck out the lowered window on his side. He's pulling in the smells, dissecting them one by one, his eyes narrowed against the wind, his long black ears flapping behind him.

We're almost to Cookeville, and I'm feeling optimistic now about the last eighty miles or so into Nashville. I stick my arm out the window and let it fly with the same abandon as Hank Junior's ears, humming a melody I've been working on the past couple days.

A sudden roar in the front of the car is followed by an awful grinding sound. Gertrude jerks once, and then goes completely limp and silent. Hank Junior pulls his head in and looks at me with nearly comical canine alarm.

"Crap!" I yell. I hit the brake and wrestle the huge steering wheel to the side of the highway. My heart pounds like a bass drum, and I'm shaking when we finally roll to a stop. A burning smell hits my nose. I see black smoke start to seep from the cracks at the edge of the hood. It takes me a second or two to realize that Gertrude is on fire.

I grab Hank Junior's leash, snapping it on his collar before reaching over to shove open his door and scoot us both out. The flames are licking higher now, the smoke pitch black. "My guitar!" I scream. "Oh, no, my guitar!"

I grab the back door handle and yank hard. It's locked. Tugging Hank Junior behind me, I run around and try the other door. It opens, and I reach in for my guitar case and the notebook of lyrics sitting on top of it. Holding onto them both, I towboat Hank Junior around the car, intent on finding a place to hook his leash so I can get my suitcase out of the trunk.

Just then I hear another sputtering noise, like the sound of fuel igniting. I don't stop to think. I run as fast as I can away from the car, Hank Junior glued to my side, my guitar case and notebook clutched in my other hand.

I hear the car explode even as I'm still running flat out. I feel the heat on the backs of my arms. Hank Junior yelps, and we run faster. I trip and roll on the rough surface pavement, my guitar case skittering ahead of me, Hank Junior's leash getting tangled between my legs.

I lie there for a moment, staring up at the blue Tennessee sky, trying to decide if I'm okay. In the next instant, I realize the flouncy cotton skirt Mama made me as a going away present is strangling my waist, and Hank Junior's head is splayed across my belly, his leash wrapped tight around my left leg.

Brakes screech and tires squall near what sounds inches from my head. I rock forward, trying to get up, but Hank yips at the pinch of his collar.

"Are you all right?"

The voice is male and deep, Southern like mine with a little more drawl. I can't see his face, locked up with Hank Junior as I am. Footsteps, running, and then a pair of enormous cowboy boots comes into my vision.

"Shit-fire, girl! Is that your car?"

"Was my car," I say to the voice.

"Okay, then." He's standing over me now, a mountain of a guy wearing jeans, a t-shirt that blares Hit Me – I Can Take It and a Georgia Bulldogs cap. "Here, let me help you," he says.

He hunkers down beside me and starts to untangle Hank Junior's leash. Hank would usually do me the service of a bark if a stranger approached me, but not this time. He wags his tail in gratitude as the big guy unhooks the snap from his collar, tugs it free from under my leg and then re-hooks it.

Realizing my skirt is still snagged around my waist, my pink bikini underwear in full view, I sit up and yank it down, nothing remotely resembling dignity in my urgency.

"What's going on, man?"

I glance over my shoulder and see another guy walking toward us, this one not nearly so big, but sounding grouchy and looking sleep-deprived. He's also wearing cowboy boots and a Georgia Bulldogs cap, the bill pulled low over dark sunglasses. His brown hair is on the long side, curling out from under the hat.

He glances at the burning car, as if he's just now getting around to noticing it and utters, "Whoa."

Mountain Guy has me by the arm now and hauls me to my feet. "You okay?"

I swipe a hand across my skirt, dust poofing out. "I think so. Yes. Thank you."

Hank Junior looks at the second guy and mutters a low growl. I've never once doubted his judgment so I back up a step.

"Aw, he's all right," Mountain Guy says to Hank Junior, patting him on the head. "He always wakes up looking mean like that."

Grouchy Guy throws him a look. "What are we doing?"

"What does it look like we're doing?" Mountain Guy says. "Helping a damsel in distress."

"I'm not a damsel," I say, my feathers ruffling even as I realize I could hardly be in much more distress than I am currently in.

Gertrude is now fully engulfed in flames, from her pointed front end to her rounded trunk. Cars are keeping to the far left lane. Surprisingly, no one else has bothered to stop, although I can see people grabbing their cell phones as they pass, a couple to take pictures, others more likely dialing 911.

"So what exactly happened?" Mountain Guy asks me.

"I just heard this loud noise and then smoke started coming out of the hood."

"Good thing you got her pulled over fast," he says.

"I didn't know they let vehicles that old on the road," Grouchy Guy says.

"She belonged to my Granny," I fire back in instant outrage, as if everything that has just happened is all his fault.

Grouchy Guy starts to say something, presses his lips together, maybe thinking better of it.

"Don't pay him no mind," Mountain Guy advises. "You live near here?"

I laugh then, the sound popping up out of me under the sudden realization that with the exception of my dog, my guitar and my lyrics notebook, I now have no other earthly possessions to call my own. Even my purse has been incinerated inside Gertrude's melted interior.

The shrill whine of a fire engine echoes from down the Interstate, and a couple of seconds later it comes roaring into sight, lights flashing. It rolls to a heavy stop just behind Gertrude, brakes squealing. Men dressed in heavy tan uniforms grab hoses and run at the burning car.

The water gushes out with impressive force. The blazing fire is a joke against the onslaught, and in less than a minute, the flames slink into nothingness. The only thing left is the charred framework of Gertrude's once sleek exterior.

As soon as the water hoses cut off, I start to cry, as if some sort of transference has turned on the flow inside of me. I cry because I've ruined Granny's car, her most prized possession. I cry because I now have no money, no means of getting any closer to my dream than my own two feet will carry me. And I cry because everybody back home was exactly right. I was born with dreams way too big for somebody like me to ever make come true.

"Hey, now." Mountain Guy pats me on the shoulder the same way he had patted Hank Junior on the head a few minutes before. "Everything's gonna be all right."

One of the firemen walks up to us. "This y'all's car?"

Grouchy Guy points at me. "It was hers."

"Sorry for your loss, ma'am," the fireman says. "Guess you'll be needing to call a tow truck."

Even Mountain Guy can't help laughing at this, and maybe if you were removed from the situation, it would be pretty funny. Me? I'm anything but removed, and I'm suddenly thankful for Mama's faithful Triple A membership and the insurance she's paid up for me through the end of the year.

"You can tell them the car is just short of Mile Marker 320."

"Thank you," I say. "And thank you for putting out the–"

"No problem, ma'am," he says quickly, as if realizing I can't bring myself to finish.

I glance at Mountain Guy. "Do you have a cell I could borrow?"

"Sure thing." He pulls an iPhone from his shirt pocket and hands it to me.

"You mind if I get the number for Triple A?"

"'Course not."

Hank Junior's leash wrapped around my wrist, I walk a few steps away and tap 411. A bored-sounding operator gives me the 800 number and then connects me free of charge. The woman who takes my "case" doesn't sound the least bit surprised that my car has burned to smithereens or that I need a tow truck to come and get us both. I wonder if she gets calls like this every day.

In between her questions, I can hear Mountain Guy and Grouchy Guy in a low rumble of discussion that sounds like it has disagreement at its edges. I know they're talking about me, and while I want to swing around and scream at them both that I don't need their help, I know the last thing I can afford to do is look a gift horse in the mouth.

The lady from Triple A tells me that Ray's Towing from Cookeville will be coming out to get the car. She asks if I will also need a ride. I tell her both my dog and I will.

I return the phone to Mountain Guy.

"Get it all squared away?" he asks.

"I think so," I say, not even sure in this context what that could possibly mean.

"How long before they get here?"

"Hour."

"Well, you can't wait by yourself. It'll be dark by then," Mountain Guy says.

"I'll be fine," I say. "But thanks for stopping. And for letting me use your phone."

"Not a problem," he says, glancing over at Grouchy Guy who is still wearing his sunglasses and has his arms folded across his chest in a stance of non-compliance.

I pick up my guitar case and give Hank Junior a little tug before backing away from them. "Thanks again," I say and head for my charred car.

I'm halfway there when Mountain Guy calls out, "You going to Nashville?"

"What gave it away?" Grouchy Guy throws out, his voice heavy with sarcasm.

I pin him with a look, then turn my gaze to his friend. "Yeah. I am."

"Well, so are we," Mountain Guy says. "No point in you staying here when we're going to the same place, now is there?"

Relief, unwelcome though it is, floods through me. I am feeling kind of sick at the thought of waiting with the car while dark sets in. Maybe I've watched too many episodes of *Disappeared*. My imagination has already started heading off in directions I'd just as soon it didn't.

But then, on the other hand, I don't know squat about the two I'm getting ready to ride off with. They could be serial murderers thinking it was their lucky day that my car caught on fire, and they happened by.

Hank Junior seems to think they're all right though. He's no longer low-growling at Grouchy Guy. And besides, what choice do I really have? I have no money, no credit card, no clothes.

Panic starts to clutch at me, and all of a sudden, I hear my Granny's voice telling me, as she had so many times when I was growing up, that we take this life one moment, one day at a time. I'm not going to look any farther ahead than that because if I do, I think I might just dissolve into a puddle of failure right here on the side of I-40.

"Let's get this show on the road," Mountain Guy says, taking my guitar case from me and placing it in the bed of the pickup.

Grouchy Guy looks at me. "He riding in the back?"

"You mean Hank Junior?" I ask.

"That his name?"

"It is."

"Yeah, Hank Junior."

"Not unless I am," I answer.

Grouchy Guy looks at Mountain Guy. "That's fine with me."

Mountain Guy laughs. "Man, you got up on the wrong side of the truck." Then to me, "He ain't always this nasty. Y'all hop on in."

Without looking at Grouchy Guy, I scoot Hank Junior up onto the floorboard, and climb in behind him, sliding to the middle. He hops onto my lap and curls up in a ball, as if he knows he needs to be as inconspicuous as possible.

It's a full truck with the four of us. My shoulders are pressed up against both guys, and I try to make myself smaller by hunching over.

Mountain Guy throws the truck in gear, checks the side mirror and guns onto the highway. "Reckon we oughta know your name," he says.

"CeCe," I answer. "CeCe MacKenzie."

"CeCe MacKenzie," he sings back with a country twang. "Got a nice little rhyme to it."

"What's yours?" I ask, aware that I will now have to quit calling him Mountain Guy.

"Thomas Franklin."

"You don't look like a Thomas," I say.

"I get that a lot."

"I'm sorry," I start to apologize.

"Hey, no problem. My folks wanted the world to take me seriously, so they never gave in on the Tom, Tommy thing."

"Oh. Makes sense."

"Attitude over there is Holden Ashford."

"Hey," Holden says without looking at me. He's still wearing the dark glasses, and I wonder if his eyes are as unfriendly as his voice.

"Hey," I reply, matching my tone to his.

"Where you from, CeCe?" Thomas asks, shooting a glance my way.

"Virginia."

"Georgia," he says, waving a hand at himself and then Holden.

"Let me guess," Holden says. "You wanna be a singer?"

"I am a singer," I shoot back.

I can't be sure because of the glasses, but I'd swear he rolled his eyes.

"What about the two of you? You headed to Nashville to be plumbers or something?"

Thomas laughs a deep laugh that fills up the truck. "Heck, no. I sing. He writes and plays guitar."

"That's why he takes himself so seriously." The words are out before I can think to stop them.

"Matter of fact, it is," Thomas says, another laugh rolling from his big chest.

"Up yours," Holden says without looking at either of us. I'm not sure if he's talking to Thomas or to me.

"What do you sing, CeCe?" Thomas asks.

"Country. What else is there?"

"Heck, yeah!" Thomas slaps the steering wheel. "Although with a dog named Hank Junior I reckon I could've assumed that."

At the sound of his name, Hank Junior raises his head, blinks at Thomas and then continues his snooze.

"What about you?" I ask. "Who're your favorites?"

"Chesney, Twitty, Haggard, Flatts. If it's got country on it, I sing it. Holden there says I have a sound of my own. I figure it's just what's managed to stick together from all my years of tryin' to sound as good as the greats."

The sun has dropped on the horizon, fading fast. The sky has a pinkish glow to it, and cars have started to flip on their headlights. A sign on the right says Cookeville – 5 miles.

Holden pulls a phone out of his pocket, taps the screen and says, "Starbucks off exit 288. I could use a coffee."

"I'll second that," Thomas agrees, and then looking at me, "We've got a gig tonight. Nine o'clock at the Bluebird."

"Seriously?" I say, not even bothering to hide my astonishment. I've been reading about the Bluebird for years and the country music stars who played there before they made it big, Garth Brooks and Taylor Swift among them.

"Yeah," Thomas says. "You oughta come. I mean unless you got other plans."

Not unless you count finding a place to stay on credit. "I'd like that."

"Cool."

Holden makes a sound that clearly conveys his disapproval.

Irked, I say, "You ever take off those glasses? It's getting dark outside."

He looks directly at me then, without removing them. "They bothering you?"

"Honestly, yes. I like to judge a person by what I see in their eyes."

"Some reason you need to be judging me?"

"I don't know. Is there?"

He lowers the glasses and gives me a long cool look. His eyes are blue, ridiculously blue, and his lashes are thick. I lean away from him like I've been struck by a jolt of electricity.

"He's just lovesick," Thomas says. "He's harmless. Well, mostly. Depending on who you ask."

"Shut up," Holden says.

Thomas chuckles. "Oh, the tangled webs we weave in our wake."

"Good thing you're not the writer," Holden mutters.

"I had a little alliteration thing going on there," Thomas sings back.

I have to admit his voice is wonderful. Smooth and rolling like I imagine a really nice wine might taste.

"That's about all you had going," Holden says.

We're off the interstate now, turning left at a stoplight before swinging into the Starbucks on our right. Thomas pulls the truck into a parking spot. "Potty break, anyone?"

"Okay if Hank Junior waits here?" I ask.

"Sure, it is," Thomas says and then to Hank Junior, "you ever tried their mini donuts? No? How about I bring you one? Plain? Plain, it is."

I watch this exchange with a stupid grin on my face and wonder if Thomas has any idea that the only thing anyone could ever do to make me like them instantly was be nice to my dog.

"I'll be right back, Hanky," I say, kissing the top of his head and sliding out of the truck on Thomas's side. I don't even dare look at Holden to get a read on his opinion of his friend's generosity. I'm pretty sure I know what it would be. And that's just gonna make me like him less.

Starbucks is crowded, tables and leather chairs occupied by every age range of person, their single common denominator the laptops propped up in front of them. The wonderful rich smell of coffee hits me in the nose, triggering a reminder that I haven't eaten anything since my last PBJ at eleven-thirty this morning. Right behind that comes the awareness that I have no money.

I head for the ladies' room, glad to find it empty. For once, the men's room has a line, and I don't relish the idea of standing in the hallway across from Grouchy Guy, exchanging glares.

A look in the bathroom mirror makes me wonder why those two bothered to give me a ride. My hair is a frizzy mess. What were wavy layers this morning have now conceded to chaotic turn screw curls that only need a BOIIING sound effect for maximum laugh value.

I pull an elastic band out of my skirt pocket and manage to tame the disaster into a ponytail. I splash water on my face, slurp some into my mouth and use my finger to pseudo brush my teeth. Looking up, I realize none of it has helped much but will just have to do for now.

I head to the front where Thomas and Holden are ordering. Line or not, they're fast.

"What do you want?" Thomas throws out. "I'll order yours."

"Oh, I'm good," I say, crossing my arms across my chest. "I'll just go let Hank Junior out."

Thomas points his remote at the parking lot and pushes a button. "That should unlock it. Sure you don't want anything?"

"I'm sure."

Outside, I open the truck door and hook up Hank Junior's leash. He bounds off the seat onto the asphalt, already looking for the nearest bush. I let him lead the way, across a grassy area to the spot of his choice. My stomach rumbles, and I tell myself this will be a good time to lose those five pounds I've been meaning to work on.

Hank Junior has just watered his third bush when I hear a shout, followed by the rev of an engine roaring off. Thomas and Holden are sprinting from Starbucks. At the truck door, Thomas looks around, spots me and waves frantically. "Come on!" he yells. "They just stole Holden's guitar!"

"They" are two guys on a motorcycle, now peeling out of the parking lot and hauling butt down the road. The guy on back has the guitar case wedged between them.

Hank Junior jumps in. I scramble up behind him. Thomas and Holden slam the doors, and Thomas burns rubber through the parking lot.

"You left the door standing wide open?" Holden shouts at me. He's not wearing his glasses now, and I have to say I wish I'd never asked him to take them off. His eyes are blazing with fury, and it's all directed at me.

"I was just a few yards away," I say. "I didn't think–"

"Something you're clearly not used to doing," he accuses between clenched teeth.

"Hey, now!" Thomas intervenes. "Y'all shut up! I'm planning on catching the sons of bitches."

And he's not kidding. Thomas drives like he was raised on Nascar, gunning around and in front of car after car.

"What's in the case?" I ask. "Diamonds?"

"Might as well be to Holden," Thomas says. "His lyric notebook."

My stomach drops another floor if that's possible. "Your only copy?"

"For all intents and purposes," he says.

By now, I'm feeling downright sick. I can feel Hank Junior's worry in the rigid way he's holding himself on my lap. I rub his head and say a prayer that we'll live to laugh about this. Every nerve in my body is screaming for Thomas to slow down, but a glance at Holden's face is all I need to keep my mouth shut.

"There they are!" I yell, spotting them up ahead just before they zip in front of a tractor-trailer loaded with logs.

"Crazy mothers," Thomas shouts, whipping around a Volvo whose driver gives us the finger.

I never liked thrill rides. I was always the one on church youth group trips to sit out the roller coaster or any other such thing designed to bring screams ripping up from a person's insides. I'm feeling like I might be sick at any moment, but I press my lips together and stay quiet.

"They just took a right," Holden barks. He unbuckles his seat belt and sticks his head out the window, yelling into the wind. I can't understand what he's saying, although I'm pretty sure it involves profanity.

"Why don't we just pull over and call 911?" I suggest.

Thomas ducks his head to see around a produce truck loaded with bushel baskets of tomatoes and cabbage. "They won't catch them before we do."

I have to admit we're gaining on them. I can now see the way the guy holding the guitar case keeps throwing looks of panic over his shoulder. He's making scooting motions, too, like he can force the motorcycle to go faster in doing so.

I drop my head against the seat and close my eyes, forcing myself not to look for a few seconds. That only makes the lack of control worse, so I bolt upright and hold onto Hank Junior tight as I can.

We're two car lengths behind them now, and the motorcycle driver has taken his craziness to another level. He zips past a mini-van, laying the bike so low that the end of the guitar case looks like it might touch the pavement. I hear and feel Holden yank in a breath.

Thomas cuts around the van and lays on the horn. We're right on the motorcycle's tail now and, in the headlights, I see that both the driver and his buddy are terrified. The front of the truck is all but touching the license plate of the motorcycle, and I don't dare think what would happen if they slammed on their brakes.

"Slow down!" I scream, unable to stand another second. At that same moment, the guy holding the guitar case sends it flying out to the right of the bike.

It skitters on the asphalt, slips under the rail and disappears from sight.

"Stop!" Holden yells.

Thomas hits the brakes, swings onto the shoulder and then slams the truck into reverse. Suddenly, we're backing up so fast my head is spinning.

"Right here!" Holden shouts and before Thomas has even fully stopped the truck, he's jumping out the door and running.

"There's a flashlight in the glove compartment," Thomas says, leaning over me.

I'm too stunned to move, and so I sit perfectly still, willing my reeling head to accept that we've stopped. Hank Junior barks his approval, and I rub his back in agreement.

Thomas hauls out, flicking on the flashlight and calling for Holden. Within seconds, he's disappeared from sight, too. I tell myself I need to get out and help look, but a full minute passes before I can force my knees to stop knocking long enough to slide off the truck seat. I hold onto Hank Junior's leash as if my life depends on it and teeter over to the spot where I'd seen them hop over the guardrail.

The drop off is steep, and vines cover the ground. I can't see much except in the swipes when cars pass and lend me their headlights. I catch a glimpse of the light way down the hill. I hear Thomas's voice followed by Holden's.

"Are y'all okay?" I call out.

"We got it!" Thomas yells.

I'm so relieved I literally wilt onto the rail, and send up a prayer of thanks. Hank Junior and I wait while they climb up. Holden appears first, looking as battered as his case. Thomas is right behind him. As soon as they reach the top, they both drop down on the ground, breathing heavily.

"Man," Thomas says. "What I wouldn't give for the chance to beat their tails!"

They gulp air for several seconds before Holden fumbles with the latches on the case and pops it open. Thomas points his flashlight at the interior, and my heart drops.

"Well, that's not good," Thomas says, his big Georgia voice dropping the words like boulders.

Holden picks up the guitar. It hangs limp and useless, broken in three places. He holds it the way a little boy would hold a baseball glove that got chewed up by the lawn mower. His expression is all but grief-stricken.

"I'm sorry," I say. "I'm so sorry."

"It wasn't your fault," Thomas consoles.

"Then whose fault is it?" Holden snaps, his blue gaze lasering me with accusation.

"Those two butt-wipes who stole it," Thomas says tightly.

"None of this would have happened if you hadn't insisted on stopping to help her!"

"Man, what's wrong with you? Her car was on fire. Chivalry ain't that dead."

Holden hesitates, clearly wrestling with a different opinion. "We didn't have to give her a ride to Nashville."

"No, we didn't," Thomas agrees. "But that ain't who we are."

I stand and dust off my skirt. I walk to the truck, Hank Junior trailing behind me. I climb up on the back tire, reach for my guitar and return to where the two of them are still sitting. I pull out my own lyric notebook and the flash drive that contains the only two song demos I've been able to afford to have made. I stick that in my pocket, close the case and hand it to Holden.

"You take mine," I say. "I know it won't replace yours, but maybe it'll work temporarily. Y'all have been real nice to me. I'm not gonna ask any more of you. Thanks a lot for everything."

And with that, Hank Junior and I start walking.

I feel like I'm in the middle of a dream. The good part where you're aware of hoping you don't wake up. That it will go on and on forever.

I'm hugging Thomas as tight as I can because I don't trust myself to thank him with words. If I do, I'll break down and sob right here in front of all these people.

He hugs me hard and stands, his arm still around my waist. I dangle in mid-air for a moment, then slide down his big thigh until my feet hit the floor. He forces me to face the crowd, and I'm blown away by the admiration and appreciation on their faces.

I feel Holden's gaze on me and make myself look at him. I guess I'm expecting him to be mad at me for horning in on their show, but that's not what I see in his eyes. What's there is the same admiration the audience has offered up, and maybe that surprises me most of all.

Mike thanks everyone again for coming, and people start to stand up and push their seats back. Several weave their way up to the circle of chairs and begin talking with the performers. A couple of teenagers ask Mike for his autograph. Next, they laser in on Thomas and Holden, giggling and looking as if they might lose their nerve at any moment.

One of the girls has red hair that hangs to her waist. Her eyes are a vivid green, and she looks at Thomas with starstruck longing. "Would you sign this for me?" she asks, handing him a Bluebird napkin.

"Why, sure, I will." Thomas raises an eyebrow at Holden who shakes his head.

"You're gonna be famous one day, Thomas," the girl says. "I just know it."

Thomas grins. "If that means I get to sing for a living, I'd be all right with that."

The redhead's friend sticks out a napkin of her own. "We'll buy anything you release."

"You don't work for a record company, do you?" Holden throws out.

Both girls giggle. "We're fifteen."

"Shoot," Thomas says. "Just our luck."

They laugh again, and then the redhead looks at me, her voice suddenly shy. "Your singing's so pretty."

Something in the sincerity of the compliment touches me, makes instant tears well in my eyes. It's stupid, I know, but after the way this day has gone, it's nice to hear that I'm not totally crazy to think I might have a place here. "Thank you," I say. "Thank you so much."

"You're welcome," she says, ducking her head again.

The two girls bounce off, clutching their napkins to their chests like they'd just found winning lottery tickets.

A man walks up and introduces himself. "I'm Clay Morrison. Y'all sounded real good tonight."

He has dark hair that's started to pepper a bit at the sides. He's dressed in jeans and a white shirt under a black jacket. His shoes are black, too, and they look expensive. Narrow frame glasses tone down his good looks and suggest he's smart.

I step out of the circle so his focus is on Thomas and Holden.

"Thank you," Thomas says. "Appreciate that."

"Saw you two here a few months ago. Have to say I like your new addition. The three of you sound pretty great together."

He swings a look at me then, and I want to sink into the floor. The last thing I want to do is barge in on their action. And it feels like that's what I'm doing. "Excuse me," I say and head for the ladies' room.

I lock myself inside, leaning against the door and pulling in a deep, shaky breath. I can still feel Holden's gaze on me, resentful, accusing.

I wash my face and dry it with a scratchy brown paper towel, taking my time with the process until I think Thomas and Holden might be ready to leave.

When I come out again, they're both waiting by the front door.

"You fall in?" Holden asks, looking me up and down.

I roll my eyes at him, pushing out into the cool of the Nashville evening.

We walk to the truck in an awkward silence, like neither of us knows what to say about what happened in there tonight.

Thomas hits the remote, and I open the door. Hank Junior leaps out and heads for the closest bush. I grab his leash and follow him.

When we return, it's clear Thomas and Holden have been talking. There's electricity in the air, the kind that sparks from disagreement.

Neither one looks at me, and I'm thinking it's time I go my own way. "Hey, thanks for everything, y'all. The help, the ride, the song. I expect to see your names in big places."

Hank Junior wants to jump in, but I stop him. "Come on, boy," I say, then turn around and start walking.

I have no earthly idea where I'm going. I just know I need to get away from those two before I bawl like a three-year old. I'm walking so fast that Hank Junior has to trot to keep up with me. He keeps looking back at the truck and then up at me as if he's wondering what in the world I'm doing. I wouldn't know how to begin to answer him. I don't have a thing to my name except for him. Should I find a pay phone, call Mama right now and ask her to buy me a bus ticket home? Could I even take Hank Junior with me on a bus?

I cross the main road in front of the Bluebird. There's a parking garage there. Maybe we can camp out for the night and see how things look in the morning, although short of me finding a winning lottery ticket in my pocket, I don't know how it could look any better.

The garage is nearly empty, a few cars parked along the other side that opens through to a Whole Foods. My stomach does a low rumble, and I know Hank Junior has to be hungry as well.

I head for a corner and lean against the wall, sliding down onto the cold concrete. Hank Junior looks at me as if he isn't sure what he's supposed to do. I pat the spot next to me, and loyal friend that he is, he curls up with me, his head on my knee.

That's when the tears start up for real. They gush from me like a geyser, and I just let them pour out, helpless to stop them even if I wanted to.

Hank Junior anxiously licks them from my cheek, and I rub his side, his sweetness making me drop my head to my knees and cry harder.

I guess it's my own sobbing that keeps me from hearing the truck until it stops right in front of us.

"This your plan?"

I jerk my head up to see Holden looking down at me with resignation on his face, like he's finally given in to the idea that they are stuck with me.

"For this minute, it is," I shoot back.

"Sleeping in a parking garage?"

"Does it look like I'm sleeping?"

"It looks like you're crying."

"Since when is that illegal?"

"Get in the truck, CeCe."

"No," I say. "I'll be fine."

"Oh, you've been doing a great job of proving that," he throws out.

"I didn't ask you to rescue me!"

"And I sure as heck didn't volunteer for the job," he says, opening the door and swinging out.

I pop to my feet, the concrete scratching at my back through my thin cotton shirt.

"Are you coming with us or not?"

"I don't need your charity, Holden!"

He leans in like a football player aiming a tackle and hefts me over his shoulder. I start kicking and wriggling, but he tightens his hold like I'm a sack of grain. Hank Junior stands there looking up at us, wagging his tail.

I'd like to think Holden is being chivalrous or some such thing. The truth is he's mad and altogether tired of me messing up his plans.

"When you two get finished with the foreplay, hop on in, and we'll go get some sleep," Thomas tosses out the open door.

Holden walks to the truck with me still slung over his shoulder. "Get in, boy," he says to Hank Junior who hops in like he's in the middle of a raging ocean, and Holden just threw him a buoy.

Holden tilts forward and drops me in beside Hank Junior. Fury has me sputtering some not so ladylike protests. My skirt is up around my waist for the second time today, and I kick and struggle to sit up and pull it down.

Thomas laughs and shakes his head. "You two are right entertaining."

Clearly, neither of us finds his assessment amusing.

Holden climbs in and slams the door. "Can we go now?"

Thomas peels out of the parking garage and turns right, gunning it. "I'm starving," he says. "Next stop, food."

He swings into a McDonald's, pulling up at the drive-through lane. At the window, he places his order, two big Macs, two fries, a large Coke, then looks at me and says, "What do you want?"

"I'm fine, thanks," I say.

Holden rolls his eyes. "Would you quit pretending like you have any other choice but to accept our help right now?"

"Seriously, CeCe," Thomas says.

The pride trying to raise a flag inside me wilts. "Unsweetened iced tea. Mushroom and Swiss burger, please. With no meat."

"No meat?" Thomas repeats, as if I'd just made the request in Mandarin.

"You mean like a cheese sandwich?" Holden says.

"Just no meat," I answer.

Both guys look at each other and shake their heads. Thomas calls out Holden's order, which is a duplicate of his own, adding, "We'll take two plain burgers and a water, too."

He pats Hank Junior on the head, and then to me, "I'm assuming our buddy here is not a vegetarian?"

"No," I say. "And thank you."

"You're entirely welcome," Thomas says, pulling forward.

We get the food and tear into the bags as if none of us has eaten in days. I open up Hank Junior's, force him to wait a few moments until it cools, then take pity on his drooling and let him have it.

Thomas drives while he eats, and it isn't until my stomach is full that I think to ask, "Where are we going?"

"We've got an apartment over by Vanderbilt," Holden says. "Don't have any furniture yet, but at least we have a floor to sleep on."

I don't even bother to object. A place to sleep right now sounds so good I melt at the thought of it, fatigue pulling at every bone, every muscle.

Thomas parks the truck on the street, and they grab their suitcases from the back. Holden hands me my guitar case, before reaching for his own. I follow them up the walk, stopping in a grassy spot to let Hank Junior do his business. They wait for us at the main door, before we climb a set of stairs to the third floor.

Holden pulls out a key and opens up the apartment, flicking on a light. The living room and kitchen aren't huge, but the place is neat and clean, the walls a newly painted beige.

"We've got two bedrooms. Holden and I will bunk up," Thomas says. "You and Hank Junior take the other one."

"I'll be happy to sleep out here," I say.

"We're good." Holden's words are short and abrupt. He heads down the hallway and disappears inside one of the rooms.

I look at Thomas and say, "I don't know how to thank you."

"You don't need to," Thomas says. "Go get some sleep."

I find the bedroom, wave Hank Junior inside and close the door. There's a bathroom that connects. I turn on the faucet and splash my face with water, leaning in to drink some, then rinse and spit since I don't have a toothbrush. I've brought in Hank Junior's McDonald's cup. I fill it with water and set it inside the bedroom, up against a wall. He saunters over and takes a couple laps, then flops down beside it, lowers his head on his paws and closes his eyes.

I make use of the toilet and flip off the light, lying down beside him on the floor and using his soft side as a pillow.

There are no curtains in the room, and a streetlight throws a beam across the middle of the floor. I try to turn off my brain, make all the what-if's and how-will-I's stop their relentless pecking, at least until morning, when I can address them with something resembling clear thinking.

I attempt sleep for an hour or more, but it's no use. My brain just won't turn off. I get up and leave the room, closing the door softly behind me to keep from waking up Hank Junior.

I walk through the living room and open the sliding glass door that leads onto a small deck. Holden is leaning on the railing, staring at the dark street below.

"Oh, I'm sorry," I say. "I didn't realize you were out here."

He looks over his shoulder at me, and I can see his hair is damp from a shower. "You can't sleep either?" he asks, his voice even now, without the threads of irritation and aggravation I'd heard in it earlier.

"No. Even though I'm pooped."

"I'm not a big sleeper," he says. "Plus Thomas snores."

"You can take the room I'm in," I say. "Really."

He shakes his head. "We were roommates in college. If I'm in sleep mode, I don't even hear him."

I step closer to the railing, folding my arms across my chest. "How long have you two known each other?"

"We met freshman year."

"Football?"

"Yeah."

"When did you start the music thing?"

"Both of us for as long as we can remember. Together, pretty much right after we met."

I nod and say, "Y'all are quite a match."

"Thanks. We kinda get each other."

"Not the easiest thing to come by."

"This what you've always wanted to do?"

"Yeah. I loved watching Uncle Dobie with his band. He told me one time that the way to know if music was going to be your life was to decide whether or not you were willing to give everything else up for it. He never got married or had a family."

"You think it's gotta be like that?" he asks, looking at me.

"I think dreams can have a high price tag or everyone would be going after them."

"Guess that's true."

"What did you leave behind to come here?" I ask.

"Why do you think I left something behind?"

"What's her name?"

He throws a glance at the street and then turns to me. "Sarah."

"Ah. Why didn't she come with you?"

"She likes predictability. Security. About the only thing I can predict is that I will write another song. Even if the one I just wrote sucks. Even if I don't think anybody's ever gonna wanna hear it. I don't know how not to write another one."

I absorb each word, recognizing the truth of them as my own. "Sometimes, I wish I knew how to unplug that need inside of me. How to reprogram myself to want to do something that wouldn't make my Mama so unhappy with my choices. That wouldn't force me to walk so far out on a ledge I'm terrified of falling off of."

He keeps his gaze on the street below us, and I have the feeling he's forcing himself not to look at me. I wonder if I've said too much, revealed enough vulnerability that I've made him uncomfortable.

But then he does look at me, his eyes locking onto mine, and I feel like he's drawing something up and out of me, a longing I've never felt before and am not even sure I could put a name to if asked. All I know is I can't make myself look away. Even though he just told me there's someone in his life. Even though every nerve ending is screaming at me to back up and go inside.

A car rolls by, its headlights throwing a shadow over us, and for a moment I see something in his face that I know as surely as I know my own name, I am in no way ready for. I sense that all I have to do to find out is place my hand on his chest, splay my fingers wide so that each tip absorbs the beat of his heart. In this moment, I want to do that as much as I have ever wanted to do anything. I close my eyes and imagine myself doing it or maybe I close them to stop myself from doing it.

"CeCe," he says.

My name is a protest, uttered to me or to himself, I don't know.

I let myself look at him then, and I feel the tug between us, as if an invisible cord now connects my heart to his. The stereo beat drums in my ears, and my pulse picks up its rhythm. I feel it in my wrists, my neck, the backs of my knees. My breathing has shortened, and I wilt forward like all the air has been let out of my bones.

His hands latch onto my shoulders, and he dips his head in, his mouth hovering over mine. I can smell the lemony scent of whatever soap he showered with. I tilt my head back, inviting him, imploring him.

When he steps away, I blink my eyes wide open and press a hand to my mouth.

"CeCe," he says, my name sounding ragged and torn. I haven't imagined that he wanted to kiss me. I can hear it in his voice, what it cost him to stop himself.

"What?" I manage, the question not really needing an answer.

"When the sun comes up, we'll wish we hadn't. You're gonna need a place to stay until you get things together. I'm okay with that. But this would just complicate everything."

He's right. I know it. "You always have this much common sense?" I ask.

"No," he says.

"Not sure I should be flattered by that."

"I can be stupid if you really want me to be." There's teasing in his voice, but something else, too. I could make him change his mind if I wanted to. I can hear that. Common sense is now raining down on me, and I take a step backwards.

"Think I'll try to get some sleep," I say.

His phone rings. He pulls it from his pocket, glances at the screen, then at me. "Goodnight then."

I step inside the apartment, close the door behind me, wondering if it's Sarah who's calling him in the middle of the night.

I start to walk toward the bedroom, then stop for a second, listening to the way his voice has changed. There's tenderness in it, longing, and I realize he must miss her.

I'm suddenly grateful for whatever bolt of logic kept us from following through on instinct just now. Holden might have moved to Nashville without Sarah, but he hasn't left her behind. Those are two very different things.

♪

Holden

I don't want to stop her.

I mean, what the hell? You don't need to be a friggin' genius to see the girl's nothing but trouble.

"You just gonna let her walk off into the night?" Thomas asks, looking at me like I just destroyed every illusion he ever had about me.

"If she wants to go, who are we to stop her?"

"You know dang well she thinks, knows, you don't want her riding with us."

"Do we really need another card stacked against us? She's a walking disaster!"

Thomas throws a glance up the highway. "Yeah, right now she is."

"See. You're already trying to figure out how to fix things for her. Every time you find somebody that needs fixing, we come out on the losing end of the deal."

"If you're talkin' about Sarah, that's your doin', man. All I ever agreed to do with her was sing. You're the one who got involved with her. Nobody made you do that but you."

I'd like to tell him to piss off, as a matter of fact. Except that he's right.

I get to my feet, slap the dirt from my jeans and yank up both cases, one containing my broken Martin, the other holding the piece of crap CeCe MacKenzie probably bought at Wal-Mart.

"You keeping the guitar?" Thomas calls from behind me.

"I'll toss it out the window when we pass her," I say.

"Oh, that's mature."

I put both the guitars in the back, giving lie to what I just said. I climb in the truck and slam the door. Thomas floors it, merging into the oncoming traffic.

Thomas hunches over the steering wheel, looking for her. I'm starting to wonder if, hope, she's hitched another ride when I spot her up ahead, her skirt flouncing left to right as she walks, that ridiculous floppy-eared hound trotting along beside her.

"Well?" Thomas throws out.

"Pull the hell over," I say.

He looks at me and grins but knows better than to say anything. Wheeling the truck to a stop in front of her, Thomas gets out and walks around back. I force myself not to look in the side mirror. I crank the radio, lean against the seat and close my eyes.

A couple of minutes pass before the two of them walk to the driver's side and climb in.

Hank Junior licks my face and I jerk forward, glaring at him. "You have to write her an invitation?" I ask. "We're supposed to be in Nashville in an hour and a half."

"Ain't no problem," Thomas says. "We'll be there with warm-up time to spare."

Thomas grabs his Starbucks bag from the dash where he'd flung it earlier. He pulls out a plain mini-donut and offers it to Hank Junior. "Believe I promised you that."

The dog takes it as if he's royalty sitting down to tea. He chews it delicately and licks his lips. "Good, ain't it?" Thomas says, pleased. "Got you one, too, CeCe."

"That's okay," she says.

"Go on, now. Hank Junior and I can't eat alone."

She takes the donut from him and bites into it with a sigh of pure pleasure. "Um, that's good. Thank you."

"You're welcome."

CeCe sits straight as an arrow, Hank Junior curled on top of her again. She's yet to look at me, and I can imagine her pride has taken a few more pokes in agreeing to get back in here with us.

"I'm real sorry about your guitar," she says in a low voice. "I mean it about you taking mine. My uncle used to play with a group called The Rounders. He gave it to me before he died."

"The Rounders?" I say, recognizing the name. "They wrote 'Wish It Was True' and 'Long Time Comin'?"

"Yeah, those were their biggest songs," she says, still not looking at me.

"That's some good music," Thomas says. "I've had both those tunes in my sets."

"Me, too," CeCe says.

I stay quiet for a moment. "Which one was your uncle?"

"Dobie. Dobie Crawford."

"Good writer," I say, not sure why it's so hard for me to release the compliment since I really do mean it. "I didn't realize he'd died."

"Two years ago," she says.

"What happened to him?" Thomas asks.

"Liver failure."

"That's a shame," he says.

"Yeah," I add. "It is. I'm sorry."

"Thanks," she says, looking at me now with surprise in her voice. "He was a good man. Aside from the drinking, I mean."

"He teach you how to play?" Thomas asks.

"He did," she says. "I was five when he started giving me lessons."

"You any good?" I ask, unable to stop myself.

She shrugs. "He thought I was."

We're looking at each other now, and all of a sudden it's like I'm seeing her for the first time. I realize how unfair I've been to her, that I deliberately set out not to see her as anything more than a noose around our necks.

"What do you think?"

"I think I'm pretty good. Not nearly as good as he was."

"Not many people have a teacher with that kind of talent."

"I was lucky," she says. "Who taught you?"

"I mostly taught myself," I say.

"Don't let him fool you," Thomas says. "He's got the gift. Plays like God Himself is directing his fingers."

"Wow." She looks at me full on, as if she's letting herself take me in for the first time, too, without the conclusions she's already made about me getting in the way. I'm uncomfortable under her gaze, and I don't know that I can say why. An hour ago, I didn't care what she thought of me.

"Thomas just likes the fact that he doesn't have to pay me to play for him," I say, throwing off the compliment.

"That's a plus for sure," Thomas says, and then to CeCe, "but I still ain't overselling him."

"I'd like to hear you play," she says, glancing at me again.

"Good," Thomas says. "'Cause he's gonna have to take you up on that guitar of yours. We're onstage in less than an hour."

"Okay then if I come watch?" she asks in a cautious voice.

"Sure, it is," Thomas says.

CeCe looks at me, expecting me to disagree, I would guess. But I don't. "I don't want your guitar. To keep, I mean. I'll borrow it just for tonight."

"You can keep it," she says. "I owe you."

"I don't want your guitar."

"Okay."

♪

WE DRIVE THE REST of the way into Nashville without saying too much of anything. Thomas has gone quiet in the way he always does before a show, playing through lyrics in his head, gathering up whatever emotional steam he needs to get up in front of an audience and sing.

We've been together long enough that we respect each other's process, and when it comes time to leave each other alone, we do.

I air guitar some chord patterns, walk through a new tune we're doing at the end of the set tonight, wonder if I could improve the chorus lyric.

CeCe's head drops against my shoulder, and it's only then I realize she's asleep. Hank Junior has been snoring the past ten miles. I look down at CeCe and will myself not to move. I don't know if it's because she's clearly dead tired or because her hair is so soft on my arm. I can smell the shampoo she must have used that morning. It smells clean and fresh, like springtime and honeysuckle.

I feel Thomas look at me, but I refuse to look at him. I know what he's thinking. That's when I move closer to the door, and CeCe comes awake with a start.

"Oh," she says, groggy, "I'm sorry. I didn't realize I dozed off."

"It's okay," I say, wondering if I could be more of an ass.

CeCe sits upright as a poker the rest of the way into the city. Hank Junior goes on snoring, and she rubs his ears, first one, then the other.

Thomas drives straight to the Bluebird. We've been coming down every few weeks for the past year or so, working odd jobs back home, saving money, gathering proof each time we come that we need to give this a real shot. This time, we're staying.

The strip mall that includes the Bluebird Café among its tenants isn't much to look at from the outside.

The lot is full so we squeeze into a grassy area not too far from the main entrance. The place is small, the sign out front nothing that will knock your socks off.

"It's not exactly what I imagined." CeCe studies the front door. "I thought it would be bigger."

"We thought the same thing first time here," Thomas agrees.

The truth is we'd felt downright disappointed. Both of us had heard about the place for years, how many dreams had come to fruition behind those doors. The physical appearance had been something of a letdown. It's not until you're inside and witness what goes on there that you get the fact that the appearance doesn't much matter.

"Hank Junior can wait here," Thomas says. "That okay?"

"Yeah," CeCe says. "Let me take him potty first."

Hank Junior follows her out of the truck as if that's exactly what he had on his to do list. They head for a grassy spot several yards away where Hank Junior makes use of a light pole.

Thomas reaches for CeCe's guitar case. "Maybe you oughta tune her up."

"Yeah," I say, taking the case and setting it at my feet. I feel weird about it even though I know CeCe wants me to use it. I pull out the guitar, pleasantly surprised by the heft of it. It's a Martin, like mine, and this too, catches me off guard. I guess I should have known if it belonged to Dobie Crawford, it was gonna be more than decent.

I sit on the curb, strum a few chords, and find there's not much to improve on. CeCe knows how to tune a guitar.

She's back then, Hank Junior panting like he's thirsty. "Either of you have a bottle of water you could share with Hank?"

I stand up, reach under the truck seat and pull out one I'd opened earlier.

"Thanks," she says, without looking me in the eye. She takes the cap off, squats in front of the dog and cups her hand, letting him drink from it. She refills her palm until he loses interest, and then she helps him up in the truck.

Thomas hits the remote. "Let's get on in there."

"Ah, would it be all right if I borrow some money for the cover charge? I. . .my wallet was in the car."

"You have no money?" I ask before I think to soften or censor the question.

She shakes her head, glancing down at her sandals. She looks up then, pride flashing in her eyes. "I'll pay you back."

"No need to be worrying about that," Thomas intervenes. "We'll spot you what you need. You don't have to pay here anyway. You're with the band."

I attempt to level Thomas with a look, but our friendship is way past the point of him giving in to me on anything he doesn't want to. "You're using her guitar, aren't you?" he tosses at me in case I need an explanation.

I start to argue that I wouldn't need her guitar if she hadn't left the truck door open. That seems pointless right now, so I march on ahead of them without bothering to reply.

There's a crowd, college kids, couples, older folks, pretty much the gamut. I step around the line, murmuring, "Excuse me, sorry." I duck through the door, trying not to bump anyone with the guitar case, Thomas and CeCe behind me.

A dark-haired girl is working the front door. She's wearing a short blue dress, scooped low, and cowboy boots that make her legs seem a mile long. She directs a high beam smile at me. "You in the round?"

"We are," I say, waving a hand at Thomas and CeCe.

"What about her?" She looks at CeCe and forces a smile the way girls do when they sense competition.

"She's with us," Thomas says.

"Are you playing?" the girl asks, meeting CeCe's gaze with a note of authority.

"I, no–" CeCe begins.

"Then you'll need to pay the cover charge," she says.

Thomas starts to pull out his wallet when she adds, "And go to the back of the line. All these other people were here before you."

CeCe's eyes go wide, and suddenly bright like she's going to bust out crying at any second. I guess it has been that kind of day for her.

I lean in on the stand, close to the girl's face and say, "Can you cut her a break just for tonight? I'm using her guitar because mine got stolen by two guys on a motorcycle."

"Hey!" Someone yells from the end of the line. "We standin' here all night or getting inside to hear some music?"

"All right, all right," the girl says, not taking her eyes off mine while she writes something on a card and hands it to me. "I'm Ashley. Call me later. I'd like to hear the rest of your story."

I slip it in my shirt pocket and start making my way through the tables to the center of the floor where other writers and singers are already set up.

"So that's why you bring him along," I hear CeCe say to Thomas.

"Gotta admit he comes in handy," Thomas shoots back with a laugh.

Thomas and I take the two chairs remaining in the circle. We've met everyone else in the round on other trips to Nashville. Darryl Taylor to my left who I just heard is on the cusp of a record deal. He writes his own stuff, and he's good. Really good. Shauna Owens sits next to Thomas. She's been a semi-finalist on Idol, and I hear the only thing keeping her from the big leagues is her stage fright. Sometimes she keeps it under wraps, and sometimes she doesn't.

Across from us is a fifteen-year old who's been coming to town with her mom for the past two years, learning the ropes, writing at first with anyone she could find. Last time we were in town, writers were starting to seek her out, which means someone up the ladder is taking notice of her.

Within ten minutes, the place is totally packed. People are turned away at the door. I look around and spot CeCe leaning against a corner wall by the bar. She looks a little lost standing there by herself, and I feel a pang of compassion for her. I instantly blink it away, reminding myself that Thomas and I both will do well if we manage to navigate the waters of this town without either one of us drowning. We threw her a life raft today. That oughta be enough. I'm not about to take on swimming her to shore.

Mike Hanson is top dog in the round tonight. He's got a publishing deal with one of the major houses in town and just recently got his first cut with a cool new band. Thomas and I met him when we started coming to town and playing at the Listening Room. He'd already been at it for a couple of years then, and starting to get some interest. I knew the first time I heard him that he had the talent to make it, but the way things work here, affirmation doesn't come until you get a publishing deal. The next rung up is a cut.

Mike blows on the microphone, taps it once and makes it squawk. "Howdy, everybody. Welcome to the Bluebird Café. I'd like to thank y'all for coming out. I'm Mike Hanson. We got some fine music for you tonight."

The crowd claps with enough enthusiasm that it's clear they believe him. I'm hoping we live up to it.

Mike introduces each of us, calls me and Thomas a duo, singer-writer team, and I start to get a rush of nerves the way I always do just before we perform.

"Y'all don't forget your waiters and waitresses tonight," Mike reminds the crowd. People clap and whistle. Mike strums a few chords. "I hope y'all will be hearing this on the radio real soon." He sets right in to the song then, and the applause grows louder. It's clear word has gotten out about his recent success.

This is one thing I've come to love about Nashville. People here take pleasure in the accomplishment of others. Sure, everyone wants to make it, or they wouldn't have come in the first place. It's more than that though, a camaraderie of a sort I haven't known anywhere else.

It's almost like running some kind of marathon together, and instead of begrudging the fact that they've crossed the finish line before you, you're somewhere behind them, throwing a fist in the air and cheering them on.

At least, the people who have been at it a while do. Don't get me wrong. The competition is fierce. Thomas and I were no different from any other newbie to the scene. We drove into town almost a year ago, thinking we'd be on the radio in no time. We'd gotten enough validation from our fans back home on the University of Georgia scene that we'd started to accept their loyalty as all we needed to verify what would happen once Nashville discovered us.

What we hadn't counted on was all the other talent riding into town on the same wave of determination and hope. And how damn good they would be.

Mike's song is enough to make me green with envy if I let myself buy into that. The lyrics are raw with truth, but polished like a diamond that's been buffed with a soft cloth. The music has an element of something different enough to make it sound fresh, make it stand out.

I don't think I'm far enough along to know exactly what it is that sets it apart from what the rest of us will play tonight. I just know there is something, and more than anything in the world, I want my stuff to be that good. A year of coming here has shown me that it's not, yet, and in some weird and kind of awful way, I guess you could call that growth.

When Mike repeats the last tag of his song, the crowd throws out a storm of applause. He's shy, and makes a pretense of brushing something off the front of his guitar, then leans into the microphone again. "Thank y'all. Thank you so much."

When the applause falls back, the fifteen-year old sitting next to Mike starts her song, and while the lyrics don't have the power of Mike's, her voice is soft and sweet, the tone unique enough that it's easy to see she's got something special. People lean forward in their chairs, caught up on the wings of it, the emotion she lets spill through each word, captivating in and of itself.

Two more writers are up before Thomas and me. They're both good, better than good, and I'm feeling the pressure of comparison. Thomas takes the microphone and glances at me the way he does when he's ready. I tip into the intro, hitting the strings so lightly, that a hush falls over the room, and I can feel them start to listen.

I wrote this song for Thomas. His little sister died of cancer when he was twelve, and I remember how I felt when he told me about it, what it was like to go to the hospital to see her, watch her be strong for him, even though she was younger than he was, even as the pain became unbearable. I tried to write the lyric as if I'd been standing in that room, as if I had been Thomas, a big brother who's got to know what it will be like where she's going, that he will see her again one day.

I wrote it from a father's point of view, somehow knowing I needed to give Thomas that distance. That he would never get through the song singing it as the brother.

It's called *Up There*, and he sings it now like his own truth. I guess that's why what the two of us have works.

I can see the faces of the people directly in front of us, the glimmer of tears in their eyes. Maybe this is what I love most about writing, that moment when you realize you've hit a universal, something everyone can feel.

I'm drawn to look up then and find CeCe's gaze on me. I see on her face what I have felt on my own so many times. That yearning to express something that reaches people the way this song is doing. I glimpse enough of myself in her then that I wonder why I've been so hard on her, why I'd assumed she would want to stay in the shallow end of this pool. The look in her eyes tells me something completely different. She's headed for the deep end, wants it with all her soul. And I don't doubt for a second that she won't give up until she's there, swimming on her own.

A long moment of silence follows Thomas's last note. One person starts to clap. More follow until the room is alive with it. Thomas never finishes this song without tears in his eyes, and tonight is no exception.

Mike is next again, and as good as his song is, I think I can honestly say, its effect on the audience doesn't top ours.

The round goes on for four more songs each. Thomas and I do a fast one, a slow one and then another fast one. When it's our turn to do our last song, he looks over at me before glancing out to where CeCe is still standing against the wall. I don't think she's moved all night, and I remember the first time I came here, how I'd just sat listening, not moving once until the end of the show.

"If y'all don't mind, I'm gonna bring a new face in for this one. CeCe, come on up, girl."

She stands frozen, her expression a confused mixture of euphoria and disbelief, as if she can't decide whether to run or sink onto the floor. Thomas isn't about to let her do either one. I'm suddenly so mad at him, I can't see straight. What the heck is he doing? She's not ready for this!

But the crowd has turned their attention to her, and someone starts to clap, urging her on. There's a whistle, then another, more clapping until the force of it peels her off the wall and propels her to the circle of chairs.

Her eyes are wide as dinner plates, and I'm starting to wonder if she's ever actually been on stage before.

Thomas pats one enormous thigh and indicates for her to sit, placing the microphone stand close in to them both.

"This here's CeCe MacKenzie. CeCe's new in town, and she's had a bit of a rough day. We'll make this her Nashville welcome. Y'all might've heard of her uncle, Dobie Crawford with the Rounders."

The applause erupts into a roar then. I'm hoping for CeCe's sake and for ours that she lives up to expectation.

"Dobie wrote a song called 'Wish It Were True'," Thomas continues. "Let's do that one for them," he says to both me and CeCe.

It's been a while since we've done this one. Luckily, I know it like I wrote it myself.

Thomas starts in on the first verse, and by the third line, I'm wondering if CeCe is going to join in. She closes her eyes and follows him into the chorus, her voice floating up in perfect harmony against Thomas's.

I'm shocked by the blend. The sound is like chocolate and peanut butter. French coffee and half and half.

They've never sung together, and they sound like they've been doing so their whole lives. They each know the song the way you can only know one when its meaning reflects something of your own life.

By the second verse, it's clear that CeCe's forgotten she's sitting on the knee of a guy she just met today. Forgotten she's singing to a crowd at the Bluebird. I don't know where she is, but it's a place that lets her sing from the heart, from the soul.

I don't hear training in her voice. It's not perfected in that way. What I hear is a girl who's been singing all her life. A girl who sings because it's what she loves more than anything.

They hit the second chorus full throttle, and they're smiling at each other, all out joy lighting their faces. The crowd is with them, sitting up on the edge of their chairs. I can see their realization that they are witnessing something they'll talk about one day. "I saw them when they were just starting out. The very first time they ever sang together."

And I have to admit, it's like that. Some kind of magic that makes me wonder if everything that happened today had been the lead in to this. If we were supposed to meet her. Both for her sake and for ours.

They trail off, note for note, and the applause that follows is the loudest of the night. CeCe has tears in her eyes when she throws her arms around Thomas's neck and hugs him so hard, he nearly sends the chair over backwards. People laugh and clap harder.

I watch for a moment longer, and then unable to help myself, I clap, too.

I feel like I'm in the middle of a dream. The good part where you're aware of hoping you don't wake up. That it will go on and on forever.

I'm hugging Thomas as tight as I can because I don't trust myself to thank him with words. If I do, I'll break down and sob right here in front of all these people.

He hugs me hard and stands, his arm still around my waist. I dangle in mid-air for a moment, then slide down his big thigh until my feet hit the floor. He forces me to face the crowd, and I'm blown away by the admiration and appreciation on their faces.

I feel Holden's gaze on me and make myself look at him. I guess I'm expecting him to be mad at me for horning in on their show, but that's not what I see in his eyes. What's there is the same admiration the audience has offered up, and maybe that surprises me most of all.

Mike thanks everyone again for coming, and people start to stand up and push their seats back. Several weave their way up to the circle of chairs and begin talking with the performers. A couple of teenagers ask Mike for his autograph. Next, they laser in on Thomas and Holden, giggling and looking as if they might lose their nerve at any moment.

One of the girls has red hair that hangs to her waist. Her eyes are a vivid green, and she looks at Thomas with starstruck longing. "Would you sign this for me?" she asks, handing him a Bluebird napkin.

"Why, sure, I will." Thomas raises an eyebrow at Holden who shakes his head.

"You're gonna be famous one day, Thomas," the girl says. "I just know it."

Thomas grins. "If that means I get to sing for a living, I'd be all right with that."

The redhead's friend sticks out a napkin of her own. "We'll buy anything you release."

"You don't work for a record company, do you?" Holden throws out.

Both girls giggle. "We're fifteen."

"Shoot," Thomas says. "Just our luck."

They laugh again, and then the redhead looks at me, her voice suddenly shy. "Your singing's so pretty."

Something in the sincerity of the compliment touches me, makes instant tears well in my eyes. It's stupid, I know, but after the way this day has gone, it's nice to hear that I'm not totally crazy to think I might have a place here. "Thank you," I say. "Thank you so much."

"You're welcome," she says, ducking her head again.

The two girls bounce off, clutching their napkins to their chests like they'd just found winning lottery tickets.

A man walks up and introduces himself. "I'm Clay Morrison. Y'all sounded real good tonight."

He has dark hair that's started to pepper a bit at the sides. He's dressed in jeans and a white shirt under a black jacket. His shoes are black, too, and they look expensive. Narrow frame glasses tone down his good looks and suggest he's smart.

I step out of the circle so his focus is on Thomas and Holden.

"Thank you," Thomas says. "Appreciate that."

"Saw you two here a few months ago. Have to say I like your new addition. The three of you sound pretty great together."

He swings a look at me then, and I want to sink into the floor. The last thing I want to do is barge in on their action. And it feels like that's what I'm doing. "Excuse me," I say and head for the ladies' room.

I lock myself inside, leaning against the door and pulling in a deep, shaky breath. I can still feel Holden's gaze on me, resentful, accusing.

I wash my face and dry it with a scratchy brown paper towel, taking my time with the process until I think Thomas and Holden might be ready to leave.

When I come out again, they're both waiting by the front door.

"You fall in?" Holden asks, looking me up and down.

I roll my eyes at him, pushing out into the cool of the Nashville evening.

We walk to the truck in an awkward silence, like neither of us knows what to say about what happened in there tonight.

Thomas hits the remote, and I open the door. Hank Junior leaps out and heads for the closest bush. I grab his leash and follow him.

When we return, it's clear Thomas and Holden have been talking. There's electricity in the air, the kind that sparks from disagreement.

Neither one looks at me, and I'm thinking it's time I go my own way. "Hey, thanks for everything, y'all. The help, the ride, the song. I expect to see your names in big places."

Hank Junior wants to jump in, but I stop him. "Come on, boy," I say, then turn around and start walking.

I have no earthly idea where I'm going. I just know I need to get away from those two before I bawl like a three-year old. I'm walking so fast that Hank Junior has to trot to keep up with me. He keeps looking back at the truck and then up at me as if he's wondering what in the world I'm doing. I wouldn't know how to begin to answer him. I don't have a thing to my name except for him. Should I find a pay phone, call Mama right now and ask her to buy me a bus ticket home? Could I even take Hank Junior with me on a bus?

I cross the main road in front of the Bluebird. There's a parking garage there. Maybe we can camp out for the night and see how things look in the morning, although short of me finding a winning lottery ticket in my pocket, I don't know how it could look any better.

The garage is nearly empty, a few cars parked along the other side that opens through to a Whole Foods. My stomach does a low rumble, and I know Hank Junior has to be hungry as well.

I head for a corner and lean against the wall, sliding down onto the cold concrete. Hank Junior looks at me as if he isn't sure what he's supposed to do. I pat the spot next to me, and loyal friend that he is, he curls up with me, his head on my knee.

That's when the tears start up for real. They gush from me like a geyser, and I just let them pour out, helpless to stop them even if I wanted to.

Hank Junior anxiously licks them from my cheek, and I rub his side, his sweetness making me drop my head to my knees and cry harder.

I guess it's my own sobbing that keeps me from hearing the truck until it stops right in front of us.

"This your plan?"

I jerk my head up to see Holden looking down at me with resignation on his face, like he's finally given in to the idea that they are stuck with me.

"For this minute, it is," I shoot back.

"Sleeping in a parking garage?"

"Does it look like I'm sleeping?"

"It looks like you're crying."

"Since when is that illegal?"

"Get in the truck, CeCe."

"No," I say. "I'll be fine."

"Oh, you've been doing a great job of proving that," he throws out.

"I didn't ask you to rescue me!"

"And I sure as heck didn't volunteer for the job," he says, opening the door and swinging out.

I pop to my feet, the concrete scratching at my back through my thin cotton shirt.

"Are you coming with us or not?"

"I don't need your charity, Holden!"

He leans in like a football player aiming a tackle and hefts me over his shoulder. I start kicking and wriggling, but he tightens his hold like I'm a sack of grain. Hank Junior stands there looking up at us, wagging his tail.

I'd like to think Holden is being chivalrous or some such thing. The truth is he's mad and altogether tired of me messing up his plans.

"When you two get finished with the foreplay, hop on in, and we'll go get some sleep," Thomas tosses out the open door.

Holden walks to the truck with me still slung over his shoulder. "Get in, boy," he says to Hank Junior who hops in like he's in the middle of a raging ocean, and Holden just threw him a buoy.

Holden tilts forward and drops me in beside Hank Junior. Fury has me sputtering some not so ladylike protests. My skirt is up around my waist for the second time today, and I kick and struggle to sit up and pull it down.

Thomas laughs and shakes his head. "You two are right entertaining."

Clearly, neither of us finds his assessment amusing.

Holden climbs in and slams the door. "Can we go now?"

Thomas peels out of the parking garage and turns right, gunning it. "I'm starving," he says. "Next stop, food."

He swings into a McDonald's, pulling up at the drive-through lane. At the window, he places his order, two big Macs, two fries, a large Coke, then looks at me and says, "What do you want?"

"I'm fine, thanks," I say.

Holden rolls his eyes. "Would you quit pretending like you have any other choice but to accept our help right now?"

"Seriously, CeCe," Thomas says.

The pride trying to raise a flag inside me wilts. "Unsweetened iced tea. Mushroom and Swiss burger, please. With no meat."

"No meat?" Thomas repeats, as if I'd just made the request in Mandarin.

"You mean like a cheese sandwich?" Holden says.

"Just no meat," I answer.

Both guys look at each other and shake their heads. Thomas calls out Holden's order, which is a duplicate of his own, adding, "We'll take two plain burgers and a water, too."

He pats Hank Junior on the head, and then to me, "I'm assuming our buddy here is not a vegetarian?"

"No," I say. "And thank you."

"You're entirely welcome," Thomas says, pulling forward.

We get the food and tear into the bags as if none of us has eaten in days. I open up Hank Junior's, force him to wait a few moments until it cools, then take pity on his drooling and let him have it.

Thomas drives while he eats, and it isn't until my stomach is full that I think to ask, "Where are we going?"

"We've got an apartment over by Vanderbilt," Holden says. "Don't have any furniture yet, but at least we have a floor to sleep on."

I don't even bother to object. A place to sleep right now sounds so good I melt at the thought of it, fatigue pulling at every bone, every muscle.

Thomas parks the truck on the street, and they grab their suitcases from the back. Holden hands me my guitar case, before reaching for his own. I follow them up the walk, stopping in a grassy spot to let Hank Junior do his business. They wait for us at the main door, before we climb a set of stairs to the third floor.

Holden pulls out a key and opens up the apartment, flicking on a light. The living room and kitchen aren't huge, but the place is neat and clean, the walls a newly painted beige.

"We've got two bedrooms. Holden and I will bunk up," Thomas says. "You and Hank Junior take the other one."

"I'll be happy to sleep out here," I say.

"We're good." Holden's words are short and abrupt. He heads down the hallway and disappears inside one of the rooms.

I look at Thomas and say, "I don't know how to thank you."

"You don't need to," Thomas says. "Go get some sleep."

I find the bedroom, wave Hank Junior inside and close the door. There's a bathroom that connects. I turn on the faucet and splash my face with water, leaning in to drink some, then rinse and spit since I don't have a toothbrush. I've brought in Hank Junior's McDonald's cup. I fill it with water and set it inside the bedroom, up against a wall. He saunters over and takes a couple laps, then flops down beside it, lowers his head on his paws and closes his eyes.

I make use of the toilet and flip off the light, lying down beside him on the floor and using his soft side as a pillow.

There are no curtains in the room, and a streetlight throws a beam across the middle of the floor. I try to turn off my brain, make all the what-ifs and how-will-I's stop their relentless pecking, at least until morning, when I can address them with something resembling clear thinking.

I attempt sleep for an hour or more, but it's no use. My brain just won't turn off. I get up and leave the room, closing the door softly behind me to keep from waking up Hank Junior.

I walk through the living room and open the sliding glass door that leads onto a small deck. Holden is leaning on the railing, staring at the dark street below.

"Oh, I'm sorry," I say. "I didn't realize you were out here."

He looks over his shoulder at me, and I can see his hair is damp from a shower. "You can't sleep either?" he asks, his voice even now, without the threads of irritation and aggravation I'd heard in it earlier.

"No. Even though I'm pooped."

"I'm not a big sleeper," he says. "Plus Thomas snores."

"You can take the room I'm in," I say. "Really."

He shakes his head. "We were roommates in college. If I'm in sleep mode, I don't even hear him."

I step closer to the railing, folding my arms across my chest. "How long have you two known each other?"

"We met freshman year."

"Football?"

"Yeah."

"When did you start the music thing?"

"Both of us for as long as we can remember. Together, pretty much right after we met."

I nod and say, "Y'all are quite a match."

"Thanks. We kinda get each other."

"Not the easiest thing to come by."

"This what you've always wanted to do?"

"Yeah. I loved watching Uncle Dobie with his band. He told me one time that the way to know if music was going to be your life was to decide whether or not you were willing to give everything else up for it. He never got married or had a family."

"You think it's gotta be like that?" he asks, looking at me.

"I think dreams can have a high price tag or everyone would be going after them."

"Guess that's true."

"What did you leave behind to come here?" I ask.

"Why do you think I left something behind?"

"What's her name?"

He throws a glance at the street and then turns to me. "Sarah."

"Ah. Why didn't she come with you?"

"She likes predictability. Security. About the only thing I can predict is that I will write another song. Even if the one I just wrote sucks. Even if I don't think anybody's ever gonna wanna hear it. I don't know how not to write another one."

I absorb each word, recognizing the truth of them as my own. "Sometimes, I wish I knew how to unplug that need inside of me. How to reprogram myself to want to do something that wouldn't make my Mama so unhappy with my choices. That wouldn't force me to walk so far out on a ledge I'm terrified of falling off of."

He keeps his gaze on the street below us, and I have the feeling he's forcing himself not to look at me. I wonder if I've said too much, revealed enough vulnerability that I've made him uncomfortable.

But then he does look at me, his eyes locking onto mine, and I feel like he's drawing something up and out of me, a longing I've never felt before and am not even sure I could put a name to if asked. All I know is I can't make myself look away. Even though he just told me there's someone in his life. Even though every nerve ending is screaming at me to back up and go inside.

A car rolls by, its headlights throwing a shadow over us, and for a moment I see something in his face that I know as surely as I know my own name, I am in no way ready for. I sense that all I have to do to find out is place my hand on his chest, splay my fingers wide so that each tip absorbs the beat of his heart. In this moment, I want to do that as much as I have ever wanted to do anything. I close my eyes and imagine myself doing it or maybe I close them to stop myself from doing it.

"CeCe," he says.

My name is a protest, uttered to me or to himself, I don't know.

I let myself look at him then, and I feel the tug between us, as if an invisible cord now connects my heart to his. The stereo beat drums in my ears, and my pulse picks up its rhythm. I feel it in my wrists, my neck, the backs of my knees. My breathing has shortened, and I wilt forward like all the air has been let out of my bones.

His hands latch onto my shoulders, and he dips his head in, his mouth hovering over mine. I can smell the lemony scent of whatever soap he showered with. I tilt my head back, inviting him, imploring him.

When he steps away, I blink my eyes wide open and press a hand to my mouth.

"CeCe," he says, my name sounding ragged and torn. I haven't imagined that he wanted to kiss me. I can hear it in his voice, what it cost him to stop himself.

"What?" I manage, the question not really needing an answer.

"When the sun comes up, we'll wish we hadn't. You're gonna need a place to stay until you get things together. I'm okay with that. But this would just complicate everything."

He's right. I know it. "You always have this much common sense?" I ask.

"No," he says.

"Not sure I should be flattered by that."

"I can be stupid if you really want me to be." There's teasing in his voice, but something else, too. I could make him change his mind if I wanted to. I can hear that. Common sense is now raining down on me, and I take a step backwards.

"Think I'll try to get some sleep," I say.

His phone rings. He pulls it from his pocket, glances at the screen, then at me. "Goodnight then."

I step inside the apartment, close the door behind me, wondering if it's Sarah who's calling him in the middle of the night.

I start to walk toward the bedroom, then stop for a second, listening to the way his voice has changed. There's tenderness in it, longing, and I realize he must miss her.

I'm suddenly grateful for whatever bolt of logic kept us from following through on instinct just now. Holden might have moved to Nashville without Sarah, but he hasn't left her behind. Those are two very different things.

♪

CeCe

I feel like I'm in the middle of a dream. The good part where you're aware of hoping you don't wake up. That it will go on and on forever.

I'm hugging Thomas as tight as I can because I don't trust myself to thank him with words. If I do, I'll break down and sob right here in front of all these people.

He hugs me hard and stands, his arm still around my waist. I dangle in mid-air for a moment, then slide down his big thigh until my feet hit the floor. He forces me to face the crowd, and I'm blown away by the admiration and appreciation on their faces.

I feel Holden's gaze on me and make myself look at him. I guess I'm expecting him to be mad at me for horning in on their show, but that's not what I see in his eyes. What's there is the same admiration the audience has offered up, and maybe that surprises me most of all.

Mike thanks everyone again for coming, and people start to stand up and push their seats back. Several weave their way up to the circle of chairs and begin talking with the performers. A couple of teenagers ask Mike for his autograph. Next, they laser in on Thomas and Holden, giggling and looking as if they might lose their nerve at any moment.

One of the girls has red hair that hangs to her waist. Her eyes are a vivid green, and she looks at Thomas with starstruck longing. "Would you sign this for me?" she asks, handing him a Bluebird napkin.

"Why, sure, I will." Thomas raises an eyebrow at Holden who shakes his head.

"You're gonna be famous one day, Thomas," the girl says. "I just know it."

Thomas grins. "If that means I get to sing for a living, I'd be all right with that."

The redhead's friend sticks out a napkin of her own. "We'll buy anything you release."

"You don't work for a record company, do you?" Holden throws out.

Both girls giggle. "We're fifteen."

"Shoot," Thomas says. "Just our luck."

They laugh again, and then the redhead looks at me, her voice suddenly shy. "Your singing's so pretty."

Something in the sincerity of the compliment touches me, makes instant tears well in my eyes. It's stupid, I know, but after the way this day has gone, it's nice to hear that I'm not totally crazy to think I might have a place here. "Thank you," I say. "Thank you so much."

"You're welcome," she says, ducking her head again.

The two girls bounce off, clutching their napkins to their chests like they'd just found winning lottery tickets.

A man walks up and introduces himself. "I'm Clay Morrison. Y'all sounded real good tonight."

He has dark hair that's started to pepper a bit at the sides. He's dressed in jeans and a white shirt under a black jacket. His shoes are black, too, and they look expensive. Narrow frame glasses tone down his good looks and suggest he's smart.

I step out of the circle so his focus is on Thomas and Holden.

"Thank you," Thomas says. "Appreciate that."

"Saw you two here a few months ago. Have to say I like your new addition. The three of you sound pretty great together."

He swings a look at me then, and I want to sink into the floor. The last thing I want to do is barge in on their action. And it feels like that's what I'm doing. "Excuse me," I say and head for the ladies' room.

I lock myself inside, leaning against the door and pulling in a deep, shaky breath. I can still feel Holden's gaze on me, resentful, accusing.

I wash my face and dry it with a scratchy brown paper towel, taking my time with the process until I think Thomas and Holden might be ready to leave.

When I come out again, they're both waiting by the front door.

"You fall in?" Holden asks, looking me up and down.

I roll my eyes at him, pushing out into the cool of the Nashville evening.

We walk to the truck in an awkward silence, like neither of us knows what to say about what happened in there tonight.

Thomas hits the remote, and I open the door. Hank Junior leaps out and heads for the closest bush. I grab his leash and follow him.

When we return, it's clear Thomas and Holden have been talking. There's electricity in the air, the kind that sparks from disagreement.

Neither one looks at me, and I'm thinking it's time I go my own way. "Hey, thanks for everything, y'all. The help, the ride, the song. I expect to see your names in big places."

Hank Junior wants to jump in, but I stop him. "Come on, boy," I say, then turn around and start walking.

I have no earthly idea where I'm going. I just know I need to get away from those two before I bawl like a three-year old. I'm walking so fast that Hank Junior has to trot to keep up with me. He keeps looking back at the truck and then up at me as if he's wondering what in the world I'm doing. I wouldn't know how to begin to answer him. I don't have a thing to my name except for him. Should I find a pay phone, call Mama right now and ask her to buy me a bus ticket home? Could I even take Hank Junior with me on a bus?

I cross the main road in front of the Bluebird. There's a parking garage there. Maybe we can camp out for the night and see how things look in the morning, although short of me finding a winning lottery ticket in my pocket, I don't know how it could look any better.

The garage is nearly empty, a few cars parked along the other side that opens through to a Whole Foods. My stomach does a low rumble, and I know Hank Junior has to be hungry as well.

I head for a corner and lean against the wall, sliding down onto the cold concrete. Hank Junior looks at me as if he isn't sure what he's supposed to do. I pat the spot next to me, and loyal friend that he is, he curls up with me, his head on my knee.

That's when the tears start up for real. They gush from me like a geyser, and I just let them pour out, helpless to stop them even if I wanted to.

Hank Junior anxiously licks them from my cheek, and I rub his side, his sweetness making me drop my head to my knees and cry harder.

I guess it's my own sobbing that keeps me from hearing the truck until it stops right in front of us.

"This your plan?"

I jerk my head up to see Holden looking down at me with resignation on his face, like he's finally given in to the idea that they are stuck with me.

"For this minute, it is," I shoot back.

"Sleeping in a parking garage?"

"Does it look like I'm sleeping?"

"It looks like you're crying."

"Since when is that illegal?"

"Get in the truck, CeCe."

"No," I say. "I'll be fine."

"Oh, you've been doing a great job of proving that," he throws out.

"I didn't ask you to rescue me!"

"And I sure as heck didn't volunteer for the job," he says, opening the door and swinging out.

I pop to my feet, the concrete scratching at my back through my thin cotton shirt.

"Are you coming with us or not?"

"I don't need your charity, Holden!"

He leans in like a football player aiming a tackle and hefts me over his shoulder. I start kicking and wriggling, but he tightens his hold like I'm a sack of grain. Hank Junior stands there looking up at us, wagging his tail.

I'd like to think Holden is being chivalrous or some such thing. The truth is he's mad and altogether tired of me messing up his plans.

"When you two get finished with the foreplay, hop on in, and we'll go get some sleep," Thomas tosses out the open door.

Holden walks to the truck with me still slung over his shoulder. "Get in, boy," he says to Hank Junior who hops in like he's in the middle of a raging ocean, and Holden just threw him a buoy.

Holden tilts forward and drops me in beside Hank Junior. Fury has me sputtering some not so ladylike protests. My skirt is up around my waist for the second time today, and I kick and struggle to sit up and pull it down.

Thomas laughs and shakes his head. "You two are right entertaining."

Clearly, neither of us finds his assessment amusing.

Holden climbs in and slams the door. "Can we go now?"

Thomas peels out of the parking garage and turns right, gunning it. "I'm starving," he says. "Next stop, food."

He swings into a McDonald's, pulling up at the drive-through lane. At the window, he places his order, two big Macs, two fries, a large Coke, then looks at me and says, "What do you want?"

"I'm fine, thanks," I say.

Holden rolls his eyes. "Would you quit pretending like you have any other choice but to accept our help right now?"

"Seriously, CeCe," Thomas says.

The pride trying to raise a flag inside me wilts. "Unsweetened iced tea. Mushroom and Swiss burger, please. With no meat."

"No meat?" Thomas repeats, as if I'd just made the request in Mandarin.

"You mean like a cheese sandwich?" Holden says.

"Just no meat," I answer.

Both guys look at each other and shake their heads. Thomas calls out Holden's order, which is a duplicate of his own, adding, "We'll take two plain burgers and a water, too."

He pats Hank Junior on the head, and then to me, "I'm assuming our buddy here is not a vegetarian?"

"No," I say. "And thank you."

"You're entirely welcome," Thomas says, pulling forward.

We get the food and tear into the bags as if none of us has eaten in days. I open up Hank Junior's, force him to wait a few moments until it cools, then take pity on his drooling and let him have it.

Thomas drives while he eats, and it isn't until my stomach is full that I think to ask, "Where are we going?"

"We've got an apartment over by Vanderbilt," Holden says. "Don't have any furniture yet, but at least we have a floor to sleep on."

I don't even bother to object. A place to sleep right now sounds so good I melt at the thought of it, fatigue pulling at every bone, every muscle.

Thomas parks the truck on the street, and they grab their suitcases from the back. Holden hands me my guitar case, before reaching for his own. I follow them up the walk, stopping in a grassy spot to let Hank Junior do his business. They wait for us at the main door, before we climb a set of stairs to the third floor.

Holden pulls out a key and opens up the apartment, flicking on a light. The living room and kitchen aren't huge, but the place is neat and clean, the walls a newly painted beige.

"We've got two bedrooms. Holden and I will bunk up," Thomas says. "You and Hank Junior take the other one."

"I'll be happy to sleep out here," I say.

"We're good." Holden's words are short and abrupt. He heads down the hallway and disappears inside one of the rooms.

I look at Thomas and say, "I don't know how to thank you."

"You don't need to," Thomas says. "Go get some sleep."

I find the bedroom, wave Hank Junior inside and close the door. There's a bathroom that connects. I turn on the faucet and splash my face with water, leaning in to drink some, then rinse and spit since I don't have a toothbrush. I've brought in Hank Junior's McDonald's cup. I fill it with water and set it inside the bedroom, up against a wall. He saunters over and takes a couple laps, then flops down beside it, lowers his head on his paws and closes his eyes.

I make use of the toilet and flip off the light, lying down beside him on the floor and using his soft side as a pillow.

There are no curtains in the room, and a streetlight throws a beam across the middle of the floor. I try to turn off my brain, make all the what-ifs and how-will-I's stop their relentless pecking, at least until morning, when I can address them with something resembling clear thinking.

I attempt sleep for an hour or more, but it's no use. My brain just won't turn off. I get up and leave the room, closing the door softly behind me to keep from waking up Hank Junior.

I walk through the living room and open the sliding glass door that leads onto a small deck. Holden is leaning on the railing, staring at the dark street below.

"Oh, I'm sorry," I say. "I didn't realize you were out here."

He looks over his shoulder at me, and I can see his hair is damp from a shower. "You can't sleep either?" he asks, his voice even now, without the threads of irritation and aggravation I'd heard in it earlier.

"No. Even though I'm pooped."

"I'm not a big sleeper," he says. "Plus Thomas snores."

"You can take the room I'm in," I say. "Really."

He shakes his head. "We were roommates in college. If I'm in sleep mode, I don't even hear him."

I step closer to the railing, folding my arms across my chest. "How long have you two known each other?"

"We met freshman year."

"Football?"

"Yeah."

"When did you start the music thing?"

"Both of us for as long as we can remember. Together, pretty much right after we met."

I nod and say, "Y'all are quite a match."

"Thanks. We kinda get each other."

"Not the easiest thing to come by."

"This what you've always wanted to do?"

"Yeah. I loved watching Uncle Dobie with his band. He told me one time that the way to know if music was going to be your life was to decide whether or not you were willing to give everything else up for it. He never got married or had a family."

"You think it's gotta be like that?" he asks, looking at me.

"I think dreams can have a high price tag or everyone would be going after them."

"Guess that's true."

"What did you leave behind to come here?" I ask.

"Why do you think I left something behind?"

"What's her name?"

He throws a glance at the street and then turns to me. "Sarah."

"Ah. Why didn't she come with you?"

"She likes predictability. Security. About the only thing I can predict is that I will write another song. Even if the one I just wrote sucks. Even if I don't think anybody's ever gonna wanna hear it. I don't know how not to write another one."

I absorb each word, recognizing the truth of them as my own. "Sometimes, I wish I knew how to unplug that need inside of me. How to reprogram myself to want to do something that wouldn't make my Mama so unhappy with my choices. That wouldn't force me to walk so far out on a ledge I'm terrified of falling off of."

He keeps his gaze on the street below us, and I have the feeling he's forcing himself not to look at me. I wonder if I've said too much, revealed enough vulnerability that I've made him uncomfortable.

But then he does look at me, his eyes locking onto mine, and I feel like he's drawing something up and out of me, a longing I've never felt before and am not even sure I could put a name to if asked. All I know is I can't make myself look away. Even though he just told me there's someone in his life. Even though every nerve ending is screaming at me to back up and go inside.

A car rolls by, its headlights throwing a shadow over us, and for a moment I see something in his face that I know as surely as I know my own name, I am in no way ready for. I sense that all I have to do to find out is place my hand on his chest, splay my fingers wide so that each tip absorbs the beat of his heart. In this moment, I want to do that as much as I have ever wanted to do anything. I close my eyes and imagine myself doing it or maybe I close them to stop myself from doing it.

"CeCe," he says.

My name is a protest, uttered to me or to himself, I don't know.

I let myself look at him then, and I feel the tug between us, as if an invisible cord now connects my heart to his. The stereo beat drums in my ears, and my pulse picks up its rhythm. I feel it in my wrists, my neck, the backs of my knees. My breathing has shortened, and I wilt forward like all the air has been let out of my bones.

His hands latch onto my shoulders, and he dips his head in, his mouth hovering over mine. I can smell the lemony scent of whatever soap he showered with. I tilt my head back, inviting him, imploring him.

When he steps away, I blink my eyes wide open and press a hand to my mouth.

"CeCe," he says, my name sounding ragged and torn. I haven't imagined that he wanted to kiss me. I can hear it in his voice, what it cost him to stop himself.

"What?" I manage, the question not really needing an answer.

"When the sun comes up, we'll wish we hadn't. You're gonna need a place to stay until you get things together. I'm okay with that. But this would just complicate everything."

He's right. I know it. "You always have this much common sense?" I ask.

"No," he says.

"Not sure I should be flattered by that."

"I can be stupid if you really want me to be." There's teasing in his voice, but something else, too. I could make him change his mind if I wanted to. I can hear that. Common sense is now raining down on me, and I take a step backwards.

"Think I'll try to get some sleep," I say.

His phone rings. He pulls it from his pocket, glances at the screen, then at me. "Goodnight then."

I step inside the apartment, close the door behind me, wondering if it's Sarah who's calling him in the middle of the night.

I start to walk toward the bedroom, then stop for a second, listening to the way his voice has changed. There's tenderness in it, longing, and I realize he must miss her.

I'm suddenly grateful for whatever bolt of logic kept us from following through on instinct just now. Holden might have moved to Nashville without Sarah, but he hasn't left her behind. Those are two very different things.

♪

Holden

Sarah's voice is soft and full of regret. I'm human, so it feels good to know that she wishes she'd come with us.

"I miss you so much," she says, and I can hear she's been crying.

"I miss you, too, baby." And I do. Way down deep to the core of me. Which in no way explains why I'd been out here wanting to kiss CeCe a few minutes ago, a girl I'd just met today.

"Everything feels empty without you. My bed, my apartment, the whole city of Atlanta feels empty without you."

Pride had kept her from saying any of this when I'd left early yesterday morning. Had it only been a day? Somehow, it feels like weeks since I had seen her.

"You know I want you here, too, Sarah. I never wanted to do this alone."

"And if I hadn't just gotten this promotion, I wouldn't have thought twice about it."

"I know." And I do. Sarah has a great job with an advertising firm in Atlanta. She's actually putting her college degree to use, and while, for her, singing with us was a side thing, something she did at night and on weekends, it's never been that for us.

For Thomas and me, music is THE thing, the ONLY thing we want to do.

Sometimes I think I could be happy living on an island eating bananas if all I had to do to survive was write and play.

Sarah grew up with a father who preached job security as the holy grail, the reason a person went to college in the first place, a means to increasing the likelihood that you would never be laid off, never wake up one morning to find that your livelihood had been snatched out from under you.

In all fairness, that's exactly what happened to him when Sarah was ten years old. They'd lost their house, their car, everything. Pretty much all they'd had left was the college fund he had put aside for Sarah. I guess the thought of her squandering it by taking a shot on something less than for sure is more than he could stomach.

The sad thing is Sarah has a voice like an angel. I don't think she has any idea how good she really is. Maybe because it's not important to her in that way. Her voice is part of who she is, like the color of her hair, her height, or that she's a good runner. It doesn't define her.

As much as I love her, I know this is always going to be the fence between us.

"Did you play the Bluebird tonight?" she asks.

"Yeah," I say.

"How did it go?"

"It went great. Thomas sang the house down." I don't mention CeCe. It feels like I've left a big gaping hole in the truth of our day. Bringing up the fact that we picked up a girl on I-40 whose car caught on fire and then let her sing with us at the Bluebird when the person singing with us should have been Sarah, isn't a direction I want to take our conversation in.

"We had some interest from some record company guy," I say.

"Cool," she says, but I can hear the reserve in her voice. I really think what she wants to hear is that we don't have a shot in hell of making it so we'll come back to Atlanta with our tails tucked between our legs.

And suddenly, I'm feeling the same irritation I'd felt that morning when I left her in bed, warm from the quick urgent way in which we'd just made love. She'd begged me not to go, and I'd begged her to come with me.

The stalemate made us both angry and torn and frustrated.

"I've got to get up for a work in a bit," she says. "I should try to go back to sleep."

"You should," I say.

"Call me later?"

"Yeah. I will."

"Holden?"

"Yeah?"

"We'll work it out."

"We will."

"I miss you like crazy."

"I miss you, too."

She clicks off without saying goodbye. We made the agreement when we first met that we wouldn't use that word with each other. Sarah liked the idea that our time together never really ended if we didn't say goodbye. We just picked up where we left off.

I picture her in the bed we'd shared in her apartment, her long legs bare beneath the expensive sheets she'd insisted were worth splurging on. I wonder if she's staying on her side of the bed or if her arm is slung over my side, if she imagines I'm there with her as she tries to go to sleep.

I push off the deck railing and slip inside the apartment. I need to sleep. I walk down the hallway to the room where I can hear Thomas snoring. The door to CeCe's room is shut, but I stop outside it, touching my fingertips to the wood surface.

"Is someone there?" she calls out.

"It's just me," I say. "Sorry."

"That's all right," she answers.

I stand for a moment while neither of us says anything else. And then I go to my own room and close the door behind me.

♪

CeCe

The sun has found its way to every corner of the room when I wake up. Hank Junior is nowhere to be seen, and I scramble to my feet on a bolt of panic.

"Hanky?" I call out, opening the bedroom door and flying down the hall.

Thomas is standing in the small kitchen, pouring a bowl of cereal. "He's out walking with Holden."

The surprise of that brings me to a stop. "Oh. What time is it?"

"Ten."

"Ten?!? I can't believe I slept that long."

"Musta needed it." He offers me a red plastic cup and spoon. "Cereal?"

My stomach is growling loud enough for him to hear, so there's no use denying I'm hungry. "Thanks."

"I bought Hank Junior a couple cans of food while I was out. He's had his breakfast."

Gratitude washes over me in a wave. "How will I ever pay y'all back?"

"We're not lookin' for a payback."

"I didn't mean–"

"I know you didn't. Got us a newspaper, too," he says. "Job search central."

We take our cups and the paper and sit on the bare living room floor, spreading the sections out between us.

The door opens, and Holden and Hank Junior appear. Hank Junior trots over and gives me a slurpy kiss on the cheek, his tail wagging like he hasn't seen me in a year.

Holden is wearing running shorts. Hank Junior flops down beside me, panting big.

"We went for a jog," Holden says.

"Thanks for taking him," I say, and I cannot meet his gaze this morning.

He can't look at me either. The awkwardness between us is thick, nearly tangible in the room. I can't imagine what it would have felt like if we had continued what we started. I am overwhelmingly grateful that we didn't.

I feel Thomas looking at me, and then Holden before he says, "Did you two–" He stops, lasers Holden with a look. "Shiiiit, man. The only hound dog in this room is you."

"Quit talkin' crap, Thomas." Holden makes a show of pouring himself some cereal.

Thomas looks at me, raises an eyebrow. "Is it crap?"

"I don't know what you're talking about," I say.

"I must look like I just fell off the turnip truck," Thomas throws out.

"As a matter of fact," Holden says, joining us on the floor with his cereal.

Even though my cheeks feel hot, I put my focus on scanning through the Help Wanted section of the Classifieds, heartened by the number of places currently looking for waitstaff. "I have to get a job today," I say.

"We got you covered until you do," Thomas says.

"Thanks," I say. "Really. I don't know what I would have done without you."

"Good Samaritans R US," Thomas adds.

"What are you looking for?" Holden asks, not quite meeting my gaze.

"Waitressing."

"Go for the high end places," he says. "Big tips, and you never know who you'll meet."

"Are y'all looking for jobs?"

"Oh, yeah," Thomas says. "Waitin' tables ain't my thing. Got an interview over at the Mill and Feed. Throwin' bags of grain on a truck bed – that's me."

I smile and think he's right. I can't picture Thomas balancing a tray over a table full of picky people. "What about you, Holden?" I ask.

"Bartending," he answers. "That way I can write during the day. And if we get a gig, hopefully I can switch with someone else."

He pulls out his phone, taps an app and holds the screen up for me to see. "I've already made a list of the better places in town. If I'm going there, you might as well apply, too. To waitress, I mean."

"Oh, well, that would be–"

"I'll drive you both," Thomas says.

First thing I need to do is call Mama and ask for money. Thomas lets me borrow his phone again, and I slip into the bedroom and close the door. I know she won't recognize the number. I'm hoping she'll answer anyway.

She does, with a tentative hello.

"It's me, Mama," I say.

"CeCe. I've been calling your phone since last night. I was worried sick. Are you all right?"

"Yeah, I am. I had a little mishap."

"What happened?"

I picture her standing in our small kitchen, her hand worrying the long cord of the wall telephone. I know she's got a cigarette somewhere nearby because I can hear the smoke of it in her voice. I tell her the whole story then, hardly drawing in a breath until it's all out.

"Oh, CeCe," she says when I explain how I left the burned up car on the side of the Interstate for Triple A to have towed. "Where are you now?"

"I made a couple of friends. They're letting me crash at their place. They're really nice."

She doesn't ask, so I let her assume they are girls.

"Do you need me to come and get you?" she asks. "I can leave right–"

"No, Mama," I say, stopping her before the hope in her voice gets too much traction. "It's gonna be okay. I just wondered if you could wire me some cash. Until I get my credit card replaced and all that."

"Did you lose your purse, too?"

"Yeah."

"Oh, CeCe. Are you sure you're with nice people?"

"I am, Mama." And that really is one thing I can say for sure.

"Where should I send the money?"

I tap Thomas's Google app and do a local search for Western Union. I give Mama the number. "I'll call you later today. I'm going job hunting. And I'll pay you back, okay?"

"I'm not worried about that, honey. You just be careful."

I know she's lonely. That she misses me. Guilt slips a noose around my neck, and I feel so selfish I can hardly stand myself. "Are you all right, Mama?"

"Why, sure I am," she says, her voice too bright, too cheery for me to believe her. "I've got choir practice tonight. We're having a coffee and dessert get together afterwards."

"That's good," I say. "What are you taking?"

We go on like this for a couple minutes until we both feel like some sort of normalcy has been reestablished between us, Mama not so worried, me not so guilty.

I miss her to the very deepest parts of me. In high school, I'd had so many friends who couldn't stand their mothers, who saw them as the one stumbling block between them and everything they wanted in life. I've never seen Mama as anything other than my biggest supporter and best friend. It's hard to leave that behind. Even to chase a dream.

Especially since I know how hard it was for her to let me go. She's never said it out loud, but I know she's terrified that I'll end up in the same place as my Uncle Dobie. That the love I have for music will be eclipsed by disillusion and defeat in the end, the two things that fueled his drinking. I've tried to reassure her many times. I've promised her I won't end up like that. But then she says that's what he said, too.

Tears well up in my eyes as I end the call. When I make it, the first thing I'll do is move Mama here and buy her a house that has everything she could ever want in it. She's so much a part of why I want to make it. I want to give her the things she's never been able to afford, provide her with a life that doesn't involve hoping there will be enough money in the checking account to pay off the month's bills.

I take a quick shower, without soap or shampoo. I stand in the tub until the water has dripped free of my skin, then squeeze out my hair, fluff it up with my fingers and pull it into a ponytail. At least I'm clean.

I feel fresh and rejuvenated. That seems like as good a place to start as any.

♪

THOMAS AND HOLDEN drive me to the Western Union, and I don't even have to wait to get my money. Mama must have left the house as soon as we hung up. Another wave of homesickness for her washes over me. Before we start hitting the restaurants for applications, I ask if we can make one more stop at a Goodwill store so I can buy some clothes.

Holden uses his local search to find one nearby, and Thomas drives there.

"You sure that's where you want to go?" he asks, looking at me with a raised eyebrow.

"You'd be surprised what you can find," I say.

They both go in with me, wandering the aisles and discussing their finds.

I'm after clothes, and I flip through the racks, not finding much at first. Then I spot a cute orange sundress in size 4 that looks like it will fit me. I grab it, along with a pair of black pants and a white shirt. A floral skirt and a light green t-shirt make up the rest of my stuff.

I head for the register and pay for my things. All of it comes to under $15.

Thomas and Holden are waiting in the truck. Thomas is flipping through an old book he'd found on how to make a guitar. Holden is writing something on one of the blank pages of his notebook.

He opens the door and slips out so I can slide in beside Hank Junior. "Find anything good?" he asks.

"I did," I say, feeling pleased with myself.

"I didn't know people actually shopped at Goodwill," Holden says.

I start to take this as an insult, except there's nothing judgmental in the assertion. It is simply that, a statement of fact.

"That's because you grew up with a silver spoon up your butt," Thomas throws out.

I expect Holden to snipe something back, but he just shakes his head. "At least I didn't grow up with cow manure between my toes."

"Neither one of them would make walking too easy," I say.

They both look at me then, and laugh, abruptly, as if I've surprised them. I rub Hank Junior's head and look down, a smile on my mouth. Something warm unfurls within me, soft and fluttery as a butterfly. I like the feeling and realize it's something I haven't felt since high school, and even then, never like this.

Friendship.

♪

Holden

Based on my research, there are five restaurants in Nashville where I'd like to bartend. I came up with those by looking at potential nightly take, whether they're known for attracting the music business crowd, and their proximity to other clubs and bars in the city.

The first two are a total bust. The managers are tight-asses who start laying down the do's, the don'ts, and the musts like they're the last stop on Planet Great Job. I don't even let CeCe finish filling out the application. In both places, we leave them on the bar and head for the truck.

Thomas looks up from the nap he'd been trying to take and gives me a look I've seen before. "I assume they didn't pass your personality test?"

"Whatever hours I have to give away to support this gig, I'm not giving to either of them."

"They seemed nice enough," CeCe says, and I can tell she thinks I might be a little nuts.

We're on 40, heading for downtown when I look at her and say, "How many jobs have you had?"

She's quiet for a few moments. "If you count the three day stint at McDonald's, two."

My eyes go wide. I can't help it. "Where was the other one?"

"Beckner's Veterinary Clinic."

I consider this and then say, "Seriously? So you have no actual waitressing experience?"

"No," she admits. "But I've watched a lot of them during shows."

"How are you planning to write that up on the app? Conducted observations of working waitresses in real-life settings? Or served breakfast, lunch, and dinner to canine and feline guests at Chez Beckner?"

Thomas lets loose a bark of a laugh, as if it surprises him. He apologizes for it, looking at CeCe and saying, "Sorry. He's an ass. But a sometimes funny ass."

CeCe doesn't seem to think so. "I'll be a great waitress," she says, folding her arms across her chest.

"Places like these usually don't want to just take your word for it."

Thomas wheels the truck into the third place on my list, backing into a shady spot at one end of the parking lot. "Can you two finish your argument on the way in so I can catch some shut-eye, please?"

I get out, pissed enough at CeCe that I start across the pavement without waiting up for her until I get to the front door.

"I don't have to apply at the same places as you," she says, stopping in front of me, an expression of stubborn pride on her face.

"I don't care if you apply here or anywhere else," I say. "I was just pointing out that you usually need some experience for places like this."

"I get that."

"Okay then," I say while we glare at each other.

I look away first, start to open the restaurant door, and then on impulse, turn back to her. "About last night–"

"Wasn't that a movie?" she quips.

"Look," I begin again awkwardly.

She holds up a hand to stop me. "You really don't need to go there. You have a girlfriend. Moment of weakness. No explanation needed."

Her straightforwardness surprises me. "Yeah. Something like that."

"So we're past it," she says. "Moving on?"

I'm not sure what I was expecting. It wasn't this. The girls I've known are way more persistent. Or maybe it's just my ego that's feeling the air leak.

I open the door and leave her to walk in behind me, just on principle.

The restaurant's foyer is low lit, and I blink a couple of times to adjust to the dimness. The dining room is big and circular, the walls a deep red, the tablecloths on each of the tables a rich gold. The bar is at the back. It's enormous, carved walnut, I think, and it looks like the kind of place where major movers and shakers would want to hang out.

"Wow," CeCe says in a low, breathy voice.

"Yeah. Wow," I agree. There's no one in sight, and so I call out a, "Hello?"

When there's no answer, CeCe says, "It doesn't look like anyone is here."

Still ticked at her, I ignore her and walk toward the bar. I call hello again, but still no one comes.

I look around the corner of the bar. There's a long hallway that looks like it has two or three offices on either side.

"Maybe we should come back," CeCe says behind me, sounding worried.

I'm anxious to get a job nailed down, and this looks like the place I was hoping for. I head down the hall, raising my voice again, "Hello?"

I hear something and stick my head inside the next office doorway. CeCe bumps into me, jostling me forward just as I realize what I am staring at.

A man on top of a woman on top of a desk, naked as Adam and Eve before the apple thing.

I catch myself just before my forehead hits the opposite end of the doorjamb, CeCe grabbing my shirt to keep from falling.

"Oh, my gosh!" she says, spotting what I've just spotted.

Both the man and the woman look at us then, and amazingly enough, neither of them jumps up in alarm or embarrassment or anything resembling either one.

My gaze snags first on her, fortyish, blonde, gorgeous, and then on the man, whose face is instantly recognizable. Case Phillips. Case-frigging-Phillips!

I jerk upright and turn my back to face the hallway. CeCe does the same, and I guess we must look like two soldiers snapping to attention after a reprimand.

"I'm sorry," I say. "We were looking for the manager or–"

"Owner?" the woman asks.

"Owner," I agree, still not looking.

"That would be me. And I'm a little–"

"Occupied. You're occupied. We can come back."

She laughs. "Why don't you do that?"

"Ah, are you looking for any bartending help?"

A couple beats of silence pass. "I think I just might be."

"Good. How about waitressing? Need any?"

"That depends on the waitress."

"That would be me," CeCe pipes up, raising a hand and waving it in the air. She starts to glance over her shoulder, but I throw my arm around her and tuck her into my side, so she can't.

"Why don't you two come see me later this afternoon when I'm not–"

"Indisposed," the man on top of her says with a chuckle. And in the notes of his laugh, I hear the voice I've heard on the radio a thousand times. Again, shit!

"Indisposed," the woman agrees, laughing.

I hear feet hit the floor, just before the door behind us slams shut. And then Case Phillips: "Shoulda shut the damn thing to start with."

"Come here and let me make it up to you," she says.

Only then do I let myself look down at CeCe. She's pressing her lips together, like laughter is about to explode out of her. I grab her arm and haul her down the hallway before she wrecks whatever opportunity we might have.

By the time we reach the dining room, we're both running full out, through the foyer, the front door, all the way to Thomas's truck before we collapse against the passenger side door and can't hold it back a second longer.

We laugh until my eyes are watering, and we've woken up Thomas. He slides out and walks around to look down at us like we're both insane.

"What the heck?" he asks.

I start to tell him, but I still can't talk.

"We just saw Case Phillips naked as a jaybird in there on top of the woman who owns this place." She tries to stop, then starts up laughing again.

"Was she naked, too?" Thomas asks, straight-faced.

"Oh, yeah," I say.

"Well, all right then," Thomas says.

CeCe is giggling so hard now she can barely breathe.

I glance across the parking lot and spot the black Ferrari tucked into a corner space. The license plate says JSTNCASE.

I point at it, and Thomas lets out a low whistle. "That's the life I want. The car and the girl."

"I hope I'm not the one that finds your bare linebacker ass on top of some hot babe," I say, wiping my eyes.

CeCe giggles a fresh giggle. "Don't need that visual."

Thomas laughs. "Don't knock it till you've tried it."

I get to my feet then, offering CeCe a hand up. She stands and for a second tips into my chest, her breasts soft and full against me. I feel the shock as if someone just stuck a hot wire to my back. Our gazes lock for a snap of a second, and I see the same awareness in her eyes.

I step away, too quickly, and hang my running shoe on Thomas's enormous cowboy boot. I catch myself before hitting the pavement, and grab onto the bed of the truck.

"Good day, man," Thomas says, "you are in such a world of trouble."

"Shut up, Thomas," I say, climbing in. "All I pay you to do is drive."

Chuckling, Thomas shakes his head and pulls CeCe around to his side, waiting while she slides into the middle of the seat.

I lower my window, keeping as close to the door as I can.

♪

CeCe

So it's decided once we get to the apartment that I will buy in as a roommate. Both Thomas and Holden say they don't mind rooming together.

"I already know how bad his boots can stink," Holden had graciously said.

"And I already know what kind of rattlesnake he is at six a.m.," Thomas throws back, matching the dig.

What it adds up to is the two of them throwing me a lifeline. Since I am now starting out in Nashville from negative ground zero thanks to the explosion of Granny's car, I don't have any choice but to take it.

And I am grateful. I tell them both as much, promising to pay them every penny I owe them.

"Ah, don't worry about it," Thomas says once we're at the apartment, and I am again scouring the classifieds, Hank Junior asleep with his head on my lap. Holden had borrowed Thomas's truck to go open up a banking account. I'm not holding out hope for the Case Phillips joint, considering that I've now seen the owner naked. Seems like a significant conflict of interest to me.

"I will worry about it," I say. "I like to pay my debts."

"In other words, you don't like letting others do something for you."

"Only a fool rejects a helping hand when it's needed, but I believe in keeping the slate clean, too."

"You and pecker head are more alike than you know."

I glance up from the paper, raise an eyebrow.

"Holden," he says, like who else would he be talking about.

I refuse to acknowledge the comparison, and say, "They've got openings at the Olive Garden."

"Love the food, but how's that going to help your music?"

"By helping me pay my way around here, feed myself and Hank Junior."

"Holden's right about putting yourself in a place where music stuff is happening."

"In Nashville, that could be at McDonald's."

"True. But the odds are greater over there where Case Phillips is getting some."

"Girl here. You and Holden are going to have to remember this isn't a locker room."

Thomas grins. "Spunk. I like it."

Just then the apartment door swings open, and Holden bursts through, his big white smile the first thing I see.

"You're not going to believe who I just saw in Whole Foods!"

Thomas and I both stare at him, waiting.

"Taylor Swift."

"Seriously?" Thomas throws out.

"Picking out apples in the produce department."

"You suck," Thomas says. "Did you ask for her autograph?"

Holden tosses him a look. "Right after I taped that sign to my forehead that says 'New to Nashville and gawking at every star'."

"Well, you've seen two already today. You might want to let someone else borrow your sign," Thomas argues, sounding irked.

I laugh. I can't help it. The two of them are pretty ridiculous. "Y'all are like two old ladies at a bachelor auction," I say.

"I've got a lyric I want to work on," Holden says, ignoring me and grabbing a Coke from the refrigerator before heading for the back of the apartment.

"To give you a heads up on the vernacular," Thomas says, looking at me, "that means don't come anywhere near him until he comes out and gives the okay."

"Ah," I say.

"If you do bother him, I recommend a shield of some sort. A baking sheet works pretty well."

"Because?"

"He's gonna throw something at you."

I laugh again. "How in the world did the two of you ever get hooked up?"

"Football was the original connect. He had a daddy to prove wrong. And I had a mama to prove right."

"How so?"

Thomas digs his spoon into the half-gallon of chocolate ice cream in front of him. "Holden's father didn't think he had what it took to play ball."

"Why?"

Thomas shrugs. "The real answer is he's pretty much a jerk. He kind of thinks being a musician waters down any athleticism gene."

"Why would he think that?"

"Heck if I know. Why does anyone think stupid stuff?"

I find myself feeling a pang of empathy for Holden. My mama and I never had much, but if I said I wanted to fly to the moon, she'd start helping me make the wings. "What did you have to prove to your mom?" I ask.

"That I was as good as she thought I was."

"That's nice."

"Better than Holden's version for sure."

"How long has he been writing?"

"Since kindergarten."

"I mean lyrics."

"Since kindergarten."

We both smile, and I say, "He's the real thing, huh?"

"As it gets."

"He's lucky to have you to write for."

"Actually, I'm the lucky one. I can sing until the cows come home, but hand me a pencil and tell me to write something that's gonna strike a chord with somebody, and my brain freezes up like lemonade in Alaska."

"You're lucky to have each other then."

"I'll go with that." He looks at me a moment, and then, "What's your dream, CeCe? Why are you in Nashville?"

"To sing and write."

"If you had to pick one, what would it be?"

"I love both, but unlike Holden, other than myself I don't have anyone else to write for, so if I had to pick one, I guess it would be singing."

"You're good, you know. Real good."

I hear the sincerity in his voice, and I start to brush off the compliment like it's no big deal. Actually, it is. I bask in it for a second or two. "Thank you for that. I appreciate it."

"I guess you know there are hundreds of others here just like us. Fresh off the bus. Totally sold on their talent. Ready to share it with the world."

"Yeah," I say, the seriousness in his voice instantly sobering me up from the high of his praise.

"So you wanna know what the difference between me and them is?"

Again, "Yeah."

"I've got the work ethic of a dozen mules. If someone offers me a gig down on the corner of Broadway at two in the afternoon, I'm gonna take it 'cause you never know who might be walking by. Every single chance I get to open my mouth and sing, that's what I'm gonna be doing. And I ain't averse to shakin' some hands and kissin' some babies either."

Laughter bursts up out of me, part delight, part amazement. "You're going the politician route then?"

"It don't matter what talent you've got if people don't like you first. If you're an ass, they won't bother looking past that long enough to see any other good in you."

"Aren't you a little young to be this wise?"

"My granddaddy was in Georgia politics. By the time I was six years old, I'd watched him win voter after voter just by being nice to them. It wasn't an act on his part. He genuinely liked people. Enjoyed hearing what they had to say. He taught me that you end up with way more in this world if you go at it by giving back first."

"You're amazing," I say and mean it.

He looks surprised by that and practically blushes. "Naw."

"You are."

"Holden's right about my boots," he says, grinning.

I laugh. "Even so."

He gets up to throw away his ice cream carton and put his spoon in the sink. I want to thank him, but the words stick in my throat, and I can't force them out. "Thomas?" I say, my voice cracking.

"Yeah," he calls back over his shoulder.

"I'm really glad y'all stopped yesterday. I don't know how I got that lucky."

He turns around then, studies me as if he knows just what I'm trying to say. And when he says, "No, CeCe, I think Holden and I are gonna turn out to be the lucky ones," I know for sure Thomas would make his granddaddy proud.

♪

Holden

CeCe hasn't said a word since we left the apartment. I'm matching her silence beat for beat, determined not to speak first.

"Don't you think this is a waste of time?" she finally asks just as we turn in at the restaurant parking lot.

"Actually, no, I don't," I say, swinging into a spot at the back. I glance at the corner of the building where the Ferrari had been parked earlier. "Looks like Case is gone anyway."

"Oh, good," CeCe says. "I've seen enough naked country music stars for one day."

"You sure about that?"

"Quite."

"I mean we could ask her when he's coming back," I say, enjoying myself.

"No, thank you."

We both get out of the truck, slam our respective doors and walk side by side into the main entrance of the restaurant. Unlike earlier, now all the lights are on, and wait staff bustle around table to table getting the place ready for evening business.

A man in a dark suit and a blazing red tie walks up and says, "Can I help you?"

"We're here to see Ms. Trace," I say.

"Is she expecting you?"

I nod yes, hoping like heck she remembers.

"Just a moment." He walks through and disappears down the hallway behind the bar.

CeCe and I stand poker still in the foyer, and if I feel like a fish out of water, it's clear that she does, too.

Ten minutes later, the blonde woman we'd met in her birthday suit just a few hours before walks in wearing a sexy-as-all-get-out black dress that leaves little to the imagination as to why Case Phillips hangs here.

"You came back," she says, looking directly at me.

I sense, rather than hear, CeCe stepping up close behind me. I move aside so Ms. Trace can see her too. "Yeah," I say. "We were hoping you'd have a moment to talk to us."

"Sure." She waves us both to the bar, pulls a chair up and sits down. "Have a seat."

Remembering my manners, I pull out one for CeCe, causing the woman to raise an eyebrow in approval. I take the next chair over.

"So you're looking to bartend," she says, her assessing blue gaze on me.

"Yes, ma'am," I say.

"And I was hoping you might have a waitressing position open," CeCe throws in.

"What kind of experience do you both have?"

"I tended bar around the University of Georgia," I say.

"You go there?"

"I did."

"Played ball, I bet."

"Yeah."

"You any good?"

"They seemed to think I was."

"But music's your real love," she says.

"Yeah," I admit, wondering how many guys just like me had sat here asking her for a job. Based on her look, I'm assuming a lot.

"How about you?" she asks, glancing at CeCe.

I hold my breath, hoping she's not going to tell her about the veterinary clinic.

"I've never actually waitressed," CeCe says, while I cringe inside. "But I am a really hard worker. I've watched some great waitresses in places where I've had gigs. I'd like to think I've filed away what works and what doesn't."

To my surprise, Ms. Trace looks impressed.

"Hm. Most girls would have told me they had experience even when they didn't."

"The truth is a lot less cumbersome," CeCe says.

"You're right about that. It just so happens I do have a couple of open spots. The bartending position is about thirty hours a week, the waitressing one more like fifteen. You okay to start with that?"

"Yeah," we both say in unison.

"Can you start tonight?"

"Yeah," we echo again.

Ms. Trace smiles. "Uniforms are in the back. The ones hanging in plastic have been dry-cleaned. See if you can find something in your size, and we'll get started."

She stands and leads the way, showing us where the uniforms are.

"All right, then. I'll tell Michael, the manager up front to show you two the ropes."

"Thank you, Ms. Trace."

"Yes, thank you," CeCe adds.

She looks at me then, her gaze direct and unless I'm mistaken, slightly interested.

"It's Lauren," she says.

"Thank you. Lauren," I say.

"You're welcome. Both of you." And with that, she turns and heads to the main part of the restaurant.

"Wowww," CeCe says once she's out of earshot.

"What?"

"That look."

"What look?

"You know what look."

"No, I don't."

"Yes, you do."

"What are we? Six?"

CeCe smiles. "She doesn't think you're six."

I roll my eyes and start looking at pants hanging in the closet. I find a pair of thirty-twos, pull out those and a white long sleeve shirt in large.

CeCe steps up and rifles through the skirts in her size. I notice that she finds a four and a white blouse in a small.

"I'm not changing in here with you," she says.

I roll my eyes again. "Like I want you to."

I leave in search of the men's room, figuring she can find the women's on her own. Once I've changed, I head for the bar. Michael, the guy in the black suit, is waiting there. He starts showing me the setup behind and spends the next ten minutes or so telling me who some of their customers are, what they like, the drinks the restaurant likes to push. Some of the names he drops are pretty impressive, I have to admit.

"Here's what's not cool," he says. "I'm assuming you're here for the music business, and this is a secondary gig to you."

I don't bother denying it.

"When these folks come in, they want to be away from all that. Not ever cool to pitch a song, ask for a card, give a card, a lyric, a CD."

I laugh. "I take it that's been done before?"

"Ohh, yeah."

"Got it. Not cool."

He turns to CeCe then where she's been waiting at the end of the bar for him to finish with me. "Why don't we start there? Did you get that part?"

"Yeeaah. I got that part. Does that include live auditions while I'm serving dessert?"

Now he laughs. "Yeah. It includes that."

CeCe smiles. "Not cool."

He looks at me. "You good?"

I nod. "Yep."

CeCe follows him to the front of the restaurant where he begins introducing her to some of the other wait staff. I watch her shake hands with them, notice how easily her smile comes when it's not being censored for me. A blonde dude with a GQ face holds her hand longer than necessary. It's clear that CeCe isn't immune to its intensity, and it feels kind of weird seeing her melt a bit under it.

I start taking glasses from the dishwasher and placing them on the shelf behind the bar. So she thinks the guy is hot. Whatever.

♪

CeCe

I think I'm gonna like waitressing. By nine o'clock, I have two hundred dollars in my tip wallet. I haven't spilled a thing. And not one person has yelled at me. I'm beginning to see why Holden insisted on making this place first choice. Two hundred dollars in three hours. Not bad.

And that's not even counting the fact that Brad Paisley and his wife Kimberly are having dinner in one of the private rooms off the main area. Not part of my station, but cool nonetheless.

From the looks of it, Holden has been knocking back some good money as well, the bar slammed non-stop. I haven't really recognized anyone, except Brad Paisley, of course. Everyone here appears uber-successful at something or other. Hair and makeup are flawless. Suits are definitely high end. And the women's shoes alone, purchase price all total, could make a ding in the national debt.

Thomas comes in around eight to get the truck keys from Holden. He's been downtown going bar to bar, trying to book some gigs. He took the bus over. The plan is for him to pick Holden and me up when we get off after eleven.

Thomas agrees to head back to the apartment and take Hank Junior out for a walk since I am sure he's about to pee in his fur.

When the last of the customers leave the restaurant, I feel as if my feet have permanently molded themselves to the insides of my shoes. Cleanup takes an hour or better, and it's after midnight before we're done. Holden finishes before I do, and he's waiting by the front door when I say goodnight to the other waiters and waitresses and head out.

In the parking lot, Holden says, "I decided not to call Thomas since it's so late. Okay with you to take the bus?"

"Sure," I say, and we walk to the curb, sitting down on the bench to wait. We're the only ones at the stop, and there's very little traffic on the street in front of us.

"So how was it?" he asks, leaning back to stare up at the sky, his arms folded across his chest.

"Actually, pretty amazing."

"You like?"

"I like."

"You're welcome."

"Thank you."

"Don't mention it."

I smile. "Did you know Brad Paisley came in?"

"I took a bottle of champagne to his table. Dom on the house."

I bolt around to face him. "No fair!"

"Fair."

"What did he say?!?"

"Thank you very much."

"Is that it?"

"That's it."

"Were you nervous?"

He raises his head to look at me. "He's a person like the rest of us."

"A person, yes. Like the rest of us, no."

"How you figure?"

"Just blazingly talented, that's all."

"Agreed. Got a pretty wife, too."

"I'm sure you noticed."

"Do I look dead?"

"Only a bit."

"Thanks," he says with a surprised grin.

"You're welcome."

"How'd you do tonight?"

"Crazy good. Three hundred and some change by the end of the night."

"Awesome."

"How 'bout you?"

"A little better than that."

"People must be generous when they're drinking."

"Alcohol is a well-known lubricant for the wallet."

The bus rolls up and screeches to a stop. Holden stands and waits for me to step through the open door. We find a seat in the back, and we're a few minutes into the ride when I make myself say, "Thanks for helping me get the job, Holden. I know I wouldn't have if you hadn't been there."

"Oh, I don't know. I think she liked your honesty."

"She liked your body."

He tilts his head to look at me with a raised eyebrow. "Yeah?"

"Yeah," I say, something warm unfurling in my chest.

"Do you like it?" he asks, his voice warm and curious.

"I think your head has been enlarged quite enough for one day."

He laughs. "It's awfully easy to yank your chain."

"Is not."

"Is, too."

I huff a big sigh and turn my head to look out the window, but I'm smiling. Holden seems to have that effect on me.

♪

Holden

We get to the apartment to find that Thomas isn't there. The truck is parked out front, but he's nowhere to be found. And neither is Hank Junior.

"Could he have taken him for another walk?" CeCe asks.

"Probably. I'll text him and see."

"Okay," she says, fixing herself a glass of ice water.

I tap the message into my phone.

> Me: Hey. Where r u
>
> Thomas: Looking 4 hank jr
>
> Me: What do u mean looking
>
> Thomas: As in I can't find him
>
> Me: Wtf
>
> Thomas: A squirrel ran out when I was walking him and he took off
>
> Me: Seriously?
>
> Thomas: So
>
> Me: We took the bus. Where r u and we'll help look
>
> Thomas: R u gonna break the news to CeCe
>
> Me: Yeah. Thanks 4 that.
>
> Thomas: Shit
>
> Me: So

She's left the kitchen, and I walk down the hall to her room. Feeling like I just swallowed a rock, I stick my head inside the open door. "Ah, CeCe?"

She comes out of the bathroom, toothbrush in her hand. "Yeah?"

"Thomas kind of lost Hank Junior."

"What do you mean lost?" she asks slowly.

"He took off after a squirrel, and Thomas dropped the leash."

Her face loses its color. "How long ago?"

"I'm not sure."

"Where is Thomas?"

"Still looking."

She grabs a pair of running shoes off the floor and tugs them on. "Can you find out where he's been so I can try a different area?"

I call Thomas this time, instead of texting. He picks up on the first ring and tells me which streets he's covered. "Why don't y'all start with the ones closest to the apartment?" he says. "In case he headed back that way?"

"Okay. Call you in a few."

We click off, and I glance at CeCe who now looks as if she might be physically sick. "Come on," I say, squelching my pity and forcing myself to focus on finding the dog. "Don't worry. He's probably not far away."

We head down Fume Street. CeCe's voice is high and sweet in the way she sounds calling for Hank Junior to come when it's time to eat. We walk to the end of Fume, then cut across to Sharp and jog all the way down. I wonder how many people we're waking up, then realize immediately that I don't care as long as we find Hank Junior.

Aside from calling him, CeCe hasn't said a word. I see in the rigid set of her shoulders and the tenseness of her jaw that she's barely holding it together.

We've just started up another street when a porch light flips on at a house we're about to pass. A woman comes out in a fluffy white robe and waves a hand at us. We both stop, and she bustles over, a worried look on her face. "Are you looking for a dog?"

"Yes," CeCe says quickly. "A Walker Hound. White with black and tan markings."

"Oh, yes." She shakes her head. "Animal control picked him up a little over an hour ago. I heard some barking and came outside. My neighbor, that crotchety old Mr. Lemmons, name fitting, I might add, had already called the pound because the dog had been in his yard for a half hour or more."

"But he had ID on his collar," CeCe says, her voice breaking on the end.

"I could see that, and I told the officer that we could call the number on the tag. He said he didn't have time to wait."

"The phone number on that tag is my cell, and I don't have it now." CeCe looks at me with eyes brimmed over with tears.

"Did you happen to see a name on the truck?" I ask the woman. "So we'll know where to go to get him?"

"Davidson County Animal Control," she says. "I asked him where he would be taking him, and he said the main facility."

"Thank you," I say to the woman, just as CeCe turns and takes off running down the street. We all but sprint the entire way to the apartment, and I have to admit I'm impressed with her stamina.

I call Thomas as soon as we're back in the parking lot of our place and tell him what we know.

"Take the truck," he says. "I'm still a few blocks away."

"Okay. I'll let you know what we find out."

"Tell her I'm sorry, okay?"

"She knows."

I end the call and wave CeCe to the truck. "Let's go. Thomas said to take it and that he's sorry."

CeCe nods, and doesn't speak because she's about to burst out crying again. I Google the animal control place and then tap the address into my GPS. It's a good haul from us, and we don't say a word the entire drive. She just sits straight up in the seat, staring ahead as if she's willing the distance between her and her dog to melt into nothingness.

The building is off the main road, and an intimidating gate blocks the entrance. The truck's headlights illuminate the sign. NO TRESPASSING. HOURS OF OPERATION 8 AM – 4 PM

A chain link fence surrounds the property, and a camera sits on one corner of the gate. "This place is locked up like Fort Knox," I say.

"There has to be some way we can get in," CeCe says, tears in her voice. She slides out of the truck and jogs over, jerking at the padlock.

I walk up behind her, put my hand on her shoulder. "We can wait here until they open."

She looks up at me, her eyes wide and hurt-filled. "But he's in there."

"I know."

"What if they–"

"He'll be okay until morning," I say, hoping like heck that I'm right.

"We could climb the fence."

"And then what? We won't be able to get in the building."

"Someone might be there."

"I doubt it since the gate is closed."

"I want to make sure." She grabs the chain link and starts to climb.

I grab her around the waist and haul her off, swinging her away from it. She slides to the ground in front of me, and I'm instantly aware of her breasts against my chest, her thighs pressing into mine. With one arm around her, I carry her to the truck. I open the driver's side door and set her on the seat, facing me. "He's gonna be okay," I say.

She starts to cry outright then, and I realize she's been doing her best to hold it in since finding out Hank Junior was missing. Hearing her cry feels like someone just stuck a knife in my heart, and I push a hand through her hair and pull her up against me. Her cheek is against my chest, and I draw her closer, wanting to absorb her pain.

I rub her back with one hand, my other anchored in her long, sweet-smelling hair. She widens the space between her knees, and I step in closer, some kind of crazy need sweeping up through me.

She raises her face to mine, and I can't stop myself from kissing her. It's not the right time. And it's not for the right reasons. I know this, but I can't stop.

I can feel how much she wants to escape from where we are, blank out what has happened tonight. I guess I do, too, or at least that's what I tell myself. It's a lot easier to know what to do with that than it is knowing what to do with the fact that I'm kissing her because there's nothing in the world I want to do more right now than exactly that.

♪

CeCe

Nothing in my life has ever felt as good as Holden's kiss. Not the top of my first roller coaster ride, right before the plunge. Or the first time I performed one of my own songs in front of a crowd. Not even the day my Uncle Dobie said he thought I had a future in country music.

At first, Holden is gentle, kissing me like he's not sure where the line is. I'm the one who deepens it. I loop my arms around his neck and pull him closer, opening my mouth beneath his and inviting him in. He accepts. I've never been kissed like this. Thoroughly. Completely. Expertly.

And that's what it feels like. As if Holden knows exactly how to coax, persuade, entice. A couple minutes of this, and my mind is blanked of everything but him. I explore the ripples of abs. His breathing quickens, and I trace the other side.

He runs his hands down my back and under my bottom to anchor me up against him, as if he needs me to know what I'm doing to him. Knowing I'm not ready for what I've so clearly asked him for, I pull away and study his far too good-looking face, my chest feeling as if I've just run a marathon.

"I'm sorry, Holden," I say.

He smooths my hair back from my face. "If this ever happens between us, it has to be for the right reasons."

Sanity begins to wash over me in a wave. And along with it, a tide of mortification. "Thank you."

He laughs. "Thank you?"

"For taking my mind off Hank Junior for a few minutes."

"It was entirely my pleasure. Should I feel used?"

"Maybe a little."

"It's not so bad, being used by you."

I smile, then just as quickly feel the tears well back up and spill down my cheeks.

Holden physically slides me to the middle of the seat and climbs in, shutting the door. He hooks an arm around me and tucks me into the curve of his shoulder. "He's going to be all right," he says. "We can wait here until someone comes to open up."

"You don't have to stay with me."

"I want to."

"Why?" I ask, my voice muffled against his shirt.

Holden glances out the window. "We had a dog when I was growing up. A yellow Lab named Lucy."

He's silent for a bit, and I say, "Yeah?"

"Our yard was fenced, but some of the kids in the neighborhood unlatched the gate one day when we weren't home. She got out, and that night after we came back, we looked everywhere. The next morning, my mom called the pound to make sure she wasn't there, and they said she wasn't. We put up flyers and kept looking for days. Every day my mom called and gave them her description again. They kept telling her she wasn't there."

My stomach drops, and I'm not sure I want to hear the rest of this. But I wait, unable to tell him that.

"Someone my dad knew called and said he'd just heard we were missing our dog. He had seen a yellow Lab at the pound when he and his family went down to adopt a puppy."

I want to say something. I can't because it feels like my voice is locked up inside me.

"My mom and dad and I jumped in the car and drove to the pound as fast as we could. Mom showed a woman at the front desk Lucy's picture, and just the look on her face made me run out of the place."

"Oh, Holden."

"We'd been calling for days, and they said she wasn't there."

I hear the bitterness behind the words, and I can barely bring myself to ask, "Did they-"

"The woman said they'd held her for the required period of time, but when the kennels became full-"

I reach up and touch my fingers to his lips. Tears run down my face, and I'm not surprised to see that the same is true for Holden. I lean in and kiss each of them away, my heart feeling as if it has splintered into a thousand pieces.

We sit silent for what feels like a long time, me absorbing, Holden reliving, I guess.

And then he finally says, "When I think about someone leading her to some room and taking her life while she's wondering where we are. While we're looking for her-"

A sob rises up out of me, this image of Lucy more than I can manage right now. Sorrow for her and renewed fear for Hank Junior swallow me.

Holden pulls me closer, and while I know I should be comforting him, he's the one comforting me. "So that's why I want to wait here with you," he says.

I've barely known Holden for any time at all. It feels like I've known him forever.

♪

WE'RE QUIET FOR the next hour or so, arms locked around one another, like we both need this mutual infusion of empathy and understanding.

The truck's digital clock says 4:07 when Holden reaches beneath the seat and pulls out a notebook. I sit up and watch him remove a pencil from the spiral binding.

"What is it?" I ask.

"Just a thought for a lyric."

He writes a line on the blank page.

So I got a few things I need to say

He's still for a bit before writing:

Never thought my life would turn out this way

His pencil is quiet again. This time several minutes pass before he writes down:

Do you ever think about the choice you made
And what those who loved her have had to pay

Then he adds:

Chorus
What you took from me
You can't give back

I wait for the next line, trying to guess what it might be. Several minutes pass before he writes:

You took the sun
You took the stars
You took the ground beneath my feet

The words are out before I realize I've said them. "You even took the air I breathe."

Holden looks at me and nods. He writes it down.

You even took the air I breathe

And then adds:

Everything, that's what you took from me

"For Lucy," I say.

"I don't know what else it will end up being. I never do at this point."

The sun has started to lighten the horizon behind the pound building. I feel a settling sense of peace that it's all gonna be okay. That very soon, I'll have Hank Junior back, that his fate will be different from Lucy's. Holden's sweet Lucy.

Sitting here with him as he writes on his rumpled pad, I have no way of knowing that in a few months, one of Nashville's most well-known artists will hear Thomas singing Holden's song, the one he started in this truck with me, at a club downtown. Or that in a year and a half, that same artist, whose wife was killed by a drunk driver, will release it, and the song will hit number one.

Looking at him now, the intensity on his good-looking face, my heart feels like it's becoming aware for the very first time of what it was made to feel. It's both terrifying and wonderful all at once.

He has a girlfriend. I know this, but my heart isn't listening. Just like it hasn't listened to all the reasons why turning my dreams over to Nashville might not have been the safest route for me to take.

Some things, our hearts don't let us have a say in. For me, music is one. And right here, right now, I believe Holden Ashford might be the other.

Someone once said every new beginning comes from some other beginning's end. The trick then has to be letting go of the safe, the known and reaching out for what we can't yet see.

I'm ready to reach.

I really am.

♪

Book Two - Hammer and a Song

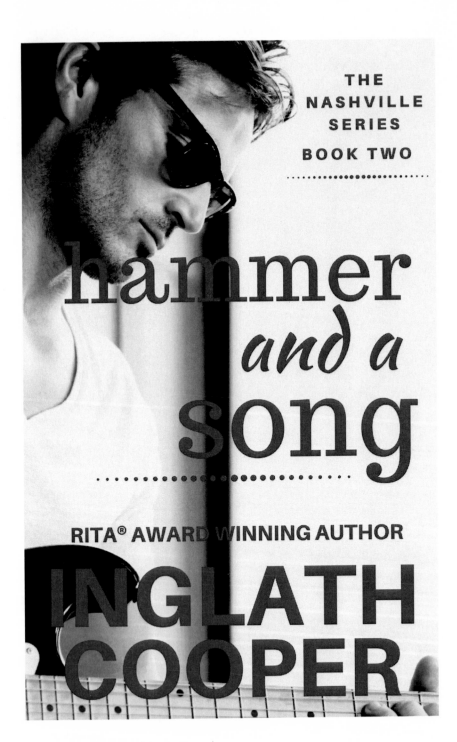

THE
NASHVILLE
SERIES
BOOK TWO

hammer
and a
song

RITA® AWARD WINNING AUTHOR

INGLATH
COOPER

Nashville – Book Two – Hammer and a Song

Inglath Cooper

*

CeCe McKenzie grew up dreaming of a life doing what she loves – singing in Nashville. When she and her Hound dog Hank Junior set out to make her dream come true, life takes some twists she hadn't counted on. Like falling for Holden Ashford, a songwriter with a gift. And also a girlfriend. Can a country music star's hunky son help her forget about Holden? Or is that even possible when her heart insists on writing the song?

Holden

I stroke her back with my right hand, and if the snoring is any indication, it's not long before she appears to be fast asleep.

"She knows," CeCe says, studying me from the other side of the truck.

"What?" I ask.

"That you saved her life."

"How do you know?"

"They just do. Hank Junior was the same way the day I got him out of the pound."

"I can't even imagine that someone could leave her in a place like that."

"Me, either. Thank you for getting her."

"If I hadn't, you would have."

She smiles at me, and it feels good to know we have this in common.

"Not sure what Thomas is gonna say about our new roommate."

"He's a softie like you."

"Oh, you think I'm a softie now, do you?"

"Yeah," she says with a smile that reaches her eyes. "I do."

I don't know that anyone has ever looked at me the way CeCe is looking at me now. I just know it feels good to have her approval. At the same time, I realize I probably shouldn't let myself dwell on that. That there's trouble down that road if I do.

"They might need to go to the bathroom," CeCe says.

"Yeah," I say and pull over at the next turn. We get the dogs out and walk them to a grassy spot where they both immediately do their business. We let them sniff for a couple of minutes and then get back in the truck.

A mile or so down the road, we pass a little country store with its lights on. I slam on the brakes. "Coffee?"

"Oh, my gosh, yes," she says.

I throw the truck in reverse and then swing into the parking lot. "Y'all wait here," I tell the dogs. They both wag their tails and stretch out on the seat as if they plan to get some shut-eye while we're gone.

The store is everything you would think a country store might be. The smell of homemade biscuits and coffee greets us at the door. Three older men in bib overalls sit on a wooden church pew across from the coffee pots, sipping from their cups and talking like they've got the world's problems to figure out by noon.

CeCe and I both choose a large, mine black, hers with cream. I find myself noting the choice for future reference and at the same time wonder what I'm doing.

A large lady with heavily teased hair greets us at the cash register. "Y'all out mighty early," she says, smiling like she's happy to see us.

"Rescue mission," CeCe says.

"Ah," she says, winking at me. "Fun stuff."

CeCe looks like she's going to add something, then thinks better of it. She insists on paying for the coffee. "You might need that last dollar for Patsy food," she teases.

"Hope the tips are good tonight," I say.

"Y'all enjoy your morning," the cashier calls out as we head back through the door.

Patsy and Hank Junior barely glance up as we climb in the truck. "They look like they could sleep for days," I say.

"Who could blame them?"

We drive for a few minutes, silent while we sip our coffee. With CeCe, there's no feeling of having to fill the silence with small talk. I have to admit I like that. It's not something I've experienced with anyone other than Thomas.

We round a curve, and the view opens up with a valley sloping down to our right.

"Let's pull over for a minute," CeCe suggests.

I turn the truck onto the gravel edge that looks as if it's been put there for people to stop and enjoy the view.

"That's just crazy beautiful," she says, opening her door and sliding out.

I follow her to the front of the truck. She climbs onto the hood and looks out at the valley below us. I step up and sit next to her. "Yeah, it is," I say.

The trees have that new leaf green that I imagine artists must yearn to get exactly accurate. A big red barn sits out to the right, and I can see horses grazing behind the white board fencing surrounding it.

"So are you," I say, the words slipping out before I can edit them.

CeCe looks at me, her eyes questioning.

"Crazy beautiful," I add.

She looks down, and I can see the color come into her cheeks. When she looks up at me, I reach out and touch her face with the back of my hand. I hear her short intake of breath, and it matches the electricity that zips through me from the softness of her skin.

We study each other for what feels like a good while, and without censoring what I'm feeling, I lean in and kiss her. It starts out light and testing, but then just as quickly ignites into something completely different. I snag her waist with one arm and reel her in to me. She opens her mouth beneath mine, and we kiss like we've both been waiting for it all our lives.

If so, it was worth every moment of the wait. If for nothing else, then to hear the raspy way she says my name now.

She slides her arms around my neck, and I haul her in closer, slipping my hands up the back of her shirt and under the lacy bra beneath. Her skin is like silk, and I have never wanted to touch anyone the way I want to touch her now.

I feel myself losing control and start to pull back, but CeCe presses her hands to the back of my head and deepens the kiss. We're both breathing like we just ran here from downtown Nashville, and I know if we don't stop now, there won't be any stopping at all.

I untangle myself and lie back on the truck hood, staring up at the morning blue sky and breathing hard.

"I'm sorry," CeCe says, lying down beside me, her voice regretful.

"I'm not," I say.

"You're not?"

"How could anyone be sorry about a kiss like that?"

She lets out a breath of what sounds like relief. "I thought I might have–"

"You didn't," I say. I sit up then and pull her up beside me.

"You're not the kind of girl a guy should take advantage of, CeCe."

The look on her face makes me smile.

"Yeah, right now, I kind of wish you were, too," I say.

"You'd never take advantage of anyone," she says. "But then I don't imagine you'd have to."

"Thanks, I think," I say, grinning.

She smiles at me then, and there's no denying the spool of feeling unraveling between us.

We study the view for a few moments before I say, "CeCe?"

"Yeah?"

"I don't make a habit of leading a girl on when I'm seeing someone else."

"Are you leading me on?"

"I don't really know what I'm doing."

"It's okay. Neither do I."

"Is there someone in your life?"

She shakes her head. "No one serious."

"Has there been?"

"Sort of."

"Which means?"

"Not serious enough for me to stay in Virginia."

I put my hand on the back of hers and lace our fingers together. "What do you really want out of this town, CeCe?"

She considers the question and then looks at me. "Just a chance to do what I love to do. You?"

"The same."

"You think anybody ever comes here just because they want to be famous?"

I laugh a short laugh. "Ah, yeah."

"That I don't get," she says.

"What is fame, anyway? People knowing who you are, seeing your face on the cover of some rag tabloid with whatever skeleton you happen to have in your closet peeking out?"

CeCe laughs. "Success, I get. That just means you get to do what you love because you've found a following of people who love the same thing."

"Which is not that easy, apparently."

"No one ever said it would be easy."

"But we're here, anyway."

"Yeah. We're here."

She's looking at me again with that look in her eyes, and I feel something low inside of me shift, like I might have crossed a line I'm going to have a whole lot of trouble stepping back from. I rub my thumb across the back of her hand, and then let go.

She slides off the hood and jumps to the ground. I follow, glancing over my shoulder. Hank Junior and Patsy are sitting in the middle of the seat, her head resting against his shoulder. "They look like a couple," I say.

CeCe smiles. "Yeah, they do."

"We better get them home."

She nods, and I like knowing that word includes all of us. Home.

♪

CeCe

I'm sitting in the middle of the truck seat with my head on Holden's shoulder when the sun begins to peep up over the Davidson County Pound building. I'm not the least bit sleepy. I'm as wide-awake as I've ever been.

Holden's hand is on my knee, his thumb rubbing back and forth over the fabric of my jeans. We haven't said anything for a good while, instead letting the music from the radio take up the space between us.

There are so many things I want to say, but I know I shouldn't. Like how is it possible to feel this kind of connection to someone you've known for such a short time? Or how I can't imagine sitting here all night, waiting to find out if Hank Junior is okay, without Holden next to me.

I know it hardly makes any sense, but it's true.

An engine sounds behind us, and I look back to see a white truck pull up. A man in a tan work uniform gets out, repositions the ball cap on his head and walks up.

Holden opens the door and steps from the truck. "Mornin'," he says to the man.

"Help you?"

"I hope so," Holden says. "Our dog is missing, and we were told an animal control officer picked him up last night. We think he might be here."

My heart does a somersault at Holden's description of Hank Junior as *our* dog. Had I really called him Grouchy Guy the first day we met?

"I'm afraid you'll have to wait until the main office opens at eight to find out."

"Are you headed down there now, sir?"

"Yeah, but I can't release him for you."

"Could we just go with you and make sure he's there?"

"I'm real sorry."

Tears well up from my chest and splash down my face before I even realize I'm crying. I jump out of the truck and stumble on a rock, righting myself with a hand on Holden's arm. "I'm CeCe," I say, sticking out my hand. "This is Holden."

We shake, and he points to the nametag on his shirt. "Kenny."

"Hey, Kenny. I'm kind of having a hard time with this. Hank was in a pound when he was a puppy. His first family left him at one, and he just sat in a corner of his kennel and shook. He wouldn't eat, and he–" I break off there, unable to speak past the knot in my throat. "Please. I need to know he's okay."

The man shakes his head. "It's against the rules."

My heart drops south, and I search for the words to make him understand. "He's my best friend," I say. "He needs me."

He looks at me for an endless string of moments. "I wish some of the folks who throw their dogs away here thought of them like that instead. If I get fired, maybe you can help me find a new job."

"I don't want you to lose your job, but I just want my dog back."

"Probably wouldn't be the worst thing that ever happened to me."

"Thank you so much," I say, the words pouring out in a gush of gratitude. "Thank you."

"Well, all right then." He pulls a set of keys from his pocket, walks over and opens the padlock on the gate, swinging each arm wide. "Y'all follow me."

I scramble into the truck, and Holden slides in behind me.

Neither of us says a word all the way to the building. I feel frozen to the seat, my heart pounding so hard in my chest that I know Holden must hear it.

Kenny pulls up to a side door, and we roll to a stop behind him. I hear the dogs from inside, a few barks starting up, and then more follow. By the time he steps in and flips on a light, all the dogs are awake and starting to bark.

"All right, now," Kenny says in a kind voice. "Y'all settle down."

His voice has an amazing calming effect. The barking subsides to a few rumbles of concern.

I scan the kennels in front of us, trying not to look at the faces. Already, my heart feels like it's swelled to the size of a pumpkin, and I'm afraid the sob sitting at the back of my throat is going to burst out at any second.

"Walk on down, and see if you see him," Kenny says.

I start down the aisle with Holden right behind me. I can tell he's trying to keep his gaze focused straight ahead. Halfway down, I spot Hank Junior curled up in the back of his kennel, shaking from the tip of his nose to the tip of his tail. Snuggled up next to him with its head on Hank's side is a chubby little Beagle.

"Hank," I say, my voice cracking.

He looks up, thumps his tail once as if he's afraid to believe it's really me.

Kenny steps in and says, "That him?"

"Yes," I say.

Kenny opens the door. I nearly leap inside, dropping to my knees and hugging Hank so hard he yelps. He licks my cheek though, still shaking.

"I'm sorry," I say, kissing his velvety ear, unable to hold back my tears.

Something nudges at my elbow, and I glance down to see the chubby Beagle looking up at me as if hoping to be included in the reunion.

Holden walks into the kennel and squats down beside us. He reaches out and strokes Hank's head, then does the same for the Beagle.

She all but melts under his touch and rolls over on her back. He smiles and scratches her belly.

"What's her name?" Holden asks, looking up at Kenny.

"Patsy," he says.

"As in Kline," I say, and we both smile.

Patsy turns her head and licks the back of Holden's hand. I see *him* melt a little.

"I hate to rush y'all," Kenny says, "but I've got to get to work."

I stand up and turn to face him. "Please let me take him now, Kenny. I can't leave him here. I just can't."

He looks at Hank and then back at me again. "So what kind of work did you say you have lined up for me?" he asks with a half-grin.

Before I can answer, he hands me a nylon leash and says, "Bring him on out."

I can't help it. I throw my arms around his neck and hug him hard. "Thank you. Thank you so much."

I slip the lead around Hank's neck, and he glues himself to my leg. Holden is still rubbing the Beagle. He stands reluctantly, following me through the door.

Kenny closes it and clicks the latch back in place. Patsy looks at Hank Junior, then up at us, her brown eyes suddenly sad, as if she knows she's being left. Clearly, not for the first time.

Holden points at the orange card with her name on the kennel door. "What does that mean?"

"Today is her day since nobody came for her," Kenny says, his voice flat now, as if he's had to practice saying these things without emotion.

"You mean she'll be put to sleep?" Holden asks, disbelieving.

"Yeah," Kenny says.

Holden's face goes white as chalk. I know in my heart how hard it must be for him to come in here in the first place and all the bad memories it must bring back. I kneel down and stick my hand back through the door to rub Patsy's head, feeling sick all the way down to the bottom of my stomach.

I don't see any orange cards on the other doors. I open my mouth to ask what her adoption fee is when Holden says, "Can I adopt her?"

Kenny glances at his watch. "The front desk people won't be here until eight. The euth tech usually comes in at seven-thirty."

Holden actually looks like he might pass out. I feel sick myself, but I put a hand on his arm, maybe to steady us both.

But his voice is strong when he says, "I don't care what the fee is. I'll put it on my credit card. Let us go on and take her. I promise I'll give her a good life."

Kenny glances at Patsy, then back at Holden, and hands him another nylon lead. "Y'all come on, so I can at least fill out the paperwork."

We follow him to the front office where he opens a drawer and pulls out two forms, one for me and one for Holden. I fill out the paperwork for Hank's release, waiting while Holden finishes the application for Patsy.

"The adoption fee is fifty dollars," Kenny says.

Holden opens his wallet and counts out the cash. I notice he has one dollar left.

Kenny takes it and says, "All right, then."

"Thank you, Kenny." Holden shakes his hand.

"For her sake, I'm glad y'all were here," Kenny says, walking around the desk and reaching down to rub Patsy's head. She looks up at him and wags her tail as if to say thank you.

"I'm happy for you, girl," he says, a rasp to his voice.

"Thank you so much, Kenny," I say and give him another hug.

He nods and walks us to the door. We step outside into the crisp morning air, Hank Junior and I climbing into the truck from the passenger side, and Holden picking Patsy up and putting her in from his side.

He backs the truck out of the spot, throws a wave at Kenny, then looks over at me and smiles. A really happy smile. I smile back, and as we roar off down the drive, it feels as if we've just done something as miraculous as cheating death. Which I guess we actually have.

♪

Holden

I stand under the shower spray way longer than I should, considering that Sarah is in my bedroom, waiting for me to come out. I let the water pummel my face into full-out awake until all threads of fatigue have dissolved.

When I can avoid it no more, I get out, dry off, put on sweat pants and a t-shirt, then open the bathroom door.

Sarah is sitting on the bed, her knees against her chest, arms wrapped tight around her legs, as if she is physically trying to hold herself together. She doesn't look at me, her gaze on her pink toenails. "Can you explain to me what just happened out there?" she finally asks.

"Nothing happened," I say, hearing the lack of conviction in my own voice.

She looks up at me then, and her blue eyes snap fire. "Holden Ashford, don't you dare play me. I deserve better than that from you. Who is she?"

"A girl hoping to make it in Nashville just like Thomas and me." I blow out a sigh and sit down on the edge of the bed. "Her car burned up on the side of the interstate. We stopped to help her, and that's how we met. That's it."

"That's it?" Sarah repeats, incredulous. "She's living in your apartment. How is that it?"

"She lost everything in her car. It made sense for us to help her out."

"I get that. And why were you out all last night with her?"

"Waiting at the pound to get Hank Junior out. Her dog. Thomas lost him while we were at work."

"We?"

"We got a job at the same restaurant."

Sarah folds her arms across her chest and stares at me hard. "I see. Wow. It sure didn't take long for you to forget all about me."

"That's not true."

"It seems like you're well on your way," she says, tears welling in her eyes.

My heart suddenly feels like it's been wrapped in one big rubber band, and I know I'm coming across as a jerk. Which considering what's been happening between CeCe and me, I guess I am. "Why did you change your mind about coming?" I ask, meeting her tearful gaze.

"I missed you," she says, and the words are so broken, so heartfelt that the wall of resistance inside me starts to crumble.

"I can't believe you drove through the night. You hate driving at night."

She nods. "Don't worry. I know it was stupid."

I feel like such an ass. I am an ass. "It wasn't stupid. I just wish you'd let me know you were comng."

"I wanted to surprise you."

And I can see that's exactly what she'd hoped to do. Just forty-eight hours ago, that would have made me ecstatic. Forty-eight hours ago, we would have already been in bed, making up for lost time.

But we're not. And we both know something feels different.

"I'm sorry, Sarah. It's been a long night. I'm just beat. I need some sleep."

"Do you want me to go?" she asks, her voice cracking a little.

I hear the question, and yet my response doesn't come immediately, as it should.

"Of course not," I say, but too many seconds have passed for me to be completely convincing. I know Sarah, and I know what she wants right now is to tell me to go to hell and leave as suddenly as she came. But I guess she's not ready to throw in the towel just yet, so she bites her lip and nods.

I open the bedroom door and call for Patsy. She trots down the hallway, looking up at me with expectant brown eyes. "Come on, girl," I say. "Nap time."

Inside the bedroom, Patsy looks around, walks to the side of the bed and lies down, stretching out with her chin on her paws.

Sarah looks at her like some unidentified object just fell through the roof. "She's sleeping in here?" she says.

"Yeah," I say.

"But you know I don't like–"

"I know you've never been around dogs, and you think you don't like them."

"That's not at all fair, Holden," she says, her voice deliberately even.

"I have a dog now, Sarah," I say. "I'm hoping you'll like her once you get to know her."

"I never should have come here!" Sarah jumps off the bed and stomps into the bathroom, where she promptly slams the door.

I reach down and rub Patsy's head. I want to call Sarah back and reassure her that she did the right thing in coming. I want to. I just don't know if it would be the truth.

♪

<!– pb_fixme –>
<!– pb_fixme –>
<!– pb_fixme –>

CeCe

It's almost eight a.m. by the time we park the truck in the back lot of the apartment complex. We get out and let Hank Junior and Patsy have a few minutes in the grass before we head up the stairs.

I'm so tired I feel like I can barely stand and at the same time so wired with feeling that I hardly know what to do with it. Has it really been less than eight hours since we left here last night looking for Hank? It seems like a lifetime has taken place since then.

Hank and I follow Holden and Patsy up the stairs, and I can't help but stare at his wide shoulders. My lips tingle with the memory of his kiss, and I have to stop myself from reaching for his shirt tail and pulling him to me.

At the apartment door, he sticks the key in the lock, then turns to me. "Weird as this sounds," he says, "it was kind of great being with you last night."

"Yeah," I say, "you, too."

He leans in, and I start to close my eyes in anticipation of his kiss. Just then, the door jerks open, and we both jump back from one another.

"Hey, you two," Thomas says in a tight voice I don't recognize. "Been wondering when you were gonna get back."

From behind him, a girl steps out, the look on her face clearly one of confusion. "Surprise," she says, only the word is flat, like a balloon someone has just let all the air out of.

"Sarah," Holden says, sounding as stunned as he looks.

"She drove all night to get here," Thomas says. "Isn't that something?"

"Is everything all right?" Holden asks.

Sarah glances from Holden to me, and her blue, very blue, eyes start to well with tears. "I thought it was," she says.

"You got a dog," Thomas throws out, as if looking for a diversion.

"Yeah," Holden says. "Her name's Patsy."

"A dog," Sarah says. "Wow. I didn't know you were–"

"It was kind of spur of the moment," he explains.

We all stand there for a few seconds like frozen popsicles, none of us sure what to do or say next. Holden moves first, stepping in to the apartment to put his arms around Sarah and hug her.

I watch, unable to move. Hank Junior whines and looks up at me, as if asking what this means. I don't dare look at him, sure I'll burst into tears if I do.

Holden steps back from the hug and waves a hand at me. "Sarah, this is CeCe. CeCe, Sarah."

We look at each other and smile, and I feel sure mine is as wobbly as hers. "Nice to meet you," we both say at the same time.

"So," Thomas says, "what a night, huh?"

"Yeah," Holden agrees, running a hand across the back of his hair.

"I bet Sarah would like to hear all about it," Thomas says. "Why don't y'all take the bedroom for some privacy, and I'll get the lowdown from CeCe out here?"

Holden looks at me, and I immediately glance away since I have no idea what to do with any of this. I feel as if a wrecking ball just landed in the center of my stomach.

"Ah, okay," Holden says. "Anything you need me to get out of your car, Sarah?"

She shakes her head. "Thomas already brought it in for me."

"You mind feeding Patsy when you feed Hank?" Holden directs the question to me.

"Sure," I say, super cheerful. "No problem."

Holden nods and walks down the hall to the bedroom. Sarah follows him. I stand perfectly still until I hear the click of the lock. Only then do I unhook Hank's leash and let out all the air in my chest.

"I'm real sorry, CeCe," Thomas says.

"You don't need to be," I say, assuming he's talking about Hank Junior, but suspecting the apology encompasses Sarah's arrival as well. "It all worked out."

"Tell me about it?" he asks, heading for the kitchen where he pulls two bowls from the cabinet and gets the dog food out of the pantry.

While Hank Junior and Patsy scarf up their food, I lay out everything that happened at the pound, including Holden's adopting Patsy at the last minute.

"I'm glad," Thomas says. "She's a cute little thing."

"I think she and Hank are in love."

Thomas smiles and then looks at me, the smile fading, "That got a little awkward out there."

I start to act like I don't know what he's talking about and then just as quickly realize how unbelievable I would be. "Yeah," I say.

"He really didn't know she was coming," Thomas says.

"Apparently."

He leans against the sink and folds his arms across his chest. "Holden is a lot of things, but he's never been a player. I think you kind of caught him off guard."

"Timing has never really been my thing."

"They've been together almost two years. I don't want to see you hurt, CeCe."

"She's beautiful," I say. "Really beautiful."

"So are you," Thomas says.

I start to shake my head, but he adds, "You are. It's just gonna be that timing thing."

I feel the tears start to well up, try my best to stop them, but they roll down my face like a faucet's been turned on inside of me.

"Hey, now," Thomas says, walking over and pulling me into his big embrace.

My tears get his t-shirt all wet, and I start to apologize, but he shushes me, rubbing the back of my hair. "I'm sorry for the hurt."

"I'll get over it," I say.

"You're strong like that," he agrees.

I want to tell him that I don't want to be strong. I want to march down the hall to that bedroom, pound on the door and beg Holden to give what we'd both felt this morning and last night a shot.

But I don't. I just press my lips together and nod. Because, what else, really, is there for me to do?

♪

Holden

We get to the Cocky Cow at just before eight. Thomas had woken me up around four so we could practice before our set. Sarah's upset with me because she wanted to have dinner alone and talk, but talking is about the last thing I want to do with Sarah since I have no idea what to say.

She's sitting at a corner table now, nursing a diet Coke and looking as if she's sorry the idea of coming to Nashville ever occurred to her.

CeCe is helping us get set up, and we're avoiding each other as if both our lives depend on it. I'm trying not to notice the way J.B. is openly flirting with her, or the way she's smiling back at him as if she likes it.

Adrienne comes over and gives me a hug, telling me how much she loves the song we wrote together. "I can't wait to hear you sing it," I say.

"Be happy to give you a private show," she says with just enough teasing in her voice to call the offer a joke if pride needs saving.

I stop short of an answer when Thomas walks over and shakes his head. "I ain't envying your position, man."

I don't bother to ask him what he means. "I had no idea she was coming," I say.

"Yeah, but didn't she have the right to?"

"I'm not saying she didn't," I admit.

"You just weren't expecting CeCe," Thomas says.

"No. I wasn't expecting CeCe."

Thunder claps outside the building, loud enough to make itself heard above the pre-show music playing in the bar.

"Whoa," Thomas says. "They're calling for some serious storms."

Thomas taps his phone screen, looks at it for a moment and then says, "Weather.com shows a tornado watch for this area."

CeCe walks up, deliberately not looking at me. "Tornado watch?" she repeats.

"That ain't no good," Thomas says.

"It's just a watch," I say. "Probably nothing."

I meet eyes with CeCe then for the first time since this morning when Sarah had greeted us at the front door. Our gazes snag for a moment, and it feels like both of us have trouble glancing away.

"You got a song in you tonight, CeCe?" Thomas asks.

She looks at him and starts to shake her head.

"Aw, come on. Just one." He names a couple her uncle wrote.

"What about Sarah?" CeCe says. "She might want to sing with you tonight."

"We'll ask her," Thomas says, "but I'm not sure she's in a singing mood."

I give him a look that makes him duck and throw an air punch at me. CeCe looks uncomfortable and says, "You should ask her."

"This a private meeting, or can I sit in?"

J.B. strolls over, one thumb hooked through the belt loop of his jeans, his gaze focused solely on CeCe.

"We're just trying to talk her into singing a song with us tonight."

"I'd sure like to hear you sing, CeCe," J.B. says, standing closer to her than seems necessary. "We still on for that drink tonight?"

"Yeah," she replies. "If we don't get hit by a tornado."

"Whhhhaat?" J.B. says.

"There's a watch," Thomas throws out.

"This place got a cellar?" J.B. asks, and from the look on his face, I'm thinking he's really worried about it.

"Shouldn't we be hitting the stage?" I say to Thomas.

"Eight o'clock. I reckon so," Thomas says.

"CeCe, you wanna hang out until Adrienne and I go on?" J.B. says.

"Sure," she answers, and if you ask me, her voice is a little too bright to be believable. Even so, her answer leaves me wishing I could remove the satisfied grin from J.B. Langley's mouth.

♪

CeCe

I should sleep.

But I can't. Don't. Won't. One of those, anyway. To close my eyes and invite sleep would be to open the current plug on my thoughts and let them come flooding in. And since I'm pretty sure I will drown in them, I opt for staying awake.

I do take a shower, and that helps wash away some of my fatigue. I try not to think about what Holden and Sarah are doing in the next room, and when my mind refuses to blank, I increase the cold water until I'm shivering and nearly blue.

When I walk back into the kitchen wearing jeans and a wet ponytail, Thomas looks up from a bowl of cereal and says, "Aren't you going to bed?"

"I don't like to sleep during the day."

"Me, either. Wanna walk over to Starbucks for a coffee? I'm meeting a couple people there."

I glance at Hank Junior who's snoozing on the sofa. "I don't really want to leave him yet."

"He can go with us. We can sit outside."

At this, I immediately agree, since the last thing I want is to stay in the apartment alone with Holden and Sarah. "If you're sure we won't be in the way."

"Course not. I think you'll like them, anyhow."

The Starbucks is only three blocks over from the apartment. We walk the short distance with Hank Junior on full sniff alert. He meets up with an elderly Pug and a regal Great Dane who both greet him like they're old friends.

We get there at just after ten and find a table on the outside patio where students from Vanderbilt sit in front of laptops, and a variety of music types talk on cell phones and text in between sips of the morning's blend.

Thomas waves at a girl standing by the main entrance. She waves back and walks over. "Hey," Thomas says while they hug.

"Adrienne Langley, this is CeCe MacKenzie," he says. "And her boy Hank Junior."

"Hey, CeCe," Adrienne says. "Hey, Hank." She bends down to rub him under the chin, and the look in her eyes tells me she's a dog-lover. I can't help but instantly like her.

"Nice to meet you," I say.

"You, too," she says, standing again. "Where's Holden?"

"He got a little detained this morning," Thomas says by way of explanation.

"Oh, I was hoping he would be here," Adrienne says, and I can see she's a verified member of Holden's ever-increasing female fan club.

A tall, dark-haired guy walks up behind her and hands her a coffee. "Tall, medium roast, sis."

"Thanks," she says, smiling at him. "Thomas, this is my brother J.B. J.B, Thomas and his friend CeCe."

J.B. shakes Thomas's hand and then settles his gaze on me. "Nice to meet you both."

He's about as good-looking as any guy I've ever met. If he were trying out for a movie role, he'd probably get it just because he's got that kind of longish, wavy hair that says box office instant success. I can't stop myself from blushing under his assessment. "You, too," I say.

"This table okay?" We pull out chairs, while Hank Junior settles himself in a slice of shade from a nearby tree, then stretches out like he's got sleep to catch up on.

"What's your pleasure, CeCe?" Thomas asks. "I'll go in and get us a cup."

"Tall blonde," I say.

"We are talking about coffee, right?" J.B. says with a grin.

"We are," Thomas says, giving him a look. "Be right back."

Adrienne pulls out a chair, and J. B. steps around to take the one between the two of us. He waits for us each to sit before sitting down.

"Where are you from, CeCe?" Adrienne looks at me and then takes a sip of her coffee.

"Virginia."

"All right," J.B. says.

"How 'bout y'all?" I ask, attempting to ignore the suggestive edge in his voice.

"North Carolina," Adrienne answers.

"How long have you been here?"

"Six months."

"And three days," J.B. adds.

"Made any headway?" I ask.

"Some, I think," Adrienne says. "We're playing out most nights. Audiences are getting bigger. Youtube hits for our videos are increasing. And we're getting ready to record a song that we're releasing under our own label."

"Cool," I say, feeling more than a little like the new guppy in the pond. "What's the song like?"

"It's actually one we wrote with Thomas's buddy Holden the last time they were in town. I'm so in love with it."

My stomach does an automatic dip at the sound of Holden's name, and my head is filled with an instant vision of Sarah stretched out alongside him in bed, their legs entwined–

"You know him?" J.B. asks, jerking my attention back to the present.

"He and Thomas kind of rescued me from the side of the Interstate a few days ago."

"Lucky them," J.B. says, flirtation at the edges of the comment.

"I'm not so sure they saw it that way."

"They're good guys," Adrienne says. "If you need rescuing, they're the ones you want riding up on the white horse."

J.B. rolls his eyes and slides down in his chair, crossing his arms across his nicely muscled chest. "That white hat thing can get kind of boring, don'tcha think?"

Adrienne looks at me and shakes her head. "Don't pay any attention to him. He likes bad girls."

"Hey now. Dissing your brother like that."

Adrienne pins him with a look. "You know it's true."

Before J.B. can answer, Thomas returns with the coffee, setting mine down in front of me.

"Thanks," I say, pulling out the chair beside me so he can sit down.

"I got Hank Junior a little cup of whipped cream," he says, and puts the cup down in front of him. Hank starts to lick, tentatively at first, and then with total enthusiasm. Thomas grins. "Thought you'd like that."

"He's going to be totally ruined," I say, even as I can't deny loving Thomas a little more each time he does something like this.

"He's yours?" J.B. directs the question to me.

"Yes," I say.

"Which one of you sings?" J.B. teases.

"He's got a good howl," I answer. "Sometimes, I'd say he's the better of the two of us."

"She's being modest," Thomas throws in. "She sings like an angel."

"Really?" Adrienne asks, and despite her smile, I hear the competitive lilt in the question.

"As you know you do, too, Adrienne," Thomas says, tipping his coffee cup at her in mock salute.

"Why, thank you, sir," she says, perking back up.

"So what is it you two wanted to talk about this morning?" Thomas asks, stretching his legs out in front of his chair.

"I was hoping Holden would be with you so we could all talk," Adrienne says, "but what we wanted to discuss was pitching both our acts to venues, kind of as a double header thing. J.B. and I think we draw a similar crowd and that we might make more of an impact that way."

"And we were hoping to write some more songs together," J.B. throws in.

"How far out are y'all booked?" Thomas asks.

"A week," Adrienne and J.B. say in unison.

"Nothing like job security, is there?" Thomas asks, and we all smile.

"We're booked over at the Cocky Cow tonight. If y'all want to play before us, we've already cleared it with the manager."

"Cool," Thomas says. "I'll check with Holden. Text you in a bit?"

"Sure," Adrienne says. "We've got an appointment with a publisher in an hour. And I need to go spiff up."

"All right, then," Thomas says. "Check you later."

Adrienne and J.B. push back their chairs and stand. Thomas and I do the same, and I wake up Hank Junior who yawns and then follows me through the maze of tables.

Adrienne and Thomas step aside to say something to one another, and J.B. turns to me with a smile. "Would you be free for a drink after our gig tonight?"

Given my no doubt accurate impression of J.B. as a player, I start to say no. But then I get an instant visual of Sarah with Holden and wonder how I can possibly stay in the apartment with them. "Maybe," I hedge.

"How do I get that changed to a yes?" he asks, looking down at me with a grin that I am sure rarely fails him.

"Do you like dogs?" I ask.

He laughs then. "Not as much as girls. But yeah, I like dogs. Is that a prerequisite?"

"Definitely," I say.

"Not a problem," he says, still grinning. "So I'll see you tonight then?"

"Sure," I answer.

"Good." He waves and gets in the convertible VW Adrienne is driving.

During our walk back to the apartment, Thomas looks at me and says, "You gotta watch that guy."

"How so?" I ask.

"His own sister won't let her friends date him."

"Ouch."

"Did he ask you out?"

"Yes."

"And?"

"I said I'd have a drink with him."

"He's not your type, CeCe."

"I don't know if I have a type yet," I say.

"And if you're doing this to get back at Holden–"

"Holden has a girl friend," I interrupt.

"I can't deny that," he says. "But don't let that make you do something you'll regret."

"It's just a drink," I say.

"Most mistakes start out that way," he says. "Let me ask you this. Would you go out with him if Sarah hadn't shown up?"

I'd like to prove him wrong by answering with an immediate yes, but we both know I'd be lying. So I don't say anything. What would be the point?

♪

Holden

CeCe and Sarah sit between Thomas and me, Sarah's back ramrod straight. I can see CeCe's trying her best not to touch shoulders with Sarah, but that's pretty much impossible since we're packed in here like books on a library shelf.

Sarah has her fingers entwined tightly with mine. I'm not sure if it's because she needs the security of my touch or if she's making a statement.

Not that CeCe appears to notice. She hasn't looked at me once since we came out of the basement. Even so, there's a cord of electricity between us that I feel and somehow know she does, too.

Thomas navigates the truck out of the parking lot and then rides with two tires on the sidewalk for a couple of blocks or so until we get around some of the vehicles that have been tossed along the street like toys.

A few people are standing outside shop doors looking shell-shocked. Thomas rolls down his window and throws out, "Y'all need any help?"

"We're good," a man answers back.

Most of the street lights are out, and it feels like a scene from one of those apocalyptic movies. The sky is still a heavy, gunmetal grey. We make decent headway until we're a couple of miles or so from the apartment. A Range Rover sits at an odd angle in the middle of the street, the driver's side door open. There's no one else anywhere in sight.

Thomas brakes the truck to a stop, and we both jump out and run to the car. There's a woman in the driver's seat. She's slumped to one side, unconscious. I realize then that it's Lauren, my boss at the restaurant.

Sarah and CeCe run over to the car. "What happened?" CeCe asks.

Before I can answer, CeCe spots Lauren and says, "Oh, no."

"Who is she?" Sarah asks.

"She owns the restaurant where we work," I answer. I lean in to feel for a pulse in her neck, my own heart pounding so hard I can hear it in my ears.

The beat is there, and I feel a quick jab of relief.

"Should we try to get her out?" Thomas asks.

"I don't know," I say, pulling my phone from my back pocket and dialing 911. An operator answers immediately and asks what my emergency is. I tell her, and she tells me the wait may be fifteen minutes or more because of the tornado and the number of emergency calls it has generated. She asks if we can get Lauren to the hospital.

"Yes," I say. "Or at least I think so."

"Call back if you can't," she says, and she's gone.

I look at Thomas and CeCe. "We need to get her to the emergency room."

"Can you take her vehicle, and I'll head for the apartment to check on the dogs?"

"Yeah," I say.

"Let's put her in the back," Thomas says. He leans in and lifts Lauren out like she's nothing more than a cotton ball and places her gently on the leather seat.

"CeCe, can you ride with her?" I ask. "At least if she wakes up, she'll know you."

"I'm going with Thomas," Sarah says, folding her arms and walking stiff-backed to the truck.

I start to go after her, tell her to come with us, but I honestly don't feel like arguing right now. And I'm also afraid of what might happen if we don't get Lauren to the hospital asap.

"Y'all get going. I'll take care of her," Thomas says, giving me a sympathetic look.

I get in the driver's seat, glance over my shoulder at CeCe who is looking a little too pale, then throw the Rover into gear. I gun it for the hospital, reminding myself how to get there.

An iPhone is lying on the passenger seat. I pick it up and check the recent calls. There's Case Phillips's name and number.

I hold it up and flash the screen at CeCe. "Think we ought to call him?"

"Can't hurt. Maybe he'll know what might be wrong."

I hit send, and put it on speaker, unable to believe I'm actually calling Case Phillips.

He answers on the first ring. "Hey, baby. Are you okay? I've been trying to call you."

I clear my throat and say, "Mr. Phillips. This is Holden Ashford. I work for Lauren at the restaurant. We found her in her car, unconscious. My friend and I are driving her to the hospital, but we thought you might have an idea what could be wrong."

"She's diabetic," he says with quick urgency. "She's passed out before. There should be a kit in her purse."

"I already looked for her purse," CeCe says from the back seat. "There isn't one in the car."

"She never goes anywhere without it," Case says, disbelieving. "Could she have been mugged?"

"It's possible," I say. "The door was open when we pulled up."

Case lets out a string of curses and then says, "Keep me on the phone until you reach the hospital."

"Okay," I agree, and then put my attention on getting us there without wrecking.

I drive well over the speed limit, deciding I'll take my chances with an explanation if I get pulled over. Right now, all I care about is getting Lauren to the ER where someone will know how to help her.

We're there in minutes, and I pull up to the main door, hopping out and running inside. I'm still holding Lauren's phone, and I let Case know we made it.

"I'm driving now. I'll meet you there," he says. "Oh, and thank you. Thank you so much."

I click off the phone, realizing that he really loves her, the fear in his voice proof of it.

I flag down a nurse and tell her what's happened and that Lauren is diabetic.

She grabs a gurney and follows me back outside where I lift Lauren out of the seat and place her carefully on it.

"Are you family?" the nurse asks me.

"No," I say. "We found her like this in her car."

"Is there someone who can give us a history?"

"Her—Case Phillips," I say. "He's on his way."

The woman's eyes widen a little before professionalism slips back into place. "Please direct him to the registration desk when he gets here," she says, and then she's wheeling Lauren toward the ER doors marked Restricted.

I let myself look at CeCe then. She's still looking a little panicky.

"Will she be all right?" she asks, clearly needing me to say yes.

"I hope so," I say and realize that's the best I can do.

We find a parking place for the Rover and then walk back inside the hospital where we wait by a vending machine. In less than five minutes, Case Phillips runs through the main doors. I wave at him, and he walks over, his face drawn with worry.

"We're the ones who brought Lauren in," I say.

"Oh. Thank you. Thank you so much. Where is she?"

I point to the restricted door. "They took her in there. The nurse asked me to tell you they'll need whatever information you can give them."

"Of course." He glances at CeCe and then back at me again. "You both look familiar. Have we met?"

"Sort of," I say, not wanting to elaborate.

But his face lights with recognition and then slight embarrassment. He glances at CeCe and says, "Ah, sorry about that."

She shakes her head. "Don't worry about it."

By now, people are starting to recognize him. There's some pointing and murmuring, a couple of giggles.

"Do you two have a ride?" he asks.

"We can get a cab," I say.

"No need. Take the Rover. We'll get it later."

"No, really."

"I insist," he says. "And Lauren would as well."

"All right," I say, still reluctant.

"I better get them what they need so I can see her."

"Sure."

"Thank you both again."

He heads for the registration desk, stares and smiles following him. And if it weren't a hospital, I'm sure people would be asking for autographs.

CeCe and I walk to the parking lot with a few feet of space between us, silent.

I unlock the Rover and slide into the driver's side. For a moment, I think she's going to get in the back again, but she opens the passenger door with some reluctance.

"I don't bite," I say.

"Hm," she says on a note of disagreement.

I back out of the parking lot and pull onto the street, the Rover engine an expensive sounding low rumble.

"I hope she'll be okay," CeCe says, looking out the window. "My mom nearly died once like that."

"I'm sorry," I say, glancing at her. "Were you there?"

"I found her when I got home from school."

"That must have been scary."

"It was," she says.

"Do you miss her?"

"A lot."

"What about your dad?" I ask.

"He's never been in the picture."

For some reason, this surprises me.

"Your parents?"

"Divorced. My mom actually lives in London."

"Do you see her often?"

"Not very."

"And your dad?"

"He's in Georgia. We pretty much try to avoid each other."

"That's sad," CeCe says and then looks as if she wants to take it back.

"Yeah, it is," I agree.

"Is it anything that can't be fixed?"

"Probably."

She wants to ask more. I can feel it. But I guess she senses I don't want to talk about it. We're quiet for a few moments, and then I say, "CeCe?"

"Hmm?"

"About Sarah."

"Don't. Please," she says, holding up a hand. "You don't need to. It's not like I didn't know you had a girlfriend."

"I didn't mean for this to happen," I say. "I'm not a guy who does that kind of thing."

"And I'm not a girl who does that kind of thing. So we need to forget about it."

"I want to," I say. "I just don't know if I can."

She looks at me then, and I see the quick flash of longing. It echoes inside me, and I swing the Rover off the street into a parking place. I turn off the engine, and we sit like this, staring straight ahead while I tell myself I'm being an idiot. That I should drive us both home. Now.

That doesn't explain why I turn to her, slip my hand to the back of her neck and pull her to me. I don't know who kisses who first. But it doesn't really matter. I can't think of anything else. I don't want anything else. Just her mouth beneath mine. And those sweet, soft sounds she's making, blocking out any other thoughts.

She slips her arms around my neck, and even with the gear shift between us, we manage to melt into one another. I've never wanted anyone in my life the way I want her now. I can't separate the want from my heartbeat, my breathing; it's so much a part of me.

It's no surprise that she's the one to pull away first. She opens the Rover door and jumps out as if it's the only sure ticket to safety. I sit for a moment, my eyes closed as I force myself to rational thought.

I let a few moments pass, then get out and walk around the vehicle where CeCe is leaning against a big round oak tree.

"We know better," she says.

"I don't deny that."

"That won't happen again," she adds, and I can't tell if she's trying to convince me or herself.

"CeCe–"

"You have someone in your life," she goes on as if I haven't spoken. "As long as that's the case, we can't be."

I know she's right. I want to argue, disagree, throw out excuses. But there really aren't any. "I'm sorry," I say, the words limp and meaningless.

We stare at each other for a string of seconds, and I feel like I'm about to lose something I never knew I was looking for. I jab the toe of my boot into the sidewalk, and wish I had an argument to stand on. But I don't. And we both know it.

"Can you give me a little time?" I ask.

"To what? Figure out how to break her heart into a hundred pieces instead of a thousand."

"No–"

"Yes, Holden. She loves you. And you probably still love her, too."

I'd like to deny it outright, tell her she's wrong. A few days ago, though, I did love her. Or thought I did.

"I don't want to be the reason you hurt her, Holden. If what you have isn't real, then it shouldn't take me to help you figure that out. And if it is real, well, it's real."

She stares at me for a few heartbeats, and I know I could sway her. Just by reaching out and pulling her to me. I also know that would make me the biggest kind of jerk. And probably a fool as well. Because she's right.

CeCe gets back in the Rover, buckles her seat belt.

I walk around and slide in the driver's side, pulling out onto the street. I hit the Satellite radio button, and music fills the interior. It's loud, and I like it that way. It keeps what I'm thinking inside of me. Silent. As it should be.

♪

CeCe

I know Holden and Sarah aren't talking. She's sitting at the back of the room, alternating staring at me with staring at him.

I'd like to go on and decide that I just plain don't like her, but then I think what it must be like to come all this way to see your boyfriend only to get here and realize that something's changed in the few days you've been apart.

I'm not saying that I think I'm responsible for that change. Maybe I'm just the bump in the road that's making Holden question whether he and Sarah are right for one another. But even I can see that he's questioning it.

I'm alternating between feeling like a rotten, relationship-wrecker and a hopeful, crush-stricken adolescent.

I sit at a table near the front of the room with J.B., nursing a Coke while Holden and Thomas bring the crowd of people in the room to life. Just about every person there is listening with the kind of intensity you only get when people really like what you're doing.

Without doubt, Thomas was born to be on stage. There's a natural ease to the way he tells something funny or revealing about himself and then segues into a song Holden has written about that exact thing. I could listen to them all night. Not just Thomas's voice but the way Holden plays the guitar as if it is the only thing he was ever meant to do. As if he feels every note. Every word. I find myself waiting for the moments when he comes in with a background vocal, his voice the perfect accompaniment to Thomas's thick, country twang.

I try not to meet eyes with them throughout the performance, but it's like there's a magnet between us. Every time I feel him looking at me, I can't help myself from letting my gaze bump his.

J.B. is apparently aware of this because every time it happens, he leans forward and says something in my ear. I get the impression that he's doing it as much to rile Holden as he is to sweet talk me.

Thomas is talking to the crowd again. I pull my thoughts back to his voice, telling myself I'm not going to look at Holden again.

"This next number, folks," Thomas says, "is a song Holden wrote one night when we both decided we didn't really care what we had to do to support our love for this business, singing and writing songs. Short of armed robbery, of course."

Laughter ripples through the crowd.

"Aside from that, anything we did, whether it's building a house or waiting tables would just be the means to the freedom to do what we love. This here's called A Hammer and a Song."

I listen to the words, and I hear Holden in each and every one of them. He has a real gift, and it's clear that this life means everything to him. I can only imagine how hard that must have been for Sarah to accept. If she has.

When the song is over, a few beats of silence follow the moment when Thomas lays down his microphone. The applause erupts all at once, punctuated by whistles and whoops. I glance at J.B. whose clapping is tentative to say the least, his voice a little clipped when he says, "That's good stuff."

"It is," I say, and then before I know it, Thomas is taking my hand and pulling me up on the stage. My heart is beating a thousand miles an hour and my hands are suddenly clammy. Thomas tells the audience about my Uncle Dobie and the great songs he had written.

"We're gonna do one of those for you, folks," he says, nodding at me.

I close my eyes and wait for Holden's intro, and then Thomas and I dip into the song together. For the next three minutes, I'm in that other place where all that matters is the music. It's a place I sometimes wish I could stay in, that sweet spot where the notes and the words all come together to create something wonderful, magical.

When it's over, the crowd gives us their approval with gratifying applause. My heart is no longer racing, and I just feel grateful to Thomas for his generosity. I hug him. He hugs me back while the audience claps harder, and I force myself not to look at Holden.

We're about to leave the stage when a sudden noise rises above the clapping. Everyone goes silent, and the sudden wail of an alarm fills the room, the noise clogging our ears like smoke in the lungs.

A man in a white shirt and black pants runs over to the stage and takes the microphone from Thomas. "Folks, I'm the manager here. A tornado has just been spotted in the downtown area. We have been advised by public safety officials to immediately take cover in the downstairs part of the building. Let's all keep our cool. Single file if you would, and follow me to the stairwell."

His voice is even and reassuring as if this is something he does every night. He steps off the stage then and heads for the main entrance to the bar.

"Seriously?" Thomas says, looking at me and then Holden.

Holden glances at the back of the room and says, "I'll get Sarah. Meet you two downstairs."

He steps down from the stage and begins winding his way through the crowd to the back of the room where Sarah stands waiting, with a panicked look on her face.

I remember then that Hank Junior and Patsy are at the apartment alone.

"The dogs, Thomas," I say, feeling a well of panic. "I need to get home."

"CeCe, that siren means we need to do what they say. I'll drive you myself as soon as we get the all clear." Thomas takes my hand, and I follow him through the lobby to the stairwell where people are hurrying downstairs.

"They'll be all right," he says over his shoulder. "And look at it this way. This will probably give us something to write about."

"Then I hope it's a song with a happy ending," I say, tears welling up.

The alarm is loud, and I'd like to cover my ears as we head down, but I'm afraid to let go of Thomas's hand. My heart is throbbing in time with the siren's wail, and I say a silent prayer that this will be over soon.

The room we're filing into is large and dimly lit. The alarm has lost its knife edge blare, and I feel like I can again think a little more clearly. We find a spot in a far corner and sit on the floor against the wall.

I see Holden come through the door, Sarah holding onto his arm. I wish for a moment that they would sit at the opposite end of the room from us, but Thomas waves them over.

Holden looks at me and says, "Think the dogs will be all right?"

"I hope so," I say, not quite able to meet his concerned gaze.

"Why wouldn't they be?" Sarah asks. "They're inside, aren't they?"

No one answers her. I'm certainly not going to since what I want to say isn't likely to make us fast friends.

Holden takes the spot next to me, leaning back against the wall. Sarah studies him for a moment, then wilts onto the floor beside him, as if it is the last place on earth she wants to be.

"How long do we have to stay here?" she asks, the words sounding like those of a petulant seven-year-old.

"Until the threat of a tornado passes, I would imagine," Thomas says, and I can hear the disapproval in his voice.

The lights in the room, already dim, flicker and extinguish all together as if someone has just blown out a candle.

Voices rise up in protest, and then that of the manager calling out for everyone to please listen. "Sorry about that, folks. Looks like we've lost our power. I know none of you came out expecting this tonight. But for the moment, it is what it is. I doubt the lights will be out for long. Let's sit tight, and give this cloud a chance to pass on over. Oh, and keep your hands to yourself, please."

This actually pulls forth a chuckle from the crowd, although I notice Sarah doesn't laugh.

From our basement haven, the wind is muffled, but its fury is still evident. I can hear something flapping at the top of the stairs.

"Sounds like a door," Thomas says.

The sounds stops, and for a second, it's silent. And then out of nowhere, another sound hits, like a train speeding through the darkness. The roar is so loud I put my hands to my ears and squeeze hard. I scream and realize I'm not the only one. An arm encircles me from either side, both Thomas and Holden are holding onto me. I feel Sarah's arms bolt around Holden's waist, the four of us linked together like a human chain of fear.

I press my face into Holden's shoulder and bite back the terror that yanks me under like a sudden, unexpected riptide.

I want to melt into him, and here in the dark, I let myself imagine we are the only two here. I remember what it felt like to be in his arms, his mouth on mine, his hands—

But we're not alone. Sarah is crying now, and Holden is soothing her with his voice, telling her it'll be over soon, that everything is going to be all right.

I pull myself out of the half circle of his arm, and Thomas hooks me up against him, comforting me with his big embrace.

I'm not sure how long we sit there. It really seems like hours, but it might just be minutes. Or even seconds.

As quickly as the roar descended, it is gone. Just like that. In the snap of a finger. And the room is terrifyingly quiet.

"Is everyone all right?" the manager speaks up, his voice by now familiar even though we can't see him. He sounds shaken, as if he's not sure what to do next.

A chorus of yes, yes, yes rises up, followed by sighs of relief. As if in unspoken agreement, everyone stays seated for a couple of minutes. No alarms. No wind. Just silence.

And then footsteps sound on the stairs, followed by an official-sounding voice. "Anyone need help down here?"

"I think we're all okay," the manager answers back. "Is it all right to come out?"

"Yes. Your building held up well. But it's a mess outside. Y'all be careful now. I brought some flashlights for you."

"Thanks," the manager says. He turns one on and shines it across the room.

I squint at the light, my eyes already adjusting to the dark. Thomas stands and offers me a hand. I get to my feet and say, "Can we go home now?" And I'm praying the tornado didn't hit our apartment building.

Thomas flicks on the flashlight someone just handed him and says, "Let's go."

Holden and Sarah follow us up the stairs. It's slow going with all the people in front of us, but we finally reach the top and walk out into the night.

A few street lights are on, others hanging limply from their poles as if they'd just taken a left hook. But that's the least of it. The four of us stand staring at the wreckage around us. Cars that had been parallel parked in front of the bar now sit on their sides, front end, and some are even rolled over on their tops.

It's like a giant lumbered down the street and picked them each up the way a toddler picks up toy cars, dropping them where he pleases when they cease to interest him.

No one says anything for a full minute, and then Thomas utters, "Good day in the mornin'."

"Let's go see if the truck is in one piece," Holden says.

We weave our way down the sidewalk to the side parking lot where Thomas had parked earlier. Amazingly enough, every car in the square lot is exactly as it had been left. The funnel cloud had made a line of carnage straight down the street, taking complete mercy on anything to either side of it.

"Thank goodness," I say.

"The only question," Holden says, "is will we be able to get out of here?"

Thomas glances around and nods once. "I didn't get her in four wheel drive for nothing."

"You can't just roll over other cars," Sarah says, sounding a little dazed.

"Y'all hop on in, and leave the driving to me," Thomas advises. And since we don't have any other choice, we do.

♪

CeCe

It's after one a.m. when we let ourselves in the door of the apartment.

Hank Junior greets us in his usual way, jumping down from the sofa and trotting to the door to first nudge me with his nose and then Holden. Loyalty keeps him from going to Holden first, even though I suspect, if he had his way, he would.

Ever since we sprang him from the pound, Hank Junior looks at Holden the way he's always looked at me. Like he knows most of the secrets to the universe.

Patsy's still more cautious. She waits for Holden to walk over to the couch and rub her under the chin. With this reminder that he's one of the nice guys, she's suddenly all wiggles and wags, hopping down to trot into the kitchen after him and Hank Junior.

I hear the refrigerator door open and the rustling of the plastic wrapping that holds the sliced turkey Holden gives Hank Junior and Patsy every night when we get home from the restaurant.

"Holden?"

I jump at the sound of Sarah's voice from the end of the hall, and reality comes crashing back like a cold ocean wave.

I call for Hank Junior and head for my room, my only regret that I have to pass Sarah on the way. She avoids my eyes on the way to the kitchen, and I step into the bedroom, wait for Hank to pad in behind me and close the door. I flip on the light and spot Thomas sprawled on the floor next to the bed in a sleeping bag.

"Hey," he says, raising up on one elbow. "Hope you don't mind me crashing in here."

"Of course not," I say. "You take the bed, Thomas. I'll be fine on the floor."

"Not necessary. Unless you wanna share it?" he says with a teasing grin.

His hair is all messed up, and there's a smile in his eyes. It occurs to me then that some girl is going to fall madly in love with him. For a second, I wish it were me. "You would so regret that in the morning," I say, heading into the bathroom.

"I'm thinking you might be wrong about that."

"You're just being nice to me," I say, putting toothpaste on my toothbrush.

"How you figure?"

"Because I was dumb enough to fall for Holden."

"Apparently, you're not aware of your obvious charms, sweetheart," he says.

I smile. "Thanks. My ego could use the boost right about now."

"He's not rejecting you, CeCe. It's just—"

"Sarah was there first," I finish for him.

"Yeah. I guess," he says.

"I get it."

"Doesn't make it hurt less though, does it?"

"No, it doesn't." I reach for my nightgown where it hangs on a hook behind the door. I push the door closed and slip out of my clothes.

I flick off the bedroom light before making my way to the bed, sliding under the covers, Hank already curled up at the foot.

A car drives by on the street outside the bedroom window, and then the room is silent again.

"Have you ever been in love, Thomas?"

"I thought it was love," he says.

"It wasn't?"

"If it doesn't last, I don't guess you can call it love."

"Yeah," I say.

"Felt good at the time though," he adds. "And I got a pretty good tune out of it. Holden got tired of seeing me mope around, so he made me write a song with him about her."

I laugh softly. "What was it called?"

"Fifty Acres and a Tractor."

"Seriously?"

He laughs. "Holden has a way of clarifying the picture."

At the mention of his name, I picture Sarah and him in the other room. I wonder if he's making love to her, and the thought is so painful, I squeeze my eyes closed tight to disrupt the image. "Thomas?"

"Yeah?"

"Can I come down there with you?"

"Well, sure. We'll both the do the sleeping bag thing. Let Hank have the bed."

I never had a brother. Never imagined what it would feel like to have someone in my life who might have my back the way a brother would. But I'd like to think he would have been like Thomas if I did have one.

I slide out of bed and scoot into the bag beside him. He raises up so I can rest my head on his shoulder. He rubs his thumb across my hair, and I know he's guessed what I'm thinking about.

"You know it'll work out how it's meant to," he says.

I nod, unable to force any words past the lump in my throat.

"Meanwhile, you got a singing career to work on."

"And starting tomorrow morning, that's all I'm going to think about. Forget this love stuff."

"There you go. It just gets in the way, anyhow."

Hank starts to snore, and we both laugh.

"I'm glad I met you, Thomas," I say.

"I'm glad I met you, CeCe," he agrees.

He gives me a kiss on the top of my head, and we let ourselves fall asleep.

♪

THE KNOCK THAT wakes us up is sharp and a little angry-sounding.

I raise up on one elbow at the same time Thomas does, and we knock heads, both of us muttering a groggy, "Ouch."

"Yeah?" Thomas barks out.

The door opens a crack, and Holden sticks his head inside. He looks from one of us to the other, his eyes going wide, before he says, "Seriously?"

Thomas rakes a hand over his face, and gives him a glare. "Don't get your panties in a bunch, man. What do you want?"

Holden looks as if he wants to slam the door and rewind these last few moments. "Lauren called, CeCe. She wants us to bring the Rover over to her house."

"When?" I ask, sleep still at the edges of my voice.

"Now."

"Why?"

"I don't know."

"Can't you take it without me?"

"She specifically said to make sure you come, too. If we want a job to go to tonight, we probably oughta do as she asks."

I roll over on my knees, arch my back like a cat and shake loose the threads of fatigue. When I flop back over, Holden is staring at me like I'm the glass of water he's crossed a desert for.

"I'm going back to sleep," Thomas says and yanks the sleeping bag over his head, leaving me bare-legged and exposed to Holden's caught-in-the-headlights stare.

"Okay," I say. "I'll be ready in ten minutes."

He closes the door without responding. I scramble to my feet, yank a t-shirt on over my head and hook a leash to Hank Junior's collar.

We head outside into the cool morning air, and goosebumps instantly break across my arms. Hank makes short work of his business. I'm ready to go back in when Holden comes out with Patsy.

Awkward doesn't begin to describe the cloud that instantly descends over the two of us. He walks Patsy over to a spot of grass near Hank and me. He's dying to ask. I can see it in his face. I have no desire to rid him of his misery, but even so, I say, "You know your best friend better than that, don't you?"

Red tints his cheeks before he says, "Yeah."

"Then why would you even think. . . ?"

"Who you sleep with really isn't any of my business anyway, is it?" he asks, his voice sharp.

"As a matter of fact, no, it isn't," I say.

"With Sarah in your bed, I don't know why you would care who's in mine." The words aren't nearly as neutral sounding as I'd intended them to be.

I don't wait for him to respond. I hightail it back up the stairs and into the apartment, slapping the door closed behind me. I let the shower water run a little extra cold this morning, more to cool my anger than to wake me up. In a few short minutes, I'm dressed, and waiting outside by the Range Rover, my hair pulled back in a wet ponytail.

When Holden comes out, he's wearing a lime green shirt that makes him look so darn good I could cry at the realization that I have fallen for a guy I am never going to have.

He walks – strides or stomps might be more accurate – around to the driver's side, hits the remote and slides in. I get in, too, and we ride the first couple of miles without speaking.

"Coffee?" he says in a neutral voice.

I nod.

He swings into a Starbucks drive-through and orders two tall breakfast blends, remembering to ask for mine the way I like it. The consideration dings my anger, and I feel it leak out of me like helium from a week old balloon.

I hand him money for my coffee. When he ignores me, I drop it in the cupholder and look out the window. We sip in silence.

Holden drives away from the city, and it isn't long before the urban roads become rural. Enormous houses begin to appear on either side of the road, wide green pastures defined by white board fencing. Horses graze the fields with lazy selectivity, as if food is plentiful and they are merely indulging their host. It's as beautiful a place as any I've ever seen anywhere. I wish the mail boxes had names on them and imagine they would read like Urban, Paisley, Parton, and Keith.

I want to comment on how amazing they are but force myself not to since we seem to be in a contest of who can hold out the silence the longest. But when the GPS on Holden's phone indicates we should make a right turn onto an asphalt driveway lined by white fencing that stretches out as far as we can see, I can't help but gasp my delight.

"Incredible!" I say.

"Yeah," Holden agrees.

A half mile or so, and a house comes into sight. It sits on a high knoll, golf course green grass cascading down to meet the pasture fencing.

"Is this Lauren's house?" I ask.

"I don't know," Holden says. "All she told me was the address."

We pull into the circular driveway, and Holden cuts the engine. The massive wood front door opens, and Case Phillips steps out. Holden and I both glance at each other like tongue-tied teenagers.

He steps out onto the stoop in bare feet and blue jeans, a t-shirt that reads *Country Boys Get the Row Hoed* stretching the width of his impressively honed chest. I'm starstruck, no point in denying it. I was lucky enough to see him in concert on my sixteenth birthday, and my mama had spent a good portion of her week's paycheck to get us on the third row. I'd sat there in a near trance-like state, listening to him woo every female in the place – including my mama – with the voice that had given him number one single after number one single.

And now I'm sitting here in front of his house. Whoa.

Case waves us out of the vehicle. We open the doors and get out our respective sides.

"Y'all come on in," he says and disappears back inside the house.

Holden and I look at each other with wide eyes, and I can tell he's as awed as I am. We bump shoulders going through the front door. Holden steps to one side and then closes it behind us.

There's music playing from a room ahead of us. Surprisingly, it's not country. It's pop with a heavy beat. A giant winding staircase sits to our right. The ceiling is high and open, and oil paintings line the walls that curve around and up.

I feel a little like Alice in Wonderland and have to force myself not to sidle up next to Holden as I would like to. He leads the way through the foyer toward the music, and we end up at the entrance to a very large room lined with bookcases on one wall and four big screen TVs on the opposite one.

There must be a dozen oversize leather chairs with matching ottomans scattered across the room. Sitting in one with her feet tucked up beneath her is Lauren.

She has a mug in one hand, a book in the other. "Hey," she says, looking up at us.

Case walks over to a wall unit and turns a button. The music lowers to barely audible.

"How are you?" I ask, thinking she still looks a little pale.

"Good," she says. "Thanks to the both of you."

Holden and I glance at each other, neither of us comfortable with the praise.

"Would y'all like some coffee or something?" Case asks, dropping down into the leather chair next to Lauren.

"No, thank you," we say in unison, and I think maybe we're starting to look and sound like twin puppets.

"Y'all sit down then," Case says and waves a hand at two chairs opposite theirs.

Holden and I sit, again puppet-like.

"So what's your story?" Case asks, his blue eyes direct on us both.

"Ah, I'm not sure what–" Holden begins.

"Why are you two in Nashville?" Case says. "Music I'm assuming."

We both nod, and Case and Lauren smile.

"Relax, y'all," Lauren says. "I know you two aren't this uptight at the restaurant."

I make an effort to do exactly that just because I feel so foolish sitting here like a bowling pin. I let my shoulders dip in and sit back in the chair.

"What's your plan for making it here?" Case asks. "You write? Sing? Play?"

"I write," Holden replies. "Sing a little."

"I sing," I say.

"I have a partner I play with," Holden adds.

"Look, the reason we called y'all over this morning," Case says, "is first to thank you for what you did for Lauren." He reaches over and takes her hand in his. I realize then that in spite of the scene we witnessed in Lauren's office, the two of them are no casual thing. They have real feelings for one another. That actually makes me happy for Lauren, even though I am one of the countless thousands of females who have no doubt had illicit dreams about him.

"If you hadn't stopped to help her–" He breaks off, squeezes her hand and then looks at us again. "Thank you."

I nod.

"I'm glad we could," Holden says.

"So when Lauren said you were both wanting to get into the music business, I thought I'd put this in front of you first. No guarantees it'll work or you'll be what I'm looking for, but even a shot is hard to come by in this town."

My heart kicks up to a level I can hear in my ears. *Thrump-ush. Thrump-ush.*

"I'm looking to develop a young group. Three or four members, raw talent in place but with the ability to still be shaped. That fit y'all at all?"

I'm actually holding my breath. Waiting for Holden to say I'm not part of his and Thomas's gig. But that's not what he says. "Absolutely," he answers, and I feel my chest release like an air valve has just been turned. I look at him with the most neutral expression I can muster, waiting to hear what he's going to say next. "We'd be really grateful to have the chance to play for you, Mr. Phillips."

"It's Case," he says. And then, "Two guys and two girls is what I'd planned to look at putting together. You got someone in mind for that?"

Holden answers without hesitating. "We do."

"All right then," Case says, slapping his hands on his thighs and standing. "Y'all come back around five this afternoon. I've got a studio here. We'll see what we come up with."

"I'll call the restaurant and get someone to take your shifts for tonight," Lauren says. "It won't be a problem."

"Thank you," I say, standing.

Holden gets to his feet and says, "Yeah, thank you so much. Both of you."

Case walks us to the door, pulls it open and once we've stepped outside, says, "Really. You have no idea how much I appreciate what you did for her last night. I can't imagine–"

"It was our pleasure," Holden says. "And you know, you don't have to do this for us just because–"

"I know I don't," he says. "But I want to."

There's a cab waiting out front by the Rover, and I realize he must have already had that arranged.

"The fare's taken care of," he says. "See you at five."
And with that, he goes back inside the house.

♪

Holden

"What exactly just happened?" I ask as we roll down the long driveway toward the main road.

"I'm still wondering myself," CeCe says. "Did we just get the kind of break that people wait years for?"

"I think we did."

"But we're not actually a group," I say, starting to panic, "and how are we going to become one before five o'clock this afternoon?"

"I don't know, but we are," I say.

"Are you talking about Sarah as the fourth person?" CeCe asks.

"Yeah," I say, and just saying it out loud makes me realize how ridiculous it is to think that she'll even consider doing it. After the argument we'd had this morning before I left, it'll be amazing to me if she hasn't already left to drive back to Atlanta.

"Do you think she will?" CeCe asks.

"She has to," I say.

"What if she won't?"

"Let's not even think that right now."

"I really don't see her wanting to be on a stage with me."

She's right, but how can I admit that? We've just been handed an opportunity that we might never get again. Just to be heard by Case Phillips, not to mention being considered as a project he's willing to develop.

"Shouldn't you call Thomas?" CeCe asks.

I pull my phone from my pocket and tap the screen for his number. He answers with a groggy, "Hello?"

"Are you still in the sleeping bag?"

"What? You're speaking to me now?"

"Not out of choice," I say.

"Maturity never was your thing," he grumbles.

"You're not going to believe this, but Case Phillips just asked us to play for him this afternoon at five o'clock."

"What?"

Thomas is awake now. I smile. "He's looking to put together a group. The only thing we have to do before this afternoon is talk Sarah into auditioning with us."

"Oh, no problem," Thomas says, blowing out a sigh. "I'll run on over to Music Row and see if I can hunt down Miranda Lambert while I'm at it."

"She's still there, right?" I ask.

"*Somebody's* running the shower in your room."

"Good. Don't let her leave, okay. We'll be there in fifteen minutes."

"We've never all played together," CeCe says as I drop my phone in my shirt pocket.

"We've never all had an opportunity like this," I say. "It's like winning the lottery. How many times do you win the lottery?"

"Odds are never."

"Exactly," I say. I just hope I can convince Sarah of this.

♪

SHE'S AT THE DOOR with her suitcase when we get back.

"Where are you going?" I ask, as if I don't already know.

"Back to Atlanta," she says, glancing at CeCe and then forcing her gaze on me.

"Did Thomas tell you what just happened?" I ask.

"Yes. And I don't see what that has to do with me."

"We need you to audition with us, Sarah. He's looking for a group. Two guys. Two girls."

Sarah tightens her grip on her purse strap and says, "This has always been your dream. It was never mine. And I came here for you. Not to be part of some ridiculous rainbow-chasing."

The words cut. I can't deny it. I'm sure the wound shows on my face, and I can feel CeCe and Thomas both looking at me with resignation, like they know she's never going to agree.

"Maybe it is, Sarah," I say. "But this is a chance that comes along about as often as the pot of gold. What do we have to lose in going for it? What do you have to lose?"

She looks at me for a long moment, and tears well in her eyes. "You," she says.

♪

CeCe

I'm not sure if I should clap or cry.

Holden doesn't look at me before he follows Sarah into the bedroom. Hank Junior and Patsy stare at me from the couch. Hank Junior jumps off and trots over to greet me with a body wag. Patsy thumps her tail but doesn't get down.

"You gonna consider that a victory or a defeat?" Thomas throws out from the kitchen where he's unloading the dishwasher.

"Victory," I say, walking over to help him.

"For the audition, yeah. Your heart, not so much."

"I'm taking my heart out of the equation."

"Easy said."

I want to say not really, but choose silence as a better alternative.

Within five minutes, Holden and Sarah walk into the kitchen. Her eyes are dry, and she looks resigned if not happy.

"We've got the rest of the day," Holden says, "to get three songs down dead and figure out how we're going to look like we've been playing together forever. Let's get on it."

♪

IF I WERE AN OUTSIDER looking in, I would have to give the four of us credit.

We do exactly what Holden said we would need to do and get down to business. We set up in the living room, Hank Junior and Patsy watching from their perch on the couch. Except for a couple breaks to take them outside and grab something to eat, we don't stop practicing.

We decide to go with two covers that everybody knows, a Rascal Flatts and a Faith Hill. On the Rascal Flatts, Thomas takes the lead, while Sarah and I do harmony. On the Faith Hill, I take a verse, Sarah takes another and Thomas joins us on the chorus.

The third song is an original of Holden's, and both he and Thomas decide that I should do the lead vocal. I feel the needles in Sarah's glare, but she actually doesn't say anything. She just goes along with every indication of being a team player. That is, until I butcher the fourth line of the first verse for the seventh or so time.

"Seriously?" She throws her hands up in the air, turns to Holden and says, "I know this song. Why is she singing it?"

She glances at me and then back at Holden. "You think she's better than I am?"

"You know that's not it," Holden says, rubbing the guitar pick between his thumb and index finger.

"Then what is it?" she asks.

Thomas shakes his head and starts to laugh. "Here's how I see it. By some stroke of good fortune," he says, nodding at me and then at Holden, "these two have managed to get us an opportunity that few people would ever get no matter how hard they worked their tails off in this town. Case Phillips wants to pay them back for pretty much saving the life of the woman he loves. And I for one am not gonna laugh in the face of that. I am totally content to ride shotgun on this one. Sarah. If I were you, I would be, too."

Sarah's fluster is immediately apparent in the red stain on her cheeks and the way her lips part as if she wants to say something, but is trying desperately hard to stop herself from doing so.

"If we get past this audition," Thomas says, "then we can look at shaking out some of the kinks that might be bothering either of us. But until then, I say spit shine the heck out of the pair of boots we've been offered to walk in. All in favor, say aye!"

No one actually gives a verbal assent, but we all nod our agreement. Sarah appears to put on emotional blinders for the rest of the session.

Three hours later, I can't believe where we are. We actually sound *really* good. Holden makes a recording on his computer and plays back what we have so far. I'm amazed at how we sound. Like we've been playing and singing together for ages. I'm not sure how that could actually be possible, but we do.

Even with all the undercurrents working so hard to pull us under, we somehow manage to rise above them, and our sound has something fresh and unique to it. I'm suddenly in love with it.

Sarah's voice is like honey, smooth and golden, fluid and flowing. My voice has grit to it, an edginess I've been told by some, that somehow synchs with Sarah's. Thomas has his own thing, a voice so big and rooted in country that the truth is he doesn't need either one of us to own the stage. I love listening to him, especially when he drops the melody for a Georgia infused rap that catches and holds the ear.

And I love the song itself.

Holden loves sound, and every line of music holds something so catchy that I know listeners will want to hear more.

It is four-fifteen by the time we put the last bit of polish on the song. We're supposed to be at Case Phillips's house at five, and neither of us has showered or changed yet.

I for one feel in need of a few minutes under the faucet to regroup and get a handle on the flutters of panic intent on welling up inside me.

We talk for a few moments about what to wear, agree that Sarah and I should opt for something simple and basic. I'm glad since I don't have a lot to choose from. Holden and Thomas agree on a light blue shirt and jeans.

In my room, I stand in front of the mirror and give myself a long hard look. From the corner of my eye, I catch Hank Junior staring at me from his spot on the bed. I shrug at him and say, "You know how I get before I sing. Well, this is like a million times more nervewracking than all the other times put together."

My sweet dog cocks his head to the right, his long Hound ear lifting like a question mark. "I know all the logical stuff. I've sung in front of people before. It's a waste of energy. You're right. But I can't help it."

I go over to the bed and sit down next to him, rubbing under his chin the way he likes me to. "This could be it, you know. This could be *the* only shot I get here. What if I'm not ready? I thought I would have all kinds of time to get better before anyone was really looking."

Hank lifts his head to lick my cheek. I lean over to give him a fierce hug. "I wish you could be there. That would make me feel better."

Hank rolls over on his side and bats me with one of his big paws as if to say, "You're being ridiculous."

"I know," I agree. "Suck it up, right?"

In the shower, I think about a book I read not too long ago on focus and how it can be the determining factor between people who are good at something and people who are great at something.

I admit it. I want to be great at singing.

I would never say this out loud because I know how it would sound. But deep down inside, I feel like I already am. Intellectually, I know how much growth I have ahead of me. But the depth and breadth and scope of my love for singing is so immeasurable that it feels like the very best part of me. Something that's good and pure. I've actually worried about what would happen to my love for music if I don't make it here. If I reach a point where I have to admit I'm never going to be able to make a living with my music. Concede defeat.

I haven't let myself think this very often because it's really too painful to consider. But I know it happens all the time. Every day in places like this, in L.A. and New York City. Kids who are drawn to the lure of fame, giving the dream everything they have. Only to find that the dream was only that. A dream.

Realizing that my thoughts are not exactly fuel for focus, I drop my head back and let the water pummel my face, beating the negativity out of me. I force myself to look at this as a gift, dropped from above, at random, perhaps, Holden and I the lucky recipients.

Something my pastor had said once in the church Mama and I went to when I was a little girl comes to me then. A gift is a wondrous thing. But it's the ways in which we share it that can give it wings.

I think about this in light of all the reasons why Holden, Thomas, Sarah, and I are such an unlikely match. And I know that if I let myself think about that for even a second longer, I'm going to waste something I may never be offered again.

And that's when I decide that no matter what happens on anyone else's part tonight, I'm going to give this everything I've got. If we fail, at least I'll know I gave it the very best I am currently capable of giving.

♪

AS A GROUP, we clean up pretty well.

We leave the dogs at the apartment and the four of us ride church-pew style out of Nashville central and into the countryside.

Thomas is driving and I'm sitting next to him, Sarah wedged in between Holden and me.

We're breaking the seat belt law. Holden had insisted he be the one to go without, even though I had argued without success to share one with Thomas. Admittedly, it would have been an interesting position necessary to make that work. Thomas and Holden had both laughed while Sarah merely rolled her eyes.

Once we table the seat belt discussion, we drive the remainder of the way to Case's house in silence. I think we're each doing what we need to do to get our best game on.

Again, we roll by estate after estate, and Thomas offers up several whistles of appreciation. Sarah's expression indicates she sees such magnificence every day of her life. Either that, or she doesn't want to let on she's impressed.

Thomas pulls up in the circular driveway, and we slide out, silent and solemn-faced. Holden lifts his guitar case from the truck bed. We walk in a straight line to the front door, Holden in the front, Thomas in the back, Sarah and I sandwiched in between.

Holden rings the doorbell, and a housekeeper answers. Dressed in a white uniform, her instant smile welcomes us. She's round-faced, round-hipped and warm as a butter biscuit. "Y'all come on in," she says. "Mr. Case is expecting you. Right this way."

She leads us through the enormous house, wood floors echoing our footsteps. At the far back right corner, she opens a heavy door behind which sits the most incredible recording studio I never thought to imagine. Red leather chairs are scattered about, dark walnut walls a backdrop to soundproofing boards disguised as artwork.

Behind an enormous recording desk sits Case Phillips and a man I don't recognize. Case stands, waves a hand at us and says, "Welcome. This is my producer Rhys Anderson. Rhys, I'll let these folks do their own introductions."

Holden shakes the other man's hand and says, "I'm Holden Ashford. This is Thomas Franklin. CeCe MacKenzie and Sarah Saxon."

The man shakes each of their hands, his smile genuine and also welcoming. "How y'all doing?" He looks smart, like someone who's been very successful in this business. His clothes agree with the assumption, his shirt and jeans carrying the stamp of some exclusive men's department.

"This here's my band," Case says, indicating the other five people in the room. "And that over there in the corner is my son Beck. He's sitting in for one of our guitar players tonight who's out sick. He might look young, but don't worry, he can hold his own."

We all smile, and Beck drops us a nod of greeting. He looks so much like his dad. No one would need to be told they were father and son. He meets my gaze and smiles, and I smile back.

"What'd y'all bring to sing tonight?" Case asks.

"Two covers and another song that I wrote," Holden says, his tone respectful and a little uncertain.

"How about we hear the original?" Case asks. "I'm lookin' to see who y'all are without the instant comparison to someone who might have sung a song before. Y'all come on in and get set up. You got a chord chart for these guys?"

"I do," Holden says, reaching inside his guitar case and pulling out the sheets.

"Good man," Case says.

The players glance at the sheets and almost immediately start to strum at the chords. Under their expertise, the song is instantly recognizable, and I notice the pleased look on Holden's face. I can't imagine what it must feel like to him, hearing people of this caliber playing a song he wrote.

"You'll be playing with them?" Rhys directs to Holden.

"Yeah, if that's okay."

"Sure, it is."

In less than fifteen minutes, Cases's guys have the song nailed and Rhys directs Sarah, Thomas, and me into the sound booth that runs along the outer wall of the room.

Sarah whispers something in Holden's ear, clinging to his arm like he's a buoy in the middle of a raging ocean. I almost feel sorry for her. It's clear that she's out of her element. Not that I'm brimming over with confidence. But maybe the difference is that I want this to be a success. And maybe she just wants to get through it.

Holden leans down and says something to her. She walks to the microphone, her expression set and uneasy.

The band runs through the song once without stopping, and I'm amazed at how it sounds like they've played it a hundred times before. Thomas, Sarah, and I wade into the melody with tentative effort. I feel their unease as part of my own. I will myself to block out everything except my role in this.

The band starts the song up again, and the three of us are a little more confident, but not much.

Case stands and holds up a hand, motioning for us to stop.

The music drops to silence, and we stop singing.

"Hey, look y'all," Case says, running a hand around the back of his neck. "The only way this is going to turn out worth a hoot is if you forget where you are. You're just singing in church back home with all your aunts and uncles. That's the you I want to hear. Okay?"

The three of us nod, mute, and I force the knot of pressure in between my shoulder blades to relent. I can't think about Thomas or Sarah and their own batch of nerves. I can only control my own. I close my eyes and picture what Case just described. The little Southern Baptist church where I grew up. The tiny pulpit from which our choir belted out old-fashioned gospel hymns every Sunday morning.

And I see myself performing solos when I was nine, the familiar faces of the congregation smiling up at me, the smell of the coffee brewing in the church kitchen wafting up into the sanctuary. The way rain pinged off the tin roof of the old building and how that sound became part of whatever music we were singing.

By going there, I forget all about the here and now. I'm just me. Singing like I always have. For the pure love of it. For the joy it makes me feel.

That's how the next several hours pass. I can hear that Thomas, and even Sarah, have found their own ways to shake off the stage fright and just sing.

It's nearly eleven p.m. when Rhys raises a hand and says, "I think we got it."

He sounds pleased, and relief washes through me.

Only then do I let myself come back to the present, the laughter and good-natured ribbing of the band members seeping into my awareness. I step out of the booth, and Cases's son, Beck, walks over and says, "Y'all rocked that."

I smile and shake my head. "Y'all made us look good."

"It seems like you've really got something," he says, his hands shoved in the pockets of his jeans, the smile on his face less confident than I would have expected from someone who'd grown up with a country music star as his father.

"Thanks," I say. "It's really an incredible opportunity."

"Yeah, well, my dad doesn't waste his time. So if he brought you here, he thought he had good reason."

I start to bring up the thing about Lauren, but decide against it since she isn't here tonight, and I'm not sure how public their relationship is.

Case walks over to the stainless steel refrigerator in one corner of the room, opens the door and starts passing out bottled beer. "If you're not old enough to legally drink this," he says, "then don't. Honor system here."

"That leaves me out," Beck says.

"Me, too," I say, shrugging.

"Can I get you something else?"

"Water would be great," I say.

"Coming right up." He turns and crosses the room, grabs a couple bottles from the refrigerator and walks back over to hand one to me.

Holden, Sarah, and Thomas are talking together several yards away. I can feel Holden's gaze on me, but I refuse to look at him.

"So what's your story?" Beck asks.

"Story?"

"Yeah. How'd you get to Nashville?"

"Wing and a prayer?"

He smiles. "How long have you been singing?"

"Longer than I can remember."

"Sounds like it," he says.

Warmth colors my cheeks. I glance down and say, "Thanks. That's nice."

"And true."

"When did you learn to play guitar?"

"When I was still sitting on my daddy's knee. He would hold me on his lap and put my fingers in position. It's kind of like breathing. Probably like singing for you."

"You're amazing with that guitar," I say and mean it.

"Thanks," he says, and he sounds almost shy. Again, not what I would have expected. "Hey, there's a party down the road some friends of mine are having tonight. You wanna go?"

My immediate inclination is to refuse, but then out of the corner of my eye, I see Sarah lean in and whisper something in Holden's ear and realize what a fool I would be to say no. "Ah, yeah," I say. "That sounds great."

"Cool. Let me see if we're about done here." He walks over to his dad and Rhys, leans down, and they talk for a minute or two.

Case slides his chair back, his long, denim-clad legs stretched out in front of him, his arms folded across his chest. "I think we got some good stuff here tonight, y'all. Rhys, you think you'll have something to listen to maybe tomorrow?"

"Sure," Rhys says. "Late afternoon?"

"All right then, I guess we can call it a night," Case says.

"We really can't thank you enough, man," Holden says. "This has been incredible to say the least."

"Paying it forward and all that." Case says, nodding at Holden. "Have y'all come up with a name yet?"

"Barefoot Outlook," Holden says without hesitating.

That was quick, I think to myself. But I actually really like it.

"Cool," Case says. "I'll touch base with you tomorrow, okay?"

Holden, Thomas, and Sarah gather up their things and walk over to where I'm still standing with Beck.

"Ready?" Thomas asks, looking at me.

"Ah, actually, I'm going to this thing with Beck." I purposely don't look at Holden, but keep my eyes focused on Thomas.

"What thing?" Holden says.

"Party down the road," Beck says. "Y'all oughta come."

"I've got a budding migraine," Sarah says.

"I'm working in the morning," Thomas adds, "but thanks, man."

Holden doesn't say anything. He just looks at me with a question in his eyes that I wonder if anyone else can read.

I glance away and Beck says, "I'll get her home safely."

"All right. Y'all have fun, man," Thomas says, and they leave the room.

"We're going to that party I told you about earlier, Dad," Beck says, taking my arm and leading me to the door.

"Y'all be careful, son," Case says, his deep, rich voice following us from the room.

"We will, Dad," Beck says. He ducks his head back around the corner and adds, "Can I take your car?"

"As long as you and it both come back in one piece."

"Will do."

We walk through the house, down a long hall lined with framed music awards and a glass cabinet full of gold statues.

"Are you amazed by this like every day?" I ask.

Beck laughs. "I probably should be. But you know, he's my dad."

I laugh then, thinking how unbelievable it is that I am actually here in this house, getting ready to go to a party with Beck Phillips, the only son of a country music legend I've had a crush on most of my life. "This is nuts," I say.

"What?"

"Just *this*. Me being here. You. Nuts."

He takes my hand and lets me precede him through the door that leads from the kitchen to the garage.

"We're not seriously taking this, are we?" I ask, spotting the Ferrari.

"You heard him."

"Oh. My. Gosh."

He laughs then, opens the door, and I slide inside, pinching myself just for good measure. Yep, I'm really here.

He goes around to the driver's side, hits the remote to the garage door and backs out. The engine sounds like pure, spun money. That Italian roar that is unique to wealth in its Nth degree.

He guns the car down the driveway, the board fences on either side rolling by in a blur of white. A beep signals the gate and the wrought iron opens at the end of the driveway like Alladin's cave.

Beck swings the car onto the road, and although I glance over to see that we're staying with the speed limit, it feels like we're flying. He lets back the sunroof, and the night air tousles our hair and cools the heat in my cheeks.

"So whose party?" I ask above the wind.

"Macey Canterwood," he answers. "She's kind of getting to be a big deal with Sony."

"Ah," I say. "I heard her new song on the radio yesterday."

"It's pretty cool."

I stop myself from countering with, "It's frigging awesome." Figuring that might come across as gushing, I say nothing.

"Most everyone here tonight will be pretty cool. I won't lie though. Some of the girls can have claws."

"Hm. Anyone in particular I should look out for?"

"I'll let them dig their own hole. Who knows? Maybe everyone will be on good behavior."

If I'm supposed to feel reassured by this, I don't. Butterflies waft up in my stomach and perch in my throat.

My phone vibrates. I pull it from my pocket. It's a text from Holden.

You okay?

Yeah. How's Sarah?

I took Hank Junior out with Patsy.

Thanks. Sorry about the Sarah question.

Is that why you went with him?

What?

To get back at me?

There's nothing to get back at you for. You have a girlfriend. Case closed.

"Everything all right?" Beck asks.

I click off my phone, realizing how rude I'm being. "Yeah," I say. "Sorry. The guys were just letting me know they'd walked my dog for me."

"What kind of dog?"

"Walker Hound."

Beck gives me a long, considering look. "You're not exactly what you first appear to be, are you?"

"What is that?" I ask.

"Like you oughta be on a walkway somewhere. In five inch heels and a mini skirt."

"Is that a compliment?"

"Actually, yeah. But it's kinda killer that you look so girly and yet you've got a hound."

"He's my best buddy."

"Lucky guy."

"The truth is I doubt I'll ever find a guy who gets me the way he does."

Beck downshifts and swings the car onto an asphalt drive. We roar up the hill, the headlights glinting off horses night-grazing a lush pasture.

The house at the top of the driveway is every bit as enormous as the one we just left. The style is different, kind of California contemporary. I would have imagined it looking out of place in this setting. But it doesn't somehow.

Beck pulls the car into a parking spot and cuts the engine. "Let's go have some fun," he says.

We walk into the house with his arm draped loosely around my shoulder. It seems a little weird to me at first because we just met. And, yeah, because he's not Holden.

But once I catch a glimpse of all the hip, young people milling about, relaxing on cushy leather sofas, talking intently by a bar, laughing at someone who's just jumped in the pool, I'm actually glad to have his arm there. It makes me feel like less of an outsider.

He introduces me around. I recognize faces, managing to contain an oh-my-gosh moment when I find myself shaking hands with one of the band members for Keith Urban. Beck throws me a grin as if he's aware of how hard it is for me not to gush.

A very tall, very gorgeous girl walks up to us, leans in and kisses Beck on the cheek. "Hey, gorgeous," she says.

"Hey, Macey," he says.

"I thought you'd decided not to come," she says, her full lips pouting.

"I sat in on a session with my dad tonight. We just finished up a little while ago."

"Cool," she says. "Who for?"

"CeCe here and a band she's singing with. CeCe, this is Macey Canterwood. Macey, CeCe MacKenzie."

"Hey," she says, offering a hand set off with perfectly manicured nails.

"It's very nice to meet you," I say, shaking her hand and noticing her smile feels a little less than genuine. "I really like your music."

"Thanks," she says, her smile now mega bright. "What kind of band are you in?"

"Little country. Little pop," I answer.

"They've got a cool sound," Beck says. I hear an undercurrent between the two and suspect there is more going on here than I first realized.

Macey's smile now appears to have a razor's edge. "Super," she says, and I wonder who the heck says super these days.

Thinking maybe they need a few moments, I excuse myself for the ladies room, winding my way through group after group of ultra-hip looking twenty-something's.

In the bathroom, I check my phone and find the rest of Holden's text message from earlier.

Be careful, okay?

All is well, I type in even as I picture him in bed with Sarah, her arms wrapped around his waist, her legs entwined with his. I touch up my lipstick and do my best to blank my thoughts of the image.

Beck is waiting for me outside the bathroom door. "Wanna dance?" he asks.

The music has changed from laid back and conversational to upbeat and thumping. I take his hand and follow him outside where people are dancing alongside the pool. He loops an arm around my waist and hooks me up close.

"Those aren't Nashville moves," I say. "More like South Beach."

He grins and says, "I like all kinds of music."

"Me, too, actually."

"I like your moves," he says, ducking his head near my ear.

I smile up at him, wondering if I'm ready to open this door. Is it even fair to him? My heart is tied up in knots over Holden, and yet I know that's a dead end road. Here I am at a hot party in Nashville, dancing with a hot guy. What is there to think about?

The music goes slow, and he swoops me in even closer. His body is fit and hard, but the first thing I register is the differences between him and Holden. Holden is broader, and I can't shake the memory of how we felt together.

I squeeze my eyes shut, wanting so very much to be here, in this moment.

"What are you thinking?" Beck says, tipping my chin up so that I am forced to look into his eyes.

"Nothing," I say, forcing a smile.

"It's that guy, isn't it?"

"Who?"

"Holden."

"Has a girlfriend."

"Does your heart know that?"

"Yes. It does," I say, my tone conceding even as I try to sound indifferent.

"I've kinda been there," Beck says, trailing his thumb across my jawline. "I know what it feels like."

I tip my head back a little farther and let a little of my pain show on my face.

"When something doesn't work, you have to move on. I'd be more than happy to help you with that." He leans in and butterfly kisses me. "I'd really like to help you with that."

"Mind if I have a turn?"

Macey Canterwood has her hand on my shoulder, the smile on her face suggesting she has no intention of taking no for an answer.

"We're kind of in the middle of something, Mace," Beck says.

"I can see that," she says, "but I have something to share with you. Just one song."

"It's fine," I say, backing away. "I'll go catch my breath."

"He's quite the dancer, isn't he?" Macey says, her smile now nowhere near reaching her eyes.

"Don't go far," Beck tells me. "This won't take long."

I make my way back inside the party, stand in line for the restroom and then use the ninety seconds before someone starts knocking to run a brush through my hair and touch up my long-gone lipstick.

Back at the bar, I ask for a bottle of water, but just as the nose-ringed bartender starts to hand it to me, a voice behind me says, "Hold off on that! Girl, if you're planning to hang with the likes of Beck Phillips, you gotta learn how to party at least a little."

I turn to find Macey smiling at me. She shakes a finger at the bartender and says, "We'll have two of what you made me earlier."

The bartender looks at Macey and raises an eyebrow, which also happens to have a ring in it. "New friend?" he asks.

"Yes," Macey answers. "CeCe, meet Huxton. Huxton, CeCe."

"Hey," he says. "Any friend of Macey's–"

"Nice to meet you," I say. "I'm fine with the water. I should go find Beck."

"He asked me to tell you he's grabbing a game of ping pong downstairs. Why don't we grab a chat and get to know each other a bit?"

You know that little voice that dings inside you when something isn't quite right, but you can't pinpoint it closely enough to act on it? I'm hearing the ding, but she is Macey Canterwood. Her music is being played all over the radio, and what do I have to lose by trying to leave here tonight with her as something closer to a friend than an enemy?

"Go snag that sofa for us," Macey says. "I'll get our drinks."

I push away from the bar and do exactly that, even as I ask myself what the two of us could possibly have in common. Except Beck, of course. And the fact that she obviously wants him, and sees me as a threat.

The couch is cushy and comfortable. I sink onto it with a sudden awareness of fatigue and exactly how long this day has been. What I really want is to go home and curl up in bed with Hank Junior.

Macey strides over in her four-inch heels – she must wear them all the time to be that competent in them – and hands me a glass that at least looks appealing. "A little something I like before a show – nothing crazy – just knocks the edge off."

"What's in it?"

"Pineapple and Goji berry juice. Which is really good for you, by the way. I'll let you guess the rest."

I've never been one to feel peer pressure. It's not something I ever bought into in high school. I had my thing – music – other kids had their thing. I didn't yearn to be someone that I wasn't.

But here, in this place, in Nashville, I realize just how far at the bottom of the totem pole I am. How high the climb is. And when someone from way on up the ladder, reaches down and offers you a hand past some of those rungs, it's pretty tempting to take it.

I sip the drink tentatively, expecting somehow that it will taste gosh-awful. Only it doesn't. "Um, good," I say.

"Told you you'd like it," she says, turning up her own glass and then stretching back on the couch. She crosses her incredibly long legs in front of her. Next to her, I definitely feel like the country mouse. "What are your goals, CeCe?"

"To sing," I answer.

She laughs. "But where?"

"Wherever anyone will listen, I guess," I answer simply but truthfully.

"I remember that feeling," she says. "But you probably shouldn't say it out loud. It has a hint of desperation to it."

"But aren't you here because you love to sing?" I ask her.

"Yes. But other things go with it that I also love."

"Such as?"

"Recognition. Adoration." She laughs. "I get how that sounds. But if you're here, trying to make it in this business, you like those things, too. Maybe you're not willing to admit it yet, but you do."

I take another sip of my drink and wonder if it's true. "I've never thought about that part of it."

"We're all a little narcissistic at heart. At least when we get the chance to be. Don't you think we're always looking for that chance?"

The edges of my vision start to fuzz, and I blink to clear it away. "I like to think I'm looking for the chance to do what I love to do."

"At the risk of someone else getting to do what they love to do though, right?"

I'm not sure how I've waded into this conversation, but it's starting to feel like quicksand, and I'd like to back out. Only my legs feel heavy and weighted, or is that my thoughts? "I don't know. I don't feel exactly–"

"What's wrong?" Macey asks, her voice sounding like it's coming to me remixed with heavy bass.

I try to stand. My legs feel as though the bones have been removed, and they won't hold me upright. I drop back onto the couch, grabbing a cushion to right myself.

Macey stands, staring down at me from what seems like a thousand feet up. I can barely hear her voice when she says, "Good luck with your ambitions, CeCe. Just don't let them get in the way of common sense, okay?"

She turns and walks away. I raise a hand to stop her, to ask her to get Beck. Only I realize I can't make the words come out. I slump back against the sofa, trying to hold my eyelids open. They're so heavy, weighted with stone. Maybe I can let them close for just a minute. Just long enough for me to work up enough energy to fight back to the surface.

But it feels so good to give in. Float along with the current carrying me away. Warm sun. Ocean breeze. Oblivion.

♪

Holden

I can't sleep.

I try, staying to my side of the bed, Sarah to hers. She's been asleep for a while as far as I can tell, but I don't think either of us wants to talk to each other, so she could be pretending, I guess.

I look at the clock. 1:15.

CeCe's not home yet. I've been listening for the door, and if I'm honest with myself, that's why I'm still awake.

I can't quit thinking about her with him. Can't quit wondering what they're doing. If he's tried to kiss her yet. If she's let him.

That last thought catapults me out of bed. I grab a t-shirt, shrug into it and leave the room. Patsy and Hank Junior are hunkered together on the sofa. They raise their heads and look at me with sleepy eyes. "Anyone up for a walk?" I ask.

Patsy ducks her head behind the pillow, giving me her answer. Hank Junior hops down and trots over.

I pick up his leash, grab my keys and cell phone from the table by the door, and we head outside. The night air is cool. At the bottom of the stairs, I hook on his leash. We walk fast down the sidewalk, and when Hank Junior clearly wants to go faster, I decide to run.

Hank's couch potato lounging could fool you about his athletic ability. The dog can run. He's made for it, and he loves it. I love it, too. We let it rip for a couple of blocks, Hank sprinting in pure joy, me trying to drain the battery of my imagination.

And it works, until we both start to tire. We drop to a jog for several blocks, and then a walk during which Hank is intent on letting others know we were here.

I'm breathing hard and heavy, but I'm right back to thinking about CeCe, wondering why she's not home yet.

"Should I call her, Hank?"

He turns to look at me with a raised ear and wags his tail.

"That a yes?"

He barks once.

"All right, then."

I tap her name under recent calls and wait while it rings. Twice. Three times. Four. Voice mail picks up.

"No answer," I direct to Hank. He looks up at me and whines.

"Yeah, me, too," I say. We turn around at the end of the block and start walking back.

It's not my place to worry about CeCe, but I am worried. About her safety or what she might be doing with Beck? Both, I guess.

Everything about what I'm feeling is so messed up. She has every right to be out with Beck Phillips or whoever else she wants to be out with. I'm the one without that right.

We're just short of the apartment building when a black Ferrari turns into the parking lot. I recognize it as belonging to Case Phillips and assume Beck drove it tonight.

The car pulls in front of the building, and the engine goes silent. I stop before they spot me, wondering if I'm going to have to wait here in the shadows while Beck Phillips makes out with CeCe.

The driver's side door opens with a *wachunk*. Beck slides out and jogs around to the passenger door. He opens it, then disappears from sight. I see him squat down, wait for him to stand back up. A minute. Two. Four. Okay, seems weird.

Deciding I'm not waiting any longer, I lead Hank through the parking lot and past the car. He turns around and barks, then starts tugging at the lead.

Beck stands and calls out, "Hey, man."

His voice doesn't sound quite right. I turn, glimpse the concern on his face.

"Hey," I say. "What's up?"

"CeCe's kind of out of it," he says, raking a hand through his hair.

I jog over behind a still tugging Hank Junior who wedges in between Beck and the car to plant two paws on the seat and begin licking CeCe's cheek.

I look past Beck to see CeCe out cold, not responding at all to Hank's licking. "What the–" I start, shoving Beck around to look at me. "What did you do to her?"

Beck holds up two hands, backing away. "Hold on, man. It wasn't me."

"Wasn't you what?" I hear my voice rising and force myself not to go ahead and punch his country-music-star-rich-kid-ass all the way back to his daddy's estate.

"A girl at the party put something in her drink to make her sleep."

"Why?" I ask, biting out the word.

"We used to date," he says, to his credit, sounding miserably sorry. "I never should have left CeCe alone with her."

"What did she give her?"

"Sleeping pill."

"Are you sure?"

"Yeah."

"How?"

"Because I told her I'd tell my dad what she'd done if she didn't tell me, and I would ask him to tell everybody he knows in the music business."

I believe him. I can see he's telling the truth, and that he feels guilty as all get out.

"Let's get her upstairs," I say.

"Yeah," Beck agrees.

We both lean in at the same time to lift her out and knock foreheads.

"Crap!"

"Ow!"

We jump back, glaring at one another while Hank Junior looks up at us like we're the two biggest dufusses he's ever had the misfortune to run across. And he might be right.

"I'll get her," I say.

Beck stands back, two hands in the air, as if in concession to the fact that I have some unspoken right to being in charge from here on out. I'm not about to tell him I don't.

I swing CeCe up in my arms and head for the stairs, Hank Junior at my heels. I hear the car door thunk closed, look over my shoulder to see Beck striding after me. "You should go home," I say.

"I'm not leaving until I know she's okay," he shoots back, and I can hear him digging in his heels.

I decide at that point to ignore him and head up the stairway with CeCe tight against my chest. I dig my key out of my pocket and decide to make use of Tag-Along, after all. I hand it to him, then barely wait for him to get the door open, before pushing past him into the living room.

I lower CeCe onto the sofa, propping her head up with a pillow. I sit down beside her then, rubbing my thumb across her jawline. "Hey, CeCe, wake up. CeCe?"

"I'll get a glass of water," Beck says, heading for the kitchen.

Hank Junior jumps up on the couch and starts licking CeCe's face.

Realizing he has a better chance at being Prince Charming than I do, I don't ask him to stop.

She moans a little, and I feel a ping of relief at the sound. She flops the back of her hand across her face in response to Hank's kissing. He wags his tail and licks harder.

But she's not responding now, and I get that sick feeling of worry in my stomach again.

Beck returns with the water, and he holds the back of her head up while I try to get her to take a sip. But she won't, and it trails down the side of her face instead.

"We could put her in the shower," Beck says.

I glance up at him with enough dagger to make him take a step back.

"With her clothes on, of course," Beck says quickly.

"I assumed as much," I say, giving him a square look.

I pick her up from the couch and carry her down the hall to her room. As soon as I open the door, the scent of her perfume meets my nose, sending a curl of memory up from somewhere inside me. And then I'm thinking about the last time I smelled this scent on her neck and how I would forever associate it with the taste of her kiss.

Hank Junior follows us into the room and hops up on the bed to survey our intentions, I would guess. I leave the bathroom door open and ease her onto the shower floor.

Beck tests the water and makes sure it's warm enough before turning on the spray. We point the nozzle at the top of her head and wait for it to work. It takes a surprisingly long time. Maybe it's seconds, but it seems like minutes. Several. I'm holding my breath, and only realize it when she begins to shake her head, batting a hand at the spray.

She moans and says, "Stop. What is that–"

"CeCe," I say. "It's me. Holden. You're back at the apartment. In the shower. We're trying to wake you up. You've kind of been out of it."

"What happened?" she asks, her voice groggy and a little slurred.

"Someone spiked your drink," Beck says, stepping into view.

She looks up, her eyelids so heavy she can barely hold them open. "Who would do that?"

I turn to look at Beck, admittedly feeling a little pleased with the guilt he feels.

"Maybe we should talk about it when you're feeling better," he says.

"Are you all right, CeCe?" I ask. "I can take you to the ER and get you checked out if you want."

"No, no," she says. "I'm okay. I'm just. . .really sleepy."

"What's going on in here?"

I turn to find Thomas standing in the doorway, wearing a pair of polka dot boxers and running his hand through sleep-wild hair.

I raise an eyebrow and drop a look at the boxers. "Seriously?"

"Gift from Mama," he says, sheepish.

"Scary," I say.

Thomas peers around me. "What the heck happened to CeCe?"

Beck hangs his head and says. "Victim of one of my messed up friends."

"You all right, CeCe?" Thomas asks.

"Yeah. Can I just go to bed?" she says. "Alone."

The three of us guys look at each other, and take a step back.

"Sure," I say. "If you need some help getting–"

"I don't. I'm all good. Really."

"All right if I call you in the morning?" Beck throws out behind me. "I have some serious apologizing to do."

"She's working tomorrow. Today." Whatever. Anything to get him to leave.

"Can I drive you?" he asks, peering over my shoulder and trying to make eye contact with CeCe.

Sarah appears in the doorway then. She's wearing a strappy pink nightgown, and her hair is tousled from sleep. "What's going on in here?"

CeCe looks at her and then glances back at me. "Nothing," she says. "Everybody go back to bed."

She starts to get up, falters a little, and grabs on to the side of the shower.

"Here," I say, reaching out a hand to steady her.

But she avoids my touch and says, "Please. Can everyone just leave?"

We back out of the bathroom, Sarah asking, "What happened to her?"

Thomas takes Sarah's arm and says, "Come on. Let's go."

They leave the room. CeCe reaches for a robe on the back of the door, pressing it to her chest, and without either looking at Beck or me, says, "Goodnight."

"Are you sure you're all right?" I start.

"Yes. Please. Go."

"I'm really sorry, CeCe," Beck says. "I'll check on you in the morning."

"Thanks," she says.

He turns and walks out of the room then.

Once he's gone, I look at CeCe and say, "I can stay. Just to make sure–"

"I don't want you to," she says. "Sarah's waiting for you. In your room. Go."

I hear the frustration in her voice. "What happened tonight, CeCe?" I ask.

"A jealous girl. That's all that happened."

"She drugged you. That's all that happened?"

"I'm fine," she says. "I just want to go to bed."

"CeCe. We need to talk."

"No. We don't. We really don't. There's nothing to talk about."

"But I want to explain something."

She bites her lip and looks at me with eyes on the verge of tears.

"He's not a guy you should be hanging out with, CeCe."

Her eyes go wide, and she laughs abruptly. "And you are? You have a girlfriend, Holden. A serious girlfriend. One who drove all the way from Atlanta to be here with you. A girlfriend who seems to want to move here to be with you. What in that equation allows anything at all for you and me?"

I want to tell her that none of that is true. Only it is. "CeCe."

"What?" she asks. "Can you deny any of that?"

"No," I say.

"Then why are you not in there with her where you belong?"

I look at her for several long drawn out moments. I think about all the things I could say. All the things I should say. But I don't want to say any of them. I just want to say the truth. "Because I want to be in here with you."

She presses her lips together, and again, I see how close she is to tears. "You don't have that right," she says.

I want to deny it, to argue with her, to bring up all the ifs, and the buts, and the maybes, but she's right. All I can say that is absolutely true is that I want her.

"Holden, I'm wet. I'm cold. I'm tired. Please."

I try to stop myself from asking this question, but I can't. The words come rolling out. "Did you go with him tonight because of me?"

Her eyes widen a little, and I can see her considering the answer. "Do you mean did I go to make you jealous?"

I shrug. I somehow know what she's going to say. And how arrogant is it of me anyway to think that would be the reason she went.

She folds her arms across her chest and sets her gaze somewhere just to the right of mine. "No," she says. "He's a nice guy. I went because I wanted to go."

Her words slam into me like baseballs being hurled from a major league pitcher. I guess I didn't want to believe that was true, but how stupid could I be? He's Beck Phillips. His father's a major country music star. What girl wouldn't want to go out with him? "Okay," I say, backing out of the room. "Goodnight, CeCe."

"Goodnight," she says.

And I don't let myself look back. Only a fool would look back.

♪

CeCe

I've never been a good liar.

But my lie is the first thing I think about when I wake up at just after ten. That and the look on Holden's face.

Considering how I've had to watch him with Sarah and act as if it doesn't bother me a single iota – the way she holds onto him, the way she looks at him as if there's no question that he is hers.

But then doesn't she have that right?

Hank snuggles up against me, and I know I need to get up and take him out. My head throbs dully. I feel like I haven't had a glass of water in two years.

Did I go with Beck last night to make Holden jealous? The question pops up like a red flag.

Not entirely.

But somewhat?

Maybe.

I throw on some running clothes, grab Hank's leash and slip out of the apartment without seeing anyone.

I know Thomas had to work this morning, but the last thing I want to think about is whether Holden and Sarah are sleeping in and what they might be doing if they are.

Since I'm already in my running clothes, I decide to pound some of last night's toxins out of me and take off at a good pace. Hank Junior is always up for a run of any kind and needs no encouragement.

We go out about two miles and I turn back. A half-mile or so from the apartment, we walk. A car pulls up alongside us, beeping its horn. I glance over and spot Beck in a convertible BMW, an uncertain look on his face.

"Hey," he says.

"Hey," I say.

"You're doing pretty well to already have a run under your belt."

"Figured my body could use it," I say.

"Yeah, about that–"

"Let's not," I say. "Better to leave it alone."

"Buy you a coffee."

"You don't have to do that."

"What if I said I want to?"

"I've got Hank."

"He'll fit nicely in the back seat."

"He's not used to rides this nice."

"It's a car. Four wheels. Come on."

"I could use the coffee. That much is true," I say.

He reaches over to open the passenger door for me. Hank hops over the seat and into the back, sitting straight as if he's prepared to enjoy the view.

Starbucks is packed with Vanderbilt students, sitting at the outside tables with laptops poised in front of them.

"Drive through okay?" Beck asks.

"Sure."

He asks me what I'd like, and I tell him a tall Veranda with one sugar. He goes for a black Pikes Peak. The girl at the drive-through window smiles big at him and asks if it's okay if Hank has a treat. I nod, and she hands Beck a cookie.

He holds it back for Hank to take, and he sits munching in happiness.

We sip our coffee in silence as we pull away from the Starbucks. We're a few blocks from the apartment when he says, "I didn't sleep last night, thinking about what could have happened."

"It wasn't your fault."

"Actually, I should have known better than to leave you with her."

"You didn't. Look, everything worked out all right. I won't be buying her latest single though."

Beck laughs. "Me, either. You could press charges against her or something if you wanted to."

"I don't want to. I just want to forget it. Maybe take it as a lesson learned about being a naïve, gullible–"

"Hey," he says. "You're not gullible. She's just bad."

We pull into the parking lot of the apartment building. Beck cuts the engine. He angles toward me in his seat and says, "I'd really like to make it up to you."

"That's not necessary."

"Please. Let me."

I sigh, reach back to rub Hank Junior under his chin. "So what do you have in mind?"

"Dad's writing with Bobby Jenkins later this afternoon. He's one of the top writers in town."

"I know who he is. That's great."

"I'm going with him. I thought maybe you'd like to come, too."

"Sit in on a session with Bobby Jenkins?"

"Yeah. He's a cool guy. He writes amazing songs."

"Wow. You don't have to do this."

"I know. I want to."

"I'm supposed to work tonight."

"Maybe you could get someone to take your shift."

"Maybe," I say. "I'll try. Give me your number, and I'll call you in a bit to let you know if I can get off."

He tells me the number, and I punch it into my phone. "Send me yours?"

"Sure."

"Thanks for the coffee." I get out of the car, motion for Hank Junior to follow me and then shut the door, stepping onto the curb.

Footsteps sound on the stairway behind us. I glance over my shoulder to spot Holden and Sarah walking toward us. Sarah has her hand tucked inside his arm. He spots us, and maybe it's only me who notices the way his eyes go a deeper blue.

"Hey," Beck says.

"Y'all are out early," Sarah says.

"Figured I owed her a coffee at the very least," Beck says.

"Yeah, I've yet to hear the real story of what happened last night," she says, looking at me with raised eyebrows. "That must have been some party."

"A little more than we bargained for," Beck replies.

"Had to have been fun if you two are already at it again," Sarah adds.

Holden is yet to speak, and the response on the tip of my tongue isn't one that would make Sarah and me friends. "Thanks again, Beck," I say.

"See you later this afternoon."

"I'll try."

"You better," he adds.

Hank and I cross the parking lot and make for the stairwell. I can feel Holden's eyes on us, but I just keep walking.

♪

AS IT TURNS OUT, I am able to switch shifts with Ainsley, one of the other waitresses at the restaurant. She's glad to do it, she says, since I offer to take her shift tomorrow night and there was something she wanted to do anyway.

I text Beck and let him know.

I feed Hank Junior early and leave Holden a note that I've fed Patsy, too.

My clothes selection isn't vast, so it doesn't take me long to decide on a simple pink sundress and flat sandals.

Beck is driving the BMW again, top down, and it feels good sliding down the Nashville streets with music from his iPhone blasting through the car's speakers.

"You look great," he says, glancing over at me, smiling his confident smile, one hand on the steering wheel.

"Thank you," I say, and feel myself blush a little.

Being with Beck feels different from being with Holden. With Holden, I always feel on the edge of something about to happen. Something I very much want but am also very much afraid of.

Not that I couldn't be intimidated by Beck. He's lived a life I know very little about. A life I have dreamed about but don't know in reality.

And he's gorgeous. Who wouldn't be intimidated by that? But he's also young. My age. And that makes him easier to talk to. Easier to be with in some ways. And then again, there's that small difference of him not having a girlfriend looming in between us.

"So the studio where we're going," Beck says, "is really cool. Bobby can pretty much write with whoever he wants considering his track record. And it's deserved. At least that's what my dad says."

"I think I know every song he's ever written," I say. "Are you sure it's okay if I'm here?"

"Positive. I checked with my dad."

It takes us twenty minutes or so to get there, the house not as far outside the city as Beck's house. When we pull into the driveway, I spot the Ferrari, indicating that Case must already be here.

Beck pulls up beside it, gets out and comes around to open my door.

"Thanks," I say, sliding out and trying to subdue the sudden flutter of butterflies in my stomach. "I'm nervous."

"Don't be. Everything's really laid back here."

The house isn't nearly as grand as Case's, but impressive all the same. It's a classic brick style with an antiqued wood front door and a mammoth knocker shaped like a guitar.

Beck knocks and a few seconds later, a pretty woman somewhere in her forties answers the door. Her smile is welcoming and we follow her through the house to a studio set up very much like the one at Beck's house. It's not as big though, and the equipment seems a little less fancy, more like the workhorse version.

Case and the man I instantly recognize as Bobby Jenkins are sitting together at a round table. I saw him once in an interview on the country music channel. Both men have guitars on their laps. Beck introduces me.

"It's really nice to meet you, Mr. Jenkins." He's older than I expect, maybe late fifties.

"So glad you could be here."

"Thank you so much. Really."

Case told him about the recording session yesterday and how I'm part of a group called Barefoot Outlook. It sounds strange hearing it as if it's really happening, and while I'd like to believe it's true, it feels more like something made of toothpicks than beams.

"Well, good luck to you," he says.

"You got anything you want to start with, Case?" he asks, picking up the guitar.

"Just a phrase," Case says. "Don't have too much attached to it yet."

"What is it?"

"Wishing time away."

Bobby nods. "Hmm. Yeah. See what we can do with that." He throws out some angles, some kind of obvious, some not so much.

I listen to the rally between them, mesmerized at the process and can't help but think how much Holden would love this. The two of them are like miners, digging, sifting, rinsing, until they find the lines of gold nuggets that begin to form a verse, a chorus, a bridge. The pieces put together with such expertise that I can't really imagine ever reaching this level of capability.

The music they create fits the words perfectly, like a glove to a fine-boned hand.

Three hours have passed when they push back their chairs and smile at each other.

"Yeah," Case says. "I like it."

"Me, too," Bobby agrees.

Beck and I glance at each other and smile. Neither of us has said a word since the start of the session, and I wonder how many times he has seen this done.

They call it a wrap. We stand, and Case throws an arm around Beck's shoulders, giving him a hug.

Beck shakes hands with Bobby who looks at me and says, "Really glad you could be here."

"Thank you," I say. "So much. It was a priceless experience."

He smiles at me and nods. When he doesn't poo poo my extravagant praise, I wonder if someone had once done the same for him, someone who was really great at writing the same as he was.

We're in the car on the way back into town when I say, "That was really incredible, Beck. I don't know how to thank you."

"I think I owed you one," he says. "It was cool for me, too. I haven't gotten over being amazed by the whole process yet. It's kind of like magic or something."

I know what he means. It is like that, watching something amazing being conjured out of thin air, the pieces coming together to form something beautiful and possibly able to resonate with so many people.

"It's early. You wanna go somewhere and hang out a while? There's a good band over at Lauren's place."

"Can we have an honest moment?"

"Sure," he says.

"I like you, Beck. I really like you. Who wouldn't? But my head is kind of somewhere else right now."

"Holden," he says.

"It's not something I won't get past. I really don't have a choice. So maybe if you could just give me a little time?"

"That's more than cool," he says. "Let's just hang out. No expectations. No demands. How's that sound?"

"I don't know. Like maybe you're too good to be true?"

He laughs. "Or maybe I just know a good thing when I see it, and I don't want to blow it." He reaches out and brushes my cheek with the back of his hand. "Let's just go have some fun, okay?"

"Okay," I say. And that sounds like a great idea to me.

♪

THE RESTAURANT IS CRAZY busy. There's a line flowing out the main door and down the sidewalk several storefronts long.

Beck knows the guy behind the rope and gets waved in, towing me along behind him.

"I feel really funny about that," I say as we slip inside the low-lit interior.

"Funny enough to go stand at the end of that line?"

"Um. Maybe not?"

The band playing on stage is country with a thumping beat, and you can't help but instantly feel it in your bones and want to move to it.

Holden isn't supposed to be working tonight, so I start at the sight of him behind the bar, filling glasses with ice. As if he feels my gaze on him, he looks up and suddenly we're staring straight at one another, my heart kicking up instantly.

In that moment of blank honesty, I see the flash of hurt in his eyes.

There's no justification for it. He has no say over who I'm here with, but at the same time, I know that feeling. It's the same one I get when I see him with Sarah, and I realize that it gives me no pleasure to make him feel that.

He turns his back and smiles at a woman at the bar. I watch its effect on her, the way she leans in and stares up at him. I turn away abruptly as my stomach does a somersault of hurt, unreasonable as it is.

As it turns out, Beck knows a couple of the band members, and we snag a table up close. During the first set, I sit as if anchored to my seat, focusing on absorbing every note of every song. The lead singer is incredible. She's got a voice that flows from her like warm honey and a range that makes me instantly envious. She also has the kind of looks that make listening to her nearly secondary to watching her.

They take a break after the first set and the singer comes over to our table.

"Hey, Beck," she says. "Glad y'all could come out."

"Hey, Tania. You're rockin' it tonight."

"Thanks," she says with an appreciative smile.

"Tania, this is CeCe MacKenzie."

"Y'all are great," I say. "I love your sound."

"Thanks," she says, turning her smile to me. "We've been working hard at it."

"No doubt," Beck says. "Y'all are really getting the polish on it."

"Thank you." She looks at Beck, her eyes suddenly teasing. "Is she why you never called me back?"

Most guys would have been embarrassed by that kind of direct arrow, but Beck shrugs and says, "Nooo. But she could be."

Tania laughs. "Don't worry. I'm on to greener pastures."

And for some reason, what's between them doesn't feel like anything other than good-natured ribbing. No daggers like there had been with Macey last night.

The rest of the show is great, and Beck seems to know half the people in the place, but I'm relieved when the band plays its last encore, and we head out into the night.

I manage to leave without meeting eyes with Holden again. "That was awesome," I say as we get in the car. "Thank you for asking me."

"Yeah, they're pretty cool." Beck cranks the music, and we speed down the highway. We both seem content not to talk, and when we get back to the apartment, he cuts the engine, insisting on walking me to the door.

"That was really fun," I say, sticking my key in the lock and turning to look up at him.

"Thanks for going with me."

"Thanks for asking."

"So we're stuck on that friends thing, huh?" he says, a smile touching the corner of his mouth.

"For now?"

"For now. I think you're worth it," he says. "The wait, I mean."

Footsteps sound on the stairwell, and I look over Beck's shoulder to see Holden come to an abrupt stop at the sight of us.

"Sorry," he says, and I can see he's caught off guard. "Excuse me." He cuts around us, pulling my key out of the lock and handing it to me. He inserts his own and opens the door. He goes inside without saying another word.

The awkwardness left in his wake is thick and undeniable.

"A little time?" I say.

"A little time," he agrees. "Goodnight, CeCe. Sleep well, okay?"

"You, too." And with that, I watch him walk away.

♪

Holden

I absolutely HATE this feeling.

Jealous guys suck. I mean, what is jealousy anyway?

Awareness that there's something you can't have. Or that someone is better at something than you are. Or has someone you can't have.

There it is. Large and looming. The truth. Ugly as it is.

Someone I can't have.

I grab a beer from the refrigerator, pull out a drawer for the opener, pop it off and take a long drink. I head for the shower then just because I don't want to be standing here when CeCe comes in.

The water is cold but does pretty much nothing to cool my misery. In my room, I wait until I hear her door click closed, and then I step out into the hall and knock.

She doesn't respond for several moments, which tells me she's considering not answering. "CeCe?" I say.

The door opens and she stands there looking at me with What? on her face.

"Ainsley asked me to remind you about her shift tomorrow."

"I know."

"Okay." Awkward silence, and then I manage, "How was it?"

"It was great. All of it. Great." She's quiet for a moment and then, "Where's Sarah?"

I glance away and then back at her. "She went back to Georgia. We kind of had a fight."

CeCe steps away, and I can see her blank her expression. "Oh. I'm sorry."

"Are you?" I ask.

"Yes, I am."

"Why?"

She throws up her hands. "Why wouldn't I be? You're obviously crazy about each other and–"

"Are we?" It's a question I shouldn't ask, but I can't help myself.

"Yes! You are!"

"Don't you want to know what we fought about?"

"No, I don't think I do."

"You," he says. "We fought about you."

She blinks once. Hard. And then, "Why would you be fighting about me?"

"Because she knows."

"There's nothing to know."

"Knows it's different. Since I got here. Since. . .since I met you."

"Holden. Don't do this. Don't hang this on me. I don't want to be responsible for you breaking Sarah's heart."

"I'm not hanging anything on you. I'm just telling you the truth."

"You love her."

"I did. Yes, I did. Now, I don't know anymore."

"She loves you," CeCe says.

"She says she does. I'm not sure what that means based on the way we've been to each other since she got here. And I wonder now if we've just been trying to make each other fit what it is we both say we want. People change, don't they? And when the change comes, how long do you deny it?"

"Holden–"

Her protest is weaker than before, and as if the words are pulled from me, I say, "I can't stand seeing you with him."

"We're friends, Holden."

"He doesn't want to be friends with you, CeCe."

"I've told him that right now that's all we can be."

"Why?"

She drops her gaze. "Because I'm not ready."

"Because," I interrupt. "You think about me the way I think about you. With every breath. Every thought."

"No, I don't. I–"

I reach out and loop my arm around her waist, splay my hand across the dip of her lower back. I reel her to me, slowly, steadily, as if the catch is inevitable. She bumps to a stop against my chest, tips her head back and looks up at me.

"Holden, don't. This is not where we should go."

"There's nowhere else I want to go," I say. "In fact, if we don't go there, if we don't go there now–" I swoop in then, finding her mouth with mine. The kiss is deep and so full of longing and want that I instantly feel inebriated by it. My head is buzzing, like I just took a shot of some fine tequila. But this buzz is better. So much better.

I lift her to me, my hands at her waist. She wraps her arms around my neck and kisses me back, fully, giving in, no longer protesting or coming up with reasons why I shouldn't be here.

We just kiss. And I feel like we could kiss like this all night long, and I wouldn't be able to get enough of her.

I pick her up, lifting and carrying her all at the same time to the bed. I both drop her and follow her down at the same time. The feel of her beneath me is like being found when I never knew I was lost.

Hank Junior makes a sound that might be disapproval and heads to a corner of the room.

CeCe and I roll to the middle, still kissing. It's pretty clear that neither of us has any desire to stop.

I feel something crumple under me and pull a piece of paper out from under my shoulder.

I'm ready to toss it when CeCe grabs my hand and says, "Hank Junior! What have you gotten into now?"

The edges of the paper have been chewed, the top right hand corner completely missing. CeCe glances at it, then pulls it in for a closer look.

Her face goes completely still. She slides up on her knees, her face growing whiter as she reads.

"What is it?" I raise up on my elbow. "What's wrong?"

She drops the paper, and it flutters back onto the blanket beneath us.

The look on her face has me spooked, and I cautiously pick up the torn page and start to read.

Patient Sarah Saxon

Age: 22

Female

Recommended course of treatment:

Radiation, chemotherapy. Initial course to be followed by reevaluation for surgical candidacy.

I sit up and swing my legs over the side of the bed, elbows on my knees, feeling suddenly and completely sick.

I hold the paper under the lamplight and read it again, just to make sure I hadn't imagined it.

"Holden," CeCe says, putting a hand on my back.

"That's why she came," I say. "To tell me. She came here to tell me. I didn't–"

"You didn't know. You didn't know."

"I all but pushed her out the door. Oh, my God." I really think I am going to be sick. I lean over and cross my arms over my stomach. I can feel the blood pounding in my temples.

CeCe gets up, stands in front of me and drops to her knees, forcing me to look at her. "You haven't done anything wrong," she says. "You haven't."

I look up at her, and it feels like I'm on one of those crazy amusement park rides that zooms you to a peak and then lets you plummet. This is the plummet part. "How can you say that?"

"Because it's true," she says, her voice breaking in the middle of the statement. "She needs you."

I let myself look directly at her then, at the tears suddenly coursing down her face. I realize they are for Sarah. For us. For it all.

♪

Book Three

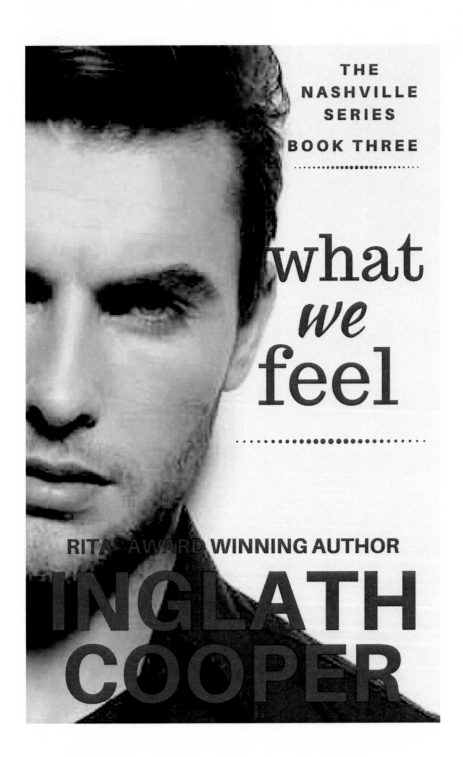

THE
NASHVILLE
SERIES

BOOK THREE

what
we
feel

RITA AWARD WINNING AUTHOR

INGLATH
COOPER

Nashville – Book Three – What We Feel

Inglath Cooper

＊

Hunky musicians Holden Ashford and Thomas Franklin rescue Nashville bound CeCe MacKenzie and her Walker Hound Hank Junior from the side of the road when her car catches on fire. A less determined girl might have let her dreams go up in smoke as well, but not CeCe. She's been singing all her life, and she just wants a chance to do the thing she loves in a place where music is part of the fabric of life. As it turns out, Holden and Thomas want the same thing, and it isn't long before they're all chasing after the dream together.

Falling in love hasn't figured in to CeCe's plans, but the moment she sets eyes on Holden, her heart is asking why not? Holden is drawn to her as well, but he already has someone in his life, Sarah who still lives in Atlanta, Sarah who loves him. Who he thought he loved back until CeCe makes him realize he hadn't really known that love could turn him inside out.

But an unexpected visit from Sarah brings to light a terrible truth and Holden is faced with a choice between doing the right thing or permanently defining himself as a guy he never thought he would be.

It is only in letting each other go that both Holden and CeCe will come to understand that in life and love, the part that's real is what we feel.

CeCe

19 months later

The Blue Bird is packed for the early show. Thomas and I are third to perform tonight. The fifteen-year-old girl currently on stage will be a tough act to follow. She sings like nobody's business. I have to wonder how it's possible for someone that age to have so much stage presence. The song isn't memorable, but her delivery is.

"Think she was singin' when she came out of her mama's womb?" Thomas asks me now.

I shake my head and smile a little. "Maybe. Is it me, or do the newbies get younger every day?"

We're both standing at the back of the room, me with my guitar, Thomas chewing gum like it's the fuel for every note he plans to reach when it's our turn to go on stage.

"They get younger every day," Thomas says.

The girl's guitar goes suddenly quiet, and she smacks out a beat below the strings, urging the crowd to follow along. They do while she does a stretch of a cappella that reveals even more fully the sweet tone of her voice.

Thomas starts to clap. "Kinda grows on you, doesn't she?"

"She's got what it takes to get her there."

"Yup."

If we've learned anything at all in the past year and a half of navigating Nashville's music industry waters, it is that talent is only a piece of it. Talent steps off the bus in this town every single day, and, with equal frequency, talent leaves. Making it here is about way more than just mere ability. "Think she'll see it through?" I ask.

"Depends on how many dents she gets in that guitar of hers and how quickly they come, I guess. Although I'd say it's gonna take some hefty whacks to derail that little girl's mojo."

I can't disagree with him. I've met some incredible singers in the past year and a half who seemed like they could take the knocks, most having arrived in Nashville full of the confidence built by small-town accolades and family praise. But most people have a vulnerability of some kind, and the music business has a way of unearthing it, even when it's hidden way down deep.

The girl ends the song, and the crowd responds with enthusiastic applause. She all but glows with it, and I wonder if my time here has already rubbed some of that shine from my enthusiasm.

She introduces Thomas and me then, my stomach plummeting as it always does right before we perform.

"If you've been in Nashville any time at all," she says, "you've probably already heard about these two. Good heavens, can they sing! Ladies and gentlemen, give it up for Barefoot Outlook!"

"Let's do this thing," Thomas says, dropping his gum in a trash can and waving me ahead of him with a gentlemanly bow.

On stage, Thomas does the introductions, his Georgia drawl full tilt. "Hey everybody, I'm Thomas Franklin. This is CeCe MacKenzie. We're Barefoot Outlook, and we're pleased as pickle juice to be here with y'all tonight!"

If the girl before us has stage presence, Thomas is the polished version of it. Since we first started performing together, I've been in awe of the way he wins the interest and attention of the crowd in front of us before he ever sings a note.

"If y'all came to Nashville to hear some country music," he says, "then hold on, 'cause here we go."

Anyone who's never seen Thomas perform with Holden wouldn't realize that he's different when they're onstage together. But I do. The two of them had this rapport that translated into something I don't think Thomas and I will ever have. Maybe it comes from having been best friends for so long and knowing pretty much all there is to know about a person. Like two people who've been married for decades and can guess what the other will order in a restaurant before they even open the menu. And like two people who fell in love and got married when they were really young, Thomas and Holden will always be each other's first for writing music and performing. I have never been under any illusion that I am a replacement for Holden.

Holden. A year and a half since he's been gone, and he still skitters through my thoughts at random points throughout every single day. He writes songs and sends them to Thomas on a regular basis, but he hasn't returned to Nashville even once since the night he left to go back to Atlanta, back to Sarah.

Our first song tonight is "Country Boys Don't Wear Thongs." Holden sent it to Thomas a couple of weeks ago. It's upbeat, twangy, and funny and immediately sets the mood for our performance. Thomas sells it like bottled water in the Sahara Desert. By the end of the last chorus, the crowd is fully hooked. It's what we wait for when we're onstage, and it's like searching for the right key and knowing the sound when the lock clicks into place.

When Thomas and I first started playing together after Holden left Nashville, we were like two people on a blind date, unsure of what to say, both letting the other go first, the result being that a couple of our shows were pretty much a muddled mess.

The next is Holden's as well, a duet called "Our Back Fence." The third is "What You Took From Me," the song Holden wrote about a man who lost his wife to a drunk driving accident. And the last song we perform is one I wrote called "Don'tcha Do That." It brings the crowd back up, and at the end, Thomas thanks everyone for being here and lets them know we'll be playing tomorrow night at the Rowdy Howdy.

Just before we leave the stage, he throws out, "Y'all come on down and let us show you a good time!"

The clapping follows us to the back of the room where Thomas gets my guitar case and hands it to me. We chat while I put my guitar away and discuss a couple of moments during the first song we think we could have handled better.

"Hey, there's someone out here who wants to talk to you two."

I look up to see the fifteen-year-old who performed before us smiling at me with the kind of smile that makes it clear life has not yet dealt her a single hard blow.

"Who is it?" Thomas asks.

She shrugs. "Some guy in a suit. Want me to tell him to come on back?"

"Sure," Thomas says. "That's fine."

She turns to go and then swings around. "Hey, by the way, y'all were awesome up there. You write your own stuff?"

"CeCe wrote a couple of the songs. The rest were written by a friend of ours."

"Wow, they're really good," she says. "I hope I can write like that some day."

"Just keep at it," Thomas says.

"I will. See y'all soon." She waves once and is gone.

My phone vibrates. I glance at the text. It's Beck, letting me know he's running a little late to pick me up.

I text back. "NP. See you in a few."

"K" is his reply.

"Beck?" Thomas asks.

"Yeah."

"Where y'all headed tonight?"

"His dad's having a thing," I say.

"A thing at Case Phillips's house is a good thing, isn't it?"

"Yeah. I guess I'm tired."

"Of Beck?"

I look up quickly. "No. Why?"

"Just seems like you haven't been seeing him as much as you were."

"We've both been busy," I hedge.

"Okay."

"We have!" I insist.

"Okay," Thomas says with a smile. "Me thinks she doth protest too much."

"Stop," I say. "And anyway, you're the one who needs to get your love life out of drought status."

"Ouch! Low blow."

"You opened that can of worms."

A knock sounds against the frame of the doorway. A man in a dark suit steps in and says, "I was told I could find you two back here."

"Yes, sir," Thomas says. "What can we do for you?"

"I'm Andrew Seeger." He walks forward and sticks his hand out to me. We shake, and he pumps Thomas's hand as well. "I'm hoping I can do something for you."

During our first months in town, this would have perked our ears up considerably. Fancy guy, fancy suit, do something for us. It's certainly not the first time we've heard it. To date, not much of it has panned out.

"Yeah?" Thomas says. "What's that?"

Andrew doesn't appear put off by Thomas's shortness. "The song you did tonight. "What You Took From Me." Did one of you write it, or both of you?"

Thomas shakes his head. "A buddy of ours wrote it."

"Oh." Andrew appears slightly disappointed. "Is he around?"

"Actually, no," Thomas says. "He lives in Atlanta now."

Andrew looks more disappointed.

"What exactly is this about?" Thomas asks.

"I'm Hart Holcomb's manager."

At the name, my eyes go wide, and I feel Thomas's surprise as well.

"A friend told us about the song," he says, his voice soft. "Hart snuck into a club downtown where you two were playing and listened for himself. Hart's wife was killed in a drunk driving accident five years ago. The message is one he feels a need to put out there, and well, he loved it. He wants to record it."

I glance at Thomas, see the look of stunned surprise on his face, and realize mine probably mirrors it exactly.

"Did you say Hart Holcomb?" Thomas asks.

"Yeah," Andrew says with a half-smile. "Hart had just finished up his new record when somebody told him about it. He's bumping another song to include this. I gotta tell you, if there's any such thing as a lucky break for a songwriter, this is it. Think you can get your friend down here, like ASAP?"

Under most circumstances, the answer would be an immediate yes, but Thomas had yet to talk Holden into coming back even once. After his last trip to Atlanta to see Holden, Thomas returned with the admission that maybe it was time he accepted that Holden was through. "He said he'd write songs for me as long as I want him to," he'd admitted, more down than I'd ever heard him, "but anything else, he's moved on."

"I'm not really sure," Thomas says now, and I flash a quick look at him.

Andrew hands Thomas a card. "My number is on there. Ask him to give me a call and let me know when we can meet with Hart."

"Will do," Thomas says.

"All right, then." Andrew drops us a nod and walks out.

Thomas and I look at each other but wait a full sixty seconds before saying a word.

"Did he just say Hart Holcomb wants to record Holden's song?" Thomas is smiling.

"Yeah, he did."

"Good friggin' day! That's like somebody dropping in to say you won the lottery when you didn't even buy a ticket."

"It's a great song," I say, deliberately keeping my voice smooth.

"It is."

"Do you think he'll come?"

Thomas's smile fades instantly. "He has to come. If I have to drive down there and drag his butt here myself, he's coming."

I don't doubt Thomas means it, but I also know that Holden has chosen another life and made it clear that this one is behind him. Something flutters low inside me at the thought of seeing him again. It shouldn't, but it does.

"In fact, I'm calling him right now." Thomas pulls his phone from his shirt pocket, swipes the screen and then taps his number.

My heart kicks into overdrive now. Which is ridiculous considering I'm not the one calling, and Holden won't even know I'm in the room. My palms instantly start to sweat. I pick up my guitar and mouth to Thomas, "I'm leaving. Beck is..."

"Hold on a minute," Thomas says. "Don't go anywhere."

Holden answers because Thomas says, "Hey, what are you doing?" A pause and, "You're still at work? I thought the corporate world went home at five." Another pause. "Are you sitting down? Well you should. We just finished up a set at the Blue Bird."

I notice he doesn't say my name.

"And you're not gonna believe what's happened. Hart Holcomb wants to record "What You Took From Me." Silence and then, "Ah, hold on, maybe you didn't understand what I said. *Hart Holcomb* wants to record your song. This is pretty much a once in a lifetime opportunity. Can you come down tomorrow, man?"

A pause before, "Seriously! Two years ago, you would have sold your eyeteeth for a chance like this. . .Yeah, I know things are different now, but do you have to stop living. . .Well, not the life you planned to live."

Another stretch of awkward silence. Thomas says, "You know what, I'm going to pretend for now that somebody hit you over the head with a two-by-four, and you're not yourself. I'll call back in the morning and hope the Holden I used to know will answer the telephone." And with that he clicks off.

It's a rare thing to see Thomas angry. I've seen him mildly aggravated a couple of times, but this is far beyond that.

"Aliens have taken over his body," he says, looking at me and shaking his head.

"He made a choice, Thomas."

"But he said she's doing well. It's like he thinks if he resumes his life, she'll get sick again."

"Maybe that's how he's made peace with it," I say, even though something at the core of me aches with a deep dull throb. I had made my own peace with it eventually; not right away, because it simply hurt too much. Watching Holden go and not come back was the first time in my life I fully understood the meaning of wanting something heart and soul and not being able to have it. Before that, if I had been asked, I would have said I knew what that felt like. There had been things in my life that I didn't get, that I yearned for at the time. I didn't get the puppy I wanted for Christmas when I was seven. I didn't make the cheerleading squad in tenth grade. And after standing in line for almost two days to audition for *American Idol*, I came down with the stomach flu and had to leave.

By world standards, those are ridiculously minuscule things, but in nineteen years of life, those events were my measuring stick for disappointment. Maybe it's their flimsiness that made wanting Holden and not being able to have him all the more excruciating.

On the morning he left, I lay in bed listening to the sounds of his going. The shower starting up in his room. The zip of his luggage. The snap of his guitar case. The squeak of the bedroom door. His footsteps in the hallway. The gush of water from the kitchen faucet. Muffled words between him and Thomas, their tones low and somber. Then the opening of the door and the clicking sound of it closing behind him. I had been holding the tears inside. With that final sound of his leaving, they had gushed up and out of me with the force of a geyser. It was as if my holding them in had only increased the pressure beneath, and I could not stop myself from sobbing. I buried my face in my pillow, but Thomas heard me and came into the room.

Sitting down on the side of the bed, he pulled me up against him. He folded his arms around me like a big, broad band of comfort, and he let me cry. I cried until there wasn't a single tear left in me. I lay limp and empty against his wide strong chest. He rubbed the back of my hair with one hand and said, "Damn, it sucks."

"I'm not just crying for me," I'd said. "I'm crying for all of it. How could someone so young, how could she-"

"I don't know," Thomas said, shaking his head. "It's a wretched fuck of a disease."

I bit my lower lip and refused to let another dry sob slip past my throat. "Will she be okay?" I asked, like a small child looking to a parent for reassurance of things simply too big to process.

He continued rubbing my hair. "I pray like hell she will."

"I didn't mean to fall in love with him," I said in little more than a whisper.

Thomas said nothing for a bit, and I wondered if he hadn't heard me. But then he said, "I don't think he meant to fall in love with you either."

And that, just that, broke the dam again. Thomas had held me and let me cry. At some point, he slipped us both under the covers, and he stayed there with me until sleep stole my tears and gave me relief. An unbreakable bond was forged between the two of us that night. Our loss was mutual. It would be a while before either of us knew the extent of it, knew that Holden wasn't coming back for good. Once that became clear, something in Thomas dimmed a little. Holden had not only been like a brother to him, but was probably the only other person in the world who understood what music meant to him and felt the same way about it. They had been on a journey together for a long time, and when Holden's path had veered off in another direction, Thomas was just kind of lost. Everything he thought he'd wanted to do in this town was now up for question.

He'd been in the living room one night when I got home from working in the restaurant. He was sitting on the couch with Hank Junior nestled up under the crook of his arm, his head on Thomas's lap. I know my Hank, and I could tell by the look on his face that he was worried about Thomas.

"Everything okay?" I asked, dropping my purse on the coffee table. Hank thumped his tail, looked up, and licked Thomas's cheek.

"I swear your dog has telepathy," Thomas said.

I walked over and rubbed Hank's head. "So what's wrong?"

"I've been thinking. Maybe I ought to hang up this gig too."

I felt my eyes go wide, my lips part in surprise. "You mean quit music? Leave Nashville?"

"Well, it's kinda not making much sense now. Without Holden, I'm not sure it will ever work for me."

I sat down on the sofa next to him. "I know you miss him," I said.

"I think maybe I never realized quite how much of the driving force he was behind the two of us. Heck, CeCe, I just like to sing. I'm not any good at writing or scheduling gigs. That was Holden's thing. And it all...well, it feels flat without him."

I wanted to disagree, but I couldn't. It was like going on vacation to a place normally completely sunny, only to have your seven days there filled with clouds and rain. Somehow, it wasn't the same. "Would he want you to leave, to give all this up?"

"Well, no, but that's not really the point. He doesn't get to say whether I do or not."

I studied him for a moment and then said, "I'm not sure you know exactly how much of a gift you have in that voice of yours. People love to hear you sing, Thomas, and you love to do it. I bet, if you asked him, Holden would keep writing for you. He loves to write. I can't imagine that he would give that up forever."

"I think he wants to forget all of it."

"You don't know until you ask."

We sat there on the couch for a good long while. Now that I was home to take over soothing duty, Hank Jr. snored softly, his head still resting on Thomas's leg.

"Assuming that he does want to keep writing," Thomas said finally, "and that's a big 'does,' what about the two of us going on with the Barefoot Outlook thing? I know you've been doing your thing, and I've been doing mine but I don't much like being solo."

"Me, either," I said. And even though it wasn't what I had once imagined for myself, I realized that I did like what we had begun putting together as Barefoot Outlook. Before Sarah's diagnosis and Holden's leaving. "Think it will fly with just the two of us?" I asked.

"Won't know until we try."

Since that night, that's what we've been doing. Holden did agree to continue writing, and most of the songs he's sent us were written to include us both. All of our communication went through Thomas. And I hadn't spoken to him since the morning he left the apartment. I guess it's better that way because what would there have been for us to say to each other?

Holden did the right thing. I have not questioned this, even at its cost to me. From the moment Sarah's diagnosis became a reality, I never once thought that he would choose me. I never once thought that he would do anything but the right thing where Sarah was concerned.

A person can only be what they are, and what I know about Holden is this. He's the guy who's going to walk the little old lady across the street, pick up the starving dog on the side of the road. He's the guy who sees right as right, and wrong as wrong, and there's no in between, no gray. Because if he hadn't been that guy, it's as simple as this. I would never have fallen in love with him.

♪

Holden

It's nine-thirty by the time I leave the office and head home. I take Peachtree Road out of downtown Atlanta, choosing traffic over the interstate. The Volvo belongs to Sarah's father's company. As an employee there, part of my compensation package includes a vehicle to drive. I had actually put up an argument over being given such an expensive ride for an entry level position, but Dr. Saxon is not a man too many people win an argument against. My job is a good one, a job most college graduates would be thrilled to get just coming out of school. And under any other circumstances, having the opportunity to work with Dr. Saxon would feel like something of a coup.

Sarah's father is a smart guy. His first invention, over twenty years ago, made him a multimillionaire. He developed a cream for burn victims that accelerated the healing process by as much as thirty percent. From there, he created other medicinal products, mostly rooted in natural sources, that were eventually sold to pharmaceutical companies and put his worth at over two hundred million dollars.

In fact, it is probably Dr. Saxon's unyielding determination to help Sarah beat her disease that got her to where she is now, in remission, feeling and looking like herself again. I wonder sometimes what would have happened had he not pushed her from clinic to clinic, including one in Mexico, trying countless methods of boosting her body's immune system. Watching him do everything in his power to help her made me wonder many times if he was fighting not only for Sarah's life, but his own as well. I really believe that if Sarah had died, he would have too.

That kind of love isn't something I ever saw growing up in my own home. My father's love had never been rooted in selflessness. I'm sure there was a reason for it. Maybe it was my mother's leaving when I was six and the house suddenly becoming a place where Dad and I basically crossed paths and little more. He saw his role as raising me, preparing me for the world and then pushing me out into it.

I know that's what a parent is actually supposed to do, but my dad's efforts always felt as if they were rooted in obligation. As for Sarah's parents, especially her father, everything he did for her stemmed from the purest kind of love, a love I have often wondered if anyone else in her life will be able to live up to.

Our apartment is in a nice section of Buckhead, in between the Buckhead Diner and Phipps Plaza. It's actually a condominium that Dr. Saxon bought for Sarah about six months after she got her first clear checkup. It's in a high-rise, its only drawback being that Patsy absolutely hates the elevator and refuses to get in unless I'm carrying her. I've discovered that an older Beagle pretty much personifies stubbornness. When the two of us moved in here with Sarah, I expected Patsy to be a permanent bone of contention between us, but somewhere along the way, Sarah decided that my having a dog wasn't such a bad thing. Although she still doesn't like for her to sit on the couch or sleep on our bed, she's okay with her. I should say they're okay with each other.

I park in the garage and take the elevator to our floor. As soon as I stick the key in the lock, I hear Patsy click, click, clicking across the tile. She is waiting just inside the door, as she is every night when I get home.

Her tail a wagging blur, she's so happy to see me that she's shaking, and I wonder, not for the first time, why anyone would choose to be lonely. All they have to do is get a dog. No one has bothered to tell Patsy that I actually did not hang the sun and the moon, and so she continues to think I did. I have to admit I don't mind. I reach down and rub under her chin where she likes to be rubbed. "Do you need to go out? Have you been out already?"

She jogs in place like a little foot soldier, and I feel a surge of pride for how good she looks. Her coat is shiny, and although she's not plump, she looks like a dog who is well-fed and well-loved. In the Davidson County pound, she had looked at least twice as old as she does now. I guess it's true that while lack of care can age beyond fairness, it is also true that the simple ingredients of kindness and love can peel away those years.

"I took her out about a half hour ago."

I look up to see Sarah standing in the kitchen doorway, a soft smile on her mouth. She's thin in skinny jeans and a pink sweater; her hair still very short, but thick and again healthy.

"Thanks," I say. "I didn't mean to be this late."

"That's okay. We had a nice walk."

"Smells great in here."

"I'm roasting some vegetables," she says. "Hungry?"

"Starving."

"Get your shower, and I should have everything ready by the time you're done."

"Sounds good," I say. I walk over and give her a kiss on the cheek, patting my leg for Patsy to follow me. Instead, she leads the way, and in the bedroom, heads for the fancy dog bed Sarah bought for her when we moved in.

Fatigue hits me in a wave as I step under the shower spray a few minutes later. I lean against the wall and let it do its best to revive me. It's not as if my work is physical. It isn't. I've been doing research for Dr. Saxon on hundreds of different topics, compiling the most relevant notes for whatever question he has presented me with. It's interesting, so I'm not exactly sure why I come home exhausted each night.

But then a thought waves itself in front of me like a white flag vying to be noticed. Round pegs, square hole. The constant forcing of a fit. Trying to make something function in a manner in which it was not designed to function. I try not to think about it, belabor it, question it.

I made a choice. Just over nineteen months ago, I made a choice. It's not one I can regret, or really ever imagine regretting.

The first weeks after I came back to Atlanta were a complete nightmare, for Sarah, for me, for her family. The diagnosis itself, the suggested forms of treatment. Chemo. Complete mastectomy with reconstruction. The prognosis itself, unwavering in its uncertainty. It wasn't an if-then proposition. If you take this treatment, then you will be cured. With her cancer, there was nothing definite except for the fact that it had taken her body hostage.

The gratitude on Sarah's face that first night back in Atlanta told me, as nothing else could, that I'd made the right choice. None of what had happened between us in Nashville mattered at that point. She never brought it up, and I never mentioned it. We went on as before, like I had never left Atlanta to go there in the first place. Like there had never been CeCe.

Her name is like a small electrical shock to my brain, because I don't let myself think it very often. There's no point in dwelling on something that can no longer be. It's not as if I were able to do it in the beginning, put her out of my mind. I think I know now that the heart doesn't give up what it wants that easily. I have no explanation for how hard I fell or how fast except that it was like finding a part of myself that I never realized was missing until I met her.

Thomas's call is suddenly front and center, and that's another thing there's no point in thinking about. I'm not going back to Nashville. The likelihood of Hart Holcomb actually cutting my song is about as probable as Georgia snow in July. To go back on the off chance that something might come of it doesn't seem worth what it would feel like to have to leave again. Easier not to go back at all.

I put on sweat pants and a t-shirt and head for the kitchen. Sarah has dinner on the table. We sit down with her telling me about a nutrition class she is taking. In addition to the juicing she's been doing, she's considering adapting to a completely raw diet.

"With the way you like salads," I say, "that shouldn't be too hard."

"I think so too," she agrees. "Some of the research the professor presented was pretty convincing."

"Then you definitely should."

She spears a red pepper, looks at me for a moment and then says, "Are you okay?"

"Yeah," I say.

"You look, I don't know, a little sad or something."

"I'm just tired."

"Daddy over-working you?"

I shake my head. "I probably didn't sleep great last night."

"Anything bothering you?"

"No. Everything's good." I'd like to think I sound convincing but she doesn't look convinced.

A couple of hours later when we're in bed, Sarah reaches across and clasps her fingers in mine. Her touch surprises me. For a long time after her surgery, she did not want me to touch her. Even after her body had completely healed physically, she avoided any opportunity for us to be close.

I've let myself think that with time, this part of our relationship would come back. So far it hasn't. We've continued to ignore it, even though it's begun to loom between us like a big black cloud that we can no longer see through. With her fingers entwined in mine, she says, "Thomas called earlier, right before you got home."

Something jumps inside my chest, and I realize there's no point in asking her what he wanted. "Did he?"

"He told me about the song," she says.

"Yeah, you know the odds of that becoming anything."

She's quiet for a minute or more before saying, "Maybe it's time we talk about some of that."

"What is there to talk about?" I ask, deliberately nonchalant. "Another time, another place."

"But it was your dream."

"Was," I say.

She sighs, turns over onto her side, and, with a fingertip under my jaw, forces me to look at her. "Dreams don't really go away, do they?"

"Sometimes they have to," I answer, my tone ragged enough that I immediately wish I had censored it.

She's quiet for several moments before saying, "Can we drop the walls and be honest with one another, Holden?"

"Sarah," I look at the ceiling, "I am being honest with you."

"I know you think you are. Holden, before I knew I was sick, what I wanted more than anything was for you to come back here because it was where you wanted to be. I never pretended that Nashville was my dream, and I guess I wanted you to decide that it wasn't yours either. But it was your dream. Still is your dream."

"You know I've put all that behind me," I say.

"I know you think you have." She squeezes my hand hard, as if bracing herself. "I want you to go back."

"What?" I hear the surprise in my voice.

"If you don't, you'll regret it," she says softly, "because you'll always wonder what might have happened."

"No, I won't," I say, firm.

Sarah turns over on her back and now she is staring at the ceiling as well. Patsy snores softly, one z after another, all that is filling the silence between us.

"Sarah, things are good now. Let's not mess it up, okay?"

"But are they? Really good? Compared to what they could have been, yes, I think they are. Good as in, I didn't die."

I sit up on one elbow. "Don't talk like that."

"I could have, it's true."

"You didn't, and you won't."

"At least not if Daddy has anything to say about it," she says, a half-smile on her mouth. "I don't know, Holden, I guess I've been thinking a lot about how I'm different now."

"What do you mean?"

"How we're all just one doctor's visit and diagnosis away from our lives being shattered as we know them. I know now how in a blink it can all change. I was so arrogant about life and what I thought I deserved."

"You weren't arrogant," I say.

"Actually, I was. I wanted you, at whatever cost, even if it meant that you would never really be happy with the life that we made together."

"Sarah," I take her hand again, "I am happy. Stop."

"You made a choice to give up all the things that you wanted. You made a choice to give up your writing and music, and I let you because I was too selfish to let you go."

"That's not true."

"It is true," she insists. "And if I couldn't let you go and be sure that you would come back, were you ever really mine to begin with?"

I'd like to answer, to reassure her with the words I know she needs to hear, but they're stuck somewhere in the back of my throat and for the life of me I cannot force them out.

"Now that I'm admitting all of this, I guess I want to be loved by someone else the way I've loved you, Holden. I don't think I want to go through the rest of my life being the one who loves the most."

"Sarah, please-"

"Let me finish. We both deserve that."

"Why are you doing this?" I ask, feeling as if I'm walking on glass and everything beneath me is going to shatter at any second.

"Because I know you won't ever do it first."

Her words fall around us like rain pinging off a roof. I try to absorb their meaning. "Are you saying everything that's happened in this past year and a half has meant nothing?"

"No," she says softly. "The opposite. It's meant everything. What you did for me when you knew that I needed you. . .I don't have any words to come close to thanking you for being who you are. But there is something I can do to pay you back."

"What?" I ask, not sure I even want to know the answer.

"Let you go. Without guilt or regret."

"Sarah-"

"Go and be who you were meant to be, Holden."

"I don't know why you're saying these things. This is a mistake."

"It isn't. And I don't want to think of any of it that way. But to hold onto each other for the wrong reasons, yes. That would be a mistake."

I slip an arm around her waist and pull her to me, a deep sadness sinking in around me. Because she's right. I know she's right.

She presses her face into my chest, and I feel her tears against my skin. "We don't have to do this," I say.

She puts a finger to my lips. "There is one more thing."

Hearing something different in her voice, I pull back to look at her. "What?"

She's silent until I start to think she's not going to tell me. "I've met someone, Holden."

The words hang in the space between us, and I see in her expression that she's not sure what my reaction will be. "A guy?" I ask, the question sounding flat and disbelieving even to my ears.

She nods once, biting her lower lip.

"Who?" I ask, and I don't think my voice sounds like my own.

She hesitates and then, "He's one of the doctors I've been seeing for my follow-up care. Nothing has happened. But he's told me he has feelings for me. And I. . .I think I might for him, too."

I sit up, swing my legs over the side of the bed, lean forward with my elbows on my knees and pull in a couple of deep breaths. "That is probably the last thing in the world I expected to hear you say."

"I didn't go looking for it. And if things were truly right between us, I don't think it would have found me."

When I can speak, I say, "Is all of this because of the very unlikely possibility of me getting a cut on my song?"

"No," she says, placing a hand on my back in what feels like a gesture of comfort. "It's just the trigger."

♪

CeCe

It's one a.m., and the party at Beck's dad's place looks like it's just getting started. There are enough famous faces in various parts of this house to keep a paparazzi photographer snapping away in every direction. The pool is shaped like a guitar, and two of the guys in Case's band are sitting on the diving board, taking requests, one song after another.

I'm in a chair at the opposite end when Beck returns from getting us both a drink. "Here you go," he says, handing me my glass of San Pellegrino and lime.

"Thanks." I look up at him with what I can feel is a weak attempt at a smile.

He sits down on the chair beside me, hip bumping me over a bit. "Hey. What's wrong?"

"Nothing." I shrug and take a sip of the fizzy water.

"Beg to differ. You haven't been yourself all night. Show at the Blue Bird not go well?"

"It went great," I say, a little too bright even to my own ears. "Everything's good."

He puts a finger beneath my chin and forces me to look at him. "Give me credit for knowing you better than that."

"I guess I'm tired. It's been kind of a long week."

"You're working a lot. Why don't you cut back on your hours at the restaurant?"

"And eat with what?" I ask with a half-smile.

"You know I want to help you out, babe. You won't let me."

"I'm good, Beck. Seriously," I say, immediately digging in my heels as I do every time he brings this up.

"Just too tired to play," he says, and for a moment, it feels like I am way older than he is.

"Responsibility calls." I immediately regret my sharpness.

Beck leans back and gives me a long look. "Whoa. Where did that come from?"

"I'm sorry," I say instantly, feeling further guilt for something I'm not even sure I can identify. Beck and I have been officially seeing each other for almost a year now, and I've never once picked a fight. We've never actually *had* a fight.

"Sorry for what?" he asks, the question sounding a little bruised.

"For being a jerk."

"You're not a jerk," he says, putting an arm around my shoulders and pulling me to him. He presses a kiss to my cheek and then nips my lower lip before kissing me full and deep. I respond as I know I should. Kissing him back and telling myself as I have a dozen times before that I would be an idiot to throw this away.

Beck Phillips is all but an actual commodity in Nashville. The only son of a major country music star. Good-looking beyond fairness. How many times have I waited for him at the end of one of his classes at Vanderbilt and seen the girls following him around like puppies after a treat jar? And every time, I've asked myself, why me? Of all the girls he could have in this town, why me?

If I've found anything close to an answer, I would say it's this. Beck doesn't like losing. He likes winning. Not in an obnoxious, arrogant sort of way. It's just what he's used to. Having what he wants. Whether it's right away. Or eventually. And maybe that's what fueled his interest in me. I've yet to give him all of me. Emotionally or physically.

He kisses my neck now, one hand looped around my waist. "Let's go up to my room," he says. "You can take a nap."

I smile and repeat one of my granny's favorite sayings. "Do I look like I just fell off the turnip truck?"

He laughs. "No, I don't guess you do," he says, kissing me full on again. He studies me without bothering to hide the need in his eyes. "What if I promise to be good?"

"I need to go home and sleep in my own bed."

"We could do that."

This time, I laugh. "No one ever said you're not persistent."

He loops an arm around my waist and lifts me onto his lap, kissing me deeply. When he pulls back, he says, "Desperation breeds persistence."

"All right, lovebirds, this is a public gathering." Case Phillips ruffles Beck's hair, saving me from a response.

"Dad," Beck protests, swatting his hand away. It's really a weird thing, knowing who Case Phillips the country music star is most of my life and then to see Beck act as if he is any regular dad who irritates him the way most dads irritate their teenage sons.

Case reaches for a chair and pulls it up next to ours. He's holding a beer in one hand, but it's nearly full. I've noticed he doesn't drink as much as the people he surrounds himself with. He sits and leans back with his long legs stretched out in front of him.

"Dad," Beck repeats, "we're kind of busy."

"I can see you're working hard in that direction," Case agrees with a raised eyebrow.

I feel the blush start in my cheeks and level out at my hairline. I slide off Beck's lap and sit beside him on the lounge chair.

"I didn't come over to ruin the party," Case says, an apology in his voice. "I actually have a proposition for you both."

"What?" Beck struggles to dampen his aggravation.

"My opening act for the upcoming tour seems to be falling apart before everybody's eyes."

"Footfalls?" Beck asks.

Case nods.

"Why?" Beck sounds more interested now. "They're crazy good."

"Agreed. Which is why a person has to wonder why they want to throw all that away by showing up for rehearsals late and loaded."

"Drugs?" Beck says, looking surprised.

"Who the hell knows? I would assume. But you know I don't stand for that crap on tour. They've been given three warnings, and it hasn't made a difference yet. Paula didn't make it through the first set this afternoon."

"I know Paula," I say, unable to hide my surprise. "We've written a couple of songs together. I can't believe she would-"

"No one ever does," Case says. "Who can figure the human psyche? Sometimes getting what you want comes with more pressure than some people can handle."

I get that, but I've had several long conversations with Paula about our love for music and the hope that we'll get to do this our whole lives. She's a small-town girl from South Carolina who has the support of a family who've given their all to help her get where she is. We were writing together the day she got the news that her band had been chosen to tour with Case. I nearly had to peel her off the wall. How could she willingly throw it all away? "That really doesn't seem like something she would do. Does she know they're at risk of being asked to leave the tour?"

"I'm afraid we're already past the at-risk phase. They're gone. Out of my hands."

"That sucks," Beck says.

"Yeah. It does suck to see someone throw away something they've worked so hard for."

My heart actually hurts for Paula and everything I know she has just lost.

"I had a thought this afternoon," Case says. "Rhys played that demo we did in the studio, what a year, year and a half ago, with you and your friends, CeCe?"

I nod. "Yes, sir."

He raises an eyebrow at me. "Wish you'd quit with the sir stuff, hon. You make me feel like a founding member of Mount Rushmore."

I smile. "Sorry, Case. You're not, you know."

His grin says he's totally aware that he's still got it as far as most American females are concerned. "I know Holden and Sarah moved back to Atlanta, but you and Thomas have a great thing going. What would you think about Beck joining the group and y'all stepping in as my opening act?"

I hear him say the words, but they don't completely sink in. I feel sure I must have imagined them. "What? Are you serious?"

"Dead," he says.

Adrenaline rushes up from the pit of my stomach, and I wish Thomas were here to take this in at the same time I am. I glance at Beck and notice his surprise. Case has pretty much done his best to keep Beck in school and out of the music business.

"Why now, Dad?" he asks, disbelief at the edge of the question.

Case sighs and shoves a hand through his dark hair. "Let's just say that after this last set of grades, it's becoming clear to me that you don't want to be in school any more than I did at your age. I know I've forced the issue. Maybe if you get out there and see what it's like, you'll want to go back at some point."

Beck raises his palm and high-fives his dad. "Heck, yeah!" he says. He looks at me then, as if he's forgotten that I have yet to say anything about his joining Thomas and me. "CeCe? What do you think?"

"I think it's an amazing opportunity," I say carefully. "Thank you, Case. I'd like to say yes this very minute, but do you mind if I talk with Thomas first?"

"Of course, that's how any good team operates," Case says, standing. "Need to know something by ten tomorrow though. Sorry for the short notice. We're running on a tight schedule now. Sound good?"

I nod. "Case, thank you again so much. I really don't know what to say."

"Say you'll do it," he says with his trademark smile. "That's thanks enough."

He leaves then, heading for a group of people chatting on the other side of the pool.

Beck leans back and looks at me with narrowed eyes. "Am I missing something, or am I the only one who thinks what just happened is incredible?"

"It is incredible," I say.

"Then why the reserve?"

"I didn't feel like I could really speak for Thomas and me both."

"I get that. Are you sure it isn't more about the fact that he wants me included?"

The question catches me off guard. "No. Why would you think that?"

"I guess it's just the vibe I'm getting."

"Beck, don't look for something that's not there."

"I'm not looking. But it's definitely there."

I want to deny it, but the butterflies in my stomach are telling me I do have some concerns. "I don't know. Maybe I'm wondering how we go from never having played together other than the demo at your dad's studio to performing in front of sold-out crowds three weeks from now."

"We'll just work our tails off until then."

"What about finishing up the semester at school? How will you manage that?"

Beck glances away and leans forward with his elbows on his knees. "Yeah. That. I think Dad is playing one step ahead of the curveball."

"What do you mean?"

He blows out a sigh and looks like he doesn't want to say what he's going to say. "My grades this semester aren't going to cut it."

"Oh," I say, more than a little surprised. "I'm sorry."

"Now you think I'm a loser, right?" he says, his voice low and unsure.

"Of course not."

"The only reason I went there in the first place is because Dad wanted me to. I guess this is his way of throwing me a lifeline."

"Pretty nice lifeline," I say, trying for a smile.

He studies me for a moment, and then says, "You don't think it's fair, do you?"

"What?"

"Being handed this."

"Of course it's fair. He's your dad. That should count for something."

"You mean that?"

"I do."

"A lot of people think I have a silver spoon up my butt."

This makes me laugh. "Well, if they do, they don't know you."

"Thanks."

"Not necessary."

His expression goes suddenly serious. "I care what you think about me, CeCe."

There's a different note in the admission, one I haven't heard before. Vulnerability. And I'm not sure I know what to do with that.

♪

BECK TAKES ME home, and we say almost nothing during the drive back into town. With the BMW's top down, the wind provides a good excuse for silence although the space between us feels thick with Beck's unusual somberness.

I don't even know why I'm acting this way, why my response to this completely out-of-left-field opportunity isn't more of what it should be. As I stare out into the night whipping past us, I realize that my thoughts have been occupied with Holden on some level since Hart Holcomb's manager came back to see us after the show at the Blue Bird. I'd like to deny it, but then I wouldn't even be honest with myself.

When we arrive at the apartment, Beck doesn't turn off the car and get out to walk me up as he usually does.

"Let me know what you and Thomas decide," he says.

I can hear that his irritation has now melted into something much more like hurt. My guilt is instant. I reach across to cover his hand with mine. "I'm sorry, Beck, for being so difficult tonight."

"Hey, it is what it is."

"But it's not. Exactly."

He leans back against the seat and pulls his hand out from under mine. "Then what is it, CeCe? No, on second thought, don't answer that. Maybe what's happened tonight will serve a couple different purposes."

"What do you mean?"

"Force your hand, I guess. Look, I think we both know I'm the one who's been pushing you along in this relationship. Maybe I didn't want to admit that exactly, but I don't think I can deny it any longer. So while you're making up your mind about whether you want this gig with my dad, why don't you figure out whether you want me or not as well? And it's not an either or proposition. I want *you* and the gig. But if I can't have both-"

I lean over and kiss him, quick and full. I feel his resistance for several long seconds, but then he gives and pulls me to him. I blank my mind of everything except him and the fact that he has been there for me during this past year. He's made me part of his life, introduced me to everyone he knows in this town. And he has been. . .even as I'm kissing him, I'm searching for the exact description. Then it hits me like a splash of ice cold water: a distraction.

I sit back in my seat just as the last two words slam through me. From Holden.

I press my hand to my lips. They tingle from the intensity of Beck's kiss.

For the first time in a year and a half, anger blooms inside me. The petals unfold like the pink blooms on Mama's Rose of Sharon tree in our backyard when spring prods it from its winter hibernation. I've imagined many times how those blooms must resist that awakening, especially when warm weather is teasing its way into existence, and there's no guarantee that nighttime won't drape them with frost.

I think maybe I'm the Rose of Sharon in this situation, refusing to open my heart fully to Beck because somewhere inside of me, I am frozen with love for Holden. And I realize then that I'm angry with myself for that. Who stays in a holding pattern for this long? Waiting for something that's already passed? That can never come back? Never be what it might have been. I know now that as surely as I'm sitting here, that's what I've been doing. Waiting.

I don't want to wait any longer. Everything I've been working for, everything Thomas has been working for, is now right in front of us. Within reach. Only a fool would turn away from it.

"I want this, Beck," I say, linking my fingers through his. "I want you."

He's looking at me as if he's sure I didn't say what I just said. "What?"

"Don't act so surprised. You know you're hot." This brings a smile to his lips, and I think I may have redeemed myself, at least a little bit anyway. He leans across and kisses me again, and there's sweetness at the edges. Beck is a cool guy, and it's not in his playbook to show insecurity. I feel that now and the responsibility of it. An immediate desire not to take advantage of it.

"You won't regret it," he says softly. "Any of it. I promise, okay?"

"I know I won't," I say. "I'll talk to Thomas and call you." I glance at the clock. "It's already after three. In a few hours."

"Okay. Goodnight, CeCe."

"Night, Beck."

And with the closing of the car door, I feel something close inside me as well. If it's not gladness that follows the click, maybe acceptance is enough.

♪

HANK JUNIOR IS asleep on the couch when I unlock the door and step inside the apartment. He raises his head and blinks sleepy hound eyes at me then thumps his tail in greeting against the sofa cushion.

"Hey, sweet boy," I say, going over to sit down beside him. I rub his soft head and velvety ears. "Need to go out?"

He rests his chin on my leg and closes his eyes in answer. I try to talk myself into leaving the conversation with Thomas until morning, but the thought of sleeping with all of this on my mind is an absolute impossibility. I knock on his door and call out, "Thomas?"

A couple of seconds pass before he answers with a groggy, "That you, CeCe?"

"Yeah. Are you alone?"

"Actually, no, I'm not."

"Oh," I say, not doing a very good job of hiding my disappointment.

"Everything all right?" he calls out.

"I was hoping we could talk for a minute."

A pause and then, "You are aware that it's three o'clock in the morning?"

"Ah, yeah."

"And this is important?" he asks, as close to grouchy as he gets.

"It is," I say.

"I'll be out in a sec."

I wait for him in the hallway, and when he steps through the door, I try to peer over his shoulder. "Who is it?" I ask.

"None of your business," he says, turning me around and pushing me toward the living room with his hands on my shoulders.

"If it's a secret, she must not be very-"

He stops me with, "CeCe, what the devil are you getting me up at this hour for? Just to give me a hard time about who's in my bed?"

"I'm not," I say. "I mean, that's not why I got you up."

Thomas plops down on the couch beside Hank Junior. I take the chair across from them. He's wearing light blue boxers with banjos on them. I squint at them and say, "Nice."

"Do you really need me to go back and put on some britches?"

"No. I'll keep my eyes chest level or above."

"Thank you. Much appreciated," he says. "Are you planning on telling me why you got me up in the middle of the night?"

"Footfalls got fired as the opening act for Case's tour. He wants us to go in their place."

If I had just dropped, "Elvis is alive and coming over for dinner," I don't think Thomas could've looked any more surprised.

"Did you say–" he starts.

"I did," I interrupt.

A grin breaks his formerly sleepy expression wide open. "For real?"

"For real."

Several moments pass, during which he looks as if he has no idea where to go from here. And then, "What's the catch?"

"We have to be ready to perform as an opening act within three weeks."

He tips his head, considers this. "We're missing electric guitar, but we ought to be able to get that filled as soon as we put it out there as part of a tour opportunity."

"Yeah," I say.

"What else?"

"What do you mean?"

"What other catch? There must be one."

I hesitate before saying, "He wants Beck to join us." This one, I can see, he did not expect.

"Ah," he says. "So what's behind that?"

"Honestly?"

"Well, yeah."

"Beck has pretty much let his grades slide this semester. His dad has always discouraged him from getting into the music business but I guess he's realizing it's kind of inevitable."

"Dude can play guitar. No doubt about it."

"Think it could work?" I ask cautiously.

Thomas rubs Hank Junior's ears, quiet for a full minute or more. "I expect it's like this. If you and I have a brain in our heads, we'll find a way to make it work."

♪

Holden

My flight lands in Nashville at five-thirty-eight p.m. As the wheels touch the runway, my heartbeat kicks up a notch, and doubt pummels through me.

Yesterday at this time I hadn't even left work. I sure didn't know that in twenty-four hours, I would have turned my life upside down again, reaching out for a rope to grab onto that might or might not be there.

As I'd done a dozen times in the past several hours, I ask myself if I'm wrong to try to pick up the edges of a dream and roll it back into something recognizable. When I woke up this morning, my first thought was that Sarah would have changed her mind. That our conversation last night would reveal itself to be nothing more than a mistake in judgment.

I think that's what I was hoping because letting go of something I wanted so badly and coming to terms with that loss hadn't happened over night. And even if our lives hadn't turned out to be everything we had once imagined they could be, I did feel extreme gratitude for Sarah's recovery and the part she had told me I played in it.

She had not decided that it was a mistake in judgment. I'm not even sure the Sarah who helped me pack my things was the same Sarah I've known since college. I don't know exactly when it happened, but I could see in her face that she'd already moved on. Wanted something other than me now.

Maybe the only reason it doesn't hurt more is that I know she's right to want something else, someone else who will love her with every speck of space in his heart.

The way I wanted to. The way I tried to. It's pretty clear now that if I hadn't realized CeCe still occupied a corner of my heart, Sarah had.

A bell chimes, and the stewardess welcomes us to Nashville. Seat belts click their release in unison, and everyone around me stands up, reaching for bags and laptops. I start to stand, but something inside me locks my legs beneath a sudden rush of uncertainty.

It feels a lot like the time Thomas and I went skydiving our freshman year in college. He went first, and I remember standing at the edge of the plane door, watching him torpedo toward the ground. I could not make myself move. It was as if my brain and my legs were no longer synchronized. And as much as I hated the thought of disappointing him, I couldn't jump.

But then he looked up, waved a hand at me, and his parachute burst open, turning his descent into a graceful sashay through wide-open space.

That was the moment I stepped over the threshold of the plane and began the free fall. As soon as I was out there, dropping through the sky, I knew I wanted to do this a thousand more times. The only thing I've ever found to compare it to is music, every phase of it, from the creation of a first note in a new song to playing it on stage in front of an audience for the first time.

If starting out after this dream again is anything like skydiving, I know I'm going to have to take a leap of faith and jump. And so I stand up and join the exodus.

♪

THERE'S A DRIVER waiting at baggage claim with a sign that has my name on it. I walk over and tell him who I am.

"Well, all right," he says with the friendliness I remember as such a part of Nashville. "I'm Mitchell. Mr. Hart is expecting you, Mr. Ashford. Can I get your bag for you?"

"It's Holden, and thanks but I'm good." I follow him out the main doors and to a waiting Hummer limo. This, I hadn't expected.

He opens the back, takes my guitar and suitcase and puts them inside, then walks around to open the door for me.

"I can ride up front," I say, feeling about a dozen different kinds of awkward.

Mitchell smiles and shakes his head. "Hey, enjoy it, young man. Clearly, you've done something Mr. Hart appreciates. No need to feel guilty. Hop on in."

I slide inside and he closes the door behind me. The interior of the Hummer is a virtual entertainment playground; big screen TV and a music system that makes what's coming through the Bose speakers hanging in four corners sound like I'm at the Ryman Auditorium.

The limo glides away from the airport and onto the interstate. Through the tinted glass, I recognize the landscape and for the first time since this morning, I let myself feel happy about the thought of being here. I do, however, feel alone. That part doesn't seem right. I started this whole journey with my best friend in the world. And I realize I don't want to have this meeting with Hart Holcomb without him.

I reach forward and press an intercom button. "Mitchell?"

"Yes, Mr. Ashford?"

"Would it be possible for you to pick up a friend of mine on the way? I'd really like for him to come with me if you don't mind stopping."

"Of course. Do you have the address?"

I give it to him and sit back in my seat, texting Thomas: Hey. Where are you?

A few seconds pass before my phone beeps.

Home. Where are you?

Nashville.

Are you kidding me?

Would I?

Yes.

Get your boots on. I'm picking you up in less than ten.

In what?

A stretch Hummer.

Dang.

Yeah.

He's waiting outside the building when we pull into the parking lot. It feels like we haven't seen each other in years, and I realize how much I've missed him. I open the door and slide out.

"You really are here," Thomas says, his grin full wattage, throwing me a high-five. "Aw, hell, brother. This deserves a hug."

He gives me exactly that, squeezing me so hard, I laugh and say, "Your neighbors are gonna get the wrong idea."

He lets me go, shaking his head, uncharacteristically at a loss for a response. "I can't believe you're really here. And in this ride?"

"Crazy, huh? Hart Holcomb sent it to pick me up at the airport."

"So you're meeting with him?"

I nod.

"Whoop!" Thomas yells. "Let's get on over there."

We climb in the back of the Hummer and Mitchell eases out of the parking lot.

Thomas can't quit grinning. "So this is what it's like when you make the big league," he says.

"I guess."

"He wants your song bad."

"I'm not assuming anything," I say.

"Would he go to all this trouble if he didn't?"

I shrug and say, "You haven't gotten any better-looking."

"And you're not any less of a smartass."

"True."

"Man, it's good to have you back. How long can you stay?"

I don't know how to begin explaining what's happened in the past day so I just start in the middle. "I guess until nobody wants to hear my music anymore."

Thomas tips his head, looking confused. "You mean you're here to stay? Like for good?"

I tell him then about Sarah and everything she'd said last night. And how I hadn't expected any of it. My voice is flat and without emotion, as if I am telling someone else's story instead of my own. When I finish, we both sit quiet for a minute or more.

"Is she okay?" Thomas asks, sounding a little shocked.

"She's better than okay. I don't know. I think it was a relief to her. To get it all said."

"Is it to you?" he asks, and I can tell he's not sure where to go with any of it either.

"It's the right thing for her," I say.

"And what about you?"

"I would have stayed."

"I know. Is your heart in one piece?"

"I think so. It's weird. I pretty much accepted that this life here was something I'd put behind me. I don't even really know how to start making music a focal point again."

"You don't think about it. You just do it. Start living it. You deserve it." He looks out the window and then back at me with a serious expression. "What you did for Sarah. I know what it cost you. In my book, they don't come any better than you, friend."

"Are you counting the part where I let myself fall in love with someone else while I was still officially with Sarah?"

"Yeah," he says, his voice firm. "I'm counting that part."

I tap a thumb against my jeans and try not to ask the question, but lose the battle. "How is she?"

"Good," Thomas says. "We've been playing somewhere about every night of the week. She's been working the lunch shift over at Lauren's."

"That's good."

"I take it you two haven't talked."

I shake my head.

"She's seeing Beck."

I'm not surprised. I expected it, really. Why wouldn't she, after all? "You like him?" I ask.

"Not much to dislike about him. But I'm pretty sure as far as she's concerned, he's not you."

"Hey, don't." I hold up a hand. "I'm not coming back here expecting anything between CeCe and me to change. If he's a good guy, good to her, that's all that matters."

"Is it?"

"Yeah," I say, wondering if I could sound any less convincing.

"If you say so."

The Hummer has left the interstate and is heading down a series of country roads that feature huge estate after huge estate. I remember that Case Phillips lives down one of the white-fenced lanes and wonder how much time CeCe has spent there with Beck, but then I cut the thought off as a dead end. There is nothing to be gained from going there.

Thomas and I make small talk the rest of the way. He tells me about the gigs they've been playing recently, and when I ask him if he's seeing anyone, he says no one special.

"Mr. Ashford?"

It's Mitchell on the intercom.

"Mr. Ashford," Thomas stage whispers, grinning at me.

"Yes?"

"We'll be arriving within a couple of minutes. Mr. Holcomb asked me to drop you at the horse barn if that's all right. He likes to ride in the evenings."

"Ah, sure. That's fine."

"Mr. Ashford at the horse barn," Thomas rap-teases.

"Shut up."

"Up yours."

"Nice to be back," I say.

"Nice to have you back," Thomas says.

♪

WE PULL INTO the cobblestone courtyard of a barn that looks more like a five-star English hotel than anything horses might live in. Boxwood bushes line each side of wrought iron-hinged sliding doors at the front. The exterior of the barn is stucco, the roof red clay tile. From either side of the entrance, horses peer over Dutch stall doors. One whinnies in our direction as we get out of the Hummer.

Mitchell walks around and says, "I'll be right out here when you're finished to give you a ride back into town."

"Thank you," I say.

At the sound of footsteps on the cobblestone, we glance up to see Hart Holcomb walking toward us. He's wearing a Stetson, Wranglers, and work boots. His shirt is wet in places, as if he's been sweating. He pulls it away from his midsection. "Sorry about the appearance. Working on some fencing out back."

"Not a problem," I say, stepping forward and sticking out my hand. "I'm Holden Ashford. This is my friend, Thomas Franklin. It's an honor to meet you, Mr. Holcomb."

"Hart, please. And thank you. For coming too." He shakes Thomas's hand as well and beckons for us to follow him into the barn.

The center aisle is also laid in cobblestone and it's so clean I'm pretty sure you'd be okay to eat off it. The interior stall doors are black with gold hinges, and they gleam with care and polish. Flies have been frequent visitors to the barns I've visited before, but I don't see one. Or even a single cobweb.

"What kind of horses do you have?" I ask, doing a quick estimate of stalls on either side of the aisle and coming up with a total of twenty-four.

"Quarter horses," he says. "We do a little cutting. Just for fun, mind you. My wife was a vegetarian, so anything that breathes on this farm isn't here to get eaten, cows included."

I hear something painful at the edges of his voice, and I'm not sure what to say to that. "She must have been a kind woman."

"She was."

"I'm really sorry for your loss."

Thomas murmurs his agreement.

"Thank you," Hart says. He stops in front of a stall to rub one of the horse's necks. "This was her baby. Whip is short for Whippoorwill. I think this horse might miss her as much as I do."

All three of us are silent for several moments before he goes on.

"It's a damn shame for the world to lose someone as fine as she was. And for no reason. When I heard your song, I felt like you might have written it for me," he says, his voice thickening with emotion.

"I can't think of a higher compliment than that," I say, and I realize how lame it sounds in comparison to this man's life-altering loss.

"I'd like for it to be the title song on my upcoming CD. You okay with that?"

I'm not sure what I had expected him to say when I got here, but it was anything other than this. I can't seem to find the words to answer him, so I simply nod.

"We'll need to go in the studio tomorrow. I've already thrown everything off schedule by adding this last minute. We'll be at HGT Recording downtown at ten. You boys want to come in for the session?"

"Yes, sir," Thomas and I answer in unison.

"Well, good deal," he says.

We shake hands. I like that his is firm, confirming.

"See you in the morning then. Mitchell will take you back into town."

He walks us to the barn entrance.

"Thank you, Mr. Holcomb, I mean Hart," I say. "This is such an honor."

"For me, too, actually," he says. "It's a hell of a song."

We climb in the back of the Hummer, and Mitchell eases out of the courtyard and down the long lane leading to the main road. Only then do I realize we never talked about money. And I don't care. If I could pay him to sing it, I would.

♪

CeCe

I'm coming up the stairs to our apartment, three Whole Foods bags in each hand when I hear their laughter.

There's no mistaking it. Thomas's big baritone. And Holden's slightly cautious follow-up.

My stomach plummets exactly the way it had on an awful elevator thrill ride I once went on at an amusement park. I can't recall how many stories it dropped. I remember it felt as if there were no bottom and we would never stop but just keep falling forever.

I pause on the top step now with that same sensation, making me light-headed, fight or flight battling it out inside me.

What is he doing here? In our apartment?

The door opens then and Thomas glances out, spots me and instantly sobers. "Oh. I heard something. Thought you were the pizza guy."

"I'm not the pizza guy," I say evenly.

"You sure aren't." He jumps forward, taking the bags from me. "Come in. I've got a surprise for you."

I can't make words come out of my mouth, but I think Thomas can see in my face I do NOT want to come in.

"We're all grown-ups," he says in a sympathetic whisper.

Just the implication that I might be acting out of immaturity is enough to send me through the door with an expression of indifference firmly in place.

Holden is sitting on the couch next to Hank Junior, who looks like manna has fallen from the sky in the form of his favorite dog treats. His chin is on Holden's knee. He glances at me with his big brown eyes, and if he could speak, his message couldn't have been any clearer. *He's back.*

Holden lifts Hank Junior's head from his knees, stands, and shoves his hands in the front pockets of his jeans. "Hi, CeCe."

"Hey, Holden." My voice goes hoarse and I clear my throat. "I didn't know you were coming to town." My tone is lemonade sweet. I so wish I could erase it and start all over.

"Kind of last minute," he says.

Thomas walks up behind me and puts a hand on my shoulder. "He's got some amazing news."

"Oh yeah?"

"Hart Holcomb is cutting "What You Took From Me" tomorrow. We just went out and met with him. It's pretty incredible how he connected with the song."

"Congratulations," I say, forcing myself to meet Holden's sober gaze. "It's an amazing song."

"Thanks."

I try to make myself look away, make an excuse about needing to put away the groceries. But my mouth won't form the words, and my feet won't obey my brain. We watch each other like two people unsure of who's going to make the first move. For a second, his guard drops, and I see in his eyes the Holden who sat outside that pound all night with me, waiting to get in and save Hank Junior. I see the Holden who kissed me that same night the way I'd always imagined being kissed; in a way I'd never been kissed before. I remember clearly how it had felt as if I'd found something I didn't know I'd been waiting for.

Just as quickly, I remember what it felt like to lose it.

"How is Sarah?" I ask.

"She's great," he says. "Actually, really great."

"That's wonderful," I say. Thomas has filled me in on her treatments, some of it good, some of it not, and I'm relieved to hear Holden say she's doing well now. "How is Patsy?"

"Bossy and opinionated," he says.

I smile at this. "What Beagle isn't?"

Holden's eyes reflect his fondness for the dog, and I'm happy for her.

"Thomas says y'all are playing all over town. Glad to hear it's going well." The words sound sincere enough, although there's a flatness there that makes me wonder if he's tried to distance himself from thoughts of it.

"We've been having fun," I say, wondering if Thomas has told him about the tour with Case.

But then Thomas says, "Yeah, about that. We've actually got some pretty cool news too, Holden. Case Phillips has asked us to replace the opening act for his tour. We've got three weeks to look like we know what the heck we're doing."

Holden's face registers surprise. "Whoa. That's amazing."

"Yeah, it is," Thomas agrees. He hesitates before adding, "Beck will be joining us."

This time the surprise in Holden's eyes is etched with something else, flashing so quickly that I can't be sure if it's admiration or regret. "Cool," he says. "I didn't know you'd been playing together."

"We haven't," I say.

"Oh," he says, as if he suddenly understands, when I'm sure he doesn't.

"Until now, it's just been CeCe and me." Thomas stops there, and then, "Now that you're here, why don't you join us? We need an electric guitar. Who better than you?"

The suggestion takes Holden as much by surprise as it does me, if the look on his face is any indication. "Hey, no. This is y'all's thing. And it's great. I'm not horning in on your action."

Thomas looks at me, trying to gauge my reaction. I don't give him one.

"Man, with the exception of Sarah, we'd have Barefoot Outlook back together. You were part of what we started here."

"And I left."

"And you're back," Thomas says.

"For good?" I say before I can stop the question from popping out.

"I don't really know yet," Holden answers.

"But what about Sarah and-" I stop and immediately apologize. "I'm sorry. That's none of my business."

"No. It's okay," Holden says. "Sarah and I are. . .we're going to be good friends."

I absorb this explanation the way I imagine a mountainside might work at absorbing a sudden deluge of rain. It is simply too much to take in so unexpectedly, and I nod once as if I understand, when I do not at all.

"Things are different now," Thomas says, in an obvious attempt to bridge a gap that cannot or will not be clearly defined at the moment. "I want you with us."

Holden and I aren't looking at each other. We both have our gazes hooked on Thomas, who's wearing a stubborn expression I recognize all too well.

"Look," he adds, "we all came here for the music. We've hit a few speed bumps and taken a couple of detours, but it still comes back to the fact that we live it, breathe it, love it. We're getting a break here with this tour. And we all know how hard those are to come by. We'll have a far better shot at going somewhere with this if you're part of it."

I let myself look at Holden, and it's clear Thomas's words mean something to him. I imagine then how it must have felt to be away from all of this for the past year and a half. To put the dream in a drawer and walk away from it, never intending to open it up again. And now. Another chance. Am I going to be the one to stand in his way? If so, what will that really accomplish?

One thing and one thing only. The protection of my own heart. My own pride. Getting over Holden, if I ever did actually reach a point where it qualified as that, took every bit of will I could scrape up from the bottom of my determination to accept something I could not change. I built a wall around my heart and told myself I never wanted to fall like that again. And I don't. The thought of being around Holden and not letting that happen is more than a little terrifying.

Even so, I remember how Holden had been against me joining up with Thomas and him when we'd first gotten to Nashville. He'd changed his mind, and I'd been grateful for the chance.

How can I be the one to close him out now?

I can't.

Not even when I'm aware of exactly how high a price I'm going to pay for making this choice.

♪

THOMAS KNOCKS ON my door at seven the next morning. I know his knock by now, and I consider pretending not to have heard it, but I lift up and mumble, "Come in."

He steps in the room, walks over and sits down on the edge of the bed. Hank Junior cracks an eye open, then puts his head back on my pillow and ignores him.

"CeCe?" Thomas says.

"Yeah?" I answer, my gaze on the wall.

"Thank you."

"For what?"

"You know what."

"I figure I owe you both for picking me up on the side of the highway."

"That was no biggie."

"Yeah, it was. I very well could have turned around and walked Hank and me back home at that point. If I believed in signs, I would have. So we're even."

"That's not a debt I would've called in."

"I know."

"I guess you also know Holden tried to do what he thought was right in going back to Atlanta to be there for Sarah. He pretty much gave up everything to do that."

I nod.

"And I know this isn't easy for you."

"I'm a big girl, Thomas. And I have someone in my life. What happened between Holden and me is part of our past. That's all."

"You sure about that?"

"Very," I say. "There is one thing though."

"What?"

"I'd like for you to be the one to tell Beck about Holden. I think it will sting less."

"Sure. We really do need him, you know. It's not like we're creating a spot for him."

I want to deny it, but the truth is we'll be lucky to have him. "We should start working today."

"As soon as we're done with the recording, I'll text you."

"Beck said we can practice at his house."

"Cool," he says, standing. "CeCe?"

"Yeah?"

"You're awesome."

"Don't forget it," I say, looking up at him with an attempt to stay stern-faced, and failing.

He leans over and kisses my cheek. "I won't," he says.

♪

Holden

"You know how you've dreamed about something for so long that it starts to feel like if it ever actually happened, it wouldn't even seem real?"

Thomas asks me the question in a low whisper while we are sitting behind Hart Holcomb's producer and a recording engineer in a Music Row studio complete with every piece of sound equipment I could ever imagine having access to. Hart is warming up inside the booth, going through parts of the song time and again, and it feels anything but real to hear him singing the words I wrote. "Yeah," I say. "That's what I'm thinking right now."

"It really is like you wrote it for him."

"Pretty sad though, you know."

"But maybe someone who hears it will think twice about having another drink and then getting behind the wheel. If one person's life is saved, that makes you a hero."

"I'm not the one who'll be selling it to people."

"No, but they're your words."

I don't say anything else because hearing Hart sing the last line makes my throat close up. With the fade of the final note, there's a collective breath blown out around the room.

"Wow, Hart," the producer says. "That's just plain powerful."

Hart clears his throat and takes a swig of water from the bottle next to him. "Thanks. And I'd like to thank Holden for writing it, y'all. He's never lived the story of this song but the way he wrote it would make you think he has. That's the mark of a great writer. I expect we'll be seeing you in big places, Holden."

Everyone is looking at me now. I don't have any idea what to say. Thomas claps me on the shoulder, and I finally manage, "Thank you so much. If this is the only song of mine that ever gets cut, I'll be all right with that. This is an honor. Really."

Hart smiles at me and through the sadness in his eyes, I glimpse a man I hope will one day know happiness again. Tragedy has clearly taken its toll on him. It's nice to think that maybe in putting out a song that might stop one person from causing the kind of pain he's known, there could be some renewal of purpose for him.

They play through it one more time before the producer says, "You ready to do it for real, Hart?"

"Ready," he says.

The studio is pin-drop quiet throughout the entire song, and I'm amazed that both Hart and the band hit every note perfectly and don't stop even once.

"Whoa," Thomas says when they're done. "Pretty impressive," I say.

By the time they lay the background vocals, it's after four o'clock. Just as the producer declares it a wrap, a guy in a jacket and jeans walks into the studio, speaks for a moment with Hart and then comes over to where Thomas and I are getting up to go.

He says hello to Thomas and sticks his hand out to me. "You must be Holden. I'm Andrew Seeger, Hart's manager. I hear things went incredibly well today."

"It was amazing to watch," I say.

"I'm glad it's all worked out." He reaches inside his jacket and pulls out a folded pack of papers. "Sorry I didn't get this over sooner but this is our standard contract. I believe you'll find the terms extremely appealing. As I'm sure you've already figured out, Hart really wanted this song."

I unfold the papers and glance through the first page, my eyes widening at the numbers there. "Wow. That's. . .thank you."

"We're expecting big things from this. Get ready. I think you're going to be amazed by the number of knocks you'll be getting on your door."

"Thank you," I say again, because I have no idea what else to add. I sign my name on the places he indicates I should sign. We shake hands and then I walk over and thank Hart again.

Thomas and I say nothing until we're in his truck and pulling out of the parking lot.

"Did that just happen?" Thomas asks.

"As far as I can tell, it was real."

"Dang."

"Yeah."

"You're gonna be famous."

"Shut up."

Thomas grins. "Don't go all modest. You earned it. It's a great song."

"Thanks, but luck has to play some part in it. You think I ever imagined something like this?"

"No," Thomas interrupts. "I don't. You still deserve it."

"You're a good friend, Thomas," I say, suddenly serious and wishing I knew how to say how much it means to me that any success either one of us has is never ruined by resentment or jealousy.

"Speaking of which," he segues, "I called Beck when you were talking with Hart after we first got to the studio."

"How'd that go?" I ask, suddenly sure I know what the answer will be.

"He was totally cool with it," Thomas says. "I gotta say, it's not what I was expecting."

"That's kind of a surprise."

"Just so you know, I don't think he's worried about you sweeping CeCe off her feet."

I consider this, weigh my conflicting responses and decide on, "He doesn't need to be."

"Doesn't he?" Thomas asks, looking over at me, dead serious.

"No."

"Can we have an honest moment here?"

"Thomas, I–"

"Hear me out, okay. I think it needs to be said." He taps a thumb against the steering wheel and then goes on with, "It took a long time for CeCe to start acting like herself again. You put a pretty big dent in her heart, friend."

There's no criticism in the statement, just flat truth. "I never meant to hurt her," I say.

"I know. If we're playing together, maybe it really would be best for things to stay the way they are. Everybody knows it's difficult for groups to stay together. And for whatever reason, Case wants Beck in on this gig. War between you two would pretty much dump the whole thing in the landfill."

"Thanks, friend."

"You can't deny it, can you?"

I want to but I actually don't think I can. "No," I say.

"It seems like Beck is good to her," Thomas says, clearly not enjoying this.

"That's good."

"It really is." He looks out the window as if thinking twice about what he's about to say. "You two could have been really good together. There's a lot of water under that particular bridge, and I'd hate to see either one of you–"

"Drown?"

"Something like that."

"You don't need to say anything else. I get it."

"Then why do I feel like such a jerk?"

♪

WE GET TO BECK'S place just as an enormous storm cloud breaks open and dumps rain so fast and hard that the driveway looks like a small river. We pull in at the front of the house behind a BMW. Beck slides out of the driver's side and runs around with an umbrella to open the passenger door. CeCe gets out and ducks under it, laughing as they run inside.

I watch them with a sense of loss that I know I have no right to feel. But it's there anyway, like a kick to the gut.

"You sure you're gonna be able to do this?" Thomas asks.

"I'm good," I say, the question prodding me to slide out of the truck. I grab my guitar case from its spot between us. Thomas walks around, and I follow him to the door. He rings the bell.

The door swings open, and Beck says, "Y'all get in out of the rain."

"Hey, man," Thomas says, walking inside.

I walk in behind him and stick a hand out to Beck. "Hey. Good to see you again."

"You too," Beck says with what looks like a genuine smile. "Glad it worked out that you can hook up with us on the tour. Dad was psyched about it."

"Thanks," I say. "I really appreciate the chance to be here." I want to be suspicious of his friendliness. I mean, why would he want me back here? If I were him, I wouldn't let me within fifty miles of CeCe. But then, maybe he's that confident of what they have going.

We follow him through the long hallway that I remember as leading to his dad's studio. CeCe is already there, warming up when we walk in. I haven't heard her sing since leaving here – correction – haven't let myself hear her sing since leaving here. Her voice has taken on new dimension and power. She sounds amazing.

She smiles at Beck and Thomas but stops short of meeting eyes with me. "Y'all ready to do this thing?"

"Let's jump on it," Thomas says. "Should we go through a playlist first?"

"Sure," Beck says.

"CeCe and I can highlight the songs we've been doing. Holden, you got any good new stuff?"

"I've got new stuff. Not sure if it's any good or not."

"Check the modesty," Thomas says. "Ladies and gents, you're looking at Hart Holcomb's prediction for one of this town's up and coming hit songwriters."

Both Beck and CeCe glance at me with a look of surprise. It's CeCe who speaks first.

"So it went well?"

"Yeah," I say. "He's an incredible singer."

"Congratulations," Beck says. "That's big stuff. Sounds like you've impressed him. I've heard my dad say that's not an easy thing to do."

"I think I got a lucky break," I say. "Right song. Right place."

We all pull up a chair at the round table in one corner of the room. From there, we start talking about songs, compiling a list of the best we have and then working out the playlist.

Beck knows all of the songs CeCe and Thomas have been singing from having been at so many of their shows. They ask me to play some of my new stuff. I put my thoughts on the individual songs and try not to think about the fact that Beck has entwined his fingers with CeCe's as if she's just been taken under by an unexpected current and it is up to him to save her.

And I wonder if he's that sure of her, after all.

♪

CeCe

We spend the next five hours practicing song after song, perfecting some Thomas and I already know well and then working on several new ones Holden says he wrote over the past year.

The songs are really good, and I'm relieved to see that he has continued to write. Our upbeat songs outnumber the ballads six to one, and we all agree that as the opening act, we want to get the audience up and ready to have a good time.

At first, I'm so nervous that I forget lines to songs I know by heart. I actually feel every single time Holden glances at me, but I manage not to look back. I know it's crazy. After all, how can I expect to get through an entire tour without looking at him? Whatever it is holding in place all of my determination to make this work feels about as fragile as baby grass under an April frost.

It's almost ten when we call it a wrap. I'm as tired from the effort of smiling and trying to act normal as I am from the rehearsing.

Once we've packed up all our things, Beck says he'll take me home.

"We're headed back to the apartment, CeCe, if you want to ride with us," Thomas offers.

I don't want to but it would be a little silly for Beck to drive all the way into town just to drop me off. And since I'm too tired to do anything other than go to bed, going out isn't an option. "Okay," I say. "That will save you a trip, Beck."

"I'm happy to take you."

I hear the edge in his voice and know we will end up talking about things I don't want to talk about right now. I take the coward's way out. "I'll see you tomorrow. Call me in the morning?"

"Sure." He walks over to kiss me full on the mouth. He takes his time in a statement to Holden. I start to pull away, but force myself not to. Can I blame him for feeling insecure? Wouldn't I, if the circumstances were reversed?

I wait for him to end the kiss and press my palm to his cheek. "Please tell your dad thank you for letting us rehearse here."

"I will," he says. "Goodnight."

"'Night," I say and follow Thomas and Holden from the room.

In the truck, I sit to the left of the middle so that my shoulder is touching Thomas's, putting two inches of space between Holden and me.

"I thought it went great," Thomas says as he pulls out of the long driveway onto the main road headed back to the city. "What did you two think?"

Neither of us answers for a few moments, both obviously waiting the other out. I give first.

"We've got some polishing to do, but I like where we're going."

"I agree," Holden says, his gaze set outside the window.

"CeCe, I really like what you did with the bridge on that last song. That's gonna get you a lot of fans, girl."

"Thanks, Thomas," I say, feeling a familiar tenderness toward him. If anyone in this world has my back now, it's Thomas.

We talk about different issues we need to address with certain parts of the songs. It makes the drive go quickly and keeps me from focusing on how close I am to touching Holden.

At the apartment, I take Hank Junior for a walk and deliberately stay out long enough that I hope to avoid seeing Holden again tonight. Hank sniffs every tree we pass and protests my turning back toward home by locking his legs and giving me a visual declaration of his displeasure.

"Come on," I say. "You'd stay out here all night if I let you."

To make up for not letting him have his way, I give him a cookie when we get back inside. He wags his tail in forgiveness and licks my hand.

"I see he still knows how to work the system."

I jump at the sound of Holden's voice and turn to look at him with what I hope comes across as mild interest. "I try not to let him get too big a head."

"Kind of a benevolent dictator, isn't he?"

It pretty much nails Hank's role in life, and I can't stop myself from smiling. "Sadly, I don't mind."

"He has that effect, doesn't he?"

I nod, making a pretense of wiping crumbs off the kitchen counter and putting the treat jar back in place. "Thomas already in bed?"

"Yeah. I think we wore him out."

"Well," I say, "I'm tired too. Goodnight, Holden."

I start past him, Hank Junior at my heels. Holden reaches out and stops me with a hand on my arm. "CeCe?"

I stop, as if instantly frozen in place. I try to say something but my voice is locked in my throat.

"Can we talk for a minute?" he asks.

"About what?" I finally manage. "There isn't anything–"

"Actually, there is."

"Holden-"

"Please."

I force myself to turn and face him then, saying nothing, waiting for him to go on.

"I want to say I'm sorry for everything that happened."

His eyes are fully sincere and something in me gives a little. "You have nothing to be sorry for," I say.

"I didn't mean to hurt you."

"I know." And I really do. "We never should have. . .we were wrong to-"

"I was wrong to," he finishes for me. "I wasn't free to let myself have feelings for you."

With those words, the urge to cry hits me so hard and so insistently that the tears are spilling from my eyes before I even try to hold them back. "Holden, don't," I say. "This is not a place either of us can afford to go."

"I still need to say it."

"Is that what's most important then?" I ask on a flurry of anger. "What you need?"

He blinks once but not fast enough to hide the flash of hurt. "That's not what I meant," he says.

"Maybe not," I say quickly. "What I need is to forget that we ever felt anything more than friendship for each other. That is the only way I can be on a stage with you every night for six weeks."

I turn abruptly then and start out of the kitchen for my room. Holden reaches out and reels me back to him. I stop only after hitting the wall of his chest.

I look up at him just as outrage surges through me. "Don't. Touch. Me. Holden."

But he doesn't remove his hand from my arm. With his gaze locked on mine, he gently pulls me forward until I am fully encircled in his embrace. I hold myself as if I have been cast in ice.

We stand that way for countless seconds. The refrigerator hums. The air conditioning kicks on. A cat meows somewhere outside and Hank Junior pads over to the window to investigate.

And then, slowly, slowly, Holden eases me in, folding me into the circle of his arms until I just melt against him.

Everything inside of me goes liquid and warm. I close my eyes and yield to the irresistible need to breathe him in, to let myself remember how I feel magnetized next to him. Completely unable to resist the pull between us.

I want to protest. My brain is telling me to protest. But my body isn't listening.

Instead, I let my arms wrap him up and I press my face to his chest. His warm, hard chest. Time falls away. I don't let myself think of anything except what is here, what is now.

He puts his cheek against my hair, and I feel him sigh, a release of breath, as if he, too, has been holding it since the last time we were in each other's arms like this.

We stay this way for a very long while. I can feel the pain and hurt of these past eighteen months absorb into the air around us and fade to acceptance.

"What was it like?" I ask, my voice little more than a whisper.

"What?" he answers, the question rough at the edges.

"Seeing her go through all of that."

"Terrifying." He's quiet for several moments and then, "I never imagined so many people having their lives destroyed by that awful disease. Going with her to the treatments, seeing others who were even sicker than she was . . . some days, I didn't think I could go back."

"It must have been hard," I say softly.

"Seeing the hope and courage of those people, and how fragile it all is, I swear, sometimes I wanted to change places with them just so their hopes weren't for nothing."

Tears fill my eyes. I bite my lower lip before saying, "I'm sorry."

"I saw things that made me realize what I take for granted in my life. Little kids who'd lost all their hair, who couldn't eat. And their parents, trying to act as if everything would be all right."

He stops there, and I can feel his grief like a wall that is crumbling inside him. I tighten my arms around his waist and hold onto him as if I am the only thing that will keep him from collapsing under its weight.

I'm not sure how much time passes with the two of us standing here, holding each other. I wish that we never had to move, that we could stay like this forever.

But I know we can't; there are people in our lives who have not asked to be hurt by us. I ease away from him, looking up into his eyes. "Sarah. She's going to be okay?"

"I think so," Holden says. "The doctors have said she's clear, and she works at the nutrition end of it. Really at doing anything she can to stay healthy."

"I'm glad," I say, and with this picture of her, I step back, loosen my hold on him. "Will she . . . is she planning to move here?"

He doesn't say anything for a few moments and I start to wonder if I've asked more than I should have.

"No," he says then. "Sarah and I, we're not going to be together."

The admission takes me by such surprise that I am sure I must have misheard him. "Oh. I thought. . .what?"

"We're not."

"But why?"

He looks away and then back at me. "Maybe she saw us through new eyes and didn't like what was there."

I don't know what to say so I don't say anything.

"There was something else," he adds. "She met someone who might have made her realize what she did want."

"Holden. I. . .I'm sorry."

"Don't be. I'm pretty sure she's going to be happy. That's what matters."

I take in the words with a feeling of disbelief. And all of a sudden, I feel the dissolving of a barrier between us. With it comes an awkwardness I have no idea what to do with. "I don't know what to say, Holden."

"You don't have to say anything, CeCe. You've moved on. I get it. I understand. And I'm not here to mess up things with you and Beck."

I know I should feel relieved. Because he's right. I have moved on. It took a long time but I've moved on. And now someone else's heart is involved. *Beck's* heart is involved. My heart is involved.

There's no unraveling all of that. Even if I wanted to.

"I'm sorry, Holden. For everything you've been through. For-"

He places a fingertip against my lips and says, "Shh. It's okay. We'll be okay. All of us."

And I want to believe him. I really do. I'm just not sure how to start.

♪

FOR THE NEXT three weeks, we practice as hard as I've ever imagined working. Thomas and I give notice at our jobs and, thankfully, neither place insists that we work it out. When Thomas asks me if I'm okay with Holden moving back in, I have no good reason to say no. He drives to Atlanta two days after our talk in the kitchen and arrives back in a rental car twenty-four hours later with Patsy in the front seat next to him.

Hank Junior is so happy to see her I don't think he quits wagging his tail for a week. He follows her everywhere, as if he's afraid if he lets her out of his sight, she'll disappear again.

We rehearse twelve to fourteen hours a day, polishing our performance until we're nailing every song, word for word, note for note.

And for those three weeks, Holden is right about everything being okay. No one has time to think about anything other than eating, sleeping, and getting ready for the tour. When we get home every night, I fall in bed and sleep like Rip Van Winkle.

My biggest worry is what to do with Hank Junior when we're gone. Since Holden has the same concern about Patsy, he, Thomas and I brainstorm options one morning while we're waiting for Beck in his dad's studio.

"We can't leave them in a kennel for six weeks," Holden says, taking a sip from the coffee the housekeeper, Nelda, made for us when we arrived.

Thomas makes a choking sound. "Yeah, right. CeCe would check *herself* into a kennel for six weeks before she'd leave Hank there."

I raise an eyebrow at him but there's no point in denying the accusation. We all know it's true.

Beck walks in, his hair still wet from the shower. He kisses me on the cheek and says, "What's up with the pow-wow?"

"Just trying to figure out what we're going to do with Hank Junior and Patsy while we're away." I hear the worry in my own voice because with every passing day, I'm more stressed by my lack of a solution.

Beck sits down next to me and pours a cup of coffee. "They could stay here with Nelda."

I lean back and look at him, not sure if he means it. "Are you serious?"

"Yeah," he says. "She loves dogs."

"But what about your dad?"

"He won't mind. They'll give Nelda someone to cook for. When dad's gone anyone left here gets overfed and then some."

"That would be amazing," I say, leaning forward to give him a hug.

Holden gets up from the table to pour another cup of coffee, his back to us. "That's incredibly nice. Thanks, man. Really."

"No skin," Beck says.

"All right then," Thomas says. "Let's get to work."

♪

Holden

The tour begins in San Francisco. Three days on the bus across country, and we're all ready to be there. I've spent most of those miles trying to focus on anything but the fact that Beck can't keep his hands off CeCe.

I get a lot of reading done.

Keeping my eyes on the page and my head in someone else's story is about the only distraction that works.

We arrive in the city on the morning of the first show. After grabbing a few hours of sleep in an actual bed, we leave for the venue where we can practice on stage and get a feel for the acoustics.

The place feels absolutely enormous. We've never played anywhere that would hold half this many people, and looking out at the thousands of empty chairs, I start to wonder if we're really up for this.

"I see what you're thinking." Thomas walks up behind me and claps a hand on my shoulder. "No reason to go there now."

"This could be a major fail," I say.

"Glass half-full, please."

"Don't tell me you're not wondering what we were thinking."

"Okay, so the thought crossed my mind," he concedes. "But we're here. We've done our homework."

"Could I get an infusion of some of your confidence, please?"

Thomas snorts. "Since when do you need confidence?"

"Since we decided we could pull off opening a show for a country music legend."

"We can. Have you heard us?" He pulls his iPhone out of his shirt pocket, swipes the screen, taps it twice and one of our songs begins playing. Thomas waits a minute and then it turns it off. "That sound good or what?"

I have to admit we sound pretty good. "Let's just hope we hit that tonight."

"Faith, man. Where's your faith?"

"Working on it."

"Stay away from CeCe until you get it in place. She's already a bundle of nerves."

Just then, she and Beck walk onstage. She looks as serious as I've ever seen her. She bites her lower lip and glances out at the sea of seats in front of the stage. Her eyes widen.

"Okay," Thomas says. "I think it's time for a pep talk. Y'all get on over here."

He waves us to the end of the stage. We all sit down in a line, facing out to where all those faces will be looking at CeCe and me, and Beck on her other side.

"Anyone here dreamed about this as long as I have?" Thomas asks.

No one says anything for a few moments, and then CeCe admits, "Yes."

Her voice has a tremble in it. Thomas reaches over and covers her hand with his.

"Anyone else?"

"Yeah," I say.

Thomas looks at Beck. "How about you?"

"I've pretty much wanted to be my dad for as long as I can remember," he says in a low voice.

The admission surprises me. It's not something I would expect a guy like Beck to say.

"So, okay," Thomas says. "We all agree this is important to us. And we don't want to screw it up. The only way that's going to happen is if we forget we're anywhere other than at home in Nashville, practicing the way we've been practicing for weeks. We've got this. Y'all know we do. Every song. Every word. Every note. We've got it. Right?"

No one says anything for a long string of moments. Somewhere behind the stage, I hear equipment being unloaded from the tractor-trailer trucks. The whine of a forklift. The clank of metal cases. Conversation and laughter from the guys working hard and fast to get it all in.

CeCe draws in a deep breath and says, "We've got it."

"Beck?" Thomas says.

"Yeah, man. We've got it."

My best friend looks at me, one eyebrow raised.

"We've got it," I say. "We've got it."

♪

CeCe

I am so scared I actually feel my knees trembling.

Two minutes until we're out there in front of thousands of Case Phillips fans, who will pretty much decide with the first song whether we're worthy of being on this tour or not.

My heart is pounding so hard I feel its throb like a bass drum in my ears. I wish with everything inside me that my mama could be here tonight. It's not that I don't understand why she isn't. She's terrified of flying, and driving across country isn't something I can imagine her doing. She'll be at the show in Annapolis, Maryland, and that's good enough. That doesn't make me crave one of her reassuring hugs right now any less though.

The four of us are standing to the side of the stage and we're all wearing varying expressions of "Is this really happening?"

The crowd tonight is two thousand or so, one of the smaller venues for the tour, but the largest by far I've ever sung in front of.

"I'm not sure I can do this," I say. Only then do I realize I've said it out loud.

Holden steps up and dips his head in close to mine. "Where's a place you've sung that made you the happiest?" he asks, his voice low and calming.

I don't turn to look at him. I lace my hands together in front of me and think hard. The memory, when it comes, is sweet and poignant. "In church on the Sunday my granny was baptized. She was eighty-three. She asked the pastor if I could do a solo of "Just As I Am.""

"Yeah?"

I nod, letting myself remember what a wonderful day that had been. "By that point, she couldn't walk very well, and it took a lot of courage for her to step down into that water. Watching her and singing the words to that song at the same time made me understand what it really meant. I was so proud to have been a part of that day."

"Don't you think she'd be proud of you now?" he asks in a low voice.

I let my gaze meet his. "I do," I say softly.

"Then think about that tonight when you're out there singing. Nothing else but that."

"Thanks, Holden," I say, and for a moment, just a moment, I let myself remember why I fell in love with him so quickly. This way he has of anchoring me in the middle of a storm I am sure is big enough to overtake me. I trust him to know the way, to lead me out. I can't explain the why of it. I just know it's true.

"Welcome to the San Francisco Bayside Coliseum and the Case Phillips' Brand New Me Tour!"

The announcer's shout-out is loud enough to soften the roar of the crowd.

"This is one ticket you're going to be so glad you bought. First out tonight, a new group Case has been talking up all over Nashville, and when you hear them, you'll understand why! Folks, let's give a big California welcome to Barefoot Outlook!"

"Yee-haw!" Thomas whoops. "Here we go, y'all!"

He leads me across the stage, one fist pounding the air, the other hand clasped in mine as if he knows there's a good chance I'll run. From the corner of my eye, I see Beck and Holden taking their places, picking up their guitars.

Thomas and I reach for our microphones, and he dips into the first song of our set – "What We Feel." I wrote this song and I know it like I know my own face in the mirror. I'm supposed to come in on the chorus but my mind has gone completely blank. I know what Thomas is going to sing before I hear the words but I can't think of how the first line of the chorus begins. He's into the pre-chorus now. I feel the impending arrival of my turn to join in like a roller coaster about to reach the top of the first hill, aware that the bottom is going to fall out at any second.

My face feels frozen and I can't make myself smile. Thomas glances over at me, his eyes questioning. I know he wants to help. There's nothing he can do.

Someone steps up behind me just then, puts an arm around my shoulders, and I realize it's Case. I'm sure he's going to signal me off the stage, take my place, but he starts into the chorus with Thomas, still holding onto me.

The crowd erupts at the sound of his voice, screaming and whooping their surprise at his appearance.

And suddenly the words are coming back to me. Case must feel my relief because he shouts out, "CeCe McKenzie, folks, this girl's got couuuuntry!"

And as if he's just handed me the baton in a relay race, I swoop into the second verse with the same level of confidence I had reached during our rehearsals of this song.

The audience begins to clap and stomp out the rhythm as I go, and all of a sudden, I'm having more fun than I've ever had on stage. My heart feels like it might burst with gratitude for Case's generosity.

He joins us on the chorus again.

It's what we feel
That makes the memories
It's what we feel

That gives us history
The part that's real
It's what we feel

Thomas and I take the bridge, and then all three of us finish it out. At the end, Case kisses my cheek and heads off the stage. The audience is cheering so loudly, I'm not sure they can even hear the beginning of our next song. But it doesn't matter, I know every word. I sing like I've never sung before, giving it heart, mind, soul, me.

♪

AFTER THE SHOW, we sign autographs for fans who received back stage passes through Case's fan club. It's a little shocking to see the line of people extending down the hallway outside the room where we're having a buffet supper set up by a catering company.

The crowd is mostly made up of girls, a few guys here and there who are most likely boyfriends forced to come along. Thomas, Holden, Beck and I are at the start of the line. Case is at the other end so that the fans get to him last.

A young girl who looks to be about thirteen holds out a t-shirt for me to sign. The front says Brand New Me Tour. The back reads Case Phillips and Barefoot Outlook. Every time I see that, my stomach drops as if released from elevator cables.

How we got here, I am still not sure.

"Your voice is amazing," the girl says, looking up at me with an awe I don't see myself ever getting used to. "I could listen to you all night."

"Thank you so much," I say, smiling at her.

"I sing too," she says.

"That's wonderful. What do you like to sing?"

"Anything I can get anybody to listen to," she admits with a shy smile. "My daddy says I could sing the stripes off a zebra."

I laugh. "That's some awfully good singing."

"Not as good as you though. How long did it take you to sound like you do?"

"I started when I was really young, like you," I say. "If it's what you love to do, it's not even work. For me, I was just always happy to be doing it. Anytime. Anywhere."

Thomas elbows me. "Hey, how about saving a fan or two for me?"

The girl giggles and says to Thomas, "You're really good too, you know."

"Thank you, ma'am," he says, bestowing a smile on her that lights her cheeks up to apple red. He signs her shirt as well and when she's moved on to where Beck is standing next to his dad, I shake my head at him.

"What?" he asks, grinning.

"You're a natural at this," I say.

"I like making people smile."

"You sure can do that." I glance around the room, not for the first time since we've been standing here, and add, "Where is Holden?"

"Said he was going to take a shower."

"He should be signing too."

"He's not much on this part," Thomas says. "Never has been."

I'm not surprised by this but it still doesn't seem right that he's not out here taking some of the credit.

A very tall guy with white-blonde hair stops in front of me and holds out a ticket stub. He looks to be in his late twenties or so. "Could you sign this please?" he asks, his voice smooth, polite.

Smiling, I look up at him. His eyes are the lightest blue I've ever seen. He's smiling back at me but something in his expression makes me instantly want to take a step back. I have to force myself not to. He's looking at me as if he can see right through me. I actually feel goose bumps shiver across my arms.

"I . . . sure," I say, taking the ticket and writing, "Happiness is a Barefoot Outlook. CeCe."

He reads it and smiles again. I can't explain what it is about him, some weird energy or maybe just my imagination. The way he's staring at me feels off somehow.

"Looks like you're living the dream. Touring with Case Phillips. That's big stuff."

I feel my heart thump an inexplicable note of alarm. "We're all grateful to be here," I say.

"You're out of Nashville, right?"

I nod. "Yes." I try to make eye contact with Thomas but he's talking with someone and not looking my way. Neither is Beck or Case.

"How long before you got your break?"

I start to ask what he means but I don't want to lengthen the conversation so I say, "I've been there almost two years."

"Two years? Is that all?" He laughs. "I'd like to get your recipe for success."

Panic flutters through me now and I am certain I need to move away from him. A hand grasps my arm and I jump before I realize it's Holden. He steps halfway in front of me. The adrenaline of instant relief pumps outward from my chest.

"Hey," the guy says with a sarcastic lilt.

Holden now turns fully toward him, standing in between us. "You should move on."

"Should I?"

"You should."

"What happens if I don't?"

"I happen." Holden's voice is steel.

The guy raises both hands in concession, still holding the ticket I signed. "Chill, dude. You go ballistic every time somebody chats up your chick?"

Holden steps forward, forcing him to move back. Case's two bodyguards, John and Miles, are now walking toward us, both hulking weightlifters whose muscle is not for show.

"Everything okay here?" John asks, looking directly at the guy.

"I was just leaving," he says, the words now as neutral as his expression.

"Why don't we walk you out?" Miles says in a voice that makes it clear his offer isn't a suggestion.

He gives me one last look, his eyes lit with amusement, before turning to walk toward the door with them.

I turn and head for the dressing room, my pace fast and uneven, my knees so shaky I think they might actually collapse beneath me. I am aware of Holden following me but I don't stop until I reach the room with my name on it.

He walks in behind me. "Are you okay, CeCe?"

"Will you close it? And lock it? Please."

He does as I ask, concern on his face. "Hey. You're okay."

I sit on the small sofa against one wall, managing a nod, shivering.

"What did he say?"

I shake my head. "It was more like the way he said it."

Holden sits down beside me and slowly pulls me into the curve of his arm. "He's gone. Everything is all right."

I nod, forcing myself to focus on those two words and their ability to melt my panic.

"He really freaked you out," Holden says, smoothing the back of his hand across my hair. "I admit he was a little creepy, but is there something else going on?"

I want to tell him, except it's been so long since I've let myself think about any of it that I'm not sure I can bring it to life again with words. "I . . . had a bad experience a few years ago. I guess he reminded me of it."

Holden studies me for a moment and then says, "What happened, CeCe?"

I look down and rub my thumb against the back of one hand. "It was right after I first started going on the road. Weekend stuff. I began noticing this man showing up in the audience, even when the shows were in different places, hours apart. At first, he just watched me and never approached me. But then he began sitting at a front table, and throughout the entire show, he wouldn't take his eyes off me."

"Did you call the police?"

"At that point, I didn't have anything to report. I started to see him in other places. At the grocery store. Parked outside my high school when I got there in the mornings. He even came to my house one night when Mama was at church. I heard a knock and opened the door before I realized–"

I break off there because my voice is shaking and I can't get the rest of the words out.

Holden puts his arm around me and pulls me into the curve of his shoulder. I hold myself rigid for a few moments but then I close my eyes and sink against him, remembering how safe I feel there.

"Did he hurt you?" he asks, his voice low and laced with anger.

I shake my head. "I was able to slam the door and call the police. There was nothing to arrest him for at that point."

"What else did he do?"

"Punctured the tires on Mama's car when I borrowed it one night to go to a show in Raleigh. Surveillance cameras proved that he did it."

"Did he go to jail?"

"For ninety days."

"That's it?" he asks, sounding disgusted.

I nod.

"Has he bothered you since?"

"While he was in jail, someone would call our house and hang up. Eventually, that stopped, and I haven't heard from him again."

"You're sure this isn't the same guy?"

"I'm sure."

We sit, quiet for a good while before he says, "I don't want you to go anywhere by yourself, okay?"

"I won't."

"He's probably some jokester with a bad sense of humor, but there's no reason to take a chance."

I pull back a bit and look up at him. "Thank you," I say.

"For what?"

"Being there."

"I'm glad I was."

He brushes his hand across my cheek, and just that light touch snags something low inside me that responds to him in a way I've never responded to anyone else. My breathing goes instantly shallow.

"You're beautiful, CeCe."

The words are like the lick of a flame along my skin, and I hear in his voice that he knows he shouldn't have said them.

"I really want you to kiss me," I say softly, deliberately.

"I really want to kiss you," he says, equally soft, equally deliberate.

I lean in a little closer. There's a moment of hesitation in us both. He answers my invitation so suddenly and with such intensity that I forget to breathe, forget everything except the instant memory of how his lips feel against mine. Heated and knowing, familiar and skilled.

I slide my palms up the expanse of his hard-muscled abs and chest, the ripples and contours clearly defined beneath the thin cotton of his t-shirt. Touching him, molding myself to him, it's almost impossible to believe I'm not dreaming. Because I've dreamed this dream so many times, only to wake up to daylight and the fact that I would never be held by him like this again, kissed by him like this again.

I feel the tears seeping from beneath my closed lids. I will them to stop, but they don't, they won't.

Holden pulls back and brushes his thumb across my cheek. "Do you want me to quit?" he asks, instantly remorseful.

I shake my head, looking down because I can't make myself meet his gaze.

"But you're crying."

"I know," I whisper.

"Baby, why?" he says, the question sounding as if it has been torn from him.

I do let myself look at him now, and I answer as honestly as I can. "Because I've missed you so much. Because I thought we would never be together like this-"

I don't finish. He is suddenly kissing me into silence. And I am kissing him back. His hands slide under the skirt of my dress and around my bottom to lift me onto his lap so that I am straddling him, my arms winding around his neck and holding him tight. There is no space between us, one heart pounding into the other. And I think if I could melt myself into him, I would. I don't ever want to feel again what it's like to know this and lose it.

Call it weakness. Call it acceptance of something I can't change, but whatever I call it, I can't deny it.

I run my hands through his hair, kiss one eyelid and then the other, nip his chin with my teeth before sinking my mouth onto his again.

And we kiss without thought of time or any other measuring stick of the world outside this room. I don't want to think past the next moment, the next sensation spiraling through me, lifting me up and out of myself to a place where there is only this, only us.

"Do you have any idea what you do to me?" he asks, dropping his head against the back of the sofa, his eyes hazed with the same need I feel.

"I know what you do to me," I say. "I know that I've never felt this way with anyone but you."

"CeCe. I promised myself I wouldn't get between you and Beck," he says, the words infused with apology. "Tell me to get up and leave, and I will."

"I wish I could," I say, hearing the broken note in my admission. "I don't want to hurt him. I never wanted-"

"Me? Is that about right?"

I go completely still at the sound of Beck's voice, closing my eyes in the hope that I imagined it.

Holden gently slides me off his lap, stands, and pulls me to my feet. We both face Beck with solemn expressions.

"Beck . . . man, we didn't mean for this to happen," Holden says. "It wasn't planned."

Beck shoves a hand through his hair and laughs, a harsh sound that I don't recognize in him. "There's fool and then there's Fool with a capital F. I guess that's me."

"Beck," I say. "Don't. It's not like that."

"What is it like, CeCe?" he asks, and I see the tears shining in his eyes.

My heart twists. I really hate myself for hurting him this way. "I don't know how to explain it."

"Maybe like this," he says with an edge in his voice. "Girl likes boy. Boy dumps girl. Girl tries to get over him with sucker boy. But that didn't work, did it?"

"Beck-"

"Don't bother, CeCe," he says. "I already know the ending to this story." He turns and leaves the room, slamming the door behind him so that the thin walls rattle with the force.

I sink onto the sofa, wondering exactly what I've just done.

Holden sits down next to me. "Do you want me to go after him?"

"No. It should be me. I need to talk to him."

"I don't want you alone with him when he's angry at you."

"It's okay. That's not Beck."

"How do you know?" he asks.

"I just do," I say, and then because the guilt is starting to choke me, I add, "You should go."

He watches me while weighing his decision. "I'm not leaving you alone right now."

"I'm fine. I . . . I need some time to think."

I can see that he wants to disagree but he finally relents with, "I'll check in on you in a little while. Are you sure you'll be okay?"

I nod.

He stands then without touching me again. He walks to the door, turns, and looks at me. His eyes are solemn and serious. "Do you want me to go back to pretending that I don't love you, CeCe?"

The question echoes from my head to my heart. I am at once joyful and stricken.

He loves me.

Oh.

He loves me.

"No," I say. "I don't."

♪

CeCe

I don't sleep.

I try, but the effort amounts to nothing more than rumpled sheets and a comforter that ends up on the floor.

My thoughts bounce back and forth. From Holden and loving every moment of being in his arms, to Beck and the look on his face when he walked in the room.

I feel horrible, and I really don't know where to begin to try and fix this. There is no fixing it. I can't erase what happened or the fact that I've hurt Beck in the process.

All I can do is apologize.

I give up the fight and get out of bed at four-thirty, heading for the shower where I stand under the spray for a good twenty minutes. I brush my teeth and dry my hair, slide into jeans and a t-shirt. I make myself wait until five-thirty before walking to Beck's room. It's still an indecent hour to wake anyone up but I can't wait any longer.

He's one floor down from mine. I take the elevator and get off, glancing at the number signs and turning right.

I hear the music from the far end of the hallway. It's blasting loud enough that I wonder how anybody can be sleeping.

It's not until I've almost reached his door that I realize the music is coming from his room. I stop instantly and decide this is a very bad idea. Just then, a girl stumbles backwards out of the doorway. She is laughing so hard she's holding her stomach, and she's having extreme difficulty staying upright on her stiletto heels.

"If three isn't a crowd, Beck Phillips," she says, her voice slightly slurred, "four is just getting the party started." She laughs as if she has nailed the best punch line ever.

I start to back away. She looks around and points at me, staring for a moment as if she's trying to focus. "Oh, my gosh! You're CeCe. Beck's singer. I mean, girlfriend."

I decide that now is the time to go. But she moves surprisingly fast for someone who would no doubt blow a DUI test. She lurches forward and grabs my hand, pulling me toward the room and then through the half open door.

I stop as if I have hit a concrete wall.

Beck and two girls are in the king-size bed that takes up the middle of the floor. One girl is sitting on top of him, naked. The other girl, also naked, is draped alongside him, one leg entwined with his.

He looks at me, and I can see that he's trying to focus, as if I am very far away, when actually it's only a few feet. "CeCe? Is that you?"

His words are every bit as slurred as those of the girl who pulled me into the room. His eyes are like slits, and he's clearly having trouble keeping them open.

I spot the traces of white powder on the coffee table and the two empty gin bottles.

I've never seen Beck with drugs, never known him to even want to be around anyone messing with them.

I start to back away as he says, "Did you think I'd just come down here and cry myself to sleep, CeCe?"

I shake my head, stung by the harsh tone in his voice.

"Or maybe you thought it was okay for you to screw around as long as I didn't know about it?"

"Beck. Please."

He vaults off the bed and stumbles to a stop in front of me, wearing black briefs and nothing else. The girls are giggling now, watching us the way they might an episode of their favorite sitcom.

He grabs my arms, holding onto me so tightly that I'm not sure if it's because he doesn't want me to go or if it's the only way he can keep himself upright.

"What did I do wrong?" he asks, staggering backwards a few inches and then swaying forward again. He rights himself when his chest bumps my shoulder.

"Nothing," I say. "Let's not do this now. I'll come back when you-"

"Don't have company?" he interrupts, waving a hand at the girls on the bed. "What's wrong with me having company? It's not like I have a girlfriend or anything."

I swing around to leave, certain now that things are only going to go downhill from here. But he whirls me back, and I collide with his bare chest, grabbing his arm to keep from falling.

I look up at him then, and my growing anger instantly deflates at the look in his eyes. The hurt I see there takes my breath away. "Beck. Oh, Beck. I'm sorry. I didn't mean to-"

"Break my heart?" he finishes softly. "Well, you did."

"Come back to bed, honey," one of the girls says, patting the mattress. "We were just about to fix it for you."

He reaches out and brushes my cheek with his knuckles. "I loved you, CeCe. No. I *love* you."

Regret forms a knot in my throat. I try to say something. The words won't come. I realize I don't have any that will make this better. "I'm sorry, Beck. I never wanted to hurt you."

"But you have. Right?"

I look down at my hands, unable to respond.

"You can't make your heart feel something it doesn't feel."

"Beck, I didn't plan tonight. I didn't expect it."

"Didn't want it?"

I start to respond. I realize I can't answer this without hurting him further. Because I *did* want it.

When I don't say anything, he raises a hand and drops onto the bed, sliding back in between the two girls who instantly welcome him with open arms.

"Go, CeCe," he says. "We're done."

♪

I DON'T KNOW WHY I'm crying. I have no right to be. I created the situation I am in. I could have asked Holden to leave tonight before anything went as far as it did.

But I didn't.

I start to go back to my room but turn for Thomas's instead. I knock on his door with tears streaming down my face. I don't bother to wipe them away because they are instantly replaced with more.

"Who is it?" he calls out, husky-voiced.

"CeCe," I say, my sobs refusing to stay silent now.

He pulls the door open and stares at me with alarm on his face. "What happened? Are you all right?"

"I think I . . . I might have just ruined everything."

He takes my hand and leads me in the room. "First, clarify everything."

"Barefoot Outlook," I say, the words breaking in half. "The tour."

"Why would you think that?" he asks, pulling me to the bed where we both sink onto the edge of the mattress. "We had a great first show. It couldn't have gone any better."

"It's what happened after the show."

"What?"

I honestly don't know where to start. Finally, I just say, "Holden."

"And you?"

I nod again, miserable.

"Like that hasn't been inevitable," he says.

"Thanks," I say.

"Well, you'd have to be blind not to see it."

"I thought you were my friend."

"I am your friend. Friends tell each other the truth. So what happened, other than you two knocking boots?"

I put my hand over his mouth and say, "We did not knock boots."

He play-wrestles with my hand for a moment and says, "What exactly did you do?"

"I . . . we were kind of headed in that direction," I admit in a low voice, "and Beck walked in."

"Dang," Thomas says, sounding completely serious now. "That's bad."

"He's really angry with me."

"Yeah." He lets out a soft whistle. "Can't say that I blame him."

"He has three naked girls in his room right now, and he's been drinking. That's probably not all."

"Girl," he says, shaking his head, "you sure know how to bring a fella down."

"I didn't mean to," I say, miserable. "I didn't want to hurt him. What happened with Holden tonight wasn't supposed to happen. Oh, Thomas, what if I've messed it all up?"

"Why would you think you've done that?"

"He's pretty mad."

"Beck has as much to gain from Barefoot Outlook hitting it as any of us do. From everything he's said to me, going back to school is the last thing he wants. I doubt he wants to give his dad a reason to say the gig's up."

I shrug. "Maybe."

"Want me to talk to him?"

"I'm not sure it will do any good."

"I think he'll see the logic. But here's my one stipulation," he says, his voice suddenly serious.

I turn my head to look at him. "What?"

"You and Holden cool it until the tour is done."

I want to argue, tell him what happened tonight won't happen again, that we both lost it and things can go back to the way they were. I can't. Because I know that's a lie.

So I nod. Once. Looking down at my hands. "Okay," I say. "Okay."

♪

CeCe

I keep my word to Thomas, but the wear of avoiding both Beck and Holden for three weeks is starting to become evident. I'm not sleeping great, and it's taking more makeup to prevent that fact from showing beneath my eyes.

I've been talking to Mama pretty much every night after the show. We talk about normal things, people back home, who's recently gotten married, had babies, bought a new car, the kind of regular stuff that keeps me from thinking about the strain within our group.

I send her tickets for the Annapolis show, and on the morning she and my Aunt Vera are scheduled to meet me at our hotel, I wake up so excited to see them, I can hardly wait.

I'm standing outside when Aunt Vera's Suburban turns in the parking lot. As soon as she pulls into an open space, I run to the passenger side door, barely waiting for Mama to slide out before throwing my arms around her and hugging her as if I can absorb every ounce of the comfort I know she will fill me with.

"Hello, honey," she says with a catch in her voice, her southern Virginia accent music to my ears. "Gracious, it's good to see you."

I nod and bury my face in her neck. She smells like home, like the bread she makes almost every day and the basil she grows in a pot by the kitchen sink where it gets lots of sun. All of a sudden, I am crying the way I did when I would go to her as a little girl, certain that whatever was wrong, she'd be able to fix.

"Aw, honey, what is it?" she asks, smoothing her hand over the back of my hair.

"Nothing," I say as convincingly as I can manage. "It's just so good to see you."

Late forties looks more like late thirties on her, and I feel proud of her, proud that she is here. She hugs me even tighter, and Aunt Vera waits a couple of minutes before she gets out and hugs me too.

She pulls back and gives me a long look. "Good gracious, child, could you get any prettier?"

I smile a watery smile and say, "You never did go see that eye doctor, did you, Aunt Vera?"

She and Mama both beam at me, and I think not for the first time how much alike they look. They're twins, and a lot of people back home can't tell them apart even though they've known them their whole lives.

I wipe my eyes and say, "It's so good to see you both."

"It's good to see you, honey," Mama says. "We want to hear all about everything you've been doing. So much excitement. I've been telling everybody in town."

"We are so overdue a gabfest," Aunt Vera says.

"There's a Starbucks down the street," I say.

"Perfect," Mama says.

We walk there, Mama and Vera each holding my hand. They set right in on sharing the local gossip. It feels so familiar, so much a part of me that I am deeply homesick. Even so, I feel better already.

♪

"WELL, IT'S NO surprise," Aunt Vera says. "A girl as pretty as you having two boyfriends."

"I don't think that's exactly what she's saying, Vera," Mama says, taking a sip of her house blend.

"Isn't it?" Aunt Vera says, looking at me with a twinkle in her eyes.

"That was never my intention," I say.

"Sometimes, these things just happen. I remember when I was young enough and pretty enough to get myself in such fixes," Aunt Vera says, with the dramatic flair she has been known for my whole life. "Those were the days."

"Hah," Mama says. "Those were the days when you'd go out with the first boy who arrived to pick you up, leaving me to deal with the second one you had then stood up."

I laugh at this image. It's so typical of their relationship. Mama, the responsible one. Vera, leaning on her to right whatever wrongs she happened to ignite.

"So which one are you standing up, my dear?" Aunt Vera says, looking at me over the rim of her Caramel Frappuccino.

"Neither," I say, some of my misery evident in the response.

"You're not seeing either one?" Mama asks, and I can hear that she's worried about me.

I shake my head. "No, but it's fine."

"How can it be fine?" Aunt Vera says with a cluck, cluck. "That's a losing proposition."

"It's complicated," I say.

"So is being unhappy," she adds.

"I'm doing what I've always wanted to do. I have nothing to complain about."

"The heart usually insists on having what it wants," Mama says in her calm, common sense way. "Don't close a door you might later wish you'd left open."

"If only it were that simple, Mama."

"The feeling itself is, honey. Sometimes, we just need to get out of its way."

♪

I SPEND THE rest of the day with them, shopping and laughing at Vera's funny stories about her own dating life. I decide after a point that if I had ever considered taking advice from her, it would have been a bad idea.

On the way back into the hotel, we run into Holden and Thomas in the lobby. I introduce everyone, and we are all polite and friendly. I try not to give Mama or Aunt Vera any clues about my feelings for Holden, but as soon as we step in the elevator, Mama looks at me and says, "It'll be hard for your heart to accept no on that one, honey."

Aunt Vera nods. "Amen to that, sister."

I'd like to offer up at least some token disagreement, but who would I be kidding?

When it's time to leave for the show, Mama and Aunt Vera go with me to my dressing room and help me get ready. It is so wonderful having them there that I know I'm going to miss them terribly once they're gone. We laugh and giggle more like high school best friends than aunt, mother, and daughter. I try to convince Aunt Vera that light blue eye shadow has not yet come back in style. She finally relents but still doesn't agree.

It's only a few minutes before I need to leave the room when a knock sounds at the door. Aunt Vera jogs over to see who it is before I can get there. She pulls it open and then stands there as if she has been lasered to the spot.

"Oh. Good. Day." Aunt Vera utters the words with wide-eyed disbelief. She takes a step back with one hand on her chest.

"Evening, ma'am," Case says, smiling at her with the very same smile that's made his CDs bestsellers.

"Hi, Case," I say. "You might need to take a little pity on Aunt Vera. She's prone to fainting spells."

His grin widens. "I heard you had some beautiful women in here with you tonight. Thought I'd stop by and say hey."

His generosity shouldn't still surprise me, but it does. Especially in light of the fact that I know he must have heard Beck and I aren't seeing each other. "This is my mama, Mira MacKenzie. And her sister, my aunt, Vera Nelson."

"Mira. Vera. Sure is nice to meet you ladies. I can't tell you how much we think of your lovely CeCe here."

"Thank you," Mama says, her smile warm and appreciative. "We think the world of her ourselves."

"I know CeCe got tickets for you tonight but I was hoping y'all might like to use these two from my VIP section. We've created a few perks for special guests, and I'd love for y'all to be a part of it."

"Case," I say. "Thank you. Really."

"Goodness gracious," Aunt Vera says. "Some days you get up and have absolutely no idea what's in store for you."

Case laughs. "I think there's a song lyric in there somewhere, ma'am."

"Be happy to work on that with you," Aunt Vera says.

"That's mighty kind," Case says, smiling. He looks at Mama then, and I notice their gazes linger a moment longer than just polite interest.

Mama glances away first, and I see her cheeks brighten with color. I can't even remember the last time I saw her affected by a man.

"Well," Case says, "I hope y'all enjoy the show."

"I am certain we will," Aunt Vera says.

"Thank you so much," Mama says.

When he's gone, Aunt Vera waits ten seconds or so before she starts to dance around the room. "Did that really happen?"

"That really happened, Vera," Mama says, shaking her head with a smile. "Now settle down before you hurt yourself."

♪

Holden

I'm not sure that I'm old enough to make a conclusion like this yet, but I'm starting to wonder if it's even possible to be completely content in this life.

I should be. In fact, this should be a high point.

We're on the fourth week of our tour, and I don't know that we could have even hoped for the kind of response we've been getting from the crowds in pretty much every city we've visited.

San Diego. Flagstaff. Denver. Omaha. Springfield. Columbus. Annapolis last night. And now tonight in D.C.

We're here for the music. And to get the kind of break we've been given is like winning the hundred million dollar lottery. It almost never happens.

To do anything other than milk every possible moment of enjoyment from this experience makes no sense at all.

Even so, I feel like I'm living in a state of euphoria combined with one of extreme misery. Thomas was right. Staying away from CeCe, with the exception of the time that we're actually rehearsing or performing, is the common sense thing to do. I don't want to blow what we have going with this tour.

It just feels so wrong to put on a show the way we do, smiling, laughing, joking with each other. Beck even manages to pull this off, and I assume that's the power of Thomas's persuasiveness.

As soon as we're off stage though, we go in our separate directions. I've heard there are big name groups who lived like this for years while they played out their contracts; a picture of unity and professionalism when they're on stage, hating each other's guts and not speaking when they're off. That doesn't make me feel any better.

If I could rewind to that night in CeCe's dressing room and push pause for everything that I wanted to happen between us, I would. We should all be hanging out together, seeing as much of the towns we're in as we can, but unless I go somewhere with Thomas, I'm alone. The same is true for CeCe. Which means we both spend a lot of time by ourselves.

I'm just getting out of the shower when I hear a knock on the door of my hotel room. I wrap a towel around my waist and answer it.

Thomas is standing in the hall, wearing an enormous Stetson and new cowboy boots. I lean back and give him an appraising look.

"You've been shopping," I say.

"Fruits of my labor," he says. "We've got the whole day to tour the city before we need to be at the arena. I thought you and me and CeCe could see what there is to see."

I wave him in. "Aren't you the one who grounded us from being together?"

"I'll be the chaperone."

"I don't know, Thomas. I doubt that CeCe would–"

"I already asked her. She said yes."

I can't hide my surprise when I say, "Oh."

"Well? Get your britches on then."

"It seems like it'll be awkward."

"Probably will since you two have trouble keeping your hands off each other. I'll sit between you."

I roll my eyes. "What about Beck?"

"He, apparently, has a date."

I should feel glad about this but I wonder if it hurts CeCe that he's obviously not wasting any time in moving on. "Where are we going?"

"Where else? To hear some music."

♪

WE WALK THE half mile or so from our hotel to the festival in downtown D.C. Thomas keeps his word and walks in between CeCe and me. We both pretend not to notice. I can't stop myself from stealing glimpses of her out of the corner of my eye. She's wearing an orange skirt and a pink tank top. She looks like she's upped her running because her arms are even leaner and more cut than they were at the beginning of the tour.

"Bark-Fest is a fundraiser for a local No-Kill rescue," Thomas says. "Sounds like they raise a boatload of money every year."

"That's great," CeCe says, but she looks distracted, as if her thoughts are somewhere else.

We've arrived at the concession area. Tents and booths are set up all around us, and the smell of funnel cakes and cotton candy permeates the air.

"I need a Coke," Thomas says, pointing at a stand not too far away. "Anybody want one?"

"I'm good," I say.

"No, thanks," CeCe says.

"Be right back," Thomas says.

"I thought he was going to stay between us," I say, the words out before I think to stop them.

A small smile touches the corners of CeCe's mouth. "He did say that, didn't he?"

I turn to let myself look at her. It's only then that I realize I haven't been looking at her full on but turning away whenever I started to take in too much of her. Our gazes catch, and we stare at each other for several long moments.

"How are you?" I ask, the question soft, tentative.

"I'm okay," she says. "Are you?"

I start to answer with something off-hand, but I can't make myself be flip. "Sometimes. The other times? Not so much."

"Kind of a mess, isn't it?" CeCe says.

"I'm sorry for what happened that night. Beck walking in and everything."

"I'm not," she says.

I don't know how to respond to this so I say, "What do you mean?"

"I'm not sorry for what happened between us. I never wanted to hurt Beck, but I'm not sorry for the way I feel about you."

"CeCe," I say, with no idea of where to go from here. I want to pull her to me and kiss her with every drop of need inside me. I'm just about to give in and do exactly that when my phone buzzes. CeCe's makes its text alert sound a second later.

I glance at the screen, see it's from Thomas.

She looks at hers. "Thomas."

We read the message at the same time.

Sorry for the deception, but tired of watching you be miserable. No more middle man. Find your way wherever you need to go. Love you both.

When we're done, we look at each other as if we're not sure what to make of it.

"But why would he change his mind?"

I shake my head. "I don't know."

We stand there for what feels like a very long time. I hold out my hand. CeCe takes it.

♪

CeCe

Holden tugboats me through the crowd, weaving and winding until we reach the edge of the festival and a high stonewall. He pulls me behind it so that we are virtually hidden from anyone passing by.

He presses me against it, one hand on each of my shoulders, looking down at me with the fiercest need I have ever seen in anyone's eyes.

It is an exact reflection of what I feel. And suddenly, I don't want to ignore it any longer. I don't want to turn away from the constant buzz of need inside me, whether I'm next to him or nowhere near. It's there when I wake up in the morning. When I go to sleep at night. No matter what I do to pretend it isn't, it never leaves. Never stops. Instead, it just continues to grow like a storm building way out in the ocean, increasing in power until there is no denying its existence, its inevitable crash into shore.

I reach for him then, cup my hand at the back of his neck and pull him in. He comes to me with an urgency that tells me he has simply been waiting for the invitation. His mouth is on mine in full assault, full surrender. I kiss him with a need I have never in my life known. All this time of denying, subduing, turning away from. I think I will surely drown in its sudden pent-up release.

He lifts me and sets me on the stone wall, stepping in between my legs and bringing us as close as it is physically possible to be in broad daylight in a public place.

I lock my arms around his waist, and we kiss each other as if we are living out our last moments on earth, almost out of time.

"CeCe." My name is ragged on his lips, and I touch his mouth, wanting to feel him say it.

"Is this real?" I ask.

"Nothing in my life has ever felt as real as you," he says. "If I don't get you somewhere alone, I think I might actually stop breathing."

I want to smile, laugh, make light of what he's just said, but I can't because I feel the very same way. "Where?" I ask in little more than a whisper.

He lifts me off the wall and, clasping my hand in his, starts pulling me down the street at a near run.

I should protest, tell him this is crazy, that we need to stop, go back. For the life of me, I cannot make myself do anything other than hold onto him and follow.

In less than five minutes, we slow to a walk just before the entrance to a very luxurious hotel front. A discreet sign says **The Montgomery Mansion.**

I remember reading about it in a magazine once. I stop suddenly and pull on Holden's hand, protesting, "We can't go here. It's a five-star hotel."

"I want to see you naked on five-star sheets."

The words send a ripple of heat through me.

That's crazy. We have to go back. Any of these responses would have been appropriate. But that's not what comes out.

"Do I get to see *you* on those sheets?" I ask.

He doesn't answer but propels me forward through the main door of the hotel and doesn't stop until we reach the front desk.

An older man with white hair and smart-looking spectacles glances up at us with a welcoming smile. "Good morning. Welcome to the Montgomery Mansion. How may I help you?"

"We'd like a room, please," Holden says.

"Do you have a reservation, sir?"

"No, we don't."

I feel my face turn four different shades of red, one layered over the other. I squeeze Holden's hand in an attempt to convey that we should leave and forget about this.

But the man smiles and says, "Let me see what I can do."

He taps on the keyboard in front of him for a minute or more before looking up and saying, "Ah, yes. We do have something available for you." He states the rate, and I blink at the amount.

Holden hands him a credit card. "We'll take that."

"Very good, sir." The man runs the card and gives it back to Holden along with a room key. "Do you have any bags we can help you with?" His expression remains neutral in the manner of someone who is expected to be discreet.

"No, thank you," Holden says.

"Enjoy your day then," the man says, nodding as we turn to leave.

Once we're alone in the elevator, Holden walks me back against one wall and begins kissing me again. I can't stop myself from kissing him, even though my cheeks are still burning from the front desk experience.

Just as the elevator dings, I say, "Like he didn't know why we wanted a room."

Holden smiles against my mouth. "Do you think we're the first?"

"That doesn't make it any less embarrassing."

"Embarrassed is the very last thing I'm feeling right now," he says, taking my hand and leading me down the long hallway.

"How many months' rent did you just spend?" I ask, breathless.

We're at the door now. He leans in. "Stop talking so I can kiss you."

I do, and he does. So slowly and thoroughly that my legs weaken beneath me, and I lean into him, not sure of anything except that I want more.

He opens the door, walks us backwards inside, and kicks it closed behind us. From there, he swoops me up as if I weigh nothing. I loop my arms around his neck and kiss him with every ounce of feeling I have for him.

When he reaches the side of the bed, he lets go of my legs and I slide to the floor.

He stares down at me with the most intense seriousness I've ever seen in him. "I wake up in the morning, and you're my first thought," he says. "When I go to bed at night, it's your voice I hear right before I fall asleep. I've tried to make myself forget you as anything other than a friend. I can't. And I can't imagine my life meaning anything near what it would mean if you're part of it."

Tears well in my eyes, and I try to blink them back, but it doesn't work. "I love you, Holden."

"I love you, baby. So much."

We fall onto the bed together, arms wrapped tight around one another. And absolutely everything ceases to exist except this need we have for each other.

I unbutton his shirt, slide it from his shoulders and wait for him to shrug out of it. I run my hand across the muscled contours of his chest then down the curve of his left bicep.

"Do you have any idea how beautiful you are?" I ask him.

He gives me a very heated look that makes me want to wrap myself around him and never let go.

"You're the one who's beautiful," he says.

"No, I mean it," I say, tracing one finger down the center of his well-honed abs. "Beautiful like art that I just want to stare at for as long as it takes to absorb every inch of what I see."

"CeCe," he starts, but I stop him with a kiss that goes on for quite some time, a slow dance of exploration, of longing, of pleasure.

Holden drops his head back when my lips find his neck. He makes a sound of need that I want to satisfy in every way I possibly can.

He rolls me over then, settles his long body onto mine and lifts my shirt over my head, pulling it off and tossing it onto the floor.

It is the first time we've been against each other this way, skin to skin, and

I feel as if I've been ignited deep inside with a heat so consuming that only he will be able to direct it in a way that does not turn me to vapor.

And we keep kissing. Long, slow, full, deep kisses that both fill me up and drain me. I want to give him everything. Be everything he needs. But I am suddenly swamped with a wave of uncertainty. I have no idea how to tell him I've never done this before.

I press a hand to his chest and say his name.

He lifts up to look down at me through eyes hazed with want. "What is it?" he asks, his voice soft and husky.

"Holden . . . I haven't been with . . . I've never done this before."

He goes completely still above me. I watch his face as he processes what I have just said. When comprehension fully registers, he rolls across the bed and lies flat on his back, staring at the ceiling and breathing hard.

"You've. . . never. . . been with anyone?"

I shake my head, feeling something well beyond embarrassed now. We lie there like that for a good bit while I wish I could blink and disappear.

Finally, Holden turns over on his side, rising up on one elbow to stare into my eyes. "CeCe?"

"What?" I ask without looking at him, feeling the heat in my face.

"Look at me," he says gently.

I turn my head, slowly, finally letting myself meet his gaze.

He reaches out and touches my cheek. "I'm glad you told me. I want this to be different," he says. "I want us to be different."

"What do you mean?" I ask, my stomach suddenly tight with worry that he will say this is a mistake.

"This isn't casual. And it never could be."

I nod once. "I know."

"I love you, CeCe. I want to be with you. Not just here and now, but every single day of my life. Every single night of my life."

Relieved beyond words, I smile and lace my fingers through his. "I want to be with you."

"Then let's make it forever," he says, taking my hand in his. "CeCe MacKenzie, will you marry me?"

I have to wonder if I've actually heard him say this or if I have imagined it. "Do you mean it?" I ask in little more than a whisper.

He loops an arm around my waist and pulls me up close until we are touching, skin to skin. "I've never meant anything more in my life."

Tears well in my eyes, seep out and slip down my cheeks. I wipe them away with the back of my hand. "Then, yes," I say. "Yes. Yes. Yes."

♪

CeCe

Case's Fan Appreciation party is wide open by the time I change into jeans and a tank top and make my way to the big white tent set up alongside two of the tour buses. I feel lit up inside with the secret I have yet to share with anyone. Holden wants to tell Thomas after the show tonight. And I am going to tell Beck. As painful as it will be, I have to tell him.

Music is blasting from two enormous stage speakers. I don't recognize hardly anyone at first, but then I spot Thomas and Beck standing next to a table loaded with trays of sandwiches and platters of fruit and cookies.

My stomach drops and I feel sick at the thought of hurting Beck. I have to be honest with him. I owe him that.

Thomas spots me and waves me over, taking my hand and pulling me in to kiss me on the cheek. "What a show. You were amazing out there tonight."

"Everyone was," I say, letting myself glance at Beck then. "I thought it was our best of the tour."

Beck nods, but doesn't answer. "Can we talk, Beck?" I ask, my heart pounding so hard I know he can hear it.

"Yeah," he says.

Thomas looks at both of us with compassion in his eyes. "Y'all go easy on each other, okay?"

And with that he walks away, stopping to talk with some of the crew where they are loading plates with sandwiches.

"Are we doing this here?" Beck asks.

"I'd rather go somewhere else," I say.

Just then Case comes in and waves for everyone's attention. The dull roar of conversation lowers and succumbs to silence.

"Thanks y'all," Case says. "I hope everyone's having a good time. You've sure earned it. I can honestly say that so far this is the best tour I've ever been a part of. I want to thank each of you for the role you played in making it happen. It's no accident that it's a success. And without the stellar fans who are celebrating with us here tonight, none of this would be possible."

Cheers start in a wave and crescendo with whistles and clapping. Someone yells out, "You rock, Case!"

Shouts of agreement follow. He raises a hand, smiling and waiting for the volume to lower to a level where he can be heard. "Thank you, again. Every one of you."

Someone starts opening Champagne and several toasts are made by Rhys, Case's producer and a few of the band members.

My eyes are drawn to a tall figure standing at the edge of the tent. The white-blonde short-cropped hair triggers instant recognition. It's the guy from our first concert in San Diego.

He walks over to one of the tables now, picks up a plate, a couple of sandwiches, steps back and starts eating.

I should let someone know the guy is here. But what am I going to say? He was mean to me and he shouldn't be here?

I'm trying to decide what to do when Case waves Beck forward.

"Come on up here, son," he calls out. "Thomas, Holden, CeCe, y'all too!"

We walk through the crowd of people to the center of the tent where Case is waiting. Holden and Thomas thread their way in, standing on one side of Case, Beck and I on the other.

"I just want to say how proud I am of these four," Case says. "They had about three weeks to put together what you've seen them do during this tour. It's clear from the way all you fans have responded to them, you'll be seeing a lot more of them."

Whistles and clapping follow. Case hands the microphone to Thomas and asks, "Anything y'all want to say?"

Thomas clears his throat and then, "Thank you for the opportunity, Case. I'm not sure we could ever do justice with words our appreciation for the shot you've given us. And how much I admire you for who you are and what you do. You live your life by paying it forward, and if I ever get the chance to do for someone else what you've done for us, I hope I'll be as generous."

"You could start by paying it forward with me," a voice calls out from the guests. "Jared Ryner."

The name rings out in the otherwise silent tent. I look into the crowd and see that it came from the blonde guy from San Diego. My heart starts to pound so hard that I can feel it against my chest.

He drops the now empty plate onto the table, wipes his hands on his jeans. "Do you know how many years I spent in Nashville trying to get someone to give me a shot?"

People start to shift where they stand, uncomfortable and unsure of where this is going.

"Eight," he says. "Eight years. Playing on street corners. Exit ramps off the interstate. Knocking on doors. Sending songs to record companies and never getting a call back."

People are now starting to back away from the center of the tent, as if they all sense that something's not quite right.

Somebody calls out, "Are you supposed to be here, Jared?"

The guy laughs then, as if something hysterically funny has just been said. "No," he says, trying to catch his breath. "I suppose that's the punch line to my eight years of working to get a break. I never actually belonged. There must have been some secret pass code no one ever bothered to let me in on."

Another man's voice rings out with authority, "Someone call Security and get him out of here."

But Jared lifts the front of his shirt and pulls a handgun from the waist of his jeans. "I'm afraid it's a little late for that," he says, raising it up and firing it once through the top of the tent.

Screams erupt and people start to push and shove to get out. He points the gun at the center of the crowd and fires again. A man in a white shirt standing a few yards away from us tilts forward and then collapses onto the ground, blood spilling from his neck like water from a hose.

All around, women begin screaming. I am frozen where I stand. Holden steps in front of me and calls out, "Jared! Man, this isn't the way. Put the gun down, and let's go outside and talk."

He looks at Holden and laughs. "Talk with you? The big hottie on stage? What would you and I have to talk about? No matter how good my music is, I'm never going to get the same chances as a guy who looks like you. How is that fair?"

"A man may die because of you," Holden says, his voice calm and even. "That's the next pressing thing on your list. You still have a chance to turn this around if you want to."

"There's no turning anything around now. It took me a while but I finally figured that out."

I hear the wail of sirens in the distance. Holden steps back and presses against me, his body fully blocking me from seeing where Jared is or what he's doing.

Case moves away from us and walks toward him. "Son. Come on. Put the gun down. You've taken this far enough."

"I suggest you stop right there," he says, pointing the weapon at Case.

Case raises his hands, saying, "Like Holden said, let's go outside and see if we can work this out."

"Don't you see, Mr. Country Music Star," he says, sarcasm underlining every word, "I've already got it worked out. Eye for an eye and all that. If I don't get my dream, then it seems right that I cancel a few others on my way out. Am I the only one that makes sense to?"

Beck reaches out and grabs his dad, pulling him back to where we're standing. "Get out of here, man! The police will be here any second."

The sirens scream like they're right outside the tent now. Car doors slam. I hear the sound of running. I step out from behind Holden and scream, "Go! Just go! End this now!"

Jared Ryner has a look on his face that I've never seen on the face of another human being. He's not leaving this world alone. His eyes say it as clearly as if I have heard him speak the words.

It happens so fast there's no time to say anything else, to move, or to run. He lifts the gun, fires, and Thomas slumps forward, then drops to the ground. I hear myself screaming, a wail I don't even recognize.

Another shot, and Case goes down, falling backwards into the people standing behind us. The next shot takes Beck. He staggers and slumps to the ground next to his dad.

It is surreal now. None of this can be happening. I feel the bullet enter my body with the realization that I have been hit, only I have no idea where. My body is instantly infused with white-hot pain, and I drop to my knees. I hear a roar of fury, and realize that it has come from Holden. He is charging the guy, but the gun is lifting and I know what is coming. I hear my scream as if I am a million miles from it. I feel the earth tremble with my fury as Holden stops with the bullet's impact. He stands for a moment, sways and then collapses.

Police are rushing into the tent, an entire force of them. Panic has taken over, and the screaming I now hear is not my own. I try to get up, lifting myself on one elbow. My face is wet, and I'm not sure if it's with tears or blood.

I see the policeman body tackle the shooter, taking him down, down, down, but not in time to prevent Jared Ryner from putting the gun to his temple and pulling the trigger.

♪

Book Four

THE NASHVILLE SERIES
BOOK FOUR

pleasure
in the
rain

RITA® AWARD WINNING AUTHOR

INGLATH
COOPER

*

Nashville – Book Four – Pleasure in the Rain

Inglath Cooper

✳

————————————————————————

Hunky musicians Holden Ashford and Thomas Franklin rescue Nashville bound CeCe MacKenzie and her Walker Hound Hank Junior from the side of the road when her car catches on fire. A less determined girl might have let her dreams go up in smoke as well, but not CeCe. She's been singing all her life, and she just wants a chance to do the thing she loves in a place where music is part of the fabric of life. As it turns out, Holden and Thomas want the same thing, and it isn't long before they're all chasing after the dream together.

Falling in love hasn't figured in to CeCe's plans, but the moment she sets eyes on Holden, her heart is asking why not? Holden is drawn to her as well, but he already has someone in his life, Sarah who still lives in Atlanta, Sarah who loves him. Who he thought he loved back until CeCe makes him realize he hadn't really known that love could turn him inside out.

But an unexpected visit from Sarah brings to light a terrible truth and Holden is faced with a choice between doing the right thing or permanently defining himself as a guy he never thought he would be.

It is only in letting each other go that both Holden and CeCe will come to understand that in life and love, the part that's real is what we feel.

Holden

I can't wrap my brain around the pain in my left side.

I can't think beyond it. Speak beyond it. Feel beyond it. It's as if my entire body is on fire with it.

I don't know if I am actually drowning in it or suspended above it, looking down at myself, connected only by this tether of savage pain.

I decide I must be above it because I can see the blood pooled on the ground next to me. Bright red soaking into the white of my shirt.

I hear the noise of sirens and screaming and crying. I just can't see where any of it is coming from. I only see me. I know this can't be right. I feel this indescribable pull toward awareness of what else I am missing. It's like I'm at the edges of a dream, but not able to push myself up from the ether of sleep.

I try. Even though there is an enormous weight on my brain, pressing down on the very spot that controls my ability to wake up.

I'm not sure how long it takes. Seconds. Hours. Maybe days. I push against it until I begin to surface. Up, up, up. Breaking through the wall suppressing me.

Then it rushes in. All of it. The screams. The cries. The sirens. Around me, I see people. Some bleeding like me. Standing, bent over, falling.

I feel something on my chest then. Manage to direct my gaze downward and realize that it's an arm.

Thomas's arm. Football player bicep and shoulder unmistakable. He's bleeding, too, his blood spilling onto my chest.

I want to raise up and see how bad it is. But I can't. I can only look from the corner of my eye. My heart starts to pound because something else is trying to press through.

I struggle to latch onto it. And then her name.

CeCe.

Oh, dear God.

Where is CeCe?

I will myself to get up. But my brain and my body are somehow not connected. I can do nothing but lie here, flat, with Thomas's arm draped across me.

I start to pray. Pieces of verses float up from the place where they have been stored in my heart so long that I had forgotten they were there. They're delivered on the voice of a Sunday school teacher who had told our class to memorize such scripture because there would come a day when we might need to call on its comfort. I realize now I doubted the truth of what she'd said. And I had been wrong.

I hear footsteps, heavy booted feet running at me. Two EMTs in rescue worker-clothing dropping down beside me. One directing his attention to me, the other to Thomas.

Their hands are quick and adept, checking my pulse, shining a light into my eyes. I try to form the question, and it takes me several seconds to force it out.

"CeCe? My-"

"Hey, man, don't try to talk. We're gonna get you out of here, okay?"

"I need. . .to know where. . . she is."

"You need to let us take care of you, son. Right now that's the only thing that matters."

"It's not," I say. Tears start to slide from the corners of my eyes. I see her face as she had looked. . .had it just been this morning? I swear I think I can feel her touch on my skin.

I have to find her.

But my protests to the EMT come out jumbled, and I'm not sure whether I'm speaking them or thinking them. I can't see through the tears that won't stop. I feel helpless. And I just pray. Every word a plea that if a life has to be taken here tonight, it will be mine and not hers.

♪

CeCe

When I was a little girl, Mama used to tell me about the bomb shelter drills they had when she was in elementary school. I would listen with a kind of half-disbelief. I don't think I really believed then that anything that bad could ever actually happen.

A bomb dropping on a school full of children?

The world, in my mind at that age, couldn't be that terrible a place. That kind of thing was limited to scary books and movies that I never had any desire to see because I couldn't understand why anybody actually wanted to feel fear. Or for that matter, wanted to cause someone else to feel fear.

I see his eyes in my mind now, the look that had been there right before he pulled the trigger. I know that fear is exactly what he wanted me to feel. Wanted everyone in the room to feel.

My heart pounds against the wall of my chest, and the force of it fills my ears with a pressure so intense I think my temples might explode beneath it. This is all I can feel. I have no idea whether I am alive or dead or dreaming or awake.

I try to scream, but no sound comes up from within me. I'm trapped in this bubble of semi-awareness.

I was the only one, wasn't I?

No, that's not right. There's something else. Something more.

More shots. There had been more shots.

Holden. Thomas.

This time, the scream breaks through, piercing my own ears with its wail. The protective bubble of denial surrounding me shatters beneath its jagged edges.

And now, I'm crying. With terror. With grief. I'm not sure which one will tear me apart first.

I feel hands on me, a woman's voice attempting to offer comfort. "Shh, honey," she says. "Hold on. Everything is going to be okay."

A needle pierces my arm, and in what seems like an instant, a soft blanket folds in around me, my vision seeping to nothing more than a pinpoint of light until blackness envelops even that.

And my crying stops.

♪

I RECOGNIZE THE smell, but I can't place it. It is clipped to a memory that nudges at me without effect.

My eyes are closed. I can't make myself open them. They are weighted with something too heavy for me to push aside. I hear voices, one abrupt and authoritative.

"Has anyone found an ID for her yet?" the voice asks. "She looks like she's probably over eighteen, but we need to know next of kin."

My brain processes the words with foggy edges. And then the source of the smell comes to me. My granny's long stay in the hospital.

Hospital.

I'm in a hospital.

And next of kin. Why do they need to find my next of kin?

"Blood pressure's dropping." This voice belongs to a woman, and she sounds worried.

"What's taking so long with the blood?" It's the man's voice again.

I hear and feel the snipping of scissors simultaneously and realize my clothes are being cut from my body. Heavy footsteps retreat from the room at a quick urgent pace.

The woman's voice, lower this time. "I guess nothing should really be a surprise in this world anymore. But can you imagine? They were just shot down like-"

"I know," another woman says, and I can tell she's on the other side of me. I feel her take my hand and lace her fingers through mine. "My brother was at the concert. He called a few minutes ago to ask if we were getting the victims. He's sixteen, and he couldn't stop crying."

"It's insane," the other woman says. "Case Phillips. I've been in love with him since I was sixteen. It sounds like he might not make it." Her words break at the edges.

"Don't you just feel fury at how senseless these things are? These people never did anything to deserve this, and one person destroying so many lives."

They're silent for a moment. "I don't understand," one of them says.

"There is no understanding. It's just hate, and a person feeling like they've been cheated. I know I shouldn't say it, but at least he's dead."

The heavy footsteps return, the pace conveying urgency. I hear motions around me but feel nothing. The women are no longer talking.

The man says, "They're waiting for her in the O.R. Let's get her up there stat."

I try to make words come out of my mouth. To ask where the others are. Holden. Thomas. Beck. But the fog again descends. And I am gone.

♪

Holden

I'm in a field. The grass is the color of a spring pasture in Kentucky, a deep, almost blue-green. It picks up the hue of the cloudless sky above. I'm walking with purpose as if I know exactly where I'm going, but there's nothing visible ahead except for the same rich grass reaching toward the horizon. I have no idea how long I walk, but it's effortless. I'm aware that I'm watching myself and at the same time walking. Searching, but not with any kind of urgency, just a peaceful sort of expectation.

And then I see her, so far away that at first I think it might be my imagination. I walk faster. Closer now, I know that I'm right. I realize that the distance must be farther than I initially thought because it seems to take a very long time for the gap to begin to close between us. My legs feel heavy beneath the desire to run. It feels like I'm fighting gravity with every step, pushing through some unidentifiable force that I can't see but know is there.

I feel infused with love for her. It's as if my entire being was created with the intent that this love would be my life source. We're close enough now that I can see its reflection in her eyes. I realize with a wash of happiness that she has been created in exactly the same way.

The distance between us dissolves, and we walk into each other's arms. It's as if I have just completed a lifelong journey to a point where I was supposed to be all along.

We don't say anything. We don't need to. She rests her cheek against my chest, and I feel the exhaustion leave her. I am her safe haven, and like a boat that's been chased to shore by waves that should have overcome it, she anchors herself to me.

I vow that I will never let her know the threat of harm again.

She tilts her head back and looks up at me. We drink each other in. We can't get enough of each other. I lean down and kiss her, aware in a way I have no explanation for that we won't be apart again; that this is permanent, forever, the way it should be when you love someone with every cell, every breath and every thought.

I have no memory of what came before, of how we got here or why. I only know it's where we both belong and that it's time for us to continue toward the horizon.

I pull back and look down at her, my hand anchored through her long hair. She smiles at me, entwines her hand with mine, and we start to walk through the vast field, purposeful, peaceful. I don't feel the passage of time, just this deep sense of contentment and rightness.

But then CeCe stops. I instantly feel the change in her and the peacefulness dissipates in an instant. She looks at me, her gaze regretful and pain-filled.

"What is it?" I ask.

"We have to go back."

"Why? We're already here."

"We can't leave him," she says. "He'll need us."

I know suddenly that she means Thomas.

As soon as his name enters my thoughts, I'm flooded with the same fear I see in CeCe's face. Selfishly, I want to tell her she's wrong, that we have to stay. It's too late. But I can't because somehow I know she's right.

I look down at our joined hands and feel the separation even as I will it not to happen. I'm torn between begging her not to go and an undeniable certainty that I have to go back as well.

In the very next instant, I feel as if a knife has been plunged through the middle of my heart. I'm in a room where everything appears to be made with stainless steel. I am on a bed of some sort. There are people all around me. They have on masks, and their hair is covered with light blue caps.

I hear a clink, like silverware dropping into a tin bowl.

"Good boy." A man's voice. "You're back. That was way too close, son."

I struggle to make sense of the statement and wonder if he's even talking to me.

"All right," the voice says. "We got him. Let's not lose him again."

I try to open my eyes to see who has said this, but they are too heavy, and I am too tired.

When oblivion returns, there is no blue-green pasture, and there is no CeCe.

♪

CeCe

"CeCe. CeCe. Honey, can you hear me?"

The voice is somewhere above me. I try to lift myself toward it. The voice is Mama's, tears attached to each word. I know how much she needs me to answer her.

I want to. Focus as hard as I can to push a response from my brain to my lips.

She continues to call. I try to respond. I have no idea how long it takes, but I finally manage to separate my eyelids just far enough that a slit of light seeps in. I try to open them wider. I can't describe how hard it is, like trying to swim upward through thick mud. It pulls at me, the suction nearly too powerful to resist.

But Mama keeps calling, and I keep trying to get to the surface, until finally I manage to open my eyes wide enough to see her. She's standing directly over me, looking down into my face, her light blue eyes tear-filled.

"That's it, honey," she says. "Come on back to us."

Her voice breaks. I stare up at her, trying to find words. Her tears trigger my own. They slide down my face. I can taste the salt on my lips.

Mama wipes them away with a tissue, paying no attention to her own. She sits down on the side of the bed, leans in closer and slides her arms up under me, pulling me up from the mattress to hug me hard. I feel her sobs, even though they are silent.

"I'm... sorry... Mama," I say, forcing the words out bit by bit, alarmed by how much energy it takes to voice them.

"Oh, baby, you have nothing to be sorry for. I'm just so thankful that you're–" She breaks off there, unable to finish, her crying eclipsing whatever else she had intended to say.

She holds me there against her for a long string of minutes, reluctant to let me go. But she finally eases me back against the pillow, pushing my hair away from my face in the same way she had when I was a little girl.

"You're going to be okay, honey. It's just going to take some time."

It's only then that I think to wonder what is wrong with me. I glance down at myself, see nothing unusual at first other than the thin hospital gown. I pat my chest and then my midsection and feel the bandages there.

"You were shot," Mama explains, "in the abdomen."

I feel the heavy tape wrapped around my torso and try to shift my body beneath it. Instantly, a pain stabs through me. I wince.

"Don't try to do anymore," Mama says.

The fog thickening my ability to think presses in on me, and I struggle to remember what it is that I need to know. It's important, I know this much. I start to get frustrated, because the thought is at the tip of my reach, but I can't quite get to it.

"Your friends," Mama says, her voice ragged at the edges. "That's what you want to know, I'm sure."

Full awareness hits me then. It feels like running into a concrete wall. I am so filled with dread waiting for her response that I cannot make myself speak. I watch her struggle with the words, my heart pounding heavily against the wall of my chest.

"I know it's not what you need to hear right now, but I can't lie to you, baby. Holden, Thomas and Mr. Phillips, they're still in critical condition."

Even as I process this, I let myself feel a ray of hope. They aren't dead. They are alive. Thank God, they are alive.

There's something else though. I struggle to wrap my thoughts around it. The look on Mama's face tells me there's more, and then I remember she hasn't said anything about Beck.

Her face crumples the moment she realizes I've noticed. Tears run down her cheeks, and she shakes her head a little saying, "I'm so sorry, honey. Your friend Beck, Mr. Phillips's son, he didn't make it."

I hear what she says, except I'm detached from the words, as if I am again unconscious and have no way of knowing whether it is part of a terrible dream or, in truth, reality. I shake my head and manage to utter, "No. That can't be. No."

Mama takes my hand between the two of hers and squeezes it hard. "I'm so sorry."

She starts to cry again then. I can't look at her tears. Grief is an avalanche inside me. One move will trigger its release. I know in this moment I will never be able to survive its onslaught. I turn my head on the pillow and stare out the window of the hospital room. The sky is bright blue, the sun happy with its job today. I wonder how that can be, why the sky isn't grey and the sun hidden from view?

Beck is gone. I can't process it, can't make sense of the three words clanging through my brain. It can't be right. He's only nineteen years old.

Maybe there's been a mistake? Mama could have gotten it wrong. He's probably in critical condition, the same as Holden and Thomas and Case. I don't even realize that I'm shaking until Mama presses her hand against my face and says "CeCe, are you all right?"

I can't answer her, my teeth are chattering so hard that I bite my tongue.

Mama pushes the nurse button, calling out in a panicky voice, "Could someone help us, please? Can you come now?"

It seems like only a blink before a nurse appears at the side of the bed. She takes one look at me. "Poor baby," she says.

I'm not aware of her leaving until she returns. I feel the needle pierce my right arm. In a moment or two, oblivion rolls in from the edges of my grief, obliterating its rawness until it is a pinpoint at the center of me. I try to hang onto it, but it slips through my fingers. I drop straight down into nothingness.

♪

CeCe

The funeral takes place at the First Baptist Church in Nashville on an early winter day that will set temperature records at a high of seventy-six degrees.

It's been twelve days since the shooting. I have gone against my doctor's orders in attending. Even so, I'm surprised by my own weakness and grateful for Mama's hand at my elbow as we walk through the doors.

I still don't feel connected to myself, my perception and awareness of what is going on around me almost separate from my physical self. Maybe it's just the pain medicine that I can't do without.

Mama thinks it's my body's natural protection mechanism, my brain only allowing me to process what I can currently handle taking in. I guess I would have to agree with her, because I'm not capable of processing very much at all. Life still seems unreal, like something that could only have happened in a nightmare, and certainly this current piece of it.

My gaze falls across the casket at the front of the church, the large framed picture of Beck playing guitar sitting on an easel next to it.

The sanctuary is full, every pew filled with people shoulder-to-shoulder. There are a few seats left in the back. I let Mama lead me to the closest one. We sit down, me with the carefulness of someone four times my age. I notice then the piano and the song being played.

The music isn't mournful. It's one of Beck's favorites, upbeat country, the kind of song he liked to drive to with the top down on his car.

Some of Case's band members walk to the front, pick up guitars, and start to play along. It's the music Beck would want. I know that, but it's not successful at lessening the aura of tragedy lying thick and heavy over the sanctuary.

I don't allow myself to look around, even though I feel gazes stray to me and snag in recognition. I don't belong, and hurting Beck as I had is something I will forever wish I could take back.

Maybe I should have asked Case for permission to come today. He would have every right not to want me here. I didn't ask because I was afraid he would say no, and honestly, I'm not sure if my need to be here is more for Beck or for myself.

I can't seem to make sense of any of it, to begin accepting that it really happened. But the finality of that casket and the soft weeping going on around me make it an undeniable fact.

The weight of acceptance begins to settle into me, pushing down on my chest. I try to draw in air, shallow scoops of it, but it doesn't seem to reach my lungs. I'm suddenly lightheaded, as if I'm going to pass out.

Mama takes my hand and laces her fingers through mine, squeezing gently. "Just close your eyes for a moment, honey. Take a deep breath."

I do as she says because I'm desperate not to make a scene here where attention will be drawn to me.

John, Case's drummer, walks down the center aisle and stops at the edge of the pew where Mama and I are sitting. He leans in and says in a low voice, "Case would like for y'all to come up front and sit with him if you would?"

I'm so surprised by the invitation that I panic a little, realizing I'll have to face Case for the first time since the shooting. But just as quickly comes the awareness that I can't say no.

Mama nods at me, stands, still holding my hand, and we follow John to the front where Case is sitting on the left side of the pew.

He looks up at me, and we both start to cry at the same time. He stands on shaky legs and hugs me hard. We cling to each other like shipwreck survivors to a lone flotation device. I can feel that we are actually clinging to the same things. Awareness of what has been lost, how it was taken, and complete bewilderment as to the fact we're still here. I can feel his brokenness, too, as if his bones are only temporarily holding his body together.

Next to him, Lauren stands, kisses me on the cheek and helps Case back into his seat. He moves carefully, barely hiding his physical pain.

Mama and I sit down on the pew. I blink back an encroaching wave of dizziness, willing it away even as I wonder if I will inevitably succumb to it.

A white-haired man in a dark navy suit walks to the podium at the front. His face is heavy with the sorrow he makes no attempt to hide.

"Good morning," he says. "I can't pretend, dear friends, that I am anything other than heartbroken today. As are all of you, I know. I've known Beckley Phillips since the day he was born. His daddy, Case," he nods in Case's direction, "called me at five-thirty one morning to tell me Beck had made his entrance into this world. Case asked if I would come to the hospital then to meet the little fella. It wasn't so much that he was so proud of his new son that he wanted to show him off, although there was that."

This comment brings a slight smile to his face. "Case wanted me to pray with him over his new baby boy, to ask for God's protection for Beck as well as wisdom for Case in knowing how to guide him through this often tangled and complicated world."

He takes a visible moment to wrestle with his own emotions, before going on with, "And we did pray that morning, both of us. I expect there will be some of you today who wonder if God ever heard that prayer. As a fellow member of the human race, I understand why you would ask that question. Tragedy does this, you see, throws into question, throws into doubt everything we believe, every bit of faith we have for our purpose here and God's love for us. I bet most of you could easily imagine Case coming to me with those questions over the past few days. But it might surprise you to know that I went to Case with those questions. I'm the one who asked him if he believes that God heard our prayers nineteen years ago, on the day Beckley Phillips was born. I'd like to tell you now what he said to me. And I have his permission to do so."

People shift in their seats. The pastor looks down and takes another moment to collect himself before he goes on.

"Case said that because we've never seen what is beyond this world, we mourn the loss of a young life taken too soon. Or at least what we can determine to be too soon. But Case believes, you see, that one day, we'll understand that the leaving from this world was a cause for celebration and joy for the person who has gone on ahead of us. That we've actually had it wrong all along, and if there's anyone to feel sorry for, it would be for ourselves and those left behind. Because, you see, that's where the true cause for mourning lies, in the fact that we no longer have the presence of someone we loved so dearly in our lives. And until our day comes to depart this world, we have to live with that. If you believe as Case believes, it would be selfish to wish our loved ones back here but understandably human to look forward to the day when we will see them again."

He pauses then, looks down at the podium in front of him, his struggle for composure clear. Behind me, I hear soft sobbing.

"This morning, dear friends," he goes on, "I am with Case in the hope that when God is done with me here on this earth, I will see Beckley Phillips once again in a place far better than this."

The pastor tips his head at Case and steps down from the podium.

Case stands, visibly weak, and walks to the chair placed next to the casket. John brings his guitar to him and, with gentle kindness, helps place the strap over his shoulder. He hands him a pick and then goes back to his seat to sit down.

Case doesn't look up. I somehow know that if he does, he will never make it through this. He keeps his eyes on the guitar strings, his voice low and emotion-filled when he says, "Beck started playing this guitar at five years old. It was nearly bigger than he was then, but he was determined to master it, and he did. This was his favorite hymn, and if y'all don't mind, I'd like to sing it to him today."

He strums the chords to *Just as I Am*, the words coming out a little unsteady at first, building courage as he goes on. And by the time he reaches the chorus, it's as if he's singing to Beck and Beck alone, no one else in the room, a father to a son he will miss until the day he dies.

Tears fall down my cheeks.

I don't wipe them away.

♪

Holden

I hear the voices calling my name. I'm at the end of a long tunnel. Ahead, far, far ahead, I see a pinpoint of light.

I start toward it, but just as I do, the light moves away. I feel a weight press into my chest, like a concrete wall that has settled just above my rib cage. I realize the wall is frustration, me reaching out to the voices, trying to tell them I'm here, just behind the light. I can't get close enough to make them hear me.

Now I hear CeCe crying. A soft broken sound that rips my heart in half. I need to get to her. I feel like I will choke on my own urgency, her torment coursing through me like the blood in my veins.

I struggle to get out from beneath the wall, but it's useless. I'm too weak, my voice not loud enough to project that far. It's like drowning, looking up to see the surface so close above you and yet not able to push yourself up high enough to break through.

I don't have the strength left to fight the descent.

♪

CeCe

The graveside service is simple and final. The sun smiles brightly at the crowd of people huddled together on a Tennessee hillside.

The cemetery is a private family spot on Case's two hundred fifty acre farm. It's enclosed with white board fencing and an enormous oak stands at the center of the spot. It has to be at least a century old. I'm grateful for the canopy of shade it drapes across us.

Mama is holding onto my elbow. For a moment, I wish I had taken her advice and let her get the wheelchair she'd rented for me out of the trunk of the car.

The pastor's words here are brief and heartfelt. Case is sitting on the front row of chairs, bent over with his elbows on his knees, his shoulders visibly shaking with grief.

There is no music here, just the soft whistle of wind through the nearby trees. A cow lows for its calf in the distance. Other than that, silence.

Family members stand and drop flower petals across the top of the casket, each person filing out of the tent until only Case is left. I notice that Lauren isn't here with him. I don't know what to make of that.

Case lifts his head, his gaze locked on the petal-strewn casket, tears streaming silently down his face. He stands then, using a cane to right himself.

Next to me, Mama draws in a quick breath that sounds more like a sob. I'm afraid to look at her because I can barely contain my own sorrow.

Case reaches down to scoop a handful of petals from the pot next to the coffin. He gently scatters them in among the others. They fall like silent rain.

I see his shoulders droop, and he starts to drop back onto the chair. Mama moves so quickly that it takes me a moment to realize she's right there beside him, helping him to sit without falling.

"It's okay," she says. "Just lean on me."

He looks at her then, and the grief in his eyes is more than any human being could possibly know how to bear.

Tears stream from Mama's eyes as well, and she takes his hand and clasps it between her own like a rudder righting a ship on an ocean's staggering waves of sorrow.

♪

I DON'T WANT TO go to the gathering at the house.

The thought of food still makes me feel sick, but even more, I can't imagine winding my way through all of the guests who will be there. Forcing a smile to my face, a polite note to my voice. I can't imagine smiling again or that the furnace of anger melting my very core can ever be snuffed out.

But Mama thinks I will regret it if I don't go in. And since I'm too exhausted to put up much of a fight, I let her get the wheelchair out of the car. I sit down in it to the hope that it will lessen the number of times I actually have to meet eyes with the other people here today.

I see Nelda, the Phillips's housekeeper standing at the entrance to the kitchen, her black dress formal in a way I've never seen her. She glances up, and as soon as her gaze falls across me, I hear the sob erupt from her chest.

She walks over to me, drops onto her knees and puts her arms around me. Her shoulders shake with the effort of trying to hold back the despair intent on breaking free from her. And I'm crying so hard that I can't catch my breath. I feel like such an imposter here. All of these people loved Beck.

I cared for him, but I hurt him. If I could take back those last moments between us, if I could just reach through time and change the ending. . .

I can't. And that is something I will have to live with.

I wonder if Nelda knows we had broken up. Would she be hugging me this way if she did?

"I am so sorry for what happened," she says. "To all of you. It is so very wrong. . .such a waste."

I nod, biting my lip.

"How are you?" she asks, brushing her hand across my cheek.

"I'm okay," I say. But I'm not a good liar. I can see she doesn't believe me.

"I have taken good care of your Hank Junior and Miss Patsy."

"Thank you so much, Nelda. I've missed them."

Case appears in the hallway, John at his elbow. "CeCe," he says, "could I speak to you and your Mama for a moment?"

I'm surprised by the question, my stomach doing a jolt of dread. I nod. Nelda gets to her feet and strokes her hand across my hair. "If you need anything, sweetie, anything at all."

"Thank you, Nelda," I say.

"Nelda, why don't you get Hank Junior for her? And Patsy, too. We'll be in here," he says, nodding at the open door of the closest room.

She says of course and walks toward the stairs at the end of the hall. Mama pushes my wheelchair into the room. John helps Case to a nearby chair.

"Call if you need me, Case," he says and leaves, closing the door behind him.

My mind is doing a kaleidoscope of possible reasons for why Case would want to see us. I can't blame him if he's angry with me. I think in a way I'd almost welcome it.

He rubs the palms of his hands against the knees of his pants and looks at me with his sorrow-filled eyes. "I hardly know what to say to you, CeCe," he begins.

I brace myself for what is to come. I deserve every word of it.

Mama squeezes my shoulder as if she knows what I'm feeling.

"I'm so sorry, CeCe," Case says.

I glance quickly up at his face, shaking my head in confusion. "For what?" I ask, the words barely audible.

"For everything. For the horror of what happened there that night. I've tried so many times to imagine what could have been done to prevent it."

"Case," I say, "you're not to blame."

"Not directly, I know," he says. "But you learn pretty early on in this business that there's resentment and sometimes envy, I guess."

"If anyone is to blame, it's me," I say, looking down at my hands. "There's something I need to tell you." I struggle to put my words in some kind of logical order. "The guy. Jared. He was at one of the shows earlier in the tour. Kind of harassing me. But Holden was there and basically put a stop to it. And I don't know," I say, starting to cry, "I should have told someone else what happened. If I had, maybe none of this-"

"CeCe," Case says, raising a hand to stop me. "And what would the charge against him have been if you had reported him that first time? Probably nothing, and he would have done what he planned to do anyway. That's the truth of it, hard as it is for any of us to accept. Almost for sure, there's nothing that we could have done." He stops there and looks off out the window.

From here, we can see the top of the tall broad oak tree sheltering Beck's gravesite.

"I just wish," he finally says, "that it had been me."

"Oh, Case," Mama says, quickly and urgently as if she can't stop herself from objecting. "You can't wish that."

He looks at her then. Really looks at her. They hold each other's gaze for a long moment before she adds, "Your son wouldn't want that."

"He wouldn't, but I do."

I have to tell him now. I can't keep it inside me any longer. I need for him to know. I fully expect him to hate me. "There's something I need to tell you, Case," I say.

"What is it, honey?" he asks in his kind Southern voice. I wonder if that voice will ever again be free of the ragged edges of grief.

The words stick in my throat. I force them out one by one. "I. . .I broke up with Beck before the shooting."

I sense his gaze on me, but I can't make myself meet his eyes. I feel too awful, too horrible, and so I sit looking at my hands and waiting for him to rain down whatever ridicule I deserve.

"Aw, honey," he says.

I jerk my gaze to his at the note of compassion in his voice. "I know about that."

"You do?"

"CeCe. . .y'all are. . . .you are so young. And so was Beck," he says, his name breaking off at the end. "Don't let yourself feel guilty about things not working out between you. You and my son spent a lot of good time together. I think you made him want to live for some things that maybe he hadn't been living for. You don't need to waste any of your sadness worrying about me being angry at you for that."

I bite my lower lip, trying to prevent the sob about to erupt from my throat. It does no good. I bend over with my arms anchored at my waist as a fresh wave of unbearable sadness flattens me.

My crying is not silent. I can't make it so. I want it to stop, but it won't.

Mama kneels down and wraps her arm around my shoulder, murmuring soothing words that I only wish could comfort.

Just then something warm and wet licks the side of my face. It's my boy. Hank Junior.

He puts his head on my lap and whines a broken-hearted whine that tells me he's had no idea where I've been or why I left him. His whole body shakes down to the tip of his tail. I lean over and hug him as tightly as I can, saying in his ear, "I will never leave you again." And I mean it.

I hear the familiar plodding little footsteps and open my eyes to see Patsy wedge her way in next to Hank Junior. She wags her tail, looking up at me with her soft brown eyes. I can see she, too, has wondered where we've been. I reach out and rub her chin with the back of my hand, telling her how much I've missed them both.

Holden's face comes to me so clearly then. I suddenly feel ashamed for not having the courage to go in and see him before leaving the hospital. I haven't allowed myself to think of him, focusing only on getting through the trip home, the service today. I couldn't face more than that, all of it like a mountain looming in front of me that I somehow had to find a way to climb.

But now, with Patsy in front of me, I let a little of my fear for Holden and Thomas in. It forms a crater in my stomach. I start to slip at its edges, barely able to prevent myself from tumbling in headfirst.

Mama reaches out and takes my hand, squeezing it hard. "We'll go back as soon as you're a little stronger," she says, reading my thoughts.

I don't know why I'm still surprised at her ability to know what I'm thinking. I nod once, not trusting myself to speak.

Mama looks at Case and says, "Thank you so much for taking care of these two. Letting them stay during the tour."

"They were good company for Nelda."

"Thank you, Case," I say.

"You're welcome, honey."

"We should probably go," Mama says. I barely recognize the note in her voice when she says to Case, "I hope you'll take good care of yourself."

He nods once, but I'm not convinced, and neither is Mama.

"Your son would want you, too," she adds.

This registers with Case, and he gives her a deep, assessing look that doesn't bother to hide his raw grief.

Mama walks over to him and puts her arms around him, hugging him with utter compassion. When she pulls back, I see the confusion in his face, and the moment when it fades to simple gratitude.

She wheels me to the door. "Just a moment," I say, and she stops.

I look back at Case. "If you need us. . .for anything."

He nods once.

We leave the room then. I wonder how he will ever survive the days ahead of him.

♪

AT THE FRONT of the house, Mama waits for a kind-eyed man to open the front door before she rolls my chair out onto the walkway. I'm protesting that I'm okay to walk to the car when I hear a familiar voice say my name.

I glance up. Macey Canterwood stares at me with naked accusation. She's wearing a black dress that might as well have couture stamped across the front. Her hair is pulled back in a severe ponytail, accentuating the anger in her expression.

"I'm surprised you'd have the nerve to come here today," she says.

"Hello, Macey," I say.

"But then if ex-girlfriends weren't invited, I don't guess I would be here either, would I?"

"We should go," Mama starts. I raise a hand to stop her. I think some part of me wants it all out in the open, the fact that I had hurt Beck.

"The only difference being, of course," Macey goes on, "that my exit from his life wasn't voluntary. And if you hadn't stepped into the picture, we might have gotten back together the way I had hoped we would."

Tears well in my eyes, but I forbid them to fall. "I'm sorry."

"Yeah, well, that hardly does any good now, does it?"

The last word breaks on a sob, and I feel sorry for her. It's clear that she really did care about Beck.

"It's time for us to go," Mama says, wheeling me down the brick walkway.

"I have my own regrets to live with," Macey calls out behind us. "But I'd sure hate to have to live with yours."

♪

ON THE DRIVE into Nashville, I sit in the back seat with Hank Junior. Patsy is up front in the passenger seat next to Mama.

Hank has his chin planted so firmly on my lap that I don't think he ever intends to move it just in case I decide to leave him again.

"He really missed you," Mama says, glancing at me in the rear view mirror.

"I missed him, too," I say, rubbing his soft ears.

Patsy whines, and Mama reaches over to give her head a reassuring pat.

We drive on in silence for a few minutes. I watch the Tennessee countryside rolling by outside my window, my thoughts stuck in neutral. I don't want to think about the past. I can't think about the future.

"You can't dwell on anything that girl said, honey," Mama says, her voice soft and compassionate. "She's just lashing out in anger at a loss she didn't expect."

"But she's right," I say in little more than a whisper.

"About which part?" Mama asks in a way that tells me she's prepared to reason this out with me.

"That I'll have to live with doing something like that to him right before—"

"CeCe. You didn't plan any of this. You're not to blame for what that man did there that night."

"I know." And I do. My logical mind accepts this. But as for hurting Beck? I am to blame for that.

"I just wish I could take it back," I say, not even sure I've spoken the words out loud.

"But what would that really mean? Don't you think you owed him honesty?"

I nod once, looking down at Hank. He's staring up at me with his liquid brown eyes. I lean over and kiss the top of his head. "Why can't love be as simple as my love for Hank?"

"The love between a man and a woman is never simple," she says. "It can be wonderful but never simple."

I'd like to deny it, but I can't.

We've just reached the city limits when Mama says, "If I've learned anything in my life, honey, it's that we shouldn't put ourselves in the position of having something to regret. If there's something we need to act on, then we should. Otherwise, we're going to have to live with the results of not doing so somewhere down the line."

"I know what you're doing, Mama." I stare out the window to avoid meeting her gaze in the mirror.

"I'm trying to say the things you need to hear."

"And make me feel better. I don't want to feel better."

"Because you think you should punish yourself?"

"Maybe."

"And what would be the point of that?"

I don't have a logical answer, so I continue staring out the window.

"All any of us can do is what's right when we have the opportunity to do so."

I look up then, meet her knowing gaze. "What do you mean?"

"Thomas and Holden. That you didn't go see them before we left the hospital."

I feel a physical pain at the sound of their names. "I wasn't up to-"

"I know," she says, kindness in her voice. "But you are leaving yourself open to another cause for regret if you don't go see them."

I try then to let myself think about the fact that either one of them, or both of them, could have died. An immediate black wall erects itself at the end of that thought, and I can't get past it. Life without Holden and Thomas? That is an unimaginable place.

But then I think about Beck, and that is unimaginable as well.

It feels as if everything that has happened is still sitting on the surface of my comprehension, none of it really having seeped in yet. It's like an enormous rainstorm that falls on sunbaked ground, the soil so dry and hard-packed that the water cannot penetrate. Instead, it begins to stream in whatever direction allows it to flow, flooding anything in its path. I guess that's where I am right now. Drowning in everything I'm trying to process.

I put my mind back in its neutral place, not looking back and not looking forward. For now, this is all I can manage.

♪

THE CLOCK ON MY nightstand blares 3:12 A.M. The minute slot flips to three, and it's now 3:13 A.M. It seems as if I've watched every minute change since I went to bed several hours ago.

Now that I've let them in, my thoughts refuse to move beyond fear for Holden and Thomas. I want to know how they are. I need to know how they are, but I am terrified to ask. What if the answer is something I'm not prepared to hear?

Hank shifts beside me, his back pressed up against my left side, his head resting on the pillow beside mine. He's snoring softly. Patsy is curled up in a ball at the foot of the bed, her snores even louder than his.

I wrestle with my fears for another hour before reaching for my phone on the nightstand. I don't let myself consider what time it is, not even daybreak yet. I just need to take advantage of this moment where I've worked up the courage to call him.

I tap the phone symbol on my screen. It rings twice before a woman answers the phone, her voice groggy and a little surprised. "Hello?"

"Hi. I hope I'm not calling at a bad time," I say. "This is CeCe MacKenzie, Thomas's friend."

"Oh, CeCe. Of course, dear. This is Thomas's mother, Ophelia."

"Mrs. Franklin, I'm so sorry to be calling at this hour."

"No, no," she says. "Thomas has been so concerned about you."

"How is he?" I ask.

"He's out of the ICU. We're so happy about that."

"Thank goodness."

"Yes. Would you like to speak with him?"

"I shouldn't wake him up."

"Let me," Mrs. Franklin says. "I know it will do him good."

I wait, hearing her say his name softly from the other end of the phone and feeling ridiculous that I called in the middle of the night when I could have waited or better yet already called before now.

I consider hanging up, but what kind of cowardly thing would that be to do? I hear a rustling sound and then, "CeCe?"

His voice is hoarse and a little disbelieving.

"Hey, Thomas," I say. "How are you?"

He coughs once and says, "I reckon I've been better, but I'm still here. Are you okay?"

"Yes. I'm all right."

"Where are you?"

"I'm back home. In Nashville."

"In Nashville?" He sounds confused. I can hear the pain medication in his voice.

"I'll be back in a few minutes, honey," I hear Mrs. Franklin say.

"Okay, Mom," he says.

We're both quiet for a moment. He speaks first. "Mom hasn't been willing to tell me too much since I started coming back around. She said Holden is still unconscious. Have you seen him?"

"No. I. . .I haven't."

He draws in a deep breath which I can hear through the phone. "What about the others?" he asks.

"Case is pretty messed up, but they say he'll be okay with time."

"The band? Beck?"

I can't answer for several moments during which my heart pounds in my ears. "I. . .he didn't make it, Thomas."

"What?" The question is barely audible.

"That's why I came back to Nashville. To go to the funeral."

"No," Thomas says. "That can't possibly be."

"They said he'd lost too much blood," I say softly. "He died before they could get him to the hospital that night." My voice breaks on the last word. A sob spills from me. I am suddenly crying full out as if I have not actually stopped since the last time this grief hit me.

"But he's just nineteen years old." And then Thomas is crying, too. It overwhelms him the same way it has me. "This isn't right," he says, the words broken and raw. "This isn't right."

"No," I say. "It's not."

♪

Holden

I recognize the voice.

I know the voice is talking to me, but I can't place who it belongs to.

"How long exactly are you planning on staying in this bed? And how many days am I gonna have to wheel this chair up to your room and ask you the same questions? Dying is not optional, so wake the heck up, Holden. You die, and I will personally kick your butt all the way to Heaven. By the time you get there, you'll wish you'd never checked out of this hard as a board hospital bed."

The name that goes with the voice surfaces then. Thomas. I try to open my eyes, but they feel so heavy. It's tempting to give in again, as I have the other times I felt the pull toward coming fully awake.

He's still talking when I finally manage to push my lids open far enough to see him. He's sitting in a chair at the side of the bed. He's probably lost twenty pounds.

"You're wearing pajamas," I say, my voice low and hoarse.

Thomas jerks his gaze from the window, staring at me as if he's sure he'd imagined my speaking. He shakes his head and then, "Beats the heck out of that sissy nightgown you're wearin'. Wait 'til you get up and go to the bathroom. I've decided the budget cuts around here must not have included fabric for the backside."

I feel myself start to smile, but then I remember why I'm here, why he's here. Everything comes crashing in, and my smile dissolves. My thoughts freeze altogether because I don't know which one to let in first.

Thomas reaches over and takes my hand, "You made it, buddy. I sure am glad."

We look at each other for several long moments. I see him processing what I'm processing. Tears start to leak from the corners of his eyes. He wipes them away. "For a while there you had me thinking you weren't going to."

I've never seen Thomas come even close to crying, and the sight of it shakes me. "What day is it?" I ask.

"Today's Friday. You've been this way for two weeks."

At first I can't make sense of that. "Like what?" I ask.

"In a coma. They couldn't tell us if you were ever going to wake up."

I raise a hand to the bandages on my chest. My thoughts don't seem to be in any particular order. I try to place what happened to put me here, to put Thomas here, but it's just out of reach.

"You don't remember, do you?" Thomas says.

"I'm not sure."

"Maybe I oughta let the doctors talk to you first." Thomas rolls the chair toward the door of the room. "They've been waiting for you to wake up. I'll be right back, okay?"

"Thomas, wait," I call out, my throat parched and dry.

But he's gone, and I try to force my thoughts into some kind of order, but they're slippery and hard to grasp.

He wheels back in, a pretty woman in a white coat right behind him. She stops at the side of the bed, looking at me with a pleased smile.

"You're back," she says. "We're so happy to see it. How do you feel?"

I touch my temples. "Fairly bad headache," I say.

"That's to be expected."

"What. . .why am I here?"

"Do you remember anything about what happened?" she asks, her voice soft.

I grapple for the answer, but it remains just out of reach.

"There was a shooting," she says. "You were shot. I'll be honest, you're very lucky to be here at all."

I glance at Thomas and see that he agrees with her. I notice his bandages again, and it occurs to me that I haven't asked what happened to him.

"Were you shot, too?"

"Yeah," he says.

"Where were we?"

"It was after the concert at Case's party."

"Just you and me?" I ask.

Thomas is silent for a moment and then shakes his head.

"Who else?"

The doctor takes a step back and says, "I'll let you two talk for a couple of minutes. I'll be back with the other doctors involved in your care. We'd like to check you out, okay?"

I nod and say thank you, before looking back at Thomas, waiting for him to answer.

"Case and Beck," he says quietly.

"Are they okay?"

"Case should be all right."

I wait for him to include Beck in the statement, but he doesn't.

"What about Beck?"

Thomas glances out the window, his grip on the arms of the wheelchair tightening until his knuckles are white.

"He didn't make it, Holden."

I try hard to process what he just said, but it won't compute. How could that be? It doesn't make any sense. Beck, dead? No sooner have the words made their way through my consciousness than her name races in right behind them. "CeCe." I say, fear instantly flooding through me.

"She's okay," he says.

The relief hits me so hard that I go weak beneath its weight. I want to ask him where she is, why she's not here. I can't. My head is pounding. I close my eyes tight to block out the pain.

I don't even realize I'm crying until I look at Thomas's face and see that he is as well.

"It's gonna be all right, man," he says, putting his hand on my shoulder and squeezing hard.

I hear the raw edges in his voice, and I know that he's not sure whether there's any truth at all to what he has just said.

♪

CeCe

For the next five days, I don't get out of bed except when Mama runs me a hot bath at night and insists that I get in.

She waits in my room just outside the bathroom door as if she's afraid I might do something unexpected. Fall or maybe hurt myself intentionally. She brings me food on a tray at regularly spaced intervals, refusing to let me get away with not eating at least something that's on the plate.

But I have no desire to eat. All I want is to sleep.

Sleep is the only thing that lets me block out all the stuff I don't want to think about. Can't bring myself to think about. The dull ache in my left shoulder that never ceases its throbbing. The image of Case at Beck's graveside, a man broken as I have never before seen one broken.

But the one looming thing that prevents me from getting out of bed is terror.

It feels as if my bones have been infused with it. Even the thought of leaving this apartment makes my heart start to race in my chest.

I feel the adrenaline surge of fear light through me like flame to gasoline.

There's this new awareness in me now that I've never felt. Before the shooting, I had read about, heard about catastrophic things happening to other people. But that was to other people. Those tragedies didn't happen in my own life. Or to anyone I loved.

You always hear people say how life can change in an instant. Go from safe and secure to something not even recognizable as the world you've been living in.

In my dreams, I see Jared's eyes and the cold blankness of them. He's become a machine that does not recognize or process human emotion. He's pointing the gun at me. I watch him pull the trigger with a total lack of ability to stop him. I feel myself falling over and over again, a movie loop on repeat. And every time I hit the ground, I hear the gunfire in another direction, knowing I'm not the only one going down. Holden. Thomas. Beck. Case.

When I'm awake, I find myself thinking of things I've only seen in the news. The Twin Towers and the moment it became clear they were going to fall.

At the time it happened, Mama hadn't let me watch footage of it on TV. She said those weren't images a little girl should have in her head. When I was older in high school, I read a book called *Tower Stories*. I wanted to learn exactly what had happened that day.

The book described the regular, normal lives of some of the people who were in the buildings. How they'd gone to work the way they always did and within minutes of getting there, found themselves facing something beyond the worst nightmare anyone could even begin to imagine.

A plane crashing into a building. Fire and smoke everywhere. Desperate, resigned people jumping from the skyscraper to certain death below. A fate they saw as preferable to burning alive.

And then there were those who missed the train that morning. Woke up sick. For whatever reason, varied from their typical day of going to work in those buildings.

They had been spared.

They must wonder why.

Like I wonder why I've been spared. Why Beck was taken and not me.

The people who made it out of the building or who didn't arrive there at all that day. How did they see their lives from that point on? How could they ever look at it the same? How can I?

I have no idea how to answer this question.

In order to do so, I will have to look beyond where I am right now. Locked in my apartment, refusing to face anything outside that door.

I honestly don't know whether I can do that or not.

♪

I'VE LOST TRACK of the number of days since I left my bedroom. The afternoon sun is streaming through the slats in my blinds when I hear a knock at the door. The knob turns before I respond with, "Come in."

I open my eyes. Thomas stands in the doorway, leaning heavily on the cane in his right hand.

"Hey," he says, "I hear you like it so much in here you've decided you're never going to leave."

For a second, I freeze at the sight of him. But then everything inside me begins to melt. The tears I haven't cried in so many days are suddenly there again, pouring from me because I'm so grateful to see him. His eyes tell me he's struggling with all the same things I'm struggling with.

He hobbles to the side of the bed and kind of collapses next to me, dropping the cane onto the floor. Hank Junior is stretched out at the foot of the bed. He raises his head, thumps his tail hard once at Thomas and then returns to his nap.

Thomas and I study each other for several moments. He reaches out, slides his arms under mine and lifts me up against him, hugging me with such love and relief that I just melt into him, needing to absorb his quiet strength. And then I realize that we're both crying, silent shaking sobs that reveal the grief still so raw and real.

"Hell and back, right?" he says against my ear.

"I don't think I've made it to the back quite yet," I say, my cheek pressed against his chest.

He leans away, looking down at me with fierce determination in his eyes. "We'll get there, all of us, because there is one thing for damn sure."

"What's that?" I ask softly.

He pushes my hair away from my face and says, "Bad guys don't win for good."

♪

Holden

I've been in the hospital for almost five weeks.

Time has pretty much stopped having any kind of meaning here. The hospital is alive around the clock, so that there's no true finite line between day and night.

Sarah came to see me the day after I woke up from the coma. She sat by the side of the bed, held my hand and cried for me. We talked for a long time, about her life and the guy she had just agreed to marry. I felt happy for her, really happy because she deserves someone who will love her the way I should have loved her.

My dad has been here at the hospital most of the time. I have to admit, this surprised me. I can't remember another time in my life when he's been away from his work for this long. Everything that's happened has changed him in ways neither one of us would ever have expected.

Lying here in this room, I've had a lot of time to think. Too much time. One of the things I've wondered most about is why it so often seems to take a catastrophic event for us humans to see things as they really are. As for my dad, it's as if a bomb went off and blew aside most of the things he's placed importance on all my life. What's left, he sees clearly for the first time, and his guilt is like a visible noose around his neck. I don't want him to feel guilty though. If I've realized anything in these past weeks, it's how little time there is in this life for regret.

I'm being released today. Dad offered to rent a car and drive me back to Nashville. But I told him Thomas wanted to pick me up. I think we were both a little relieved at this. To spend that many hours trying to find things to talk about sounds exhausting to me right now. With Thomas, I know I won't have to talk just to fill up the silence.

Dad's flight isn't until the afternoon, and so he waits with me in my room for Thomas to arrive.

A nurse helps me get dressed, and I'm sitting on the edge of the bed waiting when Thomas appears in the doorway.

"Hey," he says. "'Bout time you got out of bed."

"'Bout time you got here. You bring the mule and wagon or something?"

Thomas smiles and shakes his head. "She's not as fast as she used to be."

My dad stands to shake Thomas's hand. "How you doing, son?" he asks.

"A lot better, sir, thank you."

"You look good."

"I can't complain." Thomas looks at me and says, "How're you doing?"

"Ready to leave this place."

The nurse walks back in and says, "Everything's taken care of. This is your ride, I assume?"

"Yes, ma'am," I say.

"All right, then. We're going to miss you around here."

"I think I've outstayed my welcome and then some."

"Never. But I know you'll be glad to get back to regular life."

I nod even as I wonder if there will ever again be such a thing.

"I'll be wheeling you down to the front entrance of the hospital," she says and then directing at Thomas, "Would you like to meet us there, young man?"

"Sure," he says. "I'll take the shortcut to the parking garage and meet you down there. Nice to see you, Mr. Ashford. You have a safe trip back to Atlanta."

"Thank you for coming, Thomas. I appreciate it."

"Sure thing," he says.

Dad doesn't bother to hide the worry in his eyes. "You'll be all right, son?"

"Yeah," I say, "Thank you for being here. For everything."

He reaches out and shakes my hand, squeezes my shoulder. "We'll be talking, okay?"

I nod and watch him leave the room. I believe we really will.

♪

I'M WAITING AT THE front entrance with the nurse who's doing her best to assure me that someday not too far from now all of this will just be a bad dream. I don't know how to tell her I can't imagine that day ever coming, so I simply nod and try for a smile. Thomas drives toward us from the far end of the parking lot. It's not until he's rounding the curve under the hospital portico that I see who's in the front seat with him. Her name slams into my chest like a train into something unfortunate enough to be caught in the middle of the tracks. It literally knocks the wind from me. I have to remind myself to breathe deep and even.

"Are you all right?" the nurse asks, noticing.

"Yeah," I say, "I'm fine."

CeCe is staring straight ahead, not yet having let her gaze fall across me. I, on the other hand, cannot take my eyes off her. Her face alone tells me she's lost a significant amount of weight. Her eyes have that hollowed out look beneath, like someone who isn't able to sleep.

Thomas stops the truck, leaves the engine running, gets out and walks around. I try to stand, but feel the weakness in my knees when they refuse to do as I am trying to make them do.

"Whoa there, cowboy," Thomas says, taking my elbow and helping me regain my balance.

"Thanks," I say, even as I hate my own weakness.

Thomas opens the passenger door. CeCe slides to the middle. He helps me in. I thank the nurse.

"You take good care now, you hear?" she says.

I nod and close the door.

As soon as it shuts, I breathe in the subtle scent of CeCe, some kind of clean, minty shampoo that makes me remember pressing my face into her hair and drawing in the smell I associate only with her.

We're both looking straight ahead, keeping our shoulders tilted just enough that we don't touch. I feel the change in her, the wall that might as well be positioned in between us right now. I know the reasons for it. I can imagine every single one she has thought about and blamed herself for and felt guilty over, and I get it.

I've felt so much guilt myself over Beck and what had happened. I knew to expect these changes in her. Thomas warned me, but even if he hadn't, the fact that we haven't spoken once since that nightmare night tells me everything I need to know. She's shut me out and, knowing CeCe as I do, I doubt that she'll ever let me back in.

♪

WE'RE A FEW MILES down the highway when Thomas looks over and says, "So how long are you two planning on ignoring each other?"

I glance across at him, more an excuse to capture CeCe in my line of vision than to actually acknowledge what he's said, but nonetheless I'm compelled to answer.

"How are you, CeCe?" I ask. My voice doesn't even sound like my voice. My question has the neutrality of someone who is fairly indifferent to the answer, and that couldn't be further from the truth.

"I'm okay," she says, not directly meeting my eyes. "How are you?"

"Better," I say, although I instantly ask myself, as compared to what?

She looks down at her hands and says, "I'm sorry I haven't–"

"It's okay." I cut her off because I don't think I want to hear her try to rationalize her unwillingness to speak to me or see me since all of this happened.

I already know the why. For her to say it will only prove that I've been right all along, that what happened between us that last day in D.C. might as well never have happened. All of its meaning, all of its hopefulness and rightness disappeared that night beneath the flood waters of another human being's hatred.

"Since you two obviously aren't going to get past initial pleasantries," Thomas says, breaking the silence, "here's how I see it. We're never gonna be the same, none of us. All three of us probably should have died that night. We didn't, and I don't know why. I don't reckon there's anybody on earth other than Case and the folks who were there that night who understands what that lunatic permanently did to us. If we've ever needed each other, I suspect we're going to even more now. So if we're not the same, then I'm thinking we oughta be something even better. That's my plan anyway. I need you both to realize that I'm here for you, just like you'll be there for me. And I hope you're going to be there for each other."

He looks out the window for a second. I somehow know none of this has been easy for him to say.

"We've been given a chance to write a new chapter. I'm not going to give that asshole the satisfaction of taking anything beyond what he's already taken. Ya'll in or what?"

I turn my head, meet eyes with Thomas. He's everything I could ever imagine a brother being. I realize how lucky I am to have him as my best friend. I nod once. It's only then that I let myself look full on at CeCe. Her face is wet with tears, and I'm nearly bent double with the desire to pull her into my arms and give her the comfort she needs.

I'm going to have to wait for her to ask me. That day may never come. There's no way to know. But unlike the last time the three of us sat in this truck headed west to the city of our dreams, we have a few more knowns in front of us. And, like Thomas said, we've got each other. Regardless of what else lies ahead of us, that's something. Really something.

♪

CeCe

Holden's arrival in Nashville unleashes a storm of media interest in the three of us. Mama had told me over these past weeks about the coverage on Beck's death and its devastating effect on Case. I hadn't read any of it, knowing that every word would be like a refresh button to renew the pain bouncing around inside me.

But the morning after we get back from D.C., the knocks at our door start before seven o'clock. I hear Thomas mutter his way down the hall, open the front door and then shut it again to a string of disbelieving cuss words. No sooner has he slammed the door than my cell phone rings. I pick it up from the nightstand, glancing at the number. It's Rhys, Case's manager. I consider not answering it, but then a pang of fear for Case and that something might have happened to him, makes me.

"CeCe," Rhys says, "sorry to be calling so early. How are you?"

"I'm all right," I say.

"Look, I'll just be up front. Case is mad as fire about this, but the phones have been ringing off the hook over at the label with requests for interviews with you guys. And now that Holden is back in Nashville, I'd like y'all to do a few."

"What?" I ask, not sure I heard him correctly.

"Interviews," he says, his voice not without compassion. "About what happened."

"But that's impossible," I say.

"I know it's a lot to ask," he says. "But the label is taking the stance that this event happened while you were on tour and fans want a glimpse of it from your point of view."

The words release an instant balloon of anger inside me. For several moments, I cannot speak past it.

"Rhys, I don't want to talk about it in public, and I'm pretty sure that Thomas and Holden don't either."

Silence takes up the space between us until he says, "Here are the cold hard facts, CeCe." His voice is low and regretful. "There's a clause in the contract you signed that says you understand that media interviews are a part of promoting the tour as well as your band and that you agree to support the experience with media exposure."

I remember skimming through the clause and not thinking any more of it than what it appeared at face value, willingness to help promote it through normal channels of media exposure.

"But this is different," I say, outrage bubbling up. "This is using something horrible to profit, and I don't want any part of that."

"I know that's what it feels like, CeCe, and from your point of view, I understand. From theirs, the tour was an investment, and this is just a continuation of that."

"What does Case say?"

"He said to tell you to do it, CeCe. The label has already checked everything out with their legal guys. They have the right to request this of you. You don't want to take that on."

"So you're telling me that we have to go outside and talk to these people who are currently banging on our door?"

"No," he says. "That you ignore. If we need to send over security, we will. The interviews will be arranged and the label will decide which networks get you first."

"Get us first," I repeat.

"I'm sorry," Rhys says, taking a deep breath. "I didn't mean it like that, CeCe, it's early for me, too. I know this is awful. It's not what any of us would ask of you, but my advice is just to get it over with so you can all move on."

"And if we decline?"

"Then I'm afraid you're going to have a lawsuit on your hands. A very big one."

♪

THE NEXT MORNING at five-thirty a.m. a car service picks the three of us up to drive us to the first of the four interviews we will be doing to live up to our contractual obligations.

We don't talk during the ride there, we don't even meet eyes, and for the next few hours we simply operate on autopilot, answering the questions that are asked of us. Making predictions about how this will affect us in the future. Agreeing about the extent of the tragedy. And the interviewers are sympathetic. I realize they're just doing their job, but even so, when it's all said and done, and we're back in the car headed home, I feel as if I have been pried open and autopsied alive.

♪

Holden

The next few months pass in a blur of days spent trying to write and nights in a battle with sleep that mostly won't come.

Like the media clause in the contract with the label, we had also agreed to produce a record following the tour should the label deem it a successful enough venture to warrant one.

We drag our feet to delay going into the studios and work on a record that none of us wants to make.

We use the excuse that we're working on new material, but for eight weeks, I don't write a single word. I sit with my guitar perched on my knee and my pad and pencil on the stool beside me. Not one word comes during the whole of that time. I don't feel any sense of frustration about it, just an emptiness where the well of creativity inside me used to be. I have no idea if this will ever change or if it's gone for good.

It's been weeks since Thomas last asked me how it's going. I'm sitting on the sofa one afternoon, Hank Junior and Patsy napping next to me when Thomas walks in the room and drops into the chair across from us.

"Got anything you want to play me?" he asks.

"Not yet," I say.

"The label gave us three months to recover," he says. "Their words, not mine. How are we going to go into the studio in a couple of weeks if we don't have any material?"

"I don't know."

"We could look at songs from other writers," Thomas says. "That would take some of the pressure off."

I glance at him, concern evident in his eyes. "Is that what you want to do?"

"No, but you shouldn't be forced to write until you're ready to write."

I stand my guitar against the arm of the couch, drop my head back, running my hands over my face. Patsy scoots over and puts her chin on my leg. I rub her ears saying, "Man, I don't know why I can't. I want to."

"The fact that you can't means you're not ready to."

"So he gets to take that away from me, too?" I say angrily.

Thomas starts to say something, looks off and then back at me. "She's going to forgive herself at some point."

He doesn't need to say her name for me to know he's talking about CeCe. "I don't think so. We live in the same place, but we're basically strangers passing each other in the hallway without meeting eyes. Most of the time she's not even here."

"She's been doing a ton of demos," Thomas says. "I think anything to fill the hours between when she gets up and when it's time to go to bed. She's also going out to check on Case a few times a week."

"How's he doing?" I ask.

"Sounds like he might be drinking again."

I hate to hear that. I do. It's not a secret that alcohol once had a pretty grim hold on Case when he first started to make it in the music business.

"You know what I see?" Thomas says.

"What?"

"We're all just treading water, keeping our head above the surface to get through to the next day. And you know what that means?" I say nothing, but he goes on anyway. "It means he wins. It means that he pulled off exactly what he set out to do. Pulling everybody else down into the lake of misery he'd been swimming around in, feeling sorry for himself about all the crap the world had thrown at him."

Thomas's eyes flicker fire. I look away from it.

"That just really pisses me off. I don't think we should hand that to him on a silver plate tied up in a big red bow. But we pretty much are, all three of us, and Case, obviously. Don't get me wrong, I can't even imagine the extent of his grief, and I know he must blame himself. He almost took our lives that night. Almost. Should we just go on and concede defeat? I know you, Holden, and everything that's happened is going to give you something big to say. You just have to let yourself believe that's okay."

I want to argue with him, tell him he's wrong, but the thing about Thomas is, he has a way of seeing through to the truth of things, even when it's hard to say and especially when it's hard to hear.

I pick up the guitar, put it across my lap, pick out a few chords. "You got any ideas?" I ask without looking at him.

"Yeah, as a matter of fact I do. It's something I said to CeCe when I first got back from the hospital. Might make a good hook."

"What is it?"

"Bad guys don't win for good."

I think about the words, pluck at the guitar for a couple of minutes and then offer, "Go stand where we once stood."

Thomas raises an eyebrow and nods, "Yeah?"

I sound out a rhythm for the words, test out some chords. Another phrase comes to me, "Fill the fears."

Thomas immediately says, "Cry the tears."

And that's what we do for the next three hours. Try a line, cast it aside; try another and decide it's a keeper. By that evening we have a song. Thomas sings it like it's a song that needs to be heard. I guess maybe it is.

I remember it's true what they say about music; it consoles, it heals. And by the time we've recorded a rough demo on my laptop, I can actually feel its beginnings in me.

♪

CeCe

Three weeks later

It's after eleven when I let myself in the apartment door. I hear Hank Junior hop off the couch even as I'm turning the key in the lock. He's there to greet me, tail wagging hard.

"Hey." I keep my voice low in an effort not to wake up Holden and Thomas if they've already gone to bed. "Shh, come on boy." I pat my leg for him to follow me to the kitchen.

But I stop short at the sight of Holden sitting in a living room chair.

"Hi," I say, startled.

"Hey," he says. "How'd the demo session go?"

I shrug. "Long, but good songs. I think I'll head on to bed. I'm pretty tired."

"Could we talk for a minute, CeCe?"

My stomach drops with the question. It's been months since we've talked alone, been alone. "Now's not a good time, Holden."

He looks up at me, anger flashing across his face. "When will it be a good time, CeCe? You don't look at me, much less talk to me. I know you have your reasons, and I'm not questioning them. We've each had to do what we had to do to get through this. Cutting you out of my life wouldn't have been my method, but it's yours, so I'm respecting that. I guess I'm wondering though how we're going to pull off the first recording session for the album tomorrow."

I shake my head and keep my expression neutral. "We just each do our thing," I say.

"It doesn't work that way," he disagrees. "Our practice sessions over the last couple of weeks don't sound anything like we used to sound. Why go into the studio if we don't sound like we're all part of the same whole?"

I drop my backpack onto the floor, its contents making a harsh jangling sound. "Are we?" I ask.

"Are we what?"

"Part of the same whole."

"Can I be honest here?" he asks, frustration clouding his face.

I nod once, biting my lip, knowing somehow that I need to hear what he's about to say, but I don't want to.

"I think Thomas and I are on the same page, CeCe, part of the same whole. It's pretty clear that you're not. Is this something you still want to do? Make music with us?"

It's a fair question. I can't deny it. And one I haven't let myself exactly face these past months. I walk over to the couch and sink down onto the cushions.

"What do you want me to say, Holden?" I hear the edge of anger in my voice. It's unfair, but it's there, and as much as I try to deny it, it won't go away. Some days I wonder if it will actually swallow me whole.

He looks at me for a long time before he finally says, "Do you really think the two of us loving each other caused what happened that night?"

The question is threaded together with hurt. I've been so consumed with everything going on in my own head that I've given little to no thought to what Holden must be thinking or feeling. The selfishness of this startles me now. It's not the way I once thought of myself, as someone capable of this, but then I'm not sure I'm the same person I was before the shooting. I don't know if I will ever be that person again.

"I don't think we caused it," I say carefully. "But everything I said to you, everything I felt for you. . .now it just feels. . .tainted."

Holden visibly flinches, my words like a physical slap to his face. I'd like to take them back just to spare him the hurt, but it's taken months to get to this point of truthfulness. It would be cowardly for me to back away now.

"That's not what I was expecting you to say," he says.

"What were you expecting?"

He shakes his head. "That you need time. That there's still a chance for us."

"I don't even know who I am anymore." I look down at my hands. "I wake up every morning and tell myself it's okay for me to be here, but is it? Is it really? And what should I do to be deserving of it? It feels like my life is just this big field of land mines, and I'm trying to figure out how to weave my way through without stepping on one, without causing a blast that's going to blow up everything around me."

"I know," Holden says softly. "I don't think we're supposed to live that way though."

"A lot of things aren't supposed to happen." I hear the anger in my words. "But they do. I feel like I was so naïve before, making my plans, following my heart, like it was all going to end up in some pink bow happily ever after. We were part of that, but there is no happily ever after."

Holden leans forward, elbows on his knees. "There's good in this world, CeCe, and there's bad. What we saw that night was the very worst part of a human being, one who's given in to hatred and envy and resentment. Somebody who's let all of that take the place of hope and forgiveness. I guess that's pretty much what any of us can be reduced to if we let the punches life throws out take us down for good. But somehow we have to find a way to get back up again, to duck the next swing, and even if we take another one on the chin, keep standing, keep fighting."

I don't even realize I'm crying until Holden gets up and walks over to the chair where I'm sitting. He takes my hand and laces his fingers through mine. Even though I don't want it to, it feels like a lifeline. The first I've felt since that nightmare night.

My grip tightens into his of its own accord. He stares into my eyes, making no pretense of hiding what he's feeling: sorrow, regret, yearning and sympathy. I make an effort to hide what I'm feeling, to keep from my own eyes all of those same emotions.

I see that I've failed when he stands up, and without letting go of my hand, pulls me up in front of him. He says my name the way I've heard him say it in my dreams all these months that we've been apart. A song I associate only with my feelings for him. I let it play through me, feeling every note deep in the center of my heart.

I try my hardest to keep the wall around me in place. But when it starts to crumble, there's absolutely nothing I can do to stop its fall. I guess he knows it's happening even as I do because he's right there to catch me. I all but collapse into him, a soft cry of defeat slipping from my throat. Holden gathers me up and into him, as if I am some rare, precious find that he thought lost to him forever.

He strokes my hair with one hand and says, "Shh, baby, don't cry."

I don't know how to stop. It seems as if this is all I do when I'm alone. It's only in staying busy, putting myself in a room of people involved in normal everyday things like recording demos that I function in a way that even remotely resembles normal.

It feels so good though to stop pretending, stop trying to act like I'm on the road to putting it all behind me because here in Holden's arms I realize how far from that I am. I want to melt into him, lose myself in the comfort I feel here.

He leans back, brushes his hand across my cheek. I look up at him and, although the light in the room is dim at best, I see that his love for me still exists. It's there in his eyes like the shine of a star I thought too far away to actually see.

"CeCe," he says, "I've missed you so much."

"I've missed you, too," I say, and with the release of the words, I feel the impact of their truth and how utterly lonely I've felt. Even though we've been living in the same apartment, we might as well have been hundreds of miles apart. That's no one's fault but my own.

He runs his hand through my hair and anchors it at the back of my neck, his thumb making a soft circle of comfort. "What can I do?" he asks. "How can I help?"

I shake my head. "How do I answer that when I don't even know what's wrong with me? I get up every day thinking this will be the day when I'm my old self again, when I want to do the things I used to do, that maybe I'll actually laugh at something. And then it doesn't happen. I go to bed thinking okay, maybe tomorrow. I'll feel better tomorrow. Life will seem normal again tomorrow. But it never does."

"Maybe you're asking too much of yourself too soon," he says. "CeCe, we were all victims and, I don't know, I've done a little reading about things like this and ways to put it behind you to a point where it's okay to let yourself feel safe again."

"I don't feel safe," I say quickly. "And I don't think I ever will. Do you?" I add.

He looks off somewhere behind me, and it's several moments before he answers.

"I've been having some crazy dreams, stuff that doesn't really make sense once I wake up and try to figure out what it was all about. My heart is racing. I'm sweating as if I've just run ten miles. I guess that's my subconscious telling me that I haven't totally put it behind me, but maybe that's how my brain is trying to process it. I don't know."

"If Thomas is having trouble dealing with it," I say, "he won't admit as much to me."

"Each of us is different," Holden says. "People have to come to terms with things in different ways."

He slowly pulls me back to him and wraps me up in his arms again. I close my eyes and breathe in his scent. It feels so good to be held like this by him. I wish that we never had to move past this thought, this moment, that we could simply infuse each other with love and caring until we were both completely strong again, no nightmares, no panic attacks, no sadness.

When he pulls away to look down at me, I know he's going to kiss me. I want him to with every cell in my body. My need for him is as basic and elemental as the need for food, air, water.

I don't stop him, and his kiss has forgotten none of its hunger. It's a powerful thing, the knowledge that I have in me the ability to feed that hunger, but then he is the only one who can do the same for me. I will myself to shut off the nagging fear in my mind and simply become lost in everything Holden makes me feel. I just want to remember what this felt like when I didn't see it through the lens of guilt, and it was just so clear to me that we had been lucky enough to find something special in each other.

I loop my hands around his neck and take what he is giving. I undo the first three buttons of his shirt and slip my hands inside, just to feel the warmth of his skin. It seeps through my palms, up my arms and along my shoulders to drop down into the core of me.

"CeCe," he says. "Dear God, I have missed you so much."

"And I've missed you," I say.

He pulls my t-shirt from the back of my jeans and slides his hands around my waist. We kiss until I can't think for wanting him. He drops onto one knee and lifts the side of my shirt, his gaze finding the three-inch scar just above my belt. He stares at it and then leans in and presses his lips to it with gentle care. I clasp the back of his head with my hand and wonder why I haven't allowed myself the comfort only he can give me.

We stay like this for a long time, absorbing one another.

When he stands, he looks down into my eyes and rubs his thumb across my cheek. He leans in and kisses me as if I am priceless to him. I finish unbuttoning his shirt and start to slide it from his shoulders when Hank Junior whines, jumps down off the couch and trots to the door.

I start to pull away to see what has his attention, but Holden won't let me. He's kissing me again, and I'm lost to anything but following his lead.

"Now that's what I'm talkin' about."

I step back from Holden as if I have just been shocked by an electric current. He and I both stare at Thomas who is standing in the doorway with a girl under each arm, one blonde, one brunette, both in short tight skirts, one in stilettos and the other wearing cowboy boots.

"Looks like you finally got your act together," Thomas says, each of the words slurred at the end. The girl in the stilettos takes a wobbly step forward, pointing at me.

"You're CeCe MacKenzie. Oh my gosh, I love your voice." Her gaze sways to Holden with astonished recognition. "And you're Holden. I just read about you two in *Star Struck*." Her expression goes from delight to stricken sadness.

"It's so awful, what happened with you two. You had like this perfect love and then you," she says, looking at me, "being so broken up about Beck Philips that you blame yourself."

Holden steps in front of me, making a physical shield between the girl and me. I can't see her now but I hear her say, "Does this mean you two are back together? Oh my gosh, that's so cool! Misty, that means we witnessed it firsthand."

"Seriously, Thomas?" Holden says.

I step out from behind Holden just as Thomas reels the two girls back into his own unsteady embrace.

"You've been drinking," Holden says.

"Hey, I am legal, you know," Thomas says with an amused laugh. "Last time I checked, anyway."

"Well, you might be legal," Holden agrees, "but you're drunk."

"So?"

He stares hard at us both for a long moment. "You two think you're the only ones around here trying to figure out all this crap. Well you're not, and these two young ladies have graciously offered to make me feel better." He starts corralling them toward the hallway that leads to the bedroom. "And I've decided to let them."

Holden follows him, grabbing the back of Thomas's shirt. "Hold up there, buddy."

His response is as instantaneous as it is unexpected. He turns around swinging, his balled up fist connecting with the center of Holden's abdomen. I hear the air leave Holden's lungs in a single whoosh. Thomas staggers backwards, both girls falling away from him like drunken tinker toys.

"Damn, Holden. I didn't mean-" Thomas starts to apologize.

But Holden is a torpedo barreling toward him, head down. He connects with Thomas, shoulder to stomach, and they both go down in the hallway. I scream for them to stop while Thomas's Barbie dolls stare at the two of them fighting, like they've been given VIP seats at a prizefight.

I run at them, trying to wedge myself in between their shoulders, screaming for them to stop, but my efforts are all but laughable. They're rolling back and forth on the floor. Hank and Patsy, aroused from their sleep, are standing next to them, barking out fearful yelps.

"Stop it! You're going to kill each other!"

When it's clear that my words are having no effect, I run to the kitchen, grab a plastic pitcher from the counter and fill it with cold water. The tap is so slow I'm about to scream by the time it gets to the top. I head to the living room as fast as I can go without sloshing out all of the water and then aim the contents at their heads. The water has the desired effect. They roll apart, yelling.

"What the heck, CeCe?" Thomas throws out.

"You two acting like toddlers," I say. "That's what."

Holden and Thomas sit breathing hard and glaring at each other.

"Do I have to get another pitcher?"

"No!" they erupt in unison.

The Barbie dolls are giggling now. I actually hear one of them whisper, "Do you think we can sell this to *Star Struck*?"

"I got pictures on my phone," the other one says.

"Out!"

I don't even recognize my own voice, but I am charging the two like a mother lion protecting her cubs. They stare at me as if I have just hurled something at them in Greek, and they have no idea what I've said.

"Leave! Now. Go, out, and don't come back!"

Both girls right their miniskirts, looking immensely hurt. In another phase of my life, I would have felt guilty. In this current one, I merely feel justified. The one in stilettos yanks at the knob, saying over her shoulder in a pitiful voice, "But we don't have a car. How will we get home?"

"I'll call you a cab," I say. "Just wait out front."

"Well, all right then," she says, miffed. I slam the door behind them and then turn to look at Holden and Thomas, who are still sitting on the floor dragging air into their lungs. Patsy is licking Thomas's cheek. Hank Junior licks Holden's. I want to tell them not to waste their sympathy because any suffering Holden and Thomas are enduring, they fully deserve.

I walk in the kitchen and call a taxi, then go outside the apartment and stand at the railing until I see it pull up. I watch the two girls get inside. When I go back in, Holden and Thomas look a little less enraged at one another, their expressions mirroring something closer to shame when they both look up at me.

"CeCe," they both start at the same time.

But I stop them, holding up a hand and saying, "Y'all work it out, I'm going to bed. Come on, Hank." He gets up and trots after me. Patsy follows, too. I close the door behind us and turn the lock.

♪

Holden

Thomas drops onto the floor, one arm over his eyes. He groans and says, "Where'd you learn to punch like that, man?"

I lean back against the couch, wincing with the movement.

"Probably from you. You're the only friend I have who picks fights."

He removes his arm from his eyes and glares at me. "Me? You're the one who started it."

"So you think I should have just let you go on and have your drunken therapy session with those two-"

"Those two what?" Thomas interrupts.

"*Ladies* you would regret spending time with tomorrow," I say in an attempt at diplomacy.

"You're a jerk, you know that?" he says.

"Yeah, and if we hadn't brought you to your senses, they'd probably have a picture of you hanging naked from a light fixture in tomorrow evening's *Star Struck*."

"Maybe we could use it for the new album cover," he says with a sarcastic grin.

"Thanks, but I'll pass," I say.

We sit there, not saying anything until I finally ask, "So why'd you go out and get wasted tonight?"

Thomas shrugs. "I didn't plan it."

"Well, it's not your typical game plan."

"Nope."

"Is it about going in the studio tomorrow?"

He doesn't answer for a good bit, and when he does his voice is far off, like something he's been thinking about for a while.

"I don't know. I guess I'm wondering whether I bought my own 'we need to rise above this' speech."

"What do you mean?"

"Just whether we deserve for anything good to be happening to us."

"You want me to repeat what you said to me?"

"Hell, no."

"We can cancel it."

"Yeah, if we wanna get sued by the label."

"With everything that's happened, you really think they'd do that?" I ask.

"I really think they would," he says. "Money's money. We were an investment that hasn't paid off yet."

"We can make a crappy record, and they'd be kicking us off the label."

"We could, but what's that gonna prove other than we can suck if we want to?"

"Nothing," I say.

We're quiet for a bit, and then he asks, "Do you think we're wrong to do it?"

"I think right now it feels like we are, but I don't really think we can trust our perspective as evidenced by your choice in company tonight," I say with a half-smile.

"Speaking of company," Thomas says, "What the heck was that we walked in on?"

"I have no idea."

"She's a mess, isn't she?"

"Yeah," I agree.

"Do you think she'll go through with it tomorrow?"

I shake my head, "I really don't know. I think it could go either way."

"We've got good songs."

"You think?"

"I know."

"CeCe said anything to you about them?" I ask, hearing the uncertainty in my own question.

Thomas shakes his head. "Why?"

"She's just not owning them."

"Yeah," Thomas agrees.

"You sure the songs don't suck?"

"No, man. They rock," he says.

"Are we just wasting everybody's time by going in the studio tomorrow?"

"That," Thomas says, getting to his feet and swaying a little under the alcohol's remaining influence, "remains to be seen."

♪

THE NEXT MORNING, the three of us pile into Thomas's truck at just after eight. We're supposed to be at the studio at eight-thirty, and even though we're pushing our luck on time, Thomas insists on a Starbucks infusion. He maneuvers his big truck through the drive-through, and we each get a large coffee. Nobody opts for food, and I can only guess it's because we're all equally anxious about the morning ahead.

CeCe has yet to say a word to either of us other than an initial good morning. She sits in the middle of the seat between us, sipping at her coffee and looking straight ahead.

I fortify myself with a few sips as well before saying, "If we're not up for this today, I mean, if we're not ready for this, I think we should just go in there and tell them that."

Both CeCe and Thomas take so long to acknowledge that I've said anything, I start to wonder if they even heard me.

Driving with one hand, Thomas props his coffee cup on his knee, looking straight ahead. "Are we all ready for this?" he asks.

"You mean am I ready, right?" CeCe says, her voice low and void of emotion.

I consider not saying the truth, but it feels like the truth is pretty much the only hand we have left to play.

"You're punching the clock," I say quietly, "but your heart's not in it."

She draws in a deep breath, bites her lower lip and then breathes out again. "Is that what you think, Thomas?"

"Sorry, babe," Thomas says, "but yeah."

I stare out the window, forcing myself not to look at her. I hate hurting her. I know what we've said hurts. "You've never been about dialing it in, CeCe. That's not who you are. We need to go in there this morning and give it everything we've got. Do what they hired us to do. Or we don't go in at all. We go at it lukewarm, we're not doing anybody any favors. Not them, not us."

I feel her stiffen next to me, but then just as quickly, she sinks back against the seat, anger losing its foothold.

"You're right," she admits in a low voice. "I just don't know if I can do it."

"Do you want to do it?" Thomas asks softly.

We're on the interstate, tractor-trailers whizzing by on either side of us. We're approaching the exit when she says, "Yeah. Yeah, I guess I do."

"Then we've got your back," Thomas says. "Right, Holden?"

"Always," I say.

She nods once, biting her lower lip, and then saying, "What if I let you both down?"

"You won't." I reach for her hand and lace my fingers through hers.

She squeezes hard, as if I alone am the anchor that will keep her afloat today.

For the first time in months, it feels like we have a shot at life finding its way back to some kind of normal. It won't be the old normal. I know better, but a new normal that's yet to be defined.

Thomas hits the blinker, and we take the ramp that will get us over to Music Row.

CeCe glances at me. I let myself fully meet her gaze.

"The songs are good, Holden," she says. "They're really good."

And I wonder if she has any idea that a number one song wouldn't mean as much to me as hearing those words from her.

♪

CeCe

The launch party for the record takes place on the one-year anniversary of the shooting. Holden, Thomas and I all voiced our objections to the label. To me, it feels opportunistic and disrespectful, but their angle is a different one, and that's the one they chose to go with.

Good wins in the end. Bad guys get their due. And life goes on.

It's true that if there's a message in the music, this would be it, and although I want to believe it, I just don't know if I do.

A Hummer limo picks us up at six p.m. to drive us to an estate outside the city where the launch party is being held. It's the former home of one of country music's earliest stars, and we've been told it's an incredible place.

The label had actually sent an image consultant over earlier in the week to take us shopping for the clothes we would wear tonight and give us pointers on ways to polish – her word not mine – our appearances.

We're in the back of the limousine and on the way when Thomas says, "So this is us. Spit shine time."

"I guess," Holden says. He looks at me, and even in the dim light of the car, the color of his eyes deepens.

"You look beautiful, CeCe," he says.

"Yeah, you do," Thomas agrees.

"Thanks," I say, keeping my voice light and looking down at my hands. "You two look pretty great yourselves."

We're quiet for a couple of minutes while the car rolls on, sleek and plush beyond anything I could possibly feel deserving of.

"Anybody else feel like we're standing on the edge of a cliff about to jump off?" Thomas asks, breaking the silence.

"Yeah," Holden says. "I do."

"They're making some crazy predictions about this record," Thomas says.

"Isn't it all just guessing?" I ask.

"I agree," Holden says, "except that by now I think we know they don't do much investing in guesses."

"Well, with the album going live at midnight," Thomas says, "we'll know pretty soon whether they were right or wrong."

I glance out the window at the city's skyscrapers retreating into the distance.

"If y'all could go back," I say, "to the moment you started dreaming this dream of coming here and making it in music. Would you still go after it if you knew how the dream would end up coming true?"

The weight of the question settles around us.

"Probably not," Holden finally says in a low voice.

"No," Thomas echoes.

"Me, either. I guess we'll never know whether we would have made it to this point without the shooting and all the media stuff."

There's another question I want to ask. And that is this. If our dream is transformed into something other than what we had imagined, will it change us as well? A year from now, will we be the people we came here as?

But I keep this one to myself. I honestly don't know if I want to hear the answer.

♪

THE HOUSE IS enormous. Three stories high with wings that jut off to the right and left. Boxwoods that appear to be a hundred years old line the front like guards standing watch. Cars are parked on either side of the winding driveway, and a flutter of nerves erupts in my midsection.

"Incredible," I say, and I'm pretty certain in that moment I cannot go in that house and do what is expected of me.

As if he's felt my conclusion, Holden reaches over and presses his hand on mine. "They're just people," he says. "You've got this."

"I really don't know if I do or not."

"Yeah, you do." Thomas places his hand over my other hand. I feel unbelievably lucky to have them both in my life.

"How about I just stay between you two all night?" I ask.

"We can be a CeCe sandwich," Thomas says with the grin I have begun to see more of recently. I've missed it in these past months.

"Fine by me," Holden says, looking down at me without the usual censoring.

"Will your dad be here?" I ask, forcing myself to glance away.

"I think so," he says.

Thomas's mom stopped by the apartment earlier in the afternoon and showed us the dress she had bought to wear. She'd been so excited and proud, and I couldn't help but envy Thomas a little.

Mama won't be here tonight. She'd had a terrible sinus infection for the past ten days and didn't think she was strong enough yet to make the trip. She'd made me promise over the phone this morning that I would FaceTime her while at the party so she could see what it all looked like. I tried to hide my disappointment because I know how much she wanted to be here. Since the shooting, she's all but put her own life on hold, driving back and forth from home to Nashville to make sure I'm all right.

The driver eases the limo to a stop at the front of the house and walks around to open Holden's door.

We've arrived.

♪

AS A LITTLE GIRL, I had once visited the Biltmore Mansion in North Carolina with Mama. It's one of the most extraordinary places I've ever seen, and the inside of this house reminds me so much of it.

The foyer is huge, a winding staircase with shallow marble stairs leading up to the next floor. To the left is what looks like an enormous ballroom where at least a couple of hundred people are mingling, sipping drinks and some talking, others listening. An incredible speaker system streams music from what sounds like every direction and the song playing is one of ours from the new album. *Pleasure in the Rain.* It's strange to hear my voice filling the room.

"That's pretty dang cool," Thomas says as we walk into the main room.

Gazes begin to turn our way. A man with short cropped white hair and smart-looking eyeglasses starts toward us. I recognize him as the label President Henry Ogilvy. We've only met him once at the label's main office, but he's not the kind of man that you forget. Confident but gracious, he knows the music business and is said to be the force behind many of the names who have made it big over the past ten years in Nashville.

He walks up to the three of us, smiling his very white smile. He holds out both hands to me, forcing me to let go of Holden and Thomas. He leans in then and kisses me on both cheeks.

"Wow," he says. "If y'all don't make a picture. You look beautiful, CeCe. Good grief, America is gonna be so in love with all three of you pretty soon."

We each offer him a slightly disbelieving smile.

"Why don't we get you a drink?" He holds up a hand and beckons a waiter with a small wave. The waiter asks what we'd like. Holden and Thomas opt for a beer. I ask for a Perrier.

"Y'all get your sea legs," Mr. Ogilvy says. "Relax a little bit, and then I'd like to introduce you around if you don't mind."

"Of course." I nod as if mixing with this crowd is something we're used to when nothing could be further from the truth.

When he walks away, the three of us turn to face each other.

"How long do we have to stay?" I ask.

"I think the rule is if you leave before midnight you'll turn into a pumpkin," Holden says.

"Right now I think I'd rather be a pumpkin," I say.

We look at each other and a smile a small smile. It's a really nice moment.

From the corner of my eye, I see someone walking toward us. I turn my head. It's Mama and Aunt Vera with Case Philips. A mixture of relief and disbelief rush over me at the same time.

"Hi, honey," Mama says, reaching out to pull me into her arms. "I hope we haven't given you too much of a shock?"

I hug her hard and say, "No, it's wonderful."

Aunt Vera steps in and puts her arms around me, too. "We are so proud of you, honey."

I feel tears start to my eyes, and for the first time in a very long time, I realize they are tears of happiness. "I'm so glad you're here. But how did you-"

Case looks at me now with uncharacteristic uncertainty. "I flew over to Virginia this afternoon to pick these two pretty ladies up."

"You did?" I ask, still shocked.

"I knew this was something your mama wouldn't want to miss, so I offered to go get her."

"Oh, Case," I say, reaching out to give him a hug as well. "Thank you. How are you?"

"Doing better," he says. "I have to tell you, your mama here is one of the main reasons why."

I glance at Mama, aware that I'm not hiding my surprise very well. She and Aunt Vera both give Holden and Thomas a hug.

Case shakes their hands and says, "You three are making me very proud. I can say I knew a good thing when I saw it."

"Thank you, Case," Holden says. "We wouldn't be here if it weren't for you."

"Not true," Case says. "You're here because you've got some incredible talent, and the world's gonna want to hear it. Henry sent me a link to the new album. There's not a song on it that's not great. Y'all know how excited he is about you?"

I shake my head and try to say something in response, but nothing wants to come out of any significance, so I just murmur, "Thank you, Case." He gets the same from Holden and Thomas.

Case asks Holden about the guitar he played on the record, and the three of them are soon in deep conversation about things only guitar enthusiasts know about.

"I need to powder my nose," Aunt Vera says, heading off in search of the ladies' room.

Knowing her as I do, I'm sure she is trying to give Mama and me some time alone. I take her hand and say, "Want to get some fresh air?"

"Yes, of course," she says and follows me along the edge of the room to the open French doors that lead out onto a balcony. A wrought iron railing encloses the terrace. We stand looking out at an enormous field where horses graze in the moonlight.

"Are you angry with me, honey?" Mama asks.

"Why would I be angry with you?"

"I wanted to tell you that I was coming after all, but Case thought it would be a nice surprise."

I study her for a few moments. "Is there something you're not telling me about you two?"

Mama looks down at her hands and then back at me with a small smile on her mouth.

"I'm not sure I even believe it myself yet, but he's been coming to see me in Virginia."

"He has?" I ask, failing to hide my surprise.

"I know," she says. "It's crazy, isn't it? A man like that wanting to see me?"

"No," I say. "Of course it's not crazy."

"He just started calling me at night, and we would talk for hours sometimes. I guess he needed someone to talk to who might not judge him about how he was trying to manage his pain."

"I heard he might be drinking," I say because I can't help feeling suddenly protective of her.

"He was," Mama says.

"And he's not now?"

"No."

I shake my head, still a little stunned. "Mama, is this romantic?"

I don't know that I ever remember seeing my mama blush, but she's blushing now. And there's a light in her eyes that gives me the answer before she even says the words.

"Maybe. But honey, I'm not looking past today. I'm not even looking as far as tomorrow. For now, we're just enjoying each other's company, and that's all."

"In a romantic way," I tease.

Mama's cheeks light up again even as she says, "It's nice to hear a smile in your voice. And you look absolutely beautiful tonight."

"Thank you." I smooth a hand across the front of my dress. "You don't think it's too fancy for me?"

"I think it's perfect for you. Do you know how proud I am of you?" She reaches out to pull me to her, hugs me tight. "Promise me something."

"What?" I ask.

"That you'll let yourself enjoy this, that you won't feel guilty about it. You worked hard to get where you are. Anybody who knows you knows that."

"Thank you, Mama," I say, a crack in my voice.

"All right, then," she says, smoothing her hand across my hair. "I've monopolized you enough. You need to get back out there and enjoy your party."

"It wouldn't have been the same without you here. I'm so glad that Case came to get you."

"Me, too, honey. Me, too."

"The two of you. . .it's really nice."

Her answering smile makes me happy in a way I haven't felt in a long time.

♪

Holden

Thomas and I are standing in a circle, talking with some people who work at the label. Case walks up and steps into the group. He makes small talk with the ones he obviously knows, then looks at me, saying, "Have you got a minute, Holden?"

"Ah, sure," I say. Thomas raises an eyebrow at me. I have to admit I'm wondering what this is about.

Case leads the way. I follow him through the foyer and out the main door of the house. It's dark now, and the lights shining out from the windows throw shadows across the huge old boxwoods. We follow a rock walkway to a bench where Case sits down. I take the spot beside him. His phone buzzes. He pulls it from his pocket, turns off the volume and then sticks it back again.

"How you doin', Holden?" he asks.

"Fine," I say. "How about you?"

"Some good days. Some bad days," he admits.

"I can't imagine how hard it's been."

"Holden, you were as much a victim as any of us."

I start to reply, but not knowing what to say, I just nod once.

"Are you and CeCe seeing each other?"

His question surprises me, and at first, I'm not sure how to answer. "No, we're not," I finally say.

"Why?"

"I don't really know the answer to that."

"Is it because of Beck?"

"I think it's really just everything that happened. I guess it's been more than any of us could make sense of."

"Here's the thing, son. Life's short. We hear it all our lives, but none of us really get it until we lose someone precious to us. We don't get a second go around. If I didn't know that before, I know it now."

I nod once, not trusting my voice to respond.

"Her mama's worried about her," Case says then. "I told her I would speak to you. Neither one of us wants to overstep our bounds, but here's how I see it. A whole lot of things got broken that night. Whatever it is that you and CeCe have, that doesn't need to be one of them."

I consider this for a few moments and then say, "To be honest with you, Case, I'm not sure I have a lot of say in that."

"If you want her bad enough, then I guess you're gonna have to be willing to fight for her, son. Even if she's the person you're fighting."

"You're a good man, Case. I hope people tell you that a lot."

"Got a lot of sins to make up for," he says with a half-smile. He stands then. "I'd better let you get back to the party. They'll be wondering where you are."

I stand and stick my hand out, "Thanks, Case. I mean it. For everything. You've been incredible to us. We wouldn't be here tonight if it weren't for you."

"Don't sell yourself short. Real talent will always find its way to the top. You three have definitely got that."

"That means everything coming from you."

We walk back inside, and just as we step through the door, I see CeCe talking with Michael Parker. Parker currently has a number one song. It doesn't take a genius to get that he's into her.

Case tips his head in their direction, raising an eyebrow. "See. You'd better get on it, son."

I decide then and there that I'm going to take his advice.

♪

CeCe

Michael Parker is telling me about the ranch he grew up on in West Texas and how he used to write music out in the pastures by himself, using the cows as his audience.

He laughs and says, "You know, I actually feel guilty about that now. They were really bad songs."

I laugh, too, and the sound is completely unexpected to me. He's not exactly the way the few articles I've seen about him described him as being. He's down-to-earth, and unlike a lot of guys I've met who've started to hit it big, doesn't seem to feel the need to recite his list of accomplishments to date.

Holden walks up and drops a cool nod at Michael. "Hey, man," he says.

"Holden. Hey, buddy," Michael says, sticking out his hand. "Congrats on the record. Everybody's expecting big stuff from y'all."

"Thanks," Holden says evenly. "I appreciate it. Congratulations to you."

Michael smiles without any evidence of arrogance or pride. "Gotta say it feels about as good as they tell you it'll feel, hitting that number one spot. But I expect y'all are gonna find that out soon enough. Could you give me a few weeks to enjoy the ride before you knock me out?"

Holden looks like he's having trouble believing that could ever be the case and, honestly, so am I.

"I don't think you have to worry," Holden says.

"Don't underestimate yourselves. Once this roller coaster starts picking up momentum, it kind of takes on a life of its own. My head's still spinning from everything that's happened with us. Some days me and the guys in the band can't believe we're not playing frat nights back in Texas."

Silence takes over the conversation, and the three of us stand for a few moments while I start to feel uncomfortable.

Michael's expression has gone serious when he says, "I hope y'all know how glad everybody is that you're here tonight. You sure as hell deserve it after everything that happened–"

"CeCe, I need to speak with you for a moment if I could?" Holden says, interrupting Michael. Truthfully, I'm glad, although I do feel a little guilty about the quick flash of hurt in Michael's eyes.

"All right, then," he says, taking a step back. "CeCe, I hope to see you again real soon."

The fact that he hasn't included Holden in the statement rains another shower of awkwardness down on us.

"You, too, Michael," I say.

To my surprise, Holden takes my hand. Linking his fingers through mine, he leads me across the crowded room, weaving and winding, "Excuse me, pardon me, sorry," all the way until we reach the terrace doors again where Mama and I had gone out to talk. He pulls me outside. The cool night air assaults the heat in my cheeks with a feeble attempt at relief.

"What in the world, Holden?" I round on him, the skirt of my dress swishing out in an arc.

"Is he where you're headed next?" he asks.

"Michael?"

"Michael."

"We were just talking, Holden."

I fold my arms across my chest and stand straight and stiff, as if preparing myself for an assault. He watches me, and even in the dim light of the terrace I see emotion darkening his eyes.

"That night when Thomas came home drunk, I thought you and I were on our way back to finding each other. But you shut me out again, and I've let you do it because I thought it was what you needed."

"Holden-"

"CeCe, in that hotel room in D.C. I told you I loved you. And you said you loved me, too. When we said those words to each other, we had no way of knowing what was going to happen that night. But as bad as it was, as horrible as the months afterward have been, none of it changed how I feel about you, because I meant every word I said. Every word. Did you?"

I hear the pain in his voice and guilt tightens my throat. I don't want to lie and say that I didn't mean it because I did. "I just don't know if I'm strong enough to love you, Holden. I don't know if I'm strong enough to love anyone."

"What does that mean?" he says, a broken note in his voice.

"That love is risk. That a person has to be fearless to love the way I felt when I fell in love with you." A sob rises up out of my throat completely unexpected. "I'm not fearless anymore, Holden. I'm the opposite of fearless. I'm terrified. If the wind catches the door and slams it hard, I jump. I'm afraid to go to the mall by myself. I hate how I am now, but I don't know how to change it! I don't know how to fix it!"

He reaches out, and cupping his hand to the back of my neck, slowly pulls me toward him. "Then, baby, let me help you."

In that moment, I've never wanted anything more. Holden snags my waist and reels me closer. I tip my head back and look up at him. For the first time in so long, I look directly into his eyes, not trying to hide anything, simply letting him see everything I'm feeling: the love that is still there for him, but also the pain that I can't seem to come to terms with.

"CeCe," he says, and I hear in his voice how much he wants to take it from me onto himself. I know he would if he could. I think in this moment, if I could, I would let him.

He leans in then, kissing me softly and with incredible tenderness. I feel my heart quicken inside me. I close my eyes and let myself kiss him back. The kiss is sweet and full of longing, both of us echoing the other's need.

Here in Holden's arms, I wonder if I can actually begin to feel safe again, if the fears that constantly gnaw at me will finally start to lose their knife-edge.

He takes a step back from me, reaches in his pocket and pulls out a small black velvet box. I want to tell him to stop, and at the same time, I desperately want him to open it.

"I had this with me on the night of the shooting. I planned to give it to you after the party. I've been carrying it around ever since. I don't know if I would have found the courage to do this if it weren't for the things Case just said to me. He reminded me that none of us knows how long we're going to be here, that time isn't something we should waste."

"Holden," I start, but he raises a hand to stop me.

"Please. Let me say this. You might not ever feel the same about me again. But even if you don't, I meant everything I said to you. I love you. I think I have pretty much from the first moment I saw you. That morning in D.C., it became so clear to me that there are two things I can't live without in this world. You. And music. It used to be just the music. Now, there's no separating you from it or it from you. The truth is I don't want to. Everything that's happening here tonight is what we've all dreamed of. But without you, without us, it just feels flat. If I'm not able to share it with you, I'm pretty sure I don't even want it anymore."

"Holden, I-"

"Wait," he says, opening the box. The ring winks in the moonlight.

He removes it from the velvet setting and holds it up in front of me. "I need to know that I've done everything I can not to let you go. So I'm going to ask you what's in my heart."

I want to stop him, fear I can't control, can't even explain, pounding through me. "When I said I love you that morning," I say, "I meant it, too. But what happened that night has made me wonder if there's anything in this life that really can be trusted. The next moment, the next hour. If I reach out and take your hand with the intent of walking toward a future together, how do we know that there's any tomorrow?"

"Baby, we don't," Holden says, his voice low and compassionate. "There are no guarantees. There's just now and what we make of it or what we throw away. Don't throw us away, CeCe. Please."

A sob catches in my throat, and I'm suddenly crying. I want so badly to give myself over to the comfort I know I'll find in Holden's arms. I'm still not convinced I deserve it. But I want it, need it.

He reaches out and cups his hand at the base of my neck. "Baby, come here," he says.

And with that, just that, the ribbon of resistance inside me snaps. I fall into him as if he is the only safe haven left for me on this earth. I wrap my arms around his waist and bury my face against his chest.

He lifts me up and into him, his arms so tight around me that I am sure he will never let me go. "CeCe," he says, my name torn from him. "Thank God."

His hands are in my hair, tilting my head back so that I'm looking up at him. We stare into each other's eyes, both wet with tears.

He leans in and kisses me then. I kiss him back with every ounce of the love I feel for him. A love that took root inside me and has never let go.

He backs me across the terrace, lifts me up, all the while kissing me, and sets me on the stonewall at its edge. He slides my dress up to the top of my thighs and steps in between my legs.

I pull him to me. We kiss until we are both breathless with need for each other.

Holden slips my dress off one shoulder, his mouth making a heated trail across my neck and the top of my breasts.

I drop my head back and stare up at the night sky even as I'm trying to pull in air. "Holden," I say.

"Yeah?"

"That ring. Is it still available?"

He slowly leans back, his love-drugged eyes snagging mine. "It is. Any special reason you're asking?"

"Yes," I say.

"Yes?"

"Yes." I smile at him then. He kisses me, full and deep, at the same time reaching into his jacket pocket and pulling out the box. He doesn't stop kissing me as he pops open the lid and pulls out the diamond. Not even as he slides it on the finger of my left hand.

It slips over my knuckle, and something inside me clicks into place, like the final correct selection of a safe's combination. I feel the rightness of it. And know this part I will never have to question.

"I love you, CeCe. So much. Will you marry me?"

"I love you, Holden. And yes, I will."

He lifts my hand to his mouth, kisses the back of my wrist and rubs his thumb across the diamond's surface.

"I will live every day of my life trying to deserve you," he says softly.

"And I'll live mine trying to deserve you," I say.

Footsteps echo on the tile behind us. I look up. Thomas walks toward us with his long, purposeful stride.

"Is this make-out central?" he asks. "If so, y'all shoulda told me, so I could've brought a date."

I smile as Holden turns around and says, "It was make out central until you blew the moment."

Thomas stops and gives us both a long look. "What moment's that?"

"The moment where we finally admit we want to spend our lives together." I smile and for the first time in so very long, feel really happy.

"Well, good grief, it's about time," he says, grinning and walking over to clap Holden on the back.

I hold up my hand and wave the ring at him.

Thomas throws Holden a look. "Well, who knew you had that in you, son?"

Holden smiles and shakes his head. "You're just mad because I didn't ask your permission."

"I mighta had some handy pointers on ring-buying for you," Thomas teases. "But no, you've had my permission for a long time."

"Thanks, man."

"So where do we go from here?" Thomas asks.

"Making music," Holden says, and then for my ears only, leans in and adds, "Making love."

I smile and play swat him away.

Thomas rolls his eyes.

Holden turns to look at Thomas. "Now if we can just find you a CeCe."

"You don't think it's Misty or Dawn then?" Thomas asks with a sly smile.

"Ah, no," I say. "Most definitely."

"Well, all right then," he says, shrugging. "And oh, by the way, while you two were out here patchin' up your love life, everybody in there's waiting on us to come sing them a song. Think you can quit batting your eyelashes at each other long enough to-"

Holden throws a playful punch at Thomas's midsection.

Thomas goes double and says, laughing, "I'll go out by myself then. They're not here to hear y'all anyway."

"Oh, yeah?" I say. "I think not."

Holden holds out his arm to me in invitation. "We better get in there before this spotlight hog steals our gig altogether."

We begin walking back toward the lighted ballroom, me in the middle, Holden and Thomas on either side. "I am a really lucky girl," I say.

"We're pretty damn lucky ourselves." Thomas leans in to kiss my cheek. "It's really good to have you back, girl."

"Yeah, it is," Holden says, rubbing his thumb across the diamond on my hand.

"I'm not ever gonna be sure you actually deserve her," Thomas says, "but nobody ever said love was logical."

I laugh and pull them both in closer. We stop just outside the doors leading back into the house. "*Pleasure in the Rain?*" I ask.

Thomas nods. "That's what they're asking for."

"Ready then?"

"As ever," Thomas says.

"Let's do it," Holden says.

And we step into the room, walking side by side, arm in arm.

♪

CeCe

When I was a little girl I had no intention of ever marrying a boy. That made absolutely no sense to me because I couldn't stand them. They were loud and obnoxious and, for the most part, shorter than me, at least the ones my age.

What made sense to me was marrying my dog.

Henry, my best friend at the time, was a hound Mama and I found starving in the woods near our house. He was already old when he came to us. He had a bum front leg so that he could barely walk, and his eyes had already started to go cloudy with age. We took him to our vet in town. Dr. Finlay told us that hunters in the area would sometimes abandon a dog no longer able to keep up with the pack and that most likely this was what had happened to Henry. I couldn't believe anyone would actually do such a thing, but that old saying "one man's trash is another's treasure" could have been written about what Henry brought to our lives.

Once we got him to feeling better, and he could walk again, he became the most joyful soul I've ever known.

I didn't care about spending time with friends because Henry was the best companion I could imagine having. We would go on long hikes through the woods and up the mountain near our house. Henry had a nose for finding great stuff, a rabbit hole where we once came upon a nest of baby bunnies. Henry pointed them out with his wagging tail and never made any attempt to harm them; he just wanted to show them to me. Another time it was two baby skunks. Before we finished our oohing and tail-wagging, the mama returned and sent us both running back to the house with a highly smelly and unforgettable reminder not to mess with her babies.

It didn't seem possible that I would ever meet anyone in my life more entertaining, more loving than my Henry. It only made sense to me that we would get married one day because apparently that was what you did when you knew you were going to love someone for the rest of your life.

Henry died when I was twelve.

He just kind of went to sleep in my arms one night when I woke to the sound of him whimpering softly. He was curled up beside me on my bed. I remember slipping my arms around him and pulling him up close. He was breathing hard like he'd just run a really long way. As soon as I hugged him to me and kissed the top of his head, his breathing stopped, as if he had been waiting for me to kiss him goodbye.

My heart completely broke that night. I refused to get out of bed and go to school for a week. I realize now how lucky I was to have a mama who recognized my grief and just let me feel it until I could face getting up and going on without Henry.

Almost a year passed before I could bring myself to go back into our woods again, to walk the paths that we had made together.

I was sixteen before I let myself believe that it was okay to bring another dog into my life. Mama and I went to the pound one Saturday morning where a skinny long-legged hound curled up at the back of his kennel and shaking uncontrollably, stole my heart as instantly as Henry had.

By that age, I had begun to look at boys somewhat differently. But there is one thing about my little girl resolution to one day marry my dog that hasn't changed. And that's this: the man I decided to marry would have to be the most loyal friend I could ever hope for, as devoted to me as I am to him.

In Holden, I have no doubt this is what I've found.

He stands at the front of the small Virginia Baptist church I grew up in, waiting for me to walk down the aisle. Hank Junior and Patsy sit at his side, all three of them staring back at me with adoring expressions.

"I'm not sure which of the three loves you more," Thomas says now, looking down at me and smiling.

Thomas is giving me away today. It feels really right for him to do so. He's family in the truest sense of the word, those people in your life who would be there for you, no matter the need. Thomas is definitely that for me and for Holden, too.

"Thank you," I say, "for doing this."

"Walking you down the aisle?"

"Yes."

"Well, there stands the only guy in the world I'd hand you over to, and even then, if I had a lick of common sense, I'd probably swoop you up and steal you out from under his nose. I would say I hope he knows how lucky he is, but he does."

I reach up and kiss Thomas on the cheek, "You're amazing, you know that?"

"You may be a bit partial, Miss MacKenzie."

"No, I just know good when I see it."

The pianist strikes the first chords of the wedding march. My heart starts to beat faster, and I realize that I'm about to step forward into a life I will never stop being thankful for.

"We're on, let's do this thing," Thomas says, the same as he does every time we go on stage to perform.

We start down the aisle. The church is full of familiar faces I've known all my life and many from Nashville as well. Mama and Aunt Vera are sitting on the front row with Case in between them. Mama is crying, but they're happy tears. Her eyes shine with them.

We stop just short of Holden, Hank Junior and Patsy. The pastor smiles at us, says a few words of welcome, and just the way we practiced it last night, Thomas takes my hand and joins it with Holden's. He kisses my cheek, claps Holden on the shoulder and then steps in behind him.

Hank Junior thumps his tail on the wood floor, and the sound makes everyone seated behind us laugh softly. I reach down and kiss his head, and then Patsy's, too.

When I stand up again, I let myself look into Holden's eyes. They're so full of love and happiness that for a second, just a second, old fears flash through me. Will it last? Is this too good to be true? Can life really be this wonderful?

But I blink them away, not letting let them take root.

I know that life doesn't come with guarantees. We can only live the moment that's in front of us. I believe with all my heart that we should live that moment fully, embrace it without wasting even a second worrying about what might be beyond it.

We can't control that part, other people's thoughts, other people's actions. We can only control our own.

I choose to fill mine with love. Love for and the love of a guy I know how lucky I am to have. I don't ever want to take that for granted, but I don't think that I will.

Life is precious, love is a gift. The sun might not always shine on us. But those will be the days that we take pleasure in the rain.

♪

Book Five

amazed

RITA AWARD WINNING AUTHOR

INGLATH COOPER

Nashville – Book Five – Amazed

Inglath Cooper

*

Thomas Franklin has pretty much everything he's ever wanted in life.

Along with his two best friends in the world, he's part of Barefoot Outlook, a superstar band in the country music world. And if he's a little bit envious of the love Holden and CeCe have found in one another, he can accept the fact that he's had more than his share of good fortune.

Finding a girl like CeCe? Well, that's pretty much once in a lifetime.

In spite of Holden's constant harassment about his playboy reputation, Thomas is content to play the field. Until, that is, his past finds its way into the present when he agrees to do a charity gig in Virginia with Case Phillips. There, he crosses paths with the only girl who had ever stolen his heart for real.

The last thing Lila Bellamy expects on the night her best friend Macy takes her out for a birthday celebration is to find herself face to face with Thomas Franklin.

Seven years earlier, still haunted by the tragedy of her mother's death, Lila had found comfort in Thomas, and during the hours they were together, let herself forget for just a little while. It had taken nothing more than the light of day for her to realize that one night was all they were ever going to be.

Even though they had never seen each other again in all these years, Lila had never forgotten him. And not just because he had since become famous. Lila has another reason, one she's never wanted him to find out about. But as she well knows, life can change overnight. And Thomas Franklin is about to change hers all over again.

Thomas

Is This What I Was Waiting For?

The first time the phone rings, I ignore it.

I pull the pillow over my head and press it to my ear, trying to block the annoying screech of the Gomer Pyle *Shazam!* ringtone Holden put on my phone.

A hand reaches out to tap the side of my face. "Somebody's calling you, sugar."

I swat the manicured nails away and say nothing.

The phone begins to rattle again. *Shazam! Shazam!*

"Want me to turn it off?" I hear cigarettes in the voice, and at the same time, get a riff of stale alcohol.

"No, Sh—" I start to say her name, but realize I'm not sure I remember it. Sharla? Shauna? "I got it," I say instead, flipping over and grabbing the phone from the nightstand. Spotting Holden's number, I bark, "This better be good."

"Don't tell me you're still asleep?"

"It's the friggin' middle of the night. What else do you think I'd be doing?"

"It's twelve-thirty, shithead," comes his unperturbed reply. "As in the afternoon."

"What?"

"Since when can't you tell night from day?"

I open my eyes. The room is pitch dark. And then I see the small crack of light at the bottom of the heavy hotel room curtain. "Hell. I didn't mean to sleep this long."

"Where are you anyway?"

I try to think of the name of the town I picked off my GPS map last night when I decided I was too tired to keep driving, and can't for the life of me, recall it. "Somewhere between Nashville and Roanoke."

"That's helpful. Case needs to know what time you'll be getting in. He wants a little prep time before the show."

"Tell him I'll be there on time."

"Why don't you answer your dang phone and tell him yourself?"

I rub my hand across my eyes and stretch, bumping a long smooth leg that promptly tangles itself with mine. "What bee got in your britches this morning. . .afternoon?" I correct quickly.

"The one that tells me you got drunk again last night, and there's a girl in your bed."

"Well, yeah."

Holden blows out a sigh. "When are you going to grow the hell up and quit acting like you need to prove you're not ever gonna settle down?"

"I'm not."

"What?"

"Settling down."

"CeCe thinks you're a jerk."

"Does not."

"Does too."

"She flat out adores me."

"That might be, but she's getting sick of giving the 'he's just not ready to be serious' speech to half the female population in Nashville."

"I didn't ask her to give that speech," I say, recognizing the defensive note in my voice. "And if anybody knows, you know I'm up front about my intentions, or lack thereof."

"You're fine with letting them all think you're a heartless di–"

"Hey, now. Play nice."

"No, that's my advice to you."

"Man, just because you and CeCe got it made over there in Love Shack Central, doesn't mean you get to dole out relationship advice to the rest of us losers."

"That what you call your nightly trysts? A relationship?"

"Did you just say trysts?"

"Hookups, whatever the hell you want to call them. There is such a thing as overuse, you know. You might just end up breaking it."

I laugh, unable to stop myself. "You're the one in danger of breaking it. I barely see you two except when we're on stage. Aren't you sick of each other yet?"

"No."

I can tell immediately his answer didn't come out with the lack of care he'd intended. Where CeCe is concerned, Holden can hide nothing. I've never seen anybody so flat out high on love as those two. And I'm not jealous. I'm not. Envious? A little.

But there's no way to resent what the two of them have found in each other. That would be like resenting the sun for its existence. It can't help that we have to have it to live. That's what it's like between those two. They need each other to actually survive.

And so I let the seriousness of his response go. Decide not to call him on it, even though he's giving me ten different kinds of grief.

"Seriously, man, give Case a call. For some reason, he's got it in his head you're not going to show."

"Course I'm going to show. Why would he think that?"

"I don't know. Maybe because you were half an hour late getting on stage in Lexington last week. Or it could be the rehearsals you keep missing." And then, more serious, "What's going on with you, Thomas?"

I feel my hackles rise, start to get defensive and then it fades away as quickly as it bloomed. "Nothing."

"That's not true. You haven't been acting like yourself for the past six months. Can I be honest?"

"By all means."

"I'm worried about you. Mind if I ask you why you agreed to go down there in the first place?"

I don't answer for a stretch of moments because the truth is I'm not too sure I know the answer myself. "You remember that gig we had in downtown Roanoke when we were juniors at Georgia?" I finally ask.

"Yeah," Holden says. "It was one of our first. We sucked."

"Pretty much," I agree.

"And you met that girl."

Part of me was hoping he wouldn't remember her, and another part of me is almost glad he opened the door. She's been at the edges of my thoughts pretty much the entire two weeks since Case asked me to join up with him in a fundraiser for families of victims of gun violence. "He wanted you and CeCe to be there, too," I say.

"We would have if CeCe hadn't already committed to that Hounds for Housedogs fundraiser. But I sure didn't think you'd want to go without us."

"Yeah, well, I guess anyway I can pay Case back a little bit for everything he's done for us, I'm glad to do it."

"Hold on. Is it my imagination, or did you just totally skirt the subject of the girl?"

"She was just a girl, Holden."

"Right. Don't forget I lived with you when she wouldn't return your calls and gave you your first taste of being on the other side of a one-night stand."

"Didn't you once call yourself my best friend?"

"Best friends tell each other the truth. And I think the truth was she yanked that ol' country boy heart of yours right out of your chest. That's why nobody else has ever gotten anywhere near it."

"Are you writing fiction now instead of lyrics?"

Holden barks a short laugh. "It wouldn't be called fiction. Maybe memoirs. If I remember right, she was a beauty."

"How would you remember? You were too drunk to walk straight, much less see straight."

"I wasn't that drunk."

"You sure you're not drinking right now? I know how alcohol likes to lead you down memory lane."

"No, I'm just wondering if you might have had something other than philanthropy in the back of your mind when you agreed to do this gig."

"That hurts, you know it?"

"What? It's not like I'd blame you if you gave her a call or something."

"She's probably married with five kids by now."

"Or she could still be single. Pining for you."

"Again, yeah right."

"Odds are she's seen your ugly mug in a magazine or two."

"I repeat, is this what best friends do for each other?"

"I'm just saying maybe you should call her."

"Did CeCe put you up to this?"

"No," Holden starts to defend automatically.

"She did, didn't she?"

Holden is quiet for a couple of seconds, and then, "I'll admit that she thinks you've gone a little overboard with the number of girls on your dance card."

"What's with you and the corny euphemisms?"

"You want it a little straighter than that? Here, you go. She thinks you pick women you're never going to fall in love with. She thinks you do it on purpose. And that it's got to feel a little bit empty."

"Most of the time, it feels pretty damn good." Even as I say the words, I hear my own lack of conviction.

"I'm not buying it. And neither is CeCe."

"I don't recall asking you to."

"All right, before you get all jacked up, answer this one thing. You like the image those rag tabloids are painting of you?"

"Honest answer? I couldn't care less."

"I know as well as you do," Holden says, "that they're not worth wasting an ounce of energy on. But you gotta admit, you do give them a lot of ammunition."

"Am I telling you how to live your life?"

"No," Holden says, and I hear in his voice that he's a little ashamed of himself.

"Look, Thomas, CeCe's concerned about you. And, well, I have been too, I guess."

"Y'all don't need to be worried about me. It's all good. Okay?"

"So good you could tell me the name of the girl next to you right now if I asked you?"

"As a matter of fact, I've gotta go. She's awake, and I've ignored her long enough."

I smack the end call button and toss the phone on the nightstand.

"If you were talking about me, that sure was sweet."

The girl whose name I still cannot remember slides her hand up my chest and taps out a rhythm with her square-tipped nails.

"Especially since we've barely talked and all."

"We've talked," I say quickly, as if it's Holden who made the accusation.

She laughs a soft laugh. "I'm not sure those sounds we were making last night could actually be called words."

I run a palm across my in-need-of-a-shave face. "They could be a language in certain parts of the world."

She slides a little closer, slips her leg between mine. "We could say them again, if you like."

All of a sudden, I'm thinking about everything Holden just said. "I should hit the road."

"Awww," she says. "Can't you stay just a little longer?"

"I'd like to," I say. "But I have somewhere I really have to be." I sit up and all but vault off the bed, just as she reaches to grab my arm with a playful laugh.

"Surely, you've got ten minutes!"

"Afraid not this time."

She drops back onto the mattress, pouting against the pillow. "Will I see you again?"

I meet her hopeful gaze and make myself say the truth. "Probably not."

Her disappointment is immediately obvious. "I kinda knew you were gonna say that."

I start buttoning my shirt and find myself asking, "How?"

"Because you're one of those guys."

"One of which guys?"

"The kind who never lets his heart out to play with the rest of him," she says, still pouting.

"Is that how I strike you?"

"Yeah," she says. "It is. And I heard a little bit of what your friend was saying. So I know I'm right."

"Oh," I say. And then, "Look—"

"It's all right," she says. "No need to apologize. I'm a big girl. I figured you were too good to be true, anyway. You probably have like all kinds of skeletons in your closet."

"Oh, now I have a closet, huh?" I ask, teasing her.

She laughs, slides out of bed without bothering to take the sheet with her. "I'm going to take a shower. You decide you have that extra ten minutes, you know where you can find me."

She disappears in the bathroom then, the door clicking closed behind her. I let out a long whoosh of air and count to ten.

I get dressed, find my truck keys, wallet and phone, and then leave the room for the front desk to pay the bill. I'm out in the parking lot when I hear a screech coming from the middle of the hotel building. I look around, and the girl whose name I still cannot remember, if I ever knew it in the first place, is standing on the balcony of our room wrapped in a towel. She's waving her phone and screaming like she just won the lottery.

"I texted a picture of you to my friend, and she says you're Thomas Franklin! You are, aren't you?"

I shrug, no idea where to take this conversation from here.

"Ohhh, my word, I can't believe it!" She aims the phone at me and starts snapping pictures.

I shake my head, getting in the truck. I back up and then pull out of the parking lot. Through the rearview mirror, I can see her still snapping away.

Good. Gracious. Almighty.

♪

Lila

Got Your Back

I will be the first to admit that my job at Smart-Send is nothing to brag about. It requires the kind of mindless performance that leaves me enough energy at the end of the day to do the things I have to do when I leave here every afternoon.

For the past five years, I've worked a conveyor line in between two other women, Bertha Peters and Marsha Sowder, each of whom tip the scale at well over the two-hundred-pound mark and smell of antiperspirant that has fallen short of its declared abilities.

The highlight of their day is letting a box on the conveyor belt go before I'm ready for it so that my fingers get smashed between it and the one I'm finishing up. They consider this high entertainment.

This morning has been no different. They somehow got word that it's my birthday, and their objective has been to harass me beyond their normal acceptable standards. Bertha is sure I have a hot date lined up tonight where I'll be adorned with roses and fine jewelry.

"You takin' off early today?" she jeers, one hand propped on an ample hip. "Must take a while to get all that hair poofed and primped."

I continue placing the items in front of me in the cardboard box, choosing to ignore the taunt.

"Oh, she's not talking today," Marsha says. "She's probably picturing herself getting a diamond tonight, like that'll be her ticket outta here."

"At least that's a possibility for someone like her."

I turn to see Macy standing behind Marsha, looking like a mother bear that discovers somebody messing with one of her cubs.

Marsha turns around and gives Macy a laser look. "Anybody talkin' to you, Simpson?"

"If you're talking to Lila, that's the same as talking to me."

"And let me see if I've got this right. There's somethin' *you're* gonna do about it?"

Macy stares at her for a moment, then steps in closer so that she stands virtually knee to knee with Marsha, who is literally double her size. Macy and I have been friends since elementary school when Terrence Moyer, who sat in the desk behind me during reading class, cut the end of my braid off. Macy cornered him in the hallway after class and gave him a bloody nose for his efforts.

Somewhere along the way, I became her personal project, which is, in a way, an honor because she's continued the crusade some twenty years running. As far as the rest of her life is concerned, she has an ADD-like attention span, getting bored with relationships before they ever actually define themselves.

"Why, yes," Macy says. "There is, actually. Later on this afternoon, when I've got Garth Meadows in that place where he *reeeally* doesn't want me to stop, I'm gonna take a little break and mention that I think he ought to fire your sorry butt and free up a spot on this line for someone who'll actually work instead of running her big fat mouth all the time."

Marsha's face turns red enough that the risk of stroke seems more than a likely possibility. She starts to say something, then appears to think better of it, turning back to the conveyor belt and the box she'd been working on.

Macy walks over to me, smiling big as if the last few seconds never happened. "Happy birthday," she says, giving me a hug. "I've got a surprise for you."

I start to tell her that I don't need her riding to my rescue with Marsha and Bertha, but Macy is so full of cheer, I don't want to burst her bubble. "What is it?" I ask instead.

"After work," she says. "You'll see."

"Macy. . ." I begin to argue, hoping she doesn't have some kind of male stripper waiting in the parking lot at three-thirty. It wouldn't be the first time.

"Trust me, okay?"

I give her a look meant to remind her of the other times she's said this.

"Really. It's gonna be great."

We leave it at that, and Macy heads back to her workstation, while I wish for a believable excuse to leave early and avoid my mystery surprise.

The rest of the day unfolds as uneventful, Bertha and Martha both choosing not to test Macy's pull with Garth. When the factory bell rings at three-thirty, Macy is waiting out front for me.

"You ready for some fun?" she says.

"Don't you have some place to be?"

Macy wrinkles her forehead, and then says, "What? Oh, you mean Garth?"

"Yeah, Garth."

"I was just yanking their chain. Today, anyway," she adds, her grin mischievous."

"I've gotta pick up Lexie," I say.

"Yep. Then I'm coming over. And here's the surprise. My mama's gonna watch Lexie for you tonight, and we're going out."

"What?" I ask, disbelieving. "Macy. I can't do that."

"Why not? You know Mama will guard her with her life. And she's used to seeing her in Sunday school class."

"I know, but–"

"I know no one's the same as you, but you deserve this, Lila. And I'm not taking no for an answer."

The refusal rises up inside me. I can't even remember the last time I went out at night. But along with it, there is something else, the desire to go, to do something different. To shed responsibility, even just for a single evening. I feel guilty at the thought, but Macy pounces on my wavering like a cat on an unsuspecting mouse.

"She'll be fine. I promise. And it's your birthday, for heaven's sake. If anybody's earned a little celebrating, it's you."

"Are you sure your mom won't mind?"

"Are you kidding? You know she loves Lexie."

I feel myself caving. Maybe I do need a night out. "A couple of hours then. But I can't be too late, okay?"

Macy looks as if she wants to argue, but restrains herself. "We'll be there at six o'clock."

"All right," she says, climbing into the Land Cruiser and waving as Macy speeds away in her Mustang convertible.

♪

Thomas

Can't Blame the Fame

Case is waiting for me in front of the Hotel Roanoke when I pull up at just after five o'clock that afternoon. We'd talked a couple of times on my way down the Interstate, and I can tell by the look on his face, he hadn't actually been sure I was going to be here when I said I would be.

Each of the valet parking attendants standing nearby glances from Case to me and then back and forth again. Their expressions are just shy of neutral, when I suspect they want to run over and ask Case for his autograph.

To their credit, they refrain, and Case walks down the steps and sticks his head inside the truck window on the passenger side.

"You made it," he says.

"Yeah. I meant to get here a little earlier, but–"

"You're good. You wanna run up and get a shower?"

"I'll be fast," I say.

"No problem. Long as we leave here by six."

I get out, and one of the valet guys runs up to take my keys and give me a ticket. We walk through the lobby, and Case waits while I get checked in. We take the elevator up to the second floor together.

"I appreciate your coming, Thomas," Case says. "Means a lot to me."

"No big deal," I say. "So what's the plan for tonight?"

"The show's at a venue over near Hollins College. The place is already sold out, so it should be a good night."

"Cool," I say.

"Gotta say I was kind of surprised you agreed to come," Case says.

I shrug. "We just finished up that last record, and getting out of town for a little bit sounded like a good thing. Plus you know I'm happy to do it for you."

"Thanks, man. By the way, I heard the roughs in the studio the other day. Y'all really knocked it out of the ballpark with this one."

"That means a lot coming from you. I think we all felt like we had something to say on this record."

"Do the world good to hear it," Case says. "When the audience tonight sees that you're the surprise special guest, I'm sure they're gonna feel like they got their money's worth."

"You'll make it more than that yourself," I say. "Your boys already set up?"

"Yeah, they've been over there since lunchtime."

We're quiet for a few moments, and then I say, "Haven't seen you in a while, Case. How you holdin' up?"

"Most of the time, okay," Case says, glancing down at his boots and shoving his hands in the pockets of his jeans. "You know, some days are harder than others."

I start to say I do know, but I don't really. The shooting had a different effect on every one of us, but it's Case who lost the most. And I've never wanted to act like I could even begin to understand what he feels. "You been down to visit Ms MacKenzie lately?" I ask, hoping he and CeCe's mother are still seeing each other. I imagine if anybody could help Case through this past year, it would be Ms. MacKenzie.

"Yeah," he says, "about every weekend."

I smile, glad to hear it. "She's a pretty special lady, no doubt."

"She is that," Case says. "How are you managing bachelorhood without Holden?"

"Managing," I say.

He shakes his head. "The two of them are playin' it pretty close to home these days, aren't they?"

"They're not sick of each other yet, that's for sure. They invite me over for dinner about every night. I guess they feel sorry for me."

"I don't think you're spending too much of your time alone now, are you, Thomas?" he asks with a knowing half-smile.

I don't bother to deny it.

"It can be a heady thing in the beginning," he says.

"What's that?" I ask, even though I'm pretty sure I know what he means.

"All the attention. The women. Mostly the women," he admits with a rueful grin.

I want to deny it, but I'm not going to fool Case Phillips, so I say, "Sometimes."

"Especially when you're lonely," he adds. He looks off, and his voice is a little distant when he says, "I sure didn't know what to do with it at first. Beck was a little guy, and his mama and I weren't getting along. She couldn't handle all the attention I was suddenly getting. I started spending more nights away from home with women whose faces I can't even remember now. When I think about the time I lost with my son because I made those choices, I—"

"Hey, Case. Don't do that to yourself. Beck adored you."

"I did some things as a father that weren't all that adorable."

"The state of being human," I say.

"That hindsight thing will bite you in the butt every time. And there's just something about youth that keeps us from realizing how every choice we make matters. What I would give if I could just go back and spend those nights with Beck when he was a little boy at home."

The regret in his voice is thick and emotion-filled. I can't think of a single word that would provide him with any comfort at all.

♪

Lila

What Love Is

The digital clock blinks a groggy two-thirty on the nose.

I lay on my thin mattress, staring at the bright red numbers on the digital alarm clock, fatigue so heavy on my chest that it feels as if there is no possible way I'll be able to pull myself up in three hours and start another day.

I glance at the monitor on the nightstand, straining to hear Lexie's steady breathing through the small speaker. As always, I feel relief for this proof that my daughter is fine, sleeping peacefully. Even through the fatigue, I feel a wave of gratitude, too, for this stretch of time that is mine and mine alone.

I open the drawer on the nightstand and pull out my journal, scooting up and leaning back against the pillow with my hand on the leather cover. I smooth my thumb across the surface, its softness somehow soothing.

The book is one of the nicest things I own, a long-ago splurge that had taken a good-size chunk out of one of my paychecks and resulted in a two-week diet of Food Lion frozen green beans for me.

I open the cover and flip through the pages, the words blurring before my eyes. It's all there, the pain, the joy, the disappointment, and the elation of these past six years.

The book is nearly full now, only five blank pages left. I stare at the cream-colored emptiness, and the familiar need rises up inside me. I pull my pen from its holder along the spine of the book and set the tip to the paper.

The words flow up from some deep place, even though it's been a while since I've written anything. It's always been like this. The turning on of a tap, the rationing out of another small portion of the feelings inside me. When they come to life here on the page, it's only then that I manage to wrestle some sort of objectivity into the fears that sometimes get a chokehold on me.

When my pen finally goes still, I sit quiet for several minutes. And then I begin to write again, the verses coming in fragments, until the rough shape of a song begins to emerge. It feels easy tonight, maybe because I've arrived at another turning point, another birthday. Twenty-five. It doesn't sound that old, really. Plenty of people my age are just getting started in the world, but inside, I feel a little ancient.

I open the drawer again and pull out my old tape recorder. It's the kind with the big rectangular buttons to push for play and record. It still works fine, and I pop in a blank tape, staring at the words I'd written until a melody begins to hum in my head. I test it out, keeping my voice low, glancing at the thin door that separates Lexie's room from mine.

I used to strum the tune with my guitar. It's been years though since I let myself play. A psychiatrist would probably have an interesting take on the why of it. But without the guitar, I can accept that the lyrics and melodies I continue to write will remain confined to the walls of this twelve by sixty-five trailer. To actually play them is to bring them to life, and I'd just as soon leave them dormant.

I sound out the tune, recording bits and pieces of it, until the chorus is complete. I work on the verses then, reaching for notes that tie back to it.

An hour later, the song is complete. I sing it through one time for the tape, then take it out of the player and label it with a black marker. I add the cassette to the shoebox collection beneath my bed, then put the journal and the tape recorder away.

The clock now reads five-fifteen. As much as I want to go back to sleep, it's time to get up. I throw my legs over the side of the bed, my feet protesting the wiry brown shag carpet that covers the trailer floor. Outside, I hear a dog bark. It's Brownie from one trailer back. Lexie and I call him Brownie, anyway. Rowdy Maxwell, Brownie's human, big as a small dump truck and as unenlightened as one of its spare tires, calls him Killer.

Brownie has been chained to the same tree for the four years Lexie and I have lived here. I've never once seen him loose and free to run or play.

Rowdy yells out a string of curse words now, that are intended to silence the dog.

Brownie's barking suddenly subsides with a yelp, and the dark outside the window goes silent again. Rowdy's training methods include the throwing of whatever happens to be closest to his porch side La-Z-Boy—hammers, empty beer cans, flower pots. I let myself imagine for a moment a fitting retribution for Rowdy, a stray lightning bolt that would permanently sear him to his polyester recliner, or perhaps a bullet through the back of his oily yellow **I Hunt** cap. Since I suspect God wouldn't endorse either one, I can only hope He has a better plan in mind for Rowdy.

I get up and head for the small bathroom, flicking on the light and glancing in the dingy mirror above the sink, my eyes widening at the reflection staring back at me. My hair hangs midway down my back, the ends in need of a trim. The blonde streaks that have been there since I was a child are its main redeeming factor, one of the few positive things I'd inherited from my mother. My eyes are blue, not a vivid, blinding blue, but dark, almost navy. The lashes that frame them are dark too, a contrast that makes people question the authenticity of my light hair.

Is it my imagination, or do I look different today?

Twenty-five. The number is a little shocking. Sometimes it doesn't seem possible that I'm not still a kid, trying to figure out how to get to the places I wanted to go in this life.

I lean in closer to the mirror and stare hard at my face. I think I look my age, except for my eyes. They look far older.

I push away from the sink and turn on the shower, pulling the plastic curtain away from the side of the tub and waiting a moment for the water to warm. I step in and turn my face up, letting the spray wash away my nagging fatigue.

I pick up the shampoo bottle and squeeze out the last bit, aware that it will be a week before I get paid and can buy more. The conditioner has been out for days, and the small bar of soap is one of the cheap motel soaps that Macy pilfers from the room where she meets Garth Meadows for their weekly get-together.

Garth is the foreman over at Smart-Send, the packaging company where Macy and I both work. I have no idea what she sees in the man. He isn't even passably good-looking. He just thinks he is, and maybe in the eyes of some women, that is as much as the same thing. To boot, he's married with three kids and a wife who would probably beat the dickens out of Macy if she ever found out Macy was fooling around with Garth.

Macy is like that, though. Which does nothing to explain why we're best friends. She's always loved a challenge, all the sneaking around and pretending there's nothing between her and the boss at work. I think for her, it's all that passes for high drama in a town where not much else does.

Macy grew up on soap operas, and she can recite the complete story lines for at least three. My theory is that the moment her fling with Garth is no longer a secret, that will be the moment she dumps him for good and moves on to a new installment.

I get out of the shower, towel dry, and then go back to the bedroom for a pair of jeans and a T-shirt. I don't bother drying my hair; I simply comb it out and pull it back in a ponytail.

In the kitchen, I put on a pot of coffee and pull a box of oatmeal from the cabinet. I then head for Lexie's room where I flick on the small lamp next to her bed, standing for a moment, as I always do, to take in her sweetness while she still sleeps.

Lexie is a beautiful child. I can say this without fear of prejudice. I hear it all the time, from people on the street, in the grocery store, in the doctors' offices we visit with too-frequent regularity.

Here, still snuggled beneath her Barbie comforter, it's easy for me to imagine her as strong and healthy as any other little girl.

Her blonde hair is fine and silky, her skin like peaches at their most luminous, both pink and gold. Her hands are small and delicate, hands that look as if they might be gifted with a creative talent such as painting, or maybe she'll be musically inclined like me.

I sit down on the side of the bed, put my hand on her shoulder. "Lexie. Time to wake up, sweetie."

Lexie's eyes open and instantly find me; the light there is the payoff that keeps me struggling to get us from one day to the next. That light is our connection, proof of a bond of trust that doesn't need any words.

I put my hand to the side of Lexie's face and smile into her eyes. Lexie yawns widely. I slip my hands beneath the blanket and tickle her tummy. This is part of our morning ritual, and I need the fuel of my daughter's sweet giggles to get me going.

"Up and at 'em," I say, lifting her out of the bed and carrying her into the bathroom where I help her onto the toilet seat and wait for her to finish, before lifting her again and setting her on the special seat I had installed for the shower.

My back feels the strain, and I wonder how much longer I will be able to carry her like this. The thought brings with it a burn low in my stomach, the kind of looming problem I don't let myself dwell on. The truth is I don't know what I will do once I can no longer lift her, but then I hadn't known what I would do four years ago when a doctor told me she had cerebral palsy, that she would most likely never walk, never swim in the river I had grown up swimming in, and never ride a bike down country roads.

Most of Lexie's life has been a series of struggles to accomplish things that most people simply take for granted each day.

There are many things Lexie will never do. With God's grace, we have managed, trying not to look ahead for the next curve, but simply to keep negotiating the one we are currently in.

I turn on the faucet and let the water warm, testing it with my hand before turning the spray onto Lexie. Even at this early hour of the day, she loves the ritual, lifting her hands to try to catch the water as it sluices across her body.

Once we are done, I towel her dry and help her dress in a pair of flowery capri pants and a pink shirt. I then carry her to the wheelchair and fix her hair in matching braids.

In the kitchen, we both eat a quick bowl of cereal and drink a glass of orange juice. After that, we are out the door, and I use a small set of steps to help move Lexie to the back seat of my seen-far-better-days Land Cruiser. Once Lexie is inside, I stow the chair in the back.

"Need some help with that, Lila?"

I freeze at the sound of Rowdy's deep growl, not from fear, but something much more closely related to disgust. I close the back hatch and turn around with a clenched smile. "Got it. Thanks."

"That little girl sure is a lot of work for a tiny thing like you."

"Would you suggest I tie her to a tree?" The question is out before I can censor myself, my gaze cutting across the pitiful excuse for a yard to the bare spot where Brownie stands watching us, his tail wagging back and forth as if he still has hope that life can and will get better.

I try not to look at him because when I do I can hardly bear the thought that this is the only life he will ever know.

Rowdy walks over and leans against the Land Cruiser. He ducks a look at Lexie in the back seat, and I restrain myself from shoving him off the door. Even the thought of his eyes touching my daughter stirs me to a near rage.

"It works for my dog," he says, chuckling as if he's just delivered the funniest one-liner ever heard.

"Your dawg," I say, repeating his drawl, "is a prisoner."

"Well, how you figure, missy?" he says, getting a little irked now. "I let him loose, he'll just run off."

"You think?"

"I know."

"Gotta go," I say, starting the engine before I say something that gets me thrown out of the only roof we have over our heads.

He steps back, raises a hand. "Don't forget now. Rent's due on Monday."

As the resident landlord of the Sunflower Mobile Home Park, the name an oxymoron for the grim reality of the staggered rows of dated trailers, Rowdy takes pride in sparing no sympathy for late rent and has in fact personally escorted from the premises six families that I know of, piling their belongings in the back of his monster Chevy truck only to dump them just the other side of his property line.

I pull out of the rutted gravel driveway, feeling as if I need to go back and shower again.

Lexie's school is twenty minutes away, and we make the drive with her favorite songs playing on the Land Cruiser's old cassette player.

There is a funny rendition of "Happy Birthday," Lexie's favorite song on the tape. She claps her hands in offbeat rhythm, and I pretend for a moment that the song is for me, that Lexie knows today is my birthday.

As I wait at a stoplight in the center of town, the thought brings with it a poignant ache, one I try not to let myself feel too often. I'd long ago learned there's no point in living in the what-if. The only part of this life I have any control over is the now. And the truth is my daughter will never wish me happy birthday, will never grow up to live on her own, and will never call me to talk on the telephone.

And in all honesty, I don't know if this makes me sadder for me or for my daughter. My only comfort is that Lexie isn't aware of the magnitude of the loss.

That grief is mine alone.

♪

WE ARRIVE AT the Franklin School a few minutes later, a small yellow bus in front of us letting off a dozen or so children, each of whom has some visibly noticeable characteristic that makes them different from other children their age. I drive Lexie to school even though I could send her on this same bus.

I tried it once, thinking it would somehow help foster her independence, but something in the look on Lexie's small face as they pulled away made me feel as if I was deserting her. And so the next day, and every school day since, I've driven her instead.

Today, Lexie's classroom is already full, the other children who are like her in the restrictions they have to endure daily playing with an assortment of toys. Two little girls, one in a wheelchair, one standing with the help of a walker, smile big smiles when they spot Lexie rolling into the room.

I feel their welcome reaching out to my daughter even though no words are spoken. I've often wondered if the children are just happy to be in a place where they aren't different, where everyone else is mostly like them.

Their teacher, Mrs. Evans, walks up and says good morning to them both. She always has a sunshine smile for Lexie and the other children. To Mrs.

Evans, the students here are special in the way of something to be treasured. Not in the way of something to be pitied.

That's the one thing I never want Lexie to be. And yet, I've seen it flit across the faces of people once they see past her prettiness and notice the wheelchair and all its implications. I can almost hear them thinking, *What a waste. She could have done so much with her life.*

That's the part that hurts beyond description. Because I know they are right. Lexie could have. I would give my own life to make it so.

Mrs. Evans puts a hand on my shoulder and says, "I believe someone has a birthday today."

I meet her soft green gaze with a forced smile, appreciating the woman's thoughtfulness and yet at the same time reminded again that she remembered my birthday because she knows my daughter will not. She keeps a calendar of all the parents' birthdays so that each child can make something to give them.

"A birthday's always a good excuse to eat cake," I say.

"Clearly, you can afford to do so," Mrs. Evans says, giving me the kind of look my grandma used to give me when she thought I wasn't eating enough.

I lean down to give Lexie a kiss on the cheek. "Have a good day, sweetie," I say.

"We will," Mrs. Evans says, pushing Lexie to the center of the room.

At the door, I turn to look back, my heart contracting at the sight of my daughter surrounded by so much love. She belongs here, and it's clear that she is aware of this.

But as I leave the building, I am somehow more saddened by the thought than lifted up.

♪

Lila

One for the Road

With Lexie watching her favorite show on Noggin, I spend the better part of an hour in the trailer's stamp-size bathroom, taking a long soak of a bath with some salts I unearthed from the back of a cabinet. I wash my hair and paste on an intense conditioner I bought a couple of years before and never used. I file my nails to the short length I like them. After rinsing out the conditioner, I blow my hair dry, using a fat roller brush to straighten the slight wave of curl that settles in with the slightest onset of humidity.

I dress in the nicest jeans I own, a designer pair I discovered one day at TJMaxx with Macy. I suppose their reassignment to a discount store meant someone in Hollywood had deemed them no longer cool, but to me they're still worthy of special status. I pair a white scoop-neck T-shirt with them and then put on a little makeup, something I never bother with on a regular day.

Staring back at me from the dingy bathroom mirror is someone I rarely see anymore. I've grown used to the more-tired-than-tired reflection that greets me each morning and only manages to grow wearier by the time I brush my teeth at night. It feels nice to take time with the little things.

Once I finish getting ready, I scoop out some vanilla ice cream for Lexie to have while she watches one of the many *Barney* tapes I bought for her at the Goodwill store. No matter how many times she watches them, there is something about the big purple dinosaur that triggers happiness inside her with its own special light switch.

The phone jangles from its perch on the kitchen wall. I start to reach for it but decide to let the machine pick up the call.

I freeze at the sound of the voice.

"Lila. It's. . .it's your daddy." There is a long pause then, as if he is suddenly questioning his right to the title. "I know it's been a long time. It's your birthday. I hope you're having a good one." Another hesitation, and then, "I sure would love to see you sometime. And my grand–"

As if it has a mind of its own, my hand darts out to slap the delete button on the answering machine. Fury rises up inside me, and I can actually feel it turning my face a hot red. I draw in a deep breath and blow it back out again. With mechanical motions, I pick up the ice cream carton and place it back in the freezer.

How dare he?

These are the only three words I seem able to force through my mind, and they play over and over again, until I lean against the counter and blink them away.

All this time, and he picks today to call.

Why today?

I try to think how many years it has been, but a number won't stick in my head. A swirl of memories swim before me, pieces of the past that I long ago put in storage. My mama's face smiling down at me. . .the low growl of my daddy's truck as it pulls into our driveway every evening. . .the fights that were nearly certain to end the night.

I grab Lexie's bowl of ice cream and walk into the living room, sitting down beside her and holding it out like a peace offering.

She smiles her sweet smile, and I give her a bite.

A knock sounds at the door. "Come in," I call out, my voice shaking despite my best efforts to control it.

Macy walks through the door first, dressed in cowboy boots and jeans so tight it is a small miracle she managed to get them on. Mrs. Simpson, Macy's mother, is right behind her.

"How'd you know we weren't that awful landlord of yours?" Macy says, dropping her purse on the floor by the door.

"I'd have smelled him coming."

Macy laughs. "Oooh. Lila's sassy tonight, Mama. I think we're gonna have some fun."

"Now you girls have to behave," Mrs. Simpson says, her voice Southern soft, like the satin edges of a baby's blanket. "Just because it's Lila's birthday, you don't go out and forget your raisin'."

Grey hair pulled back in a bun, navy slacks and a white blouse, wire-framed glasses that tended to stay too low on her nose, Mrs. Simpson defines old-fashioned femininity. She can recite multiple books of the Bible – that is books, not verses – and actually makes as much effort to live what she believes as anyone I've ever known.

Macy, on the other hand, likes to test her mama's convictions on a regular basis. I've often wondered how Mrs. Simpson puts up with Macy's wild child lifestyle, but her patience is endless. She refuses to give up on getting her daughter back into church "one of these Sundays soon."

Mrs. Simpson steps forward and sits down on the couch next to Lexie, reaching in her oversize purse for a tissue and dabbing the white ice-cream mustache from Lexie's upper lip. "There you go, dear."

I kiss Lexie's forehead and stand up, certain that if I wait another moment to go, I won't be going at all.

Mrs. Simpson and Lexie are a picture of contentment as Macy and I walk out the trailer door a couple of minutes later. Macy leads me by the hand as if she knows I might bolt at any second.

She has no idea how right she is.

The guilt is by far the worst thing. There are times when I so much long for temporary freedom that it feels like acid eating a hole inside me. And then as soon as I get a little, the guilt sets in, and all I want to do is go home and hold my little girl until it goes away.

"Quit," Macy says, thwacking me on the arm as we slide into her yellow Volkswagen.

"What?" I say, clicking my seat belt.

"Thinking. Tonight is not about thinking. Tonight is about doing."

Macy backs up and pulls away from the trailer with a spit of gravel. I glance over at Rowdy's place, and there sits Brownie, chained up and watching us go, with the kind of longing on his face that needs no words for expression.

"And quit looking at that dog," Macy says, shifting gears so that we are breaking Rowdy's twenty-five mile-per-hour speed limit and then some. "Short of shooting that fat slob, Rowdy, there's nothing you can do to save him."

"That's what I love about you, Macy. Your endless stream of hope and optimism."

Macy reaches in the center console to pull out a pack of cigarettes, lights one and offers me the pack.

"No, thanks," I say. "I thought you quit those nasty things."

"I did. I'm quitting again tomorrow."

"Wouldn't it be a lot easier to quit for good?"

"Lets me practice my willpower."

"I'm sure one day I'll understand that."

Macy takes a deep pull and blows it out her partially lowered window. "You ready for your surprise?"

"How about we just catch a movie or something?" I say, wondering again if Macy has planned a night I will surely regret.

"A movie?" she says, looking at me as if I've just cast a curse on the whole plan. "Movies are for lame chicks who couldn't get picked up with a front-end loader."

"I like movies, and the last thing in the world I need is to be picked up."

"And when was the last time you experienced either one?"

I think for a moment. "Forrest Gump on DVD?"

"My point exactly."

I reach in my purse and pull out my cell phone, checking to make sure it has a signal. Macy snatches it from my hand and sticks it in her shirt pocket. "If it rings, I'll let you know. Otherwise, you'll will it into ringing, just so you'll have a reason to go home."

I roll my eyes and lean my head against the seat. "What's the point in celebrating another birthday anyway?"

"Well, the point is that we're still here, still kicking, capable of raising some serious hell."

"I'm capable of twelve hours worth of sleep, and that's about it."

"Oh, you've still got it, girl. We just gotta dig it up."

We take the 220 north ramp toward Roanoke. Macy cranks the music, and we drive the twenty minutes or so with Rascal Flatts as our soundtrack. I close my eyes and listen to the words, finally relaxing under their spell. I would be content with just this being my birthday surprise, riding in Macy's car with the wind blowing through the windows, the music making my pulse pound, nothing more than that expected of me.

In Roanoke, we head down 581 to the Peters Creek Road exit. A mile or so from Hollins College, Macy turns into a parking lot filled with cars. College kids stand in clusters, brown bags covering the bottles in their hands.

"Aren't we a little old for this place?" I ask. "And when are you going to tell me exactly what we're doing?"

"Now," she says. "We're seeing Case Phillips. He's doing a fundraiser here tonight. And he's got a special guest who hasn't been announced yet."

"Seriously?" I say, leaning back to give her a disbelieving look.

"Would I lie to you?"

"You've been known to," I say, smiling.

"Only when I thought it in your best interest," she says, defending herself.

"Macy, this is incredible. You shouldn't have done it. The tickets must have cost a fortune."

"Would you stop? Let me enjoy giving you your birthday present."

"Sorry. I didn't mean to sound ungrateful."

"We're here to have a good time. Let's get on it," she says, opening the car door and sliding out.

"How did you know about this?" I ask, getting out on my side.

"I keep my finger on the pulse," she says, smiling.

"I didn't know there was a pulse where we live."

We both laugh, and I realize it's been a long time since I laughed like this. I again feel instantly guilty for the thought, because while it's true, my life is as full of good moments as it is difficult ones.

We're parked next to a Saab convertible where a guy and girl are leaning against the hood, making out as if their curfew is imminent. The guy looks up at us with the slow-mo response of alcohol-numbed senses.

"Hey," he says, once he finally focuses, eyeing us both with interest. He steps back from the girl, and she makes an attempt to right the mini-dress that has made its way higher up her legs than even the designer must have intended. They both have the look of well-fed, well-groomed college students, and that air of confidence only found in people who have never had their status or their expected destination in life questioned.

"Hey," Macy shoots back, giving him a look and a smile that automatically raises the college girl's hackles. She puts a hand on the guy's arm, reestablishing her claim.

"You girls headed inside?" the guy asks.

"We are," Macy says, giving him a once-over that brings a new light of interest to his eyes. He steps away from the college girl as if he's been playing in the kiddy yard and just recognized an opportunity to move up to where the big boys play.

The girl glares at him and walks off. He shrugs and says to Macy, "See you in there?"

Macy grins. "You just might."

Halfway across the parking lot, I shake my head and say, "Was that nice?"

"Nothing wrong with a little teasing."

"Is he even legal?"

"He looks like he knows his way around the block."

"Like that means anything."

We reach the entrance where a line wraps around the side of the building. Macy takes one look at the chain of college students and walks directly up to the bouncer-guy sitting on a stool at the door.

"Ladies," he says, "end of the line's back there."

Macy gives him a smile that could melt an icecap. "Evenin'. That sure is a long line."

"Yes, ma'am, it is. Gettin' longer by the second," he says, tipping his head toward the throng of guys piling out of an old green Cadillac.

"My friend and I are real anxious to see Case Phillips. If we stand in that line, we might miss some of the performance."

"Good chance you will," he says, taking an ID from the next girl in line who barely looks old enough to drive. He gives it a cursory glance and then waves her in.

"I guess so with the careful scrutiny you're going to have to give all these IDs," Macy says. "I'm sure it's nearly impossible to tell a real one from a fake." She waggles her cell phone in the air. "Course I'd be happy to call up the local law enforcement and ask them to come on over and help you check their validity. We'd probably get in a lot faster."

Bouncer-guy looks at Macy through narrowed-eyes, clearly trying to decide if she is bluffing.

"Let me just check and see if they can help out." Macy starts punching numbers.

"All right, all right," he says, hitching his thumb toward the smoky interior behind him. "Devil only knows how many times you've pulled this one."

Macy kisses him on the cheek and saunters by. "Never failed yet."

He has the audacity to check out her behind, and as I follow her through the open door, meek as a church mouse, it occurs to me that it is always this way with Macy. She can take a guy to the mat, rob him of any last smidge of pride, and he actually ends up admiring her for it.

Macy grabs my hand and leads me through the throng of partying students, a few locals like us in the mix.

It's been years since I've been in a place like this, certainly not for Macy's lack of trying. It's hard, though, to go back to a place, or time for that matter, where I clearly don't belong anymore. It seems a far easier thing to keep my eyes focused forward.

Macy orders us each a beer from a lightning-fast bartender – Corona with lime – pays for them, then hands me one. She clinks the side of her bottle against mine and says, "Cheers! And Happy birthday!"

"Thanks, Macy," I say and take a sip, the beer ice cold going down. "Have you checked my cell phone to make sure there aren't any messages?"

Macy pulls the phone from her pocket, taps the screen and says, "No calls."

"May I have it back, please?"

"Nope. Just as sure as I give it to you, you'll be calling my mama and findin' some excuse for us to get back home."

I roll my eyes and tell myself to be gracious. Macy has gone to some trouble to pull off this night.

She takes my hand and leads me over to a circle of guys who part like a wave beneath an oncoming cruise ship to allow us entrance. "Hey, fellas," she says, cranking the wattage on her smile.

There isn't one among them who has hit the twenty-one mile marker, and for Macy, it isn't an issue. For me, it would be too much like seducing the Sunday school class.

"How you girls doin'?"

I feel sure even Cesar Millan would declare this guy the leader of the pack. He isn't the tallest in the bunch, although at first glance, you'd think so. He holds himself the way a dominant dog does, body stretched tall and taut, the message clear, first to eat, first to pick from whatever female buffet happens his way.

Pack Leader gives Macy a once-over, approval glinting in his eyes, and then turns his attention to me. It only takes him a second to make his decision, and he is back at Macy, turning his veneered smile up to impossible-to-resist level. To his credit, Macy seems impressed, and the two of them step outside the circle to engage in a duel of wit.

"That didn't appear to hurt your feelings."

The man who utters this astute observation isn't part of the Sunday school class. Apparently, he's been watching from the sidelines.

He adds, "Frankly, I think he made the wrong choice."

"Well, thanks, but maybe you didn't hear my sigh of relief from where you were standing."

He laughs then, and I notice that he has a nice one. It is deep and resonant, if that's the right word. It echoes inside me, leaving something good behind.

I've always found a good laugh attractive, maybe because it's something a person can't fake. It either works, or it doesn't.

"Could I get you another beer?"

"Thanks, but I'm fine," I say, glancing over my shoulder.

"Waiting for someone?"

I direct my attention back to the guy in front of me. "No. No, I'm not."

"I'm David Graham by the way."

"Lila Bellamy."

"You from around here?" he asks.

"Half hour or so away."

"So what do you do when you're not hanging out listening to country music?"

Just the thought of trying to answer his question with any kind of accuracy weights me with exhaustion, so I shake my head and say, "Oh, you know, just normal stuff."

He leans back, gives me a long look. "Why do I get the feeling there's more to the story?"

Before I can answer, the thrum of noise in the club rises to another level, and then everyone starts to clap and cheer. I look toward the stage where band members are walking out to pick up their instruments.

"Do you know who the surprise guest is?" I ask.

"I do, as a matter of fact."

"Who?"

He smiles. "You'll see in a moment. I work for Case Phillips, actually. I'm his road manager."

"Oh," I say, feeling suddenly silly. "Wow. That's great."

The crowd starts to yell again, whistles and hoots. I look at the stage where a tall guy in a baseball cap has just walked out and picked up a guitar.

I go completely still, as if I've been instantly frozen in place.

My heart kicks once, and then takes off at an erratic gallop. I feel sweat bead on my forehead. No way. It. Can. Not. Be.

"Thomas Franklin," David says close to my ear, "from Barefoot Outlook."

I try to respond, but for the life of me, I can't make a sound come out. I watch as he takes the stool in front of the mike while one of the players begins to strum a guitar. The crowd has gone completely silent, as if a mute button has been pushed. He starts out soft, the chords immediately grabbing me.

His voice follows, and the song spins its spell. I want to leave. I need to leave, but it's as if my feet are glued to the floor, and no matter what directives my brain tries to give, they aren't listening.

As soon as he hits the last note, the crowd goes wild with applause and cheering.

From the corner of my eye, I spot Macy walking toward the stage. I watch as she walks straight over to Thomas. And then I realize what this whole night has been about. She wouldn't. She wouldn't!

I open my mouth to call her name, but no sound comes out.

They chat for a few moments, and then I see the look of surprised disbelief cross his face. Macy points my way, and his gaze spotlights where I'm standing until he finds me. His eyes widen, and then a slow smile breaks across his face. He taps the microphone to get the crowd's attention and says, "I've just been told there's a special birthday girl in the house tonight. Lila, this one's for you."

He sings a solo rendition of the song I've heard every year of my life in one version or another, none of which ever affected me like this. His voice caresses each word, and by the time he's sung the last words – "happy birthday to you" – I feel as if I've just received a deep-tissue massage, and it is all I can do to keep my legs from buckling.

There is a pause then as the last notes fade away, and he says into the microphone, "Lila Bellamy. Could you come up front, please?"

Too stunned to move, I stand perfectly still. David leans back and gives me a questioning look before saying, "Go on. He won't bite."

At the side of the stage, Macy starts clapping and then others start to join in. Before long, the whole place comes alive with it, and what else can I do except start walking?

I use the time it takes me to weave my way through the crowd plotting various ways to pay Macy back for this act of kindness. As I walk past her, fully intent on ignoring her, Macy takes my arm and forces me to look at her, her face and voice uncharacteristically serious. "Go for it, okay?"

She then puts her hands on my back and pushes me forward. Suddenly, I'm on the stage with Thomas Franklin beckoning me over.

My feet have become concrete blocks, and it's all I can do to force myself to pick them up and walk the short distance to where he's waiting. My mind races with possible scenarios of what will happen once I get there. A sweet peck on the cheek. A serenade, maybe. Macy is nothing if not imaginative, and persuasive too.

But what actually happens, all but knocks the wind from my chest.

"Hey, Lila," Thomas says in his buttery, sandpaper voice, his eyes capturing mine. "I hear you know how to sing a song."

I stare at him as if he has just released a string of Greek words I've never heard before. "I—no, not really."

He hands me a guitar a band member has just passed him. He then offers me the stool. "Happy birthday," he says away from the microphone. "Although I feel like I'm the one getting the present."

If it is possible for fear to actually freeze the blood in a person's veins, then that's exactly what happens to me. Terrified, I can barely grasp the neck of the guitar because my fingers are shaking so badly.

While I want to be furious with Macy, tell Thomas this is a crazy mistake, that I had no idea she was going to do this, I can't even begin to find the words.

"The stage is yours," he says. "Let's hear what you've got."

Something in his tone connects with my terror and yanks the plug on it. It drains from me like water from a tub, and I realize people are staring at me, waiting to see what I'm going to do.

It hits me then that this is probably the last time I will ever have the opportunity to sing in front of anyone other than the reflection staring back at me from the bathroom mirror.

I feel the tug of long-ago dreams, and I sit down on the stool, positioning the guitar on my knee. It is a very nice one, a little big for me, but really nice. I test a few chords and instantly recognize the guitar's superiority to anything I've ever played.

I strum a beginning, leaning in to the mike and saying, "This song is called "Amazed." It's about how I want to live my life without ever becoming jaded about the things that really matter."

My voice cracks, and I tell myself I can't do it. It's been years since I sang in any kind of public setting. This is insane.

Silence hangs in the room, and I catch Macy's gaze, trained on me with such conviction. She believes in me, in the way that only the truest of friends can, and with that as my guidepost, I take a deep breath, and start over. This time my voice lifts and carries each word of the song to its intended place.

The room goes completely silent except for the tinkle of glass from the bar area. I remember then what it feels like to captivate an audience, show them a small piece of me, watch as understanding lights their faces. Just as I let the song fade with a few emotional notes, I feel the relief I always felt years ago when I realized I had made that connect.

The crowd begins to clap, the noise rising to the rafters of the room. Several voices call out for more, and others join in. I glance out from the stage where Thomas stands next to Macy.

He walks over, dips his head to my ear and says, "Damn, girl. I had no idea."

"Why would you?" I say, keeping my voice light. "We didn't exactly concentrate on conversation that night, did we?"

I feel him flinch a little, and then he says, "Will you wait for me after the show?"

"I can't stay," I say quickly, suddenly certain of that fact if nothing else. "And if you don't get back behind the mike, this crowd is going to stage a riot."

I finally let myself fully look at him, and only then realize I've been avoiding it. He has the kind of good looks that don't really seem fair when he's also been blessed with such an incredible voice. But they go together, that's for sure.

I stand up from the stool and force myself to meet his gaze. "Thank you, Thomas. That was the best birthday present I've ever had."

The band starts up, and I hand the microphone to him. "It was nice seeing you again."

"Lila, wait," he starts, but I'm already leaving the stage and making my way through the crowd to where Macy is standing. The look on her face tells me she has no idea whether I am going to hug her or slug her.

"One day you'll thank me?" she says with a questioning smile.

"Did you know he was going to be here?"

"Maybe?"

I sigh, shaking my head, even as I try to understand that her intentions where I'm concerned are always good. "I know you think you were doing a good thing for me, but Macy, you know what I have to lose."

"Do I? The way I see it, there's only room for you to gain a little."

"I don't want anything from him. I never have."

"That's not the point."

My cell phone rings from its place in Macy's shirt pocket. She snatches it out and turns her back to answer it.

"If that's your mama, give me the phone," I say, trying to reach for it.

Macy dodges my effort, but then goes suddenly serious. I watch her face fall and feel the contents of my entire being drop to the floor.

"What is it?" I ask, barely able to suppress the panic in my voice.

"We'll be right there, okay?" Macy says and snaps the phone closed.

She looks at me then, putting a hand on my shoulder as if she might need to steady me. "It's Lexie. She's had a little bit of a seizure. Mama's at the hospital with her now."

Panic floods through me. "What? Oh, no! We have to go. We have to go!"

Macy takes my hand and starts leading me through the crowd. She plows through the bar, like a swimmer caught in a riptide, determined to break the current. The exit seems as if it's miles away. And all I can think is that I never should have come to this place tonight.

I don't belong here.

I should have been home with my daughter.

That is the only place where I belong.

♪

Thomas

You Just Never Know

It's all I can do to get through my set. There are a few times when I actually think I'm not going to be able to remember the words to the next verse in front of me. All I can think about is following Lila.

But I keep my feet planted firmly on the stage. I promised Case, and I can't go back on my word to him. So I force myself to tune out everything except the forty-five minutes in front of me.

When the end of the set finally comes, I thank the crowd for their attention and walk off stage to where Case is waiting just out of sight, guitar strapped across his shoulder.

"So, who is she?" he asks me with a half-smile.

I make an attempt to shrug as if it's all casual. "Someone I met several years ago when Holden and I were playing here in Roanoke."

"I take it she made an impression on you."

"Never saw her again as a matter of fact, until tonight."

"She's got quite a voice."

"Yeah, that was a surprise to me."

"Planning on seeing her tonight?"

"I don't really think she's interested in seeing me."

Case pulls back and gives me a long look. "Well, that certainly sets her apart from the crowd. All the more reason you better go after her," he says, with the first real smile I've seen on his face in a long time. "Must be something special about her. Hey, thanks for the performance," he adds. "You were awesome out there."

"A little distracted, I'm afraid," I admit.

"Then nobody realized it but you. I'm on. See ya' later."

Case walks out and the place erupts in a roar of applause. I grab my things and head outside to the truck. I had parked in the back of the building where Case and the band bus parked. Thankfully, no one is around as I hit the remote and unlock the door. I slide inside and sit for a minute with my arms draped across the steering wheel, trying to absorb everything that happened in there tonight.

Gut instinct tells me I should just drive back to the hotel, head up to bed, and order some room service. But I keep picturing her face and hearing her voice on the notes of that song, and I really want to see her again.

The likelihood of the two of us running into each other tonight has to be somewhere in the same statistical range as this small Virginia city getting hit by a meteor.

So how had it happened?

My guess is her friend had something to do with it. I know without a doubt that Lila had no idea I would be here. Or she wouldn't have agreed to come.

To this day, I have no idea why she took such an aversion to me. After the fact, anyway.

I left her that morning almost seven years ago, fully expecting that we would see each other again. I *wanted* to see her again. But when she refused to answer my phone calls or return my emails, I eventually chalked it up to her deciding I had been a very bad idea.

And at the time, I probably was.

Considering all of that, I'm pretty sure I should leave her alone now. There's not an ounce of logic to me pursuing her an inch farther. Even so, I know I'm going to.

So how do you find somebody who doesn't want you to find them?

I pick up my phone and tap the screen.

Google. Of course.

♪

I FIND THE ADDRESS in the White Page Directory, tap the information into my GPS, surprised to see that it's some forty-five minutes away.

I'm pretty sure that this could be a really bad idea. Who's to say there's not a husband waiting for her at home? Maybe she and her friend were simply having a girl's night out.

I can't picture that scenario, but maybe that's more because I'm hoping it isn't true. When in all reality, it could be.

I crank the radio and drive with the window down, letting the music and the cool night air blow away all my reservations as to why this is a really bad idea.

I'm there before I'm ready to be. The GPS on my phone indicates a left-hand turn just ahead. I hit my blinker and brake at the same time, spotting a sign painted on an old board that reads: "Rowdy Pike's Sunflower Mobile Home Park. Enter at Your Own Risk."

I'm wondering if the GPS has steered me wrong, but the address is 150 Pike Road, so I guess it's right. I let the truck roll slowly down the gravel road, first one tire, then another dropping into pothole after pothole.

A quarter mile or so down, I see two long rows of trailers, one on my left, one on my right. Each is marked with a painted number on the top corner.

I turn into the small parking spot for the one marked 150, the lights of the truck sweeping across the rusted exterior of the seen-far-better-days mobile home.

There's no other car here, and all the lights are off. I should leave. No doubt about it. I should leave.

But I open the door and slide out, something I can't even explain pulling me to the front of the trailer where I knock softly and say her name, "Lila?"

There's no answer, and I step off the small porch just as I hear a door hinge creak open.

A voice calls out, "You got a reason to be hangin' around here in the dark?"

The question is a little slurred and a lot accusing. "I'm looking for Lila Bellamy."

"Well, I reckon you can see she ain't here."

A dog whines from somewhere behind him. In the dark, I can just make out the silhouette of a dog chained to a barrel that appears to be doing an impersonation of a dog house.

"You know when she'll be back?" I ask.

"I ain't her secretary."

The dog whines again, and the man snarls over his shoulder, "Shut up, you stupid mutt."

Anger unfurls inside me, and my fists clench automatically. "Do you expect that she'll be back tonight?" I ask, keeping my tone deliberately even.

"My guess would be no, since the rescue squad came in here earlier and took that kid of hers to the hospital again."

"Kid?" I ask, realizing the word sounds as stunned as I feel.

"Always something wrong with her."

"What do you mean?"

The man shrugs, his impatience level obviously rising. "I don't know. She's crippled up or something."

"Would you happen to have any idea which hospital they took her to?" I force the words out in as neutral a tone as I can manage, when what I'd like to do is relocate his nose for him.

"No, I wouldn't happen to have any idea which hospital they took her to," he mocks back. "Unless you got some reason to be here, this is private property, so you'd best be going."

The dog whimpers again. This time, he throws the beer can he's holding in the direction of the barrel-doghouse. It pings off the side, making a bullet sound that sends the dog flying inside the center of the barrel.

I have never wanted to hit someone so badly in all my life.

I ball my fists into a knot and walk back to the truck, putting one foot in front of the other until I'm safely inside and backing out of the driveway.

I allow myself the pleasure of envisioning a few possible responses to dealing with that scumbag, all involving actions that would most likely land me in jail most of the rest of my life.

I take the pothole-strewn driveway at a speed that spits a stream of gravel behind me. I can only hope one hits him in the head.

I'm back on the main road, trying to figure out where to go from here when my phone rings. Holden's name appears on the screen at the same time Gomer Pyle declares Shazam! I answer without letting myself consider all the reasons I don't need to be talking to him right now.

"How'd it go?" Holden asks right off.

"It was a good show," I say, keeping my voice neutral.

"You back at the hotel?"

"Not exactly."

"Another town? Another girl?"

"Not exactly."

"You sound weird."

"It's been a weird night," I admit.

"What? You run into Lila?" He asks the question in a joking voice, as if it's the very last thing he expects me to say yes to.

"Actually, yeah, I did."

"What?"

"Yeah, for real," I say.

"How the heck did that happen?"

"It's her birthday. A friend of hers brought her to the show. She asked me if Lila could sing a song."

"Lila sings?"

"Yeah," I say. "Pretty great, actually."

"Are you with her now?"

"No. Just looking for her."

"All right, you lost me somewhere between Lila sings and looking for her."

"She left the show before I was done, and I decided I'd look her up."

"And?"

"And some IQ-challenged redneck just told me she has a daughter who got taken to the hospital tonight for something."

"She has a daughter?" Holden sounds as shocked as I'd felt.

"Apparently."

"Is she married?"

"Rowdy the Redneck didn't mention it. I guess she could be."

"How old is the girl?"

"I don't have any idea."

"Maybe you oughta find out."

"Why?" It occurs to me then what he's implying. "Are you crazy? I was with her one night, Holden. After which, she gave me the boot."

"Last I heard, it only takes one night. Boot or not."

"That's insane," I say.

"If you're that sure, then I recommend you point the truck toward Nashville and floor it."

"I am sure," I say.

"Okay. So we'll see you back here tomorrow?"

"CeCe wants to know if you can come over for dinner tomorrow night. Heads up, there's someone she wants you to meet."

"You know, maybe I just need to swear off women for a while."

"You could do that," Holden says. "But you won't. CeCe thinks you'll like this girl."

"I thought she was busy warning every female she meets that I'm bad news."

"Hey, are you asking me to explain the way girls think?"

"No, because I don't think you have any more idea than I do."

"You're right about that. So we'll see you here tomorrow night then?"

"Later," I say, hanging up without giving him a definite answer either way.

A convenience store sits up ahead, and I pull into the parking lot so I can think for a minute. I don't have a single doubt in my mind that the smart thing for me to do is exactly what I just implied to Holden I would do. Head on back to Nashville.

I lean back and stare up at the night sky through the sunroof, my thoughts at war. I keep seeing her face as she sang that song tonight. And I can't quit thinking how right she had looked there. How happy it had obviously made her. But then seeing where she's living, next to that sorry excuse for a human being. And finding out that her daughter has some kind of problem.

The jerk's words come back to me then. "I don't know. Crippled up or somethin'."

Why would she be living in a place like that? Clearly, she could use some help. Whether she'll let me or not, I have no idea. But all of a sudden, I'm absolutely sure that I want to offer. And not because I think for a second that the child could be mine. She would have told me. I don't see her keeping something like that from me. Probably some guy who refused to take responsibility, leaving her to do the best she could.

I pick up my phone and do a local search for the nearest hospital, give the GPS the address and then pull back onto the road. I'm just going to let her know I'd like to help out. Find out where I can send her some money. Then be on my way back to Nashville.

And eventually, it will seem like this night never happened. Just like the only other night I ever spent with her.

♪

Lila

Just One Song

She looks like an angel.

I've thought this so many times. Sitting by the hospital bed, running my hand through my daughter's silky blonde hair while she sleeps, I wonder how I could ever think I needed anything more than this child in my life. Just the thought of losing her makes me feel as if my chest has been opened with a kitchen knife and my heart removed with bare hands.

This isn't the first time we've been here, or the first seizure Lexie has ever had. I never handled one any better than the other. They terrify me and leave me as emotionally exhausted as they leave Lexie physically spent.

I glance up and find Macy and her mother watching us from the doorway. Mrs. Simpson had done all the right things, called 911 immediately, but I can see that she's shaken.

I know the feeling of realizing that you are the only person standing between my beautiful little girl and possible death. I feel guilty for putting that responsibility on Macy's mother.

Macy steps around her mom and comes into the room. She stops at the bed and watches Lexie for a moment, taking in the even rise and fall of her breathing. "Thank God," she says.

"I know." My voice breaks under the words, and Macy squeezes my shoulder in understanding.

"Promise me something?"

"What?" I ask, glancing up at her.

"That you're not going to let this be a sign that you can't ever go out again and do something for yourself."

"I won't," I say, completely unconvincing even to my own ears.

"You will, too."

I don't bother to deny it this time. I don't believe in signs, but I do believe in reminders. This is that for me. A reminder of where I am supposed to be.

Macy sits on the corner of the bed, places a hand on Lexie's thin leg beneath the blue hospital bedspread. "You were incredible tonight, you know," she says.

I shake my head. "Some things aren't meant to be revisited. I never should have done that."

"You can't take this to mean that," she says, exasperation in her voice.

"Sometimes, Lila Bellamy, I think I need to get out one of my good dresses and throw you a big ol' pity party!"

If I wasn't so tired and guilt-riddled, I might have actually smiled, except it's clear Macy isn't trying to be funny. "I'm not asking for pity, Mace."

"No. You don't ask for anything. Good heavens, girl, you had those people eating out of your hand with one song. Just one song! That's a gift, Lila. And you've thrown it all away. It might as well not even exist."

"I did no such thing. It didn't go anywhere. But my life isn't just about me. I thought you understood that."

"Of course, I do. I love this little girl nearly as much as you do. But I also love you. And what I don't understand is why you think you have to give up all your dreams just because you got pregnant and had a child. Is it really fair that Thomas has gone on with his life when you haven't?"

"We were one night. And I've gone on with my life in exactly the way I wanted to. Lexie is everything to me."

Macy is quiet for a bit, and I can tell she's weighing what to say next.

"Do you really think it's right that you've kept her from him?"

I pull back and give her a long look. "Are you questioning what I've done just because Thomas is playing in Roanoke for one night? He's passing through. That's the life he leads."

"I'm questioning it because you're barely able to make ends meet! It's too much for one person, Lila. Too much for you."

"Stop. Macy, stop," I say, pushing back my chair and standing. "I don't want her to hear this."

"She's asleep, Lila. And you need to hear it."

"Hey."

We both turn to the doorway at the same time. Thomas is now standing there next to Mrs. Simpson, hands shoved in his pockets, a look of complete uncertainty on his face.

"What are you doing here?" I ask, panic welling up inside me so fast that I feel instantly sick.

"I'm not really sure," he says, his voice low and honest.

Macy walks to the door, reaches for his hand and pulls him inside the room. "Come in, Thomas. Mama and I were just leaving. Lila, I'll touch base with you later."

With that, she leads her mom down the hall and to the elevator.

The air in the room has become electrified. My heart is beating so fast I can feel it in my throat. I want to pause everything and rewind to earlier in the day when I could have refused to go out with Macy. When I could have stayed home with Lexie, and none of this would have happened.

I watch as he turns his head to look at Lexie where she is still asleep in the hospital bed. He stares at her and then walks over to stand beside her, looking down at her sweet face for a long time.

I see the recognition as it dawns on him. His lips part slightly, and he sucks in a short whoosh of air as if someone has just slammed a fist into his midsection.

It will do no good for me to deny what he is thinking. He is there in her features. I am there in her features. The blend of the two of us is unmistakable.

When he does turn to face me, he suddenly reaches for my elbow and propels me out of the room. I feel the anger in him, tight and coiled. He walks me to the end of the hall where a small waiting room for families of patients is currently empty. He closes the door behind us and locks it.

I force myself to walk to the opposite corner, staring out the window at the cars four floors below us, my arms wrapped around my waist as if I can hold all my fear inside.

"How could you do this?" he finally asks, each word forced from him through gritted teeth.

"Thomas—"

"How could you not tell me?"

I try to draw in a deep breath, but the air feels trapped in my chest. "Because I didn't need your help."

"My help? I'm fifty percent of what it took to make that little girl. My help? I had a right to know, damn it!"

"One night doesn't give you the right—"

He slams his fist through the air, connecting with the palm of his other hand. "Yes, it does give me the right! It took two of us to make her."

"And one of us to mess her up? Are you going to add that?"

"What? No. I—"

I start to cry then, sobs rising from inside me so quickly that I cannot hold them back.

"What do you mean, Lila? She's beautiful. She's perfect." And then in a panicky voice, "What's wrong with her? Is she going to be all right?"

I press my fist to my lips and will myself to stop crying. When I finally answer him, my voice is so low that he leans in closer to hear me. "She has cerebral palsy, Thomas."

"What?" Shock reverberates through the question.

"I didn't know until just after she turned three."

"What is it? I mean I've heard of it, but—"

I cross my arms tight around myself and try to find the words. "It's caused by a brain injury. Most likely before she was born. While her brain was still developing."

He says nothing for a long time, as if he's processing every word of what I've just said. "And you never thought you might need my help?" he says, the words low and uneven.

"I didn't want you to feel obligated—"

"But wasn't I?"

It's not what I expected him to say. And so I don't know how to answer. Finally, I manage, "I won't say that night was a mistake, Thomas. I would give my life for my daughter, but we both know it was never something that was meant to last. I didn't want to be a girl who trapped you into—"

"Damn it, Lila! That was an awfully big decision for you to make for me."

"I had to do what I thought would be best for Lexie and for me."

"And you couldn't even give me the opportunity to do the right thing?"

I meet his gaze then, and the hurt there is not what I expected to see. "Thomas. Do you think you would be where you are now if I had told you? You would never have gone after your dream. And I would be the one who kept you from doing it."

"That's not fair," he says.

"Maybe not. But I do believe it's true."

He stares at me for a long, uncomfortable string of moments, his jaw set and hard. "You have no way of knowing that."

I can see that I've hurt him, and that was never my intention. Had I been wrong to shut him out? Suddenly, I don't know, and a tidal wave of confusion washes over me, taking with it any ability I have to find logic in this.

But before I can say another word, Thomas yanks open the door and walks out, his boots making a hollow, echoing sound on the hospital's spotless tile floor.

♪

Thomas

What You Can't Get Back

I've never wanted to hit something so much in my whole life.

My fists itch with the need, and I keep them balled up until I reach the truck in the hospital parking lot. I yank open the door and slide inside, gunning the engine as soon as I hear it crank.

The truck fishtails onto the street, and I floor it through the first stoplight. But then common sense crashes over me, and I hit the brake hard, slowing down to meet the speed limit.

I don't know what to think first.

I have a daughter.

A little girl.

A beautiful little girl.

Her name is Lexie.

She's been alive for six years, and I knew nothing about her.

How can that possibly be?

I think about the look on Lila's face when she'd seen me standing in the doorway. The instant terror in her eyes. Could she really think I might try to take Lexie away from her? Or that I would reject them both?

My heart and brain balk at this, but then how would she have known any different? Other than the fact that the chemistry between us had been instant and electric, we knew little else about each other. We hadn't even been together for twelve hours.

And yet those hours had been completely life-changing. Life-creating.

I flick on the radio in an effort to slow my thoughts long enough for me to process them.

CeCe's voice flows into the truck on the words of our latest single. My voice comes in behind hers, and I reach over to turn it off, not needing the reminder of why Lila might have thought I wasn't ready to be a father.

I'm halfway back to Roanoke when I pull into a McDonald's parking lot. I find an out-of-the-way spot and cut the engine, dropping my head onto the back of the seat and staring up at the sky.

I pick up my phone to call Holden, but just as quickly decide I'm not ready for that. I need to know what I think about this first, take the pieces apart and look at them one by one until I can absorb the complete truth.

For whatever reason, Lila hadn't trusted me with the fact that she was pregnant. No matter how I try to process this, the realization has painfully sharp edges.

Had she gone through it all alone? I remember that she told me her mother had died. That she was an only child. I can't remember if she said anything about her father.

All the anger that propelled me out of the hospital less than half an hour ago suddenly slides away, like mud down a rain-pummeled hillside. In its place, I just feel an incredible sadness. Like a loss. Grief for something I know I will never get back.

The birth of my daughter. The first six years of her life. And the opportunity to be a part of doing whatever could possibly be done to help her.

I don't want to judge Lila for the decisions she made. None of it can be redone, and if I'm not sure of anything else, I'm sure of her love for Lexie.

Maybe she was right to shut me out back then. I'll never know the answer to that. But I'm not going to be shut out again. I want to know my daughter. I want her to know I want her.

♪

I WATCH HER FROM the doorway for a few seconds, wishing I could somehow freeze-frame this picture.

Lila is leaning over the bed with her cheek on Lexie's hand. Her eyes are closed, and I'm not sure if she's asleep or just resting.

"Lila," I say eventually, keeping my voice low so that I don't wake up Lexie.

She sits up with a start, stands and puts a hand to her chest. "Thomas. I didn't know you were there."

"Can we talk for a minute? This time I promise to be rational."

She looks as if she wants to say no, but nods once and waves me out of the room. We go back to the waiting area, and it's still empty.

"Thomas," she says with regret in her voice. "I know I haven't been fair to you. I never meant to-"

"Don't," I say.

She looks at me, uncertainty clouding her eyes. I walk closer and reach out to her. She resists me at first, holding herself so stiff that I wonder if she might break if I force her to yield. But the truth is I need to comfort her as much as she needs me to do it. So I reel her in slowly, but with determination, until she folds herself into my arms, burying her face against my chest where my shirt muffles the sound of her crying.

I don't know how long we stand there, but I feel myself absorbing every ounce of the pain I feel inside her. Several minutes pass before I can bring myself to ask the question I have to ask. "I know it was just one night, but did I really seem like the kind of guy who wouldn't have done the right thing?"

Even before she says a word, I think I know the answer. I know who I was then. And how I must have looked to her. At the very beginning of chasing a dream I had every intention of catching. I remember some of the things I said to her that night. And from here, I guess I can understand what she would have thought. That even if I did agree to be a part of Lexie's life, I might eventually come to resent it for the things it kept me from doing.

I can see this, and I want to flat out deny it, but I don't know if I can. Because right now, I'm at the top of the mountain. The view from here can in no way be compared to the view from where I stood then.

I'd like to think I would have said the right thing, done the right thing. But I don't know if I would have or not.

"I'm sorry," I say, rubbing her back in an effort at comfort. "I shouldn't have said those things I said earlier. I can see how much you love her. You've devoted your life to her, and I—"

"—wasn't given the chance," she finishes for me. She pulls back, wipes a hand across her face and says, "I should have given you that chance. But I—" She stops, glances off, and then, drawing in a deep breath, says, "I wanted to believe that you would want to know, but I guess it's been my experience that most of the time, people just end up disappointing you."

We stand there, quiet, for a long while. I want to argue with her. But I hear the conviction in her words. Have no idea what she's basing them on. I just know she believes they're true. And it feels good to hold her like this. I don't want to pull away. I don't want her to pull away.

"How about we start from here," I say, "and you give me a chance to be a stand-up guy? I promise you I'll do my best to live up to it."

She looks up at me then, and I see the fear in her eyes. "You can't take her from me, Thomas. She's all I have."

"Lila," I say, hearing my voice break across her name. "I would never. . ." I stop and then say, "Let's just start from here. We'll figure out how as we go."

♪

Lila

A Rowdy Retribution

The doctors release Lexie at just after seven the next morning. Thomas left the hospital at four to drive back to Roanoke to shower and change clothes, promising to be back within a few hours.

I should call him and ask for a ride home, but I can't bring myself to do it. I'm use to taking care of us myself, and the thought of leaning on him at all will take some getting used to.

I call the town cab instead. Harmon Quinn is thrilled to have a passenger before noon, and we head out of town with Lexie's wheelchair sticking out of the trunk.

"It sure is worrisome when these young'uns get sick, ain't it?" Harmon says now, glancing in the rearview mirror at Lexie where her head rests on my shoulder.

"Yes, it is," I say, rubbing my hand across the back of my daughter's hair. She's been more subdued than normal this morning, and I worry there is something the doctors might have missed.

"No man in the picture to help you out with her raisin'?"

"Ah, no, Harmon," I say automatically.

Harmon is what the locals call a picker. He collects information about the passengers who ride in his cab and distributes it out to the rest of the county as he sees fit. Everybody knows if you don't want your business spread far and wide, then you don't share it with Harmon.

For the rest of the ride, I answer his questions with a polite yes or no. When he pulls up in front of the trailer a short while later, the look of disappointment on his face actually makes me feel guilty for not giving him even a morsel of gossip to share with his next passenger.

Harmon pulls Lexie's wheelchair from the trunk and sets it next to the back door. I slide out and then reach inside to lift Lexie up and put her gently in the seat. "How much, Harmon?" I ask, reaching inside my purse and pulling out my wallet.

"For you, five dollars, Miss Lila."

"Now that'll hardly pay for your gas."

"Five is good."

"Thanks, Harmon."

"You're surely welcome."

He gets back in the old red cab and pulls away with a wave out the window, and I feel guilty for not giving him a little more fodder for gossip.

I roll Lexie toward the trailer, glancing over at Rowdy's place where Brownie sits inside his sorry excuse for a doghouse. I hear his tail thump against the barrel side, but he doesn't get up and come out the way he usually does. "Hey, boy," I say.

The door to Rowdy's trailer opens, and Rowdy comes out with a chicken leg in each over-sized paw.

"About time you showed some manners," he throws Brownie's way, finishing off the remains of a leg and hurling the bone in Brownie's direction. The bone hits Brownie in the face. He yelps and retreats deeper inside the barrel.

"Chicken bones aren't good for dogs," I say, gripping the chair handles so hard I can feel my pulse pounding in my palms.

"What the hell you supposed to feed them then? Filet mignon?" he shoots back, giving both words a long "e" in a class-act effort to make them sound more French.

"The bones splinter in their throat," I say, dumb-ass in my tone if not in the actual words.

"Maybe that'll keep him from yappin' his mouth so much," Rowdy says with a big chuckle.

I hurry, wheeling Lexie toward the ramp leading to the trailer door.

"Awful lot of ruckus over here last night," Rowdy says in a louder voice. "And you not even here for your little girl when she needed you."

I let myself envision for a moment another fitting retribution for Rowdy, a severe case of food poisoning traced back to his bucket-a-day-fried-chicken habit. And maybe an internal parasite or two to boot.

♪

Lila

The Unexpected

Inside, the trailer is stifling hot. I turn on the air conditioning window unit, and then roll Lexie to her room. The doctor had recommended she rest for the remainder of the day, and I can see she needs it. Her eyes are heavy, and her shoulders droop. I pick her up and put her in bed, not bothering to change her clothes because she's still wearing her pajamas from last night.

Lexie snuggles under the covers and immediately falls asleep. I watch her, grateful for her soft, even breathing. I brush the back of my hand across her cheek, and she makes that snuffling noise I love to hear.

Lexie had been born six weeks early, and I'd been told she might not live out the week. Those first few days of her life, I never left her side. It's hard to explain the kind of bonding that happens when you're the only link between such a tiny being's survival and her succumbing to what's stacked against her.

Lexie had beaten the odds from day one, and every time I get scared like this, I remind myself my daughter is a fighter. She always pulls through. Always. This is just another temporary setback, and before long, she'll have that light in her eyes again.

I sit though for a long time, watching her sleep, until I no longer feel as if a pair of hands is at my throat. I get up finally and walk back to the kitchen to pour myself a glass of orange juice, taking long, thirsty gulps until it's gone. The fatigue hits me then, and I collapse on the living room couch, staring at the yellowed ceiling tiles.

The tears find their way up, sliding down my cheeks. I made a pact with myself the first time Lexie had one of her seizures that I would never again let her see me cry. She already has enough to be afraid of in this world.

But now, alone, I can't hold it back, and the sobs come out in great heaving gasps that don't have an ounce of dignity to them. I'm not proud of them. I hate giving in to weakness.

So I do what I always do. Get my song journal from the bedroom and bring it back to the living room. I don't know where they come from, but the words are there, and I put them on the page, feeling better with each one. There is something in the making of a song that renews the will to fight inside me, bringing me back to a point where I can start swinging again.

Thoughts of last night fill my head, and I remember what it felt like to be in front of that crowd, singing a song I wrote. The only thing I can compare it to is what it felt like to spend the weekend at my grandma's house when I was a little girl, a safe haven for the time I was there, a place none of the hard stuff of regular life could touch. A place where my daddy didn't stripe my legs with a belt. A place where I could just be me, and that was okay.

That's what it had been like the night I first met Thomas in a downtown bar right before closing time when better judgment should have dictated that I head home. But I had been on the front row of the audience watching Thomas and Holden play, and it was so easy to lose myself in his voice, in the words of the songs he sang with such simple comfort. I don't think I moved throughout both of their sets. And when he made eye contact with me, giving me one of his wide, questioning smiles, I didn't look away.

When the show was over, and I reluctantly began looking for Macy, the guy at the front door told me he'd seen her leave about an hour before with a guy in a Jeep. Since she had the car keys, there was nothing I could do except go outside and wait.

Thomas came out of the club exit door with three or four other guys, two of whom were complaining that it was too early for the place to shut down. One of them had looked at me and made a less than polite suggestion to join them in the back of somebody's truck for a continuation of the party.

Feeling uncomfortable, I got up and started walking away from the club. Thomas followed me and, when the others started after him, he'd turned around and told them to take off. The drunkest guy rattled out a protest along the lines of "So you get to have her all to yourself?"

"Get lost, boys," Thomas said, his tone no longer light. I had the feeling there was another phrase he would have preferred to use but refrained from doing so because of me.

The guys backed away, hands in the air, one of them muttering something about the singer always getting the girl.

I started walking again, even though I had no idea where to go.

"Hey," Thomas said. "I'll walk you to your car and make sure nobody else bothers you."

"Are you sure you're with them?" I'd asked.

"Not really," he said. "I got ditched by my buddy Holden for the girl he was hitting on in the front row."

I'd looked down and said, "I'm waiting on my friend. I'll be fine. Really."

"Where's your car?"

I pointed at the parking lot across the street. "Macy has the keys."

"Ah, dilemma," he said.

"Yeah."

"Can I get you a cab?"

"I actually live about an hour from here."

"Well, I'm staying at the Hotel Roanoke just across the bridge. Their bar might still be open. We could hang out there until she comes back."

"I don't think I need a bar," I said.

"Me either, actually," he agreed. "Coffee then, just until your friend comes back?"

That would have been the time to say no, make my way back to the bench until Macy returned with the car keys. But all it took was me letting myself meet his hopeful gaze to choose his company instead. A few minutes later, we were crossing the indoor bridge from downtown to the Hotel Roanoke.

Once we were inside the hotel, Thomas led the way to the Pine Room bar, but it had already closed.

We had both looked at each other a little awkwardly then. Thomas ran a hand across the back of his hair and said, "We can go up to my room and order some room service?"

Ordinarily, it would never have occurred to me to do anything remotely like that with someone I had just met, but he was nice, and it had been so long since I'd let anyone other than Macy past the walls I'd put up around myself.

Thomas led the way to the elevator, and we rode to the third floor in silence. At his door, he slipped the key in the lock and waved me inside. Jeans, T-shirts and a pair of running shoes littered the floor. He said sorry, embarrassed, and picked them up, opening the closet door and tossing them inside.

"I wasn't expecting company," he said.

"It's fine," I said.

He opened the minibar. "Cokes and stuff in here. Would you rather order coffee or–"

"Actually, Coke would be fine. Thanks."

He pulled out two, handed me one and then popped the tab on his. The soda bubbled up and sloshed out. He shook his head and grinned. "I'm not making much of an impression, am I?"

I smiled. "You're doing fine."

"You're being kind."

I shook my head and laughed a little. "When you were on that stage tonight, I'm pretty sure you could have picked any girl in the audience." I heard the flirtatious note in my voice and wondered where it had come from. When was the last time I had flirted with anyone?

He studied me for a moment, and then, serious, said, "There was only one I wanted."

I could hear the truth of it in his voice, even though it seemed a little hard for me to believe. I had watched him perform earlier with the absolute certainty that he would go on to big things. He had that kind of presence, that kind of voice. "Now you're being kind."

"I'm being honest."

We watched each other for a good long bit, just absorbing what it felt like to be this close, to want and wish.

I was the one who reached out first. My hand went to the side of his face, my palm encountering the rough stubble there, my thumb smoothing across his cheek.

I felt his sharp intake of breath, recognized it as a signal of my effect on him. It felt amazingly good to know that I could make him feel something. For a long time now, I had felt so little, and I wanted so badly to feel something real, something good.

He dipped his head towards mine, stopped just short of my mouth. I could feel the warmth of his breath on my lips, and I closed the distance between us, kissing him softly.

He put his hands on my waist, and I felt instantly anchored by him. As if I had been drifting on a stormy sea only to find myself in this peaceful harbor where I couldn't be turned upside down by circumstances out of my control.

He deepened the kiss and pulled me tight against him. I made a soft sound of relief that he wanted to hold me as much as I wanted him to.

We found our way to the bed, stretching out alongside each other, the light from the street below shining through the open curtain. We looked at each other, staring into each other's eyes without saying any words. We didn't need to.

Even then, I couldn't explain the connection between us. I just knew I felt it, knew I needed it. That no matter what it would mean beyond this night, I needed it.

I began to unbutton his shirt with shaking fingers. He stayed completely still while I worked my way to the very last one, pulling it out of his jeans and sliding my hands across the muscles in his back. I pulled him to me so that there wasn't an inch of space between us. That was when I felt the little collapse within him, felt him take the lead in where we would go from here.

And I followed. Touch for touch. Kiss for kiss. Trying to give as much as I was taking. Relieved to know that I still had something to give.

Weeks later when I discovered that I was pregnant, I let myself play back every moment of it, closing my eyes and making myself remember it for what it had been. Something beautiful. Something at once temporary, and as it would turn out, lasting.

♪

Thomas

There Is a Tomorrow

When I get back to the hospital, Lila has already left with Lexie. I guess I shouldn't really be surprised, but it's plenty of evidence for the fact that Lila is no pushover. She's not going to let me into her life if I don't earn her trust first.

I take my time driving out to her place. I'm not sure if it's because I'm worried about my reception or if I'm starting to think I might be crazy to believe I can make a difference in either of their lives.

Since the shooting, and nearly being killed, I've pretty much chosen to live like there's no tomorrow. Because I know now that there might not be a tomorrow. Or a next hour. Or even a next minute. I haven't been making the smartest choices for somebody interested in living a long, fulfilling life.

I guess I've been trying to pack in as much living as I possibly could. But I'm starting to wonder if you can even call what I've been doing living at all. Really living, I mean.

I can't even remember the names of the girls I went out with a month ago. Seeing Lila and the commitment she's made to Lexie makes me realize I've been shallow and directionless.

Where the music is concerned, I've given that my all, and it's paid off. But as far as having someone in my life who really knows me, really cares about the me beneath the country music success, I don't have that.

So the truth is, right now, I'm not feeling too successful at all.

I wonder which me Lila sees. The one I've shown to the public or the one I showed her the night we spent together almost seven years ago.

With the exception of that night with Lila, the truth is I haven't shown that me to anyone else in the world except Holden and CeCe.

♪

WHEN I GET TO the trailer, the landlord's piece of crap truck is parked out front.

I decide to leave the stuff I've brought with me on the front seat until I make sure Lila and Lexie are here. I knock at the front door, then step back, swinging around to find the landlord glaring at me.

"If you're selling something," he says, "you're breaking the law. Didn't you see the 'No Soliciting' sign at the entrance?"

"I'm not selling anything," I say.

"Well if you ain't selling nothing, what are you doin' standing on the lady's porch?"

"Is that actually any of your business?" I ask with a narrow smile.

"Well, I'm the landlord of this here park. So I reckon it does, and if I walk over there and let my dog off its chain, you might wish you'd gotten in that truck of yours and left a little sooner."

The door to Lila's trailer opens, and she steps out, glancing from me to the landlord. "Rowdy, I don't recall anything in my lease stating I can't have visitors."

"Does this mean you want him in there? Or maybe you're just afraid I'll follow through on my threat to make Killer over there get off his hind end long enough to do some of the guard work he's supposed to be doing here anyway?"

"Come in, Thomas," Lila says, turning her back to Rowdy.

I follow her, closing the door behind us. "Is it even legal to be that much of a—"

"Jackass?" she finishes for me.

"Yeah," I say, "that."

"Unfortunately, I believe it is," she says. "No one has ever been out here to arrest him for it anyway."

"Maybe you ought to try reporting it."

She actually smiles a little at this.

"And Killer?"

"We call him Brownie. It's a name that actually fits him."

We're quiet for a moment, awkward, before I say, "How are you?"

"Okay."

"Lexie?"

"She's asleep."

A truck engine cranks up, and Lila goes to the window to glance out. "Good. He's leaving," she says.

"He doesn't seem like the most stable individual to live next to," I say, worry underscoring my words.

"I'm not scared of him."

"What if I'm scared for you?"

She looks up at me, her lips parting in surprise. "You don't need to be. He's just a big bag of hot air."

I shrug and nod a little, but I'm not sure I agree with her assessment that he's harmless.

"I brought a few things. Want to help me get them?"

"Sure," she says, shrugging and not quite meeting my gaze.

We walk out to the truck, and I open the door, reaching for the paper bag on the middle of the seat. "Maybe we should start with this before Napoleon gets back. I brought Killer a snack."

Lila's gaze widens. "Brownie?"

"Killer Brownie," I concede.

We walk over to the rusted barrel where Brownie sticks his head out, his tail thumping instantly at the sight of Lila. He whines softly and steps onto the dirt, the heavy chain attached to his collar clanking.

"Hey, Brownie," Lila says, dropping down onto her knees next to him.

The dog looks at me, cowering a little, uncertain.

"It's okay," Lila says, rubbing under his chin. "Look what he brought you."

I drop down next to her and pull a wrapper from the bag.

Brownie leans closer, sniffing with a hopeful tail wag.

"It's for you, boy," I say. "A Big Mac with no sauce. No pickle, lettuce, or tomato either. How's that sound?"

I break off a bite and hold it out to him. Brownie takes it gently, as if he's not sure it's something to actually eat. But he swallows it and immediately asks for more.

"There you go," I say, handing him another bite and then feeding him one after another until it's all gone.

"He loved it," Lila says, rubbing under the dog's chin.

"Kinda wish I'd brought him more," I say.

"That was really nice of you," she says without looking at me. Her words are cautious, as if she's not quite sure it could be true.

"Not gonna make up for what he takes from that jerk though."

"I'm still hoping for spontaneous combustion or something," she says.

I smile at the unexpectedness of this from her. "Now there's a mental picture."

We sit and rub on Brownie for a few minutes before Lila stands and says, "I'd better check on Lexie."

I follow her inside the trailer, glancing over my shoulder just before I step inside. Brownie wags his tail, just a quick shake of the tip, as if he's not at all sure happiness can be trusted.

♪

Lila

He Loves Her

Lexie is awake when I go in her room. She smiles up at me, her blue eyes crinkling at the corners, and my heart melts just as it does every single time she smiles at me. I sit on the corner of her bed and smooth my hand across her silky blonde hair.

"Hi, sweet pea. Did you have a good nap?"

She nods, smiling at me and pulling the pink bunny she never sleeps without into the curve of her arm.

"There's someone I'd like for you to meet, sweetie."

She glances at the doorway and then back at me, and I see the curiosity in her eyes. "He's waiting for us in the living room."

She scoots up in the bed the best she can, and I help her put her legs over the side, then pull her chair closer and lift her into it. Lexie loves company. She loves people, and every time I realize this, I wonder if I've sheltered her from the world too much. I've worried about what people will say to her, how it will make her feel, shape her self-image.

I worry now that Thomas won't think she's as perfect as I think she is.

With my heart clenching inside me, I roll her chair down the short hallway. Thomas is standing in the middle of the room with his hands in his pockets, worry clearly etched in his face. I understand suddenly that he is afraid she might reject him when I've been worrying about him rejecting her.

I stop the chair just short of where he's standing and lift her onto the couch. As I squat down beside her, I realize I have no idea what to tell her to call him. I look up at Thomas. He kneels down in front of her and holds out his hand. "Hi, Lexie. I'm Thomas. It's really nice to meet you."

She is slow to lift her hand to his, but she does so with deliberate effort. He takes it gently, and I can see him melt beneath her touch.

"She doesn't talk," I say in a soft voice. "But she understands everything you say to her."

Thomas nods once, reaching for the bag behind him. He slides it to her, and then pulls the edges open. She leans toward it and peers inside. She starts to flap her hands in the way that she claps, a big smile breaking across her face. Thomas reaches inside and pulls out an enormous stuffed toy.

"I used to have a Bassett Hound when I was growing up. I thought you might like this one."

He sets it down next to her, and Lexie rubs its soft ears. Her smile is all for Thomas.

"We could take him for a walk," I say.

Lexie looks at me, her eyes lit up.

"Would you like to do that?" I ask Thomas.

"Sure," he says.

I get Lexie's chair, and start to lift her into it, when Thomas says, "All right if I do that?"

I step back, and he picks her up as if she weighs no more than a feather, setting her on the wheelchair seat. He nestles the Bassett Hound in beside her, and I roll the chair to the door. He holds it open while I maneuver it onto the ramp.

"There's a fairly smooth path that we use to go for a walk. It leads down to the creek. It's pretty there."

"Sounds good," he says. "Lead the way."

We walk in silence for a minute or two, Lexie's chair making its whir-whir sound. She has the Bassett Hound clutched tightly to her chest, her cheek pressed against its head.

"I don't think you could have found anything she liked more."

"I wasn't sure what to get," he says, looking at me with relief.

I struggle to find the words for what I want to say and finally settle on just the honest truth. "I know where I live is a dump. You must think it's awful. It is awful."

"Lila," Thomas begins.

I interrupt him, needing to explain. "Just the deductible for Lexie's medical bills pretty much zaps my paychecks. I've needed to make that a priority. I've been able to save a little, and hopefully, we'll be able to move-"

"Lila," he says again, stopping me in a gentle voice. "I'm hardly in a position to judge you for anything. Not that I would anyway. But I could have helped make things easier. Made it so you didn't have to live in a place like this. Even if you didn't want me in your life. I would have done that for you both."

There's hurt in his voice, and yes, this surprises me. I'm not sure what to make of it. It's definitely not what I expected. But the realist in me prompts me to say, "I've seen the kind of life you lead in Nashville, Thomas. What would you do with this kind of responsibility? I didn't want to put that on you."

"You mean the kind of life the tabloids say I lead? I'm no saint, but then again I don't have the stamina to maintain what those losers say I'm up to."

I laugh a little, unexpectedly, the sound surprising us both. "That would definitely take some stamina."

He shakes his head, his expression hovering between disgusted and amused.

We walk on for a bit, and when he looks over at me, he is serious again. "Will you tell me about her, Lila? About when she was born? What happened and how you found out about the—"

"Cerebral palsy?"

He nods, and I can see it's hard for him to say the words. It use to be hard for me to say them. Until I was able to accept that they weren't a death sentence for Lexie.

We walk at a slow and even pace. Trees line either side of the wide path, shady shadows teasing us with streaks of sunlight.

"She was born at thirty-five weeks," I say, keeping my gaze focused straight ahead. Somehow, looking at him makes it hard for me to talk about it. "She weighed five pounds and was twenty inches long. Compared to some preemies, she didn't look premature at all. But her lungs weren't completely developed yet, and she wasn't strong enough to breastfeed."

"Is that why—"

He breaks off before finishing the question, but I know what he's asking. "The doctors don't know if the brain injury happened during pregnancy or afterward. Sometimes, I wish I knew, just to know whether it was something I did, or—"

Thomas reaches for my hand, slips it into his and squeezes hard. "Don't do that, Lila. I have no doubt that you did the best you could to take care of yourself and of her while you were pregnant. Just like you're doing now."

The words fill me with overwhelming gratitude. Tears spring to my eyes. Other people have said this to me before. But somehow, coming from him, maybe because he is half-responsible for her existence, I feel completely grateful.

"Thank you, Thomas."

"I should be the one thanking you. I don't know why things happened the way they did," he says. "Questioning it now seems like a waste. I think I'd rather choose to be grateful for the fact that you're both here and okay. And hope that you'll give me a chance to make things a little easier for you."

"I don't expect anything from you, Thomas."

"I think you've made that pretty obvious," he says.

We stop at the end of the path where the edge of the creek begins. Lexie points at the big rock in the middle of the water that I've carried her out to many times.

"Lexie likes to sit there in the sun," I say, looking up at Thomas.

"Looks like a good place to me," he says. "All right if I take her out?"

"Sure," I say.

We lean down and take off our shoes, then roll up our jeans. I unbuckle the belt on Lexie's chair and step back so he can lift her up.

She looks into his face and smiles. He smiles back at her, and the resemblance they share makes me wonder how I could ever have thought he didn't deserve to know his daughter. Or that he might reject her.

"Lead the way," he says, glancing at me, his eyes bright with something I don't remember seeing in them until now. Like when someone has discovered something that was supposed to be a part of them all along.

♪

Thomas

The Day We Met

I stay until dark. Lila makes us something to eat, but I'm not hungry. I feel full with something not quite like anything I've ever felt before. It's this satisfaction, this completeness that I feel every time I look at Lila and Lexie.

When she indicates that it's Lexie's bedtime, I stand to leave, wishing I didn't have to go. Lila walks me to the door, and we step out onto the porch.

I look at her for a few moments, absorbing her pretty face, the light in her eyes that's been there since this afternoon at the creek.

"Thanks for letting me come," I say.

"I should thank you for coming."

I rake a hand through my hair, draw in a deep breath and blow it out slowly. "Lila. We need to figure out where to go from here."

"I don't expect anything from you, Thomas."

"You should."

"But I don't."

I study the deliberate blankness in her expression, asking, "Who let you down so badly? Other than me, I mean."

"You didn't let me down. I never gave you a chance to do the right thing."

I start to deny it, but we both know it's true. "Who then?"

She walks over to lean against the porch railing, propping herself up with both elbows. She stares out into the encroaching night, and it's a long time before she says anything.

"When I was a senior in high school, I came home from school one afternoon with Macy. We were going to work on an English project. We were laughing when we walked through the front door. I don't even remember at what now. Something silly. Meaningless. My mom almost always came out to give me a kiss when I got home from school. But she didn't that day. And she didn't answer when I called her even though her car was in the driveway."

I have a sudden feeling of dread in my stomach, and I want to stop her. Tell her I don't want to hear the rest, but I don't. I can't.

"We found her on the living room floor," Lila says, her voice now barely audible. "There was so much blood. I never knew one person could hold that much blood. And she was so pale, her beautiful skin this pasty, chalky, unearthly white."

Lila is completely still, her gaze on something far away that I cannot see. I want to say something, but I can't force out a single word. I feel like I've been thrown back to the night of the shooting, to the moment when the shooter pointed his gun at me, and I knew he was going to pull the trigger.

"I dropped to my knees because all the air left me," Lila says. "I crawled to her. It felt as if my legs weighed a thousand pounds each, and I could barely pull them behind me. I draped myself across her, trying to match her shape with my own as if I could infuse her with my own life, but my clothes just soaked up her blood."

"My God. Lila." I want to tell her to stop, that she doesn't have to go on. But I can see that she needs to, and so I stay quiet.

"I don't remember what happened over the next couple of days. I guess the doctors at the hospital gave me something that made me sleep, so I basically missed the torturous necessities of removing my mom's body from the house, cleaning up all the blood, and arresting my dad.

"When I finally came home from the hospital, there wasn't one speck of evidence that any of it had ever happened. Our living room was just as it had always been. I fully expected her to call out from the kitchen, 'Cookies in the oven. Do you want milk with yours?' Her voice was so real to me that I ran around the house looking for her, sure that all of it had been a nightmare of some kind and that she wasn't really gone."

"Lila," I say. "Stop. You don't have to tell me anymore."

"I want you to know. I think I need for you to know," she says, hesitating. And then, "I ended up staying in a psychiatric hospital for six weeks. The goal, the doctors said, was to basically protect me from myself, give me time come to terms with what had happened. I hated every single drug-numbed moment I spent there. I wanted to feel it, all of it, the rage and the all-consuming sadness. My mother deserved to be mourned."

Her shoulders start to shake. I reach out and pull her to me, banding her against my chest as if I can absorb the pain she is feeling.

"That's when I met you," she says. "I had just gotten out of the hospital that day."

I try to take this in, but I can't seem to get any of it to process. "And I was—"

"Comfort," she says. "You didn't know. And I needed you. So actually, I guess it was me taking advantage of you, if we're both truthful."

I hold her tight against me, while the night sounds start up. A whippoorwill somewhere behind us. The frogs at the creek where we'd walked earlier today.

"Your dad?" I finally ask. "What happened?"

"He's in prison. Life without chance of parole."

"Lila. Dear God," I say against her hair, wishing I had words, any words, that would actually mean something in light of everything she's just told me. "All this time, have you had anyone? Any family?"

"Macy. And her mom. They're like family to me."

I hold her as long as she'll let me. I want to absorb her pain, every speck of it so that she never has to feel it again. "How did you make it through all of that, Lila? I can't imagine—"

"Most of the time we're stronger than we think," she says softly. "I suspect you already know that, though."

"Yeah," I say, realizing she's talking about the shooting.

"I wanted to tell you how sorry I was for what happened to all of you, but I thought you might not want to talk about it."

"It's okay," I say. "I don't think it'll ever be easy, but I'm in a different place from the one I was in a year ago."

"I'm glad you had your friends to be there for you."

"We've been there for each other. And yeah, I don't know what I would have done without them." I hesitate and then say, "I wish I had known what happened to you, Lila."

"But you didn't. And I didn't want you to. I just wanted that night to be what it was. An escape."

"It turned out to be a lot more than that, didn't it?"

"It did. But I don't question it. I can't imagine my life without Lexie, Thomas. In most ways, I think she saved me. Gave me a reason to go on."

I nod once, feeling the truth of this, even as I realize I don't quite know how to process it all, weave it together in my head. I just know that like Lila, I can't question what happened between us now. Or her decision to keep Lexie from me. Somehow I think I know that if I had been her, I would have done the same thing.

When she finally pulls away from me, I feel her emotional withdrawal in addition to the physical.

"I have to get Lexie to bed," she says.

"Can I come back tomorrow, Lila?"

She looks away, considers the question for several moments, as if doubting the wisdom of telling me yes.

I tip her chin up with one finger, forcing her to meet my eyes. "Please?"

"Okay," she says, stepping back. "Goodnight, Thomas."

"Goodnight, Lila."

When the door closes, I walk out to the truck and get inside. It's only then that I allow the knot in my chest to find relief through the tears that slide down my face.

I look at the sorry excuse for a doghouse Brownie is tied to. He's sitting outside of it, watching me. I wish I could walk over there, unhook him and put him in the truck with me, get him away from that sorry excuse for a human he belongs to.

It sucks to be a victim.

♪

Lila

Not Just About Me

It's after eleven o'clock when I hear the knock at the door. I get out of bed and pull the living room curtain back to see Macy's car parked outside.

She's in mid-knock when I undo the deadbolt and let her in.

"Girl, don't you ever answer your phone?"

"Sorry. I let the battery die."

"And how am I supposed to know you're okay?" she asks, walking over to the couch and plopping down with an accusatory glare. "How is Lexie? I've been worried sick about her."

"She's okay," I say. "She's asleep. What are you doing out so late? We have to work tomorrow."

"I couldn't go to sleep without knowing the two of you were all right."

"Sorry, Mace," I say, contrite now.

"I smell expensive cologne," she says.

"I don't smell anything."

"Thomas was here, wasn't he?" she says, sitting up with an ah-ha smile.

"So what if he was?"

"So *everything* if he was. What happened? I want to hear all."

"Macy. Please don't start making something out of this that it's not going to be."

"You're the one who needs to make something out of it."

"I don't want anything from him."

"You're not the only one involved, Lila. Not trying to be mean here, but you've got Lexie to think of. And God knows, you need help."

"We're doing fine."

"You call this doing fine?" she asks, throwing a hand in the air.

"I didn't say it was the Taj Mahal."

"That it isn't. Plus that creep Rowdy next door. He gives me the heebies."

"He's harmless. Gross, but harmless."

"Lila?"

"Yeah?"

"Don't let pride talk you out of letting Thomas in. I know how hard it is for you to accept anything from anyone, but it's time you changed that."

I want to argue with her, but I'm too tired, and I drop onto the sofa next to her. She slides over and puts her head on my shoulder. "I love you. You've got to quit being so dang tough."

"It's gotten me through so far," I say, trying to sound lighthearted but hearing my own failure.

"Just the fact that he came over here must mean something."

"He wanted to meet Lexie."

"I don't doubt that a bit. And why wouldn't he? You never gave him a chance to be a stand-up guy. You know I love you, girl, but I've never thought that was fair to him or to Lexie."

"If you thought I was so wrong, why are you just now saying it?"

"Truth?"

"Truth."

"I was afraid he might be a jerk and reject you both. I don't think I could stand to see you go through another horrible thing that you don't deserve."

I reach out and put my hand over hers.

"But he hasn't," Macy says. "Rejected you, I mean."

"Yet."

"You doubt his sincerity?"

"I think he wants to help. What exactly that means, I'm not sure. What if Lexie gets attached to him and then he decides—"

"If we play the what-if game," Macy interrupts, "we'll just sit here and depress ourselves into a stupor. You've gotta give him a chance, Lila."

"Be real. He's got this life in Nashville that has in no way included having a daughter."

"Yeah, so he's a player. You could change all that."

"Right."

"You could."

"Have you seen some of the girls he goes out with?"

"They airbrush everybody in those magazines," Macy says, dismissing my concern with a wave of her hand. "You can't tell me that he didn't take one look at our Lexie and fall in love."

I'd like to deny it, but I can't. I had seen the look in his eyes. Watched the transformation on his face. "No. I can't."

"So let it happen, Lila. Let it happen for Lexie, if not for you."

♪

Thomas

I Have a Daughter

I call Holden on the way back to the hotel. He answers on the first ring.

"What up?"

"Got a minute?"

"Sure. I'm fixing dinner. CeCe's upstairs taking a bath."

"And you're not up there with her?" I crack.

"Not yet," he comes back, and I hear the grin in his voice.

I release a long breath, not sure where to start.

"Something wrong?" he asks, concern edging out the humor now.

"I don't know if you'd call it something wrong or something right," I say.

"Don't tell me you finally found a woman who'd have you and eloped?"

"Shut up."

"If not that, then what?"

"I have a daughter."

Silence hangs on the line for several moments before Holden says, "Did you just say you have a daughter?"

"I did say that."

"Thomas. What the. . ."

"It's Lila."

"Wait. Are you telling me you and Lila have a daughter?"

"Yeah."

"Are you serious, Thomas. How?"

"The usual way, dumb ass."

Holden barks a short laugh. "You know what I mean."

"That one night. She had a baby."

"And never told you?"

"No."

"Whoa. How did you find out?"

"I found out she left the show because her daughter had been taken to the hospital. I went by to see if they were all right. Turns out her daughter is also my daughter."

"Did she tell you that?"

"She didn't have to tell me. All I had to do was look at her."

"Damn."

"Yeah."

"I guess that's why she blew you off so badly, huh?"

"I guess."

"So what are you going to do now?"

"I want to help her out."

"Lila or the little girl?"

"Her name is Lexie. And both."

"What exactly does that mean? Both."

"That's the part I haven't figured out yet."

"Man, don't get in over your head. You don't really even know her."

"Aren't you the white knight?"

"I just don't want to see you get taken advantage of."

"She lives in a friggin' trailer park, Holden. With this ass-wipe of a landlord who looks at her like he wants to eat her for lunch."

"That ain't good."

"I want to get them out of there. I have to get them out of there."

"And bring them here?"

"I don't know. Maybe. I've barely got any of this straight in my head yet. It seems like we need a little time to sort things through here."

Holden is quiet for a few seconds, before saying, "Remember that lake we went to the afternoon before the show? Smith. . ."

"Mountain," I finish for him.

"Yeah. That's it. I think I remember hearing that people rent houses out there. Maybe you could get a temporary place there."

I instantly like the idea. "That might be good."

"How long will you stay?"

"I'm not sure."

"We've got the tour for the new album coming up next month. We're gonna need you in rehearsals."

"I know. Just give me a few days, okay."

"Want us to come down there?"

"No," I say. "At least, not yet."

"You know we'll leave tonight if you say the word."

"I appreciate that. And yeah, I know."

"What's she like? Lexie?"

"Beautiful," I say. "Sweet." I don't add the rest because I don't feel ready to share it. And it's not that I'm ashamed of her. I guess the word would be more like protective. I don't want Holden to form an impression of her that doesn't include experiencing her smile, the light in her eyes.

"Send us pictures."

"I will. Hey, thanks, man. For the talk."

"You don't ever need to thank me for being there for you, Thomas. It's just the way it is. And always gonna be."

We talk music and work for a few minutes, and when I finally click off the call, I realize Holden has always been more brother to me than friend. I'm grateful he's in my life. Right now, I can use both.

♪

Lila

On a White Horse

Bertha and Marsha are in rare form this morning.

They've somehow gotten wind of my performance on my birthday, and they're reaching new highs in the department of ridicule.

Bertha leans over the conveyor belt so that she's right in front of my face when she sneers, "If you can sing so good, Miss Extra-ordinary, why you still workin' at Smart-Send? You hopin' they'll hire you to yodel their commercials for them?"

"I'm still holding out hope, Bertha," I say, without meeting her gaze. I could tell her that she might want to take a closer look at her dental hygiene practices, but I refrain.

"That would be something," her sidekick Marsha offers from her spot just up the line. "Head Yodeler for Smart-Send. Every girl's dream come true."

I keep my gaze on the box in front of me, fold the edges in and seal them with my tape gun.

"Aw, now we ain't done hurt your feelings, have we?" Bertha says, blowing another whoosh of bad breath my way.

I lean back and stay quiet.

"What?" Marsha jabs. "You playin' the mouse this morning since Mother Macy ain't here to defend you?"

"Any particular reason she might need defending?"

Surprise jolts through me. Thomas walks toward us, a ball cap pulled low on his head. It is completely ineffective as a disguise. I feel everyone around us looking at him. "What are you doing here?"

"Visiting you," he says.

"But you're not supposed to be back here in the factory."

He smiles at me with the very same smile that caused me to end up having his baby.

"Turns out the receptionist likes country music."

"Ah," I say.

Bertha throws me a glare and then narrows her gaze at Thomas. "You with that Barefoot Outlook band?"

"I am," he says, his smile now wary.

"So what are you doin' in a place like this?" she asks, waving a pudgy hand at our surroundings.

"Here to see a girl," he says, eyes narrowed as if he's decided to play along for a bit.

"That girl?" Bertha asks, pointing at me.

"That girl," he agrees.

She considers this and looks at me. "Only one reason I can think of for a girl like our Miss Lila to get a dude like you in a place like this. And that makes her way smarter than I ever gave her credit for."

"You get yourself knocked up, Lila?" Marsha jumps in.

I feel the flush in my face, the heat as it scalds my cheeks. I grapple for a response, but can't make one come out.

Bertha snorts and shakes her head, her extra chin jiggling as she does. "Well, let's just hope he was able to give you one that's not damaged like that one you got now."

The air around us goes completely still. I feel Thomas's rage bubbling up. Just as I move to step between him and Bertha, he body slams her against the conveyor belt, his hands out at his sides as if he is forcing himself not to wrap them around her neck.

"This how you get your kicks all day long? You're a class act, you know it? Be glad you're not a man, or I'd already have you taped up and riding this assembly line to that truck waiting on the other end."

Her eyes narrow to ugly slits, her voice venomous when she says, "You lay a hand on me, and I'll file enough charges against you to wipe out your fat Nashville bank account."

"Thomas, stop!" I say, ducking under the machine to grab his arm and try to pull him away. "It's not worth it."

"If I ever lay a hand on you, ma'am," he says, still glaring down at Bertha, "you'll sure as heck know it. You breathe one more word about my daughter, and I'm not making you any promises. We clear?"

She lifts her flabby chin in defiance, but for the first time ever, manages not to say anything.

Thomas steps back, as if he can't stand another moment that close to her. He reaches for my hand and says, "Come on."

"I can't leave now, Thomas. I'll be fired."

He pulls me along behind him as if I weigh nothing at all. "They can't fire you. You quit."

"I don't quit," I say. "I can't!"

He turns and looks down at me. "You don't need this place. You don't need that," he says with a pointed glare back at Bertha.

"I do need this paycheck."

"Not anymore."

"Thomas. You can't just come in here and upend my life! It might not be much, but it's what I've got."

"You deserve more."

"What does that have to do with reality?" I ask, suddenly furious at him for sparking in me a desire for more, for something I gave up hope of a long time ago.

"I'm not leaving you here with that crazy—"

"You don't have a choice!" I say, turning abruptly and heading for my spot on the assembly line.

But he's way faster than I am, and before I even realize what he's doing, he's swooped me up in his arms and is striding back down the aisle. Clapping sounds all around us.

"Yay, Lila!" someone yells from behind us.

"Get on out of here while you've got the chance!"

Whistling accompanies the clapping.

I struggle to slip out of his arms, but that's not happening.

At the end of the assembly line, Thomas stops and turns around, still holding me in his arms. "Oh, and ma'am?" he calls back to Bertha. "You might want to try out this new invention called a toothbrush."

♪

Thomas

Conduct Becoming

I don't put her down until we reach my truck in the parking lot. When I finally do, she is so mad I think she might take a swing at me.

"What are you doing?" she screams, forcing her hands into fists at her side.

"Something you probably wouldn't ever do for yourself."

"What does that mean?" she throws back, her eyes shooting fire.

"Making you leave that place. Is that what you think you deserve? Being treated like that every single day by that witch in polyester?"

"I never said it was about what I deserve! I *need* the paycheck!"

"No, you don't."

"Yes, I do!" she yells.

I walk around to the front of the truck, leaning against the hood and folding my arms across my chest. "When you cool off, we'll talk."

"When I cool off?"

"Yeah."

"Has your ego really been nursed to these proportions by all those fans of yours? That you think you can just come in here and smash to smithereens everything I've done to take care of Lexie?"

"It doesn't have anything to do with ego, Lila. She's my daughter too."

"Yeah, and I have no idea what you're going to think about that in a week, a month. If you're going to get tired of responsibility and start longing for your playboy life? You're not a sure thing, Thomas! Lexie and I need a sure thing. What I've built for us here might not be much, but it is a sure thing. *Was* a sure thing until you messed it up!"

"Lila—" I start, but she's turning for the factory and marching across the parking lot to the main entrance.

I go after her, blocking her path and forcing her to stop. "Give me a chance," I say. "I know you have no reason on earth to believe this, but if you'll just put your trust in me, I promise I won't let you down."

Tears well in her eyes and slide down her cheeks. She wants to believe me. I can see that she does. But I don't have any other words to convince her with. The only thing that's going to do that is time.

I step out of her way, giving her the choice of going back. I realize now I can't make her do this. It has to be her choice.

She looks at the door to the factory. She looks at me.

I hold out my hand.

We stand here this way long enough that I'm pretty sure she's going back inside. When she starts walking toward the door, my heart drops in my chest. I can't bring myself to say her name.

I force myself to turn and start walking to the truck, my steps heavy.

But then I hear her running toward me, and I don't look back. I just hold out my hand. And she takes it.

♪

Lila

Say Yes

We don't say anything for the first five minutes after we pull away from the factory. Thomas just drives, and I stick my head out the window, letting the wind blow my hair straight back.

I feel like I've been set free, but even as I acknowledge this, I know what I've just done is bona-fide crazy.

I finally sit back in the seat and look over at him. "I can't let you take care of me," I say. "I have to be able to take care of myself."

He doesn't answer for a moment, and when he does, his voice is full of understanding. "I never thought you would. But you can let me help."

"I have to have a job."

"You have an incredible voice, Lila. What about that?"

"I appreciate that, Thomas. But it's not a job."

"It could be."

"I've been away from music a long time."

"When it's in you, I don't think it ever leaves you."

I want to deny this, but I can't. I've never stopped loving writing songs. Even when I knew I'd never sing them out loud for anyone but myself.

A tidal wave of anxiety washes over me. "This is nuts, Thomas."

"We have very different lives. In very different places. And you have a full life with your career. How often are you actually going to want to visit here?"

He taps his thumb on the steering wheel, and I can see that he's nervous, as if he's trying to get up the courage to say something he's having trouble saying. "What would you think about moving to Nashville? You and Lexie, I mean?"

The question takes me so by surprise that I can only stare at him, sure I must have heard him wrong. "What?"

"I know it sounds like a huge step, but you're right. It would be hard for me to get here as often as I'd want to. With you there. . .we have a great children's hospital at Vanderbilt. And your music . . . you could work on that. I could hook you up with some producers for demo work right away. That would give you an income while you work on your own stuff. I mean, I know it's important to you to be independent."

"Wow," I say, letting out a long breath. "I don't know what to say."

"Just say yes. And we'll make it happen."

"It's really that simple for you, isn't it?"

"This is. Yeah. I want to know my daughter, Lila. Is that so wrong?"

I shake my head, not trusting my voice to answer him. "I don't want to keep you from her, Thomas. But I don't know if I can do what you're asking."

"Why not?"

I shrug, unable to find the exact words. "I just. . .I guess I'd gotten to a place of acceptance where my life is concerned. That some things aren't going to turn out the way I once hoped they would. My consolation has been Lexie. No dream I ever had compares to what I have in her."

"I can see that," he says. "I'm grateful that you're her mother, Lila. I mean that. I'm not proud to admit this, but I've known some girls who would never be the kind of mother you've been."

"Thank you," I say. "That actually means a lot to me."

"I'd like to pay you back, Lila, in whatever way I can. In whatever way you'll let me."

"You know I don't expect that."

"I know."

We drive for a few minutes before I force myself to say, "If any of this actually happens, our connection with each other will be as parents to Lexie. This doesn't mean there will be any kind of romantic thing between us."

"No," he says, quickly enough that I wonder if he's glad I'm getting this out of the way.

"You probably already have a girlfriend. Girlfriends," I correct. "And I don't want to get in the middle of any of that."

"As a matter of fact, I'm currently unattached, but I appreciate the concern," he says with some irony.

"And I. . ."

"Will of course be free to date whoever you want to."

"Of course."

"Is there. . .anybody in the picture?"

"No one serious," I say, trying to sound as if that could change at any moment.

"Lila. I know it's a lot to think about. But give me a chance, okay? We'll take it one day at a time. Figure out how to make all this work. I've rented a house at the lake for a week. Would you and Lexie come out and stay with me there a few days? So we could all spend a little time together?"

I feel myself falling farther and farther down this rabbit hole. Alarm skitters through me when I think of all the potential hazards along the way. How very likely it is that Thomas will eventually yearn for the life he had before Lexie and me.

But a few days at the lake sounds so wonderful that I cannot bring myself to say no. I can only imagine how much Lexie will love it.

And so I nod. Once. And then look back out the window.

♪

Thomas

All it Takes

I get to the trailer the next morning at nine. I'll admit I didn't sleep hardly any all night. I kept thinking Lila would call and say she'd changed her mind. That she didn't think spending a week with me was a good idea.

Not that I would blame her.

I've basically turned her life upside down, and I just hope I'm doing it for all the right reasons.

I knock at the door, looking over my shoulder where Brownie is curled up inside his barrel-house. I think about Hank Junior and Patsy. The life they have with CeCe and Holden. And it seems so damn unfair that this dog is never going to know that kind of care and love.

Lila opens the door, notices the direction of my gaze and says, "I'm just gonna steal him one day."

"Definitely be the best thing that ever happened to him."

"If I didn't think I'd be the first person Rowdy would accuse, I'd do it today."

"Think he'd sell him?"

"I've already tried that. He's offended that I don't think this life is good enough for him."

"Ass."

"Yeah," she says.

I notice how she looks then, the jean shorts that show off her long legs and suddenly have me remembering the feel of them wrapped around me. Awareness must register on my face because she backs inside and clears her throat.

"I was just finishing up getting Lexie's things."

"Take your time," I say, my voice a little uneven. "No hurry."

"She's in her room. Want to say hi and help her get in her chair?"

"Yeah. That'd be great."

"Go ahead," she says, smiling softly.

I walk down the short hall, stopping in the doorway of her room. She's sitting on the bed, playing with the Basset Hound toy I had given her. He appears to be having a conversation with her bunny.

"Hey, Lexie. How are you?"

She looks up at me and smiles, a full, happy smile that tells me she's glad to see me. My heart does a flip and then ties itself in a knot. "Your mama tell you we're going to the lake?"

She makes a swimming motion with one arm.

"You like the water?"

Another nod, her smile now a little shyer than it was at first.

"We're gonna have us some big-time fun," I say.

She scoops the bunny up under one arm, the Basset Hound under the other. I can see that it's not easy for her to hold onto them, but she manages.

"All right if I carry you out to your chair?"

She nods again, her smile sweet and happy, indicating I'll need to pick up all three of them.

And I melt. That's all there is to it. I just melt.

♪

Lila

Glass Houses

You know how you can be having a dream right before you wake up in the morning? And you're aware that it's a dream, but it's so good you don't want to open your eyes? You just want it to keep going?

That's what it feels like when we pull up in front of the house Thomas has rented at Smith Mountain Lake.

"This is incredible," I say.

"I thought it would be nice for everything to be on one level," he says, glancing back at Lexie, who is looking at the big house with awe in her eyes.

"That was really thoughtful," I say.

The center of the house is glass so that you can see right through the middle to the lake view on the other side. A ski boat pulls a skier across the smooth surface. A pontoon boat motors lazily along in the distance.

"Thomas, this is too much," I say, finding my voice.

"You don't like it?" he asks, instantly worried.

"No, it's not that. It's just. . .we're not use to things like this." The part I don't say is that deep down I'm worried that being here will make Lexie see our real life as it truly is: unable to compare.

But I know that's selfish. I don't want to deny her this experience. And so I look at Thomas and smile. "It's amazing. Really. Thank you."

"Let's go see if it lives up to its billing," he says, getting out of the truck. He gets Lexie's chair from the back and walks around to her side, opening the door and unbuckling her seat belt. She holds her arms out to him, and my heart does a little flip at the way in which she is already bonding with him.

Part of me is really happy about that. Another part of me, the insecure part, worries that she will start to see me as less.

Thomas rolls Lexie's chair along the sidewalk to the front door, fishing the keys out of his pocket. He unlocks it and swings it open, waving me ahead of them. "You first," he says.

I step into the foyer and stare, at a loss for words.

The glass on this side of the house runs the width of the enormous living room so that it looks like the surface of the lake is within reach. Sunlight glints diamonds across the stretch of blue-green water.

Oversize chairs face the view, and I think I could sit there all day long, just taking it in.

"I've never seen anything so beautiful," I say, finally finding the words.

Thomas puts his hand on my shoulder, squeezes once. "Let's just enjoy it," he says. "I'll get our things out of the truck. You check everything out."

I roll Lexie over to the glass door that leads out onto the deck, open it, and we're outside, a light breeze lifting our hair, the sun warm on our skin.

Lexie makes a sound of delight, pointing at a parasail in the distance. We watch as it glides through the air, high above everything down here. That's kind of how I feel right now, like I've been granted a temporary view of something normally out of my reach.

A few minutes later, Thomas joins us on the deck. He leans forward with his elbows on the railing. "It's so peaceful," he says.

"I've lived in this county my whole life and barely ever seen this lake. I had no idea it was so beautiful."

He looks at me then, our gazes holding. I see in his eyes a mixture of things I'm not sure I want to take apart and identify. I don't want his pity. Of anything I could possibly ever want from him, it's not that.

"So here's what I propose," he says, his voice low and persuasive. "For the next few days, there's just this and the three of us. No past. No future. Just the present. Can we do that?"

I have no idea how to do that, but I know that I want to. I really want to. "Yes," I say. "We can."

♪

Thomas

It's the Simple Stuff

We spend the afternoon motoring around the lake on the pontoon boat that came with the house rental.

I've never driven a boat before, so there's a good deal of figuring out as we go. How to get it out of the hanging slip. Where the lifejackets are stored. How to accelerate without giving us all whiplash. My novice efforts result in a good bit of laughter on Lila's part, and just the sound of it makes my bumbling worth it.

Smith Mountain Lake is enormous with more than five hundred miles of shore line. We're staying near the center where the widest part flows out beneath its namesake, a beautiful green flow of mountain that reminds me of Lake Como in Italy where my mom had taken me when I'd graduated from high school.

I find a cove at the foot of the mountain and anchor the boat. There's not another boat in sight.

Lila is stretched out on one of the front seats, her face to the sun. Lexie is playing with some toys on the floor under the covered part of the boat.

I beach the pontoon on a strip of sand and look at Lila, trying to keep my gaze on her face, which takes no small amount of willpower considering that she's wearing a blue bikini that leaves little to the imagination. Not that I need to imagine. I remember.

"This look like a good spot to swim?" I ask.

She sits up on the seat, taking in the view. "It's perfect," she says. "Lexie? Do you want to swim?"

Her smile is the only answer we need.

She's wearing a life jacket with a strap between the legs for extra security. Lila picks her up and walks to the front of the boat.

I slide off into the water, my feet hitting the bottom instantly.

Lila leans down and hands Lexie to me and says, "I'll get the floats."

Lexie's face is lit with happiness. She hits the water with one hand, giggling when it splashes on me. I drop into the water until it reaches her shoulders, and she's laughing now, flicking the water at me.

Lila hops in next, sliding a float my way. She climbs on the other, lying face down, her chin on her arm, watching us. "She loves water," she says.

"I can see that." I lift her up and set her on my shoulders. For the next little bit, we play shark with Lila and King of the Mountain. And at times, Lexie is laughing so hard, she can barely catch her breath.

I think about all the things I've done in my life so far that have given me satisfaction. There have actually been quite a few. Playing college football. Starting a band with Holden. Moving to Nashville and carving out a career there. Our first concert tour. All of it was great, and I'm thankful for every moment of it.

But I can honestly say, carting this little girl around on my shoulders while she makes her mama laugh, none of it compares to this.

♪

Lila

Awareness

I guess I never let myself imagine what Thomas would be like as a father. If I had, I don't think I would have done him justice.

He talks to her and not at her, as I've noticed so many adults doing. And she hangs on his every word. Her eyes follow him as if she can't wait to see what he does next.

On that score, I can surely identify with her. I swear, he looks like he could be one of those models for Abercrombie and Fitch. The ones on the life-size posters outside their stores. He's wearing swim shorts that hang low on his hips. His abs are cut. Ditto for his chest and biceps. I'm taking all of this in one stolen glance at a time.

I've pretty much gotten away with a full-body appraisal when he catches me dead on, his gaze snagging mine and forcing me not to look away.

Lexie is on his shoulders, and he's got his arms stretched out wide, holding her hands in his. He returns my visual assault, starting with my face and then letting his gaze drop with deliberate acknowledgment of what he's taking in.

He says nothing, but he doesn't need to.

I feel my face go bright red. I bite my lower lip and then quickly wipe the back of my hand across my mouth in case he took that as an invitation of some sort.

I'm not sure how long we stand there, staring at each other, but it's long enough that my heart is beating so hard in my chest that I can feel it in my ears. I do the only thing I can think to do to douse the fire that has erupted inside me.

I sink into the water until it completely covers my head.

Even so, I can still hear Thomas's soft laughter.

♪

WE SPREAD QUILTS ON the sandy shore and eat the sandwiches Thomas made for us.

Lexie's is peanut butter and jelly. Ours tomato and Havarti cheese with some kind of basil mayo that is just downright yummy.

"And you cook too," I say, taking a sip of my bottled water.

"Not sure this actually qualifies, but I can make some pretty mean sandwiches," he says.

He's also brought along some kind of brownie with pink icing on top.

"I don't know who's happier," I say. "Lexie or me."

"Who doesn't love brownies?" he asks, taking a bite and then licking a morsel of chocolate from his lower lip. I find myself wishing I could do that for him. No sooner has the thought crossed my mind than I feel my face heat up again, and I look away, aware that he can probably read every lascivious thought I'm having.

"Tell me about your music," he says out of the blue.

I look at him, surprised. I shrug. "There's really not much to tell these days."

"Macy said you've kept writing. That you never stopped."

"It's just a part of my day."

"I'd love to hear some of your songs."

"I don't think they're up to your standards," I say.

"Say what?"

"I mean, you've got one of the best writers in Nashville creating your stuff."

"Well, I agree Holden is as good as they get. But he's been writing his whole life, too. Just like you."

"He's got a gift."

"He does. Macy says you do, too. I know that voice of yours is a gift."

"Thanks, Thomas. But Macy is a little biased."

"Hey, we all need someone in our corner. That girl's got your back and then some."

"There have been times in my life when I don't know what I would have done without her."

"Play me a few songs tonight, after Lexie goes to bed?"

"I don't know," I say, shaking my head. "I'm not sure I can."

"Why not?"

"Because you make me nervous."

"I make you nervous?"

"Yeah," I say, trying not to smile. "You do."

"You got any idea why?"

"Not really."

He laughs his low, sexy laugh.

And I think he has a very, very good idea why.

♪

WE LEAVE THE wonderful spot at the foot of Smith Mountain and head over to a nearby marina to put gas in the boat.

The young guy who greets us at the pump jumps in to remove the gas cap, smiling at Lexie who waves a small hand at him.

"Bet you haven't seen our fish," he says to her.

"We haven't," says Thomas, stepping into the conversation.

"She'll love it," he says, pointing to the back of the small metal building that apparently houses the marina's snack bar. "They like popcorn. You can get that inside."

"Thanks," Thomas says, picking up Lexie and following me off the boat.

We buy three bags of popcorn inside from a very nice lady who recognizes Thomas the moment we walk in the door.

"Well, my goodness," she says. "You're Thomas Franklin with—" she shakes her hand as if that will jar her memory for the name. "Barefoot Outlook!"

He smiles at her, looking a little awkward, and I realize he's never really gotten use to this part. But then I wonder if you ever do. She asks him to autograph one of the marina ball caps and thanks us for coming in.

We walk around to the back of the building and onto a dock. Hundreds of fish swim in a circle, their mouths pointed upward at us, lips opening and shutting in a silent request for us to share our popcorn.

Lexie points at them and makes cooing sounds of joy. Thomas opens a bag for her, and she sticks her hand inside, showering the fish with it. They begin flapping, all in the same quest to get the treat. Thomas upends the rest of the bag, and they flap harder. Lexie laughs in pure delight.

The three of us sit down on the edge of the dock. Lexie dangles her feet, and one of the enormous fish swims up, mistaking her toe for popcorn.

Lexie flaps her hands and laughs. And then it becomes a game where she lets fish after fish tickle her toes.

We feed the rest of the popcorn a handful at a time, our audience of fish faces staring up at us in rapt attention. Lexie reaches down every minute or two to touch a head.

"Is it weird being famous, Thomas?" I ask, without looking at him.

"A little," he admits.

"I can see how it would be."

"You know just because you achieve some success doing something you love to do, and people you don't know all of a sudden know who you are, you haven't actually changed inside your own head. I'm still the me who couldn't get a date my whole freshman year in college."

"I find that hard to believe," I say.

"True fact. You can ask Holden."

I give him a skeptical look.

"And the first time Holden and I played this little dive club in Atlanta, we got booed off the stage. They actually threw baskets of pretzels at us. The hard kind."

"Did not," I say, trying not to laugh.

"Did, too," he says, grinning. "What's the difference between us then and us now? I couldn't tell you. We've got a little more polish, I guess. But I don't think we're that different."

"Maybe it's that social proof thing. People need to know other people think you're good before they can think you're good?"

"Kind of like the chicken or the egg. Which comes first?"

"I find it hard to believe anyone ever denied your talent."

"And I would say the same about you."

"We are so not in the same league, Thomas."

"Just because you don't see yourself that way doesn't mean the rest of the world won't."

"You don't have to say that."

"I know I don't. But I'm saying it because it's true. Play me a song tonight?"

I look at him then and smile a little. "Maybe."

♪

Thomas

Kiss So Good

It turns out to be one of those days I know I will never forget. A day I wish didn't have an ending, but might stretch on into infinity.

I don't think I can even explain what it feels like to be with Lila and Lexie. But it's like we've always been. Maybe it's because Lexie is a part of us both, the cord that ties us together. There's no awkwardness, just this comfort that feels like I've found a place where I belong.

We get back to the house around seven. Lila takes Lexie to her room to give her a bath, while I offer to make the only pasta dish I know how to make. Spaghetti with olive oil and Parmesan cheese.

Lila brings her back in a bit, smelling sweet in her pink pajamas, her wet hair in pigtails.

We eat outside on the deck, and my cooking appears to be a hit.

Lila cuts Lexie's noodles into bite-size pieces and puts a spoon in her hand, now and then helping her scoop some up. We talk about the fish we saw, and at the first mention of them, Lexie's eyes light up. She points at her toes and smiles.

"That's right," I say. "You almost lost a few today, didn't you?"

She giggles, and the sound of that fills my heart with overwhelming love.

As soon as she's finished eating, she starts to rub her eyes, her blinks heavy and slow.

"I think the sun wore you out," Lila says. "Why don't we get you to bed?"

"Want me to help?" I ask.

"That's okay," Lila says. "I'll tuck her in."

I kiss Lexie on the top of her head and tell her good-night.

I clean up and get the dishwasher started. I'm out on the deck, leaning on the rail and looking out at the night closing in on the water beyond the house when Lila comes back out.

"Hey," she says, walking over to the rail, but leaving space between us.

"Hey. She down for the count?"

"Pooped."

I look at her for a moment, taking in the contentment on her face, recognizing it as the same thing I'm feeling. "It was a good day," I say.

"A great day," she agrees. "Thank you, Thomas."

"You don't have to thank me. I loved it. Although, you do owe me a song."

The darkness has settled in around us. A boat or two whirs in the distance. A bird whose sound I don't recognize starts up a melody.

"Are you just doing this to be nice?" she asks.

"Actually, I'm not. I really want to hear you."

"I don't have my guitar."

"You don't need it."

She sighs and shakes her head. "Okay, but I can't face you."

I smile a little. "I'll turn the other way."

I get up and position my chair so that it's facing the lake. "Anytime you're ready, take off."

She clears her throat, and I hear her fidgeting. She starts off with a soft hum, and then dips into the first verse. The night goes silent around us. I close my eyes and focus on the sweet tone of her voice, the words so rich with emotion that my heart is instantly snared. And the chorus:

I want to live this life amazed

Hear the song

like it's never been played

I want to live this life amazed

See the world

Like it's my very last day

When she lets the last note fade from her lips, I slowly turn around and begin to clap. "That was incredible," I say. "You're incredible."

For a moment, just a moment, she lets me see how much the words mean to her. But then she shakes her head and says, "You really don't have to say that."

"No. I really don't. But I mean it."

I stand and push my chair back, walking over to stop in front of her. "It's okay to want it, Lila. To want something for yourself."

"There was a time when I did. When there was nothing I wanted more in the world. But that's not true anymore."

"Because of Lexie?"

"You can't have everything in this life, Thomas. I use to think that you could."

"In a town like Nashville, there are no guarantees. But you've got talent, Lila. The real thing. And loving Lexie doesn't mean you can't be who you are. You're a singer. A writer. Repeat after me. I'm a singer. I'm a writer."

She play slaps me, laughing softly. "Stop. Why do you want to go getting a girl's hopes up when she's perfectly happy with things the way they are?"

"Are you?"

"What?"

"Perfectly happy?"

She turns away from me, leaning against the deck railing and staring out at the night-dark lake. "Don't," she says.

I step in to stand beside her, my arm against hers. "Don't what?"

"Make me want something I don't want anymore."

"If that's really true, I'll shut up right now. But you see, I don't think it is. I think you put your dreams away to do the right thing by Lexie. I can't tell you how grateful I am for the way you've taken care of her, even though I wish you would have let me help. We can't go back and redo any of that, but we can do things a little different from here."

"You and Macy have a lot in common."

"We both want good things for you, if that's what you mean."

"I don't mean to sound ungrateful. It's just that dreams come with price tags. Always."

I turn with my elbow on the deck rail, studying her profile as she stares out at the lake. She knows I'm watching her, but she won't look at me.

"Lila?"

"Hm?" she says, still without looking.

I put my hand to her cheek, slowly turn her toward me.

"Thomas," she starts, but I don't let her finish, settling my lips on hers before either one of us has a chance to rethink it.

My first thought?

I never forgot her. Never forgot this.

That little sound she makes when my mouth touches hers. The full, softness of her lips.

I half lift her to me, pressing her against the rail as our bodies remember the fit of each other.

She slides her hands up my chest, linking them at the back of my neck and letting me deepen the kiss. We lose ourselves to it, everything else falling away, my life in Nashville, her life here. It's just us. Finding each other again. And I wonder how we could have let this slip away the first time we found it.

"Baby, I could kiss you all night," I say, finding the side of her neck and breathing in her sweet scent.

She turns my face back to hers, and this time, she's kissing me. With need. And hunger. And more than anything I've wanted in a long time, I want to fill that need. Satisfy that hunger.

"Lila," I say, lowering my head to kiss her neck and then her ear.

"We shouldn't be doing this," she says, her voice husky and uneven.

"Why not?" I ask, running my hands down her back to settle at her waist.

"Because. . .we. . .got ourselves in trouble the last time we messed around when we knew better."

"But you smell so good. . .and kiss so good."

Despite her protests, she interrupts me and finds my mouth again, and we both forget about all the reasons why this might not be such a good idea. She loops her arms around my neck, and it feels as if she could melt right into me.

The night is quiet around us, and I think we could be the only two people on earth.

I'm actually the one who pulls back first because I know if I don't, we're dropping over the edge, and we won't be coming back anytime soon.

"Lila. Dang, girl. You have any idea what you do to me?"

"If I do," she says, breathless, "I don't get it."

"What do you mean?" I ask, tipping my forehead against hers.

She pulls away then, turning against the deck railing to stare out at the dark lake. "Haven't you dated just about every single female singer in Nashville?"

"That would be a slight overestimation."

She shakes her head, and I see the smile on her face. "Slight."

"More than slight, then."

"Hmmm."

"Who I might have or have not dated has nothing to do with the fact that I'm clearly attracted to you."

She turns a little to face me then, her elbow on the rail. "Could we possibly live in more different worlds?"

"Again, I don't see what that has to do with–"

"It has everything to do with it," she says in a soft voice. "And even if that didn't concern me, the two of us starting this up again is nothing but a recipe for disaster."

"How do you figure that?" I ask, reaching out to run my finger along her cheek. She draws in an instant breath, as if I've scorched her skin. I have to admit I like seeing the effect I have on her.

"Lexie," she says. "If you're going to be a part of her life, Thomas, I want it to be because you really want to be in her life. Not because–"

"I'm trying to get you in bed?"

She doesn't answer my question, and all of a sudden, a wave of anger sweeps over me.

"Is that how you see me, Lila? You think I would play with her heart like that?"

I can see that she is regretting her choice of words, but I can also see that she really does think it's a possibility that I would. I move back a couple of steps in an attempt to sever the physical connection I still feel to her.

"I guess I don't really know," she says.

"Whoa," I say, running a hand through my hair and across the back of my neck. "You sure know how to put a fire out."

"Thomas, I'm sorry, I didn't mean—"

"It's okay," I say, letting out a deep breath. "You're probably right. We need to focus on Lexie and what's best for her. I'm sorry."

"You don't need to apologize, Thomas. I wanted to kiss you too."

"Well, that makes me feel a little better, anyway," I say, managing a half smile.

"We should go to bed," she says.

"We should," I say.

We study each other for a few, very long moments while a whole lot of things go unsaid.

Lila takes a step back, pointing over her shoulder. "I'm heading in then."

"I'm staying right here then."

She smiles and shakes her head. "You're a bad boy."

"What? No, this is me being a really good boy."

She turns and walks in the house, but I hear her laugh as she goes.

♪

Lila

Dreaming Awake

For the life of me, I cannot go to sleep.

And it's not for lack of trying.

I start to get up and take a shower as a diversion, but I can still smell a hint of Thomas's cologne on my skin, and I don't want to wash it off. I close my eyes instead and let myself be lulled into reliving his kiss.

It was every bit as good as I had remembered.

I'm not sure how that's even possible, because during the past six years, I had all but decided my memory had embellished his skill.

Apparently not.

The few guys I've been out with never once struck a chord of interest inside me. Of course the wall of resistance I put in place for them to attempt to climb over was pretty much unscalable, but I'm wondering now if the real reason was that I knew not one of them was ever going to compare to Thomas.

I'm not thrilled with my insight.

Because I'm nothing, if not realistic.

Me setting my sights on Thomas is the same as me deciding I'm not going to know a speck of happiness in life unless I win the lottery.

It's not like I don't know the odds of that happening.

And still. . .

The heart wants what the heart wants.

♪

THE NEXT THREE days are like something out of a dream.

You know how you sometimes have that feeling of having done something before? Deja vu? More than once, I feel like I've already experienced something we're doing. Like I've lived the moment before. And because that's not possible, I wonder if I dreamed it somewhere along the way. Maybe it's wish fulfillment.

Whatever the explanation, my dreams couldn't have done the real experience justice. It's like the rest of the world has fallen away, and we're in this perfect place where nothing matters except the fact that we're together.

I watch Lexie falling in love with Thomas. See her smile when he does some goofy thing that she finds adorable. Watch her slip her hand into his when we're sitting on the deck eating breakfast.

And part of me wants to stop her from falling for him. What if he decides he doesn't want to be a part of her life? Her heart will be shattered into a million pieces. At the same time I'm questioning it, I know I can't stop it. I have no choice but to let it happen.

And so I do.

We spend long, lazy days puttering around the lake on the pontoon boat. Getting out now and then in a secluded cove to float on the perfectly smooth water. Thomas never lets Lexie out of reach, and I'm amazed at how thoroughly I trust him with her safety.

Already, I know, that like me, he would lay down his life for her. Is there any more complete definition of love than that?

♪

Thomas

Can't Miss Another Thing

If I ever doubted my own self-control, I think I've pretty much affirmed its existence since our first night here at the lake when I kissed Lila out on the deck. And when Lila kissed me.

I'm not going to leave that part out, because it's true that we wanted each other. Still do if the invisible electric current I constantly feel between us is anything to go by.

But every time I look at Lexie, I think about what Lila said, and I realize she's right. This isn't just about the two of us. There's our daughter to consider. I guess I'm starting to see my attraction to Lila through the lens of what happens if I screw up. If we don't work. If one of us decides it's not what we thought it was.

I've missed the first six years of Lexie's life. If I know anything, it's that I don't want to miss another day of it.

And so, I put myself in the friend zone, not letting my gaze linger on Lila when it has the opportunity to do so. Making a constant effort to neutralize the desire I have a great deal of trouble keeping off my face.

One thing I'll say is this: it sure as hell isn't easy.

♪

Lila

What This is About

I invite Macy over for dinner on our fourth night at the lake house.

She knocks at the door a few minutes after six. I let her in, and she looks at me with a slightly dazed expression. "This place is incredible," she says.

"Temporary," I say. "Don't worry. I'm not letting myself get use to it."

"I could certainly get use to it," she says, glancing up at the high ceilings and wide, open, living room in front of us.

"Come on in. Thomas and Lexie are on the deck."

She follows me out, and I admit it feels a little awkward showing her this place. It's not mine, after all, and neither of us has ever known this kind of living before.

When I open the sliding glass door, Thomas picks up Lexie and walks her over to give Macy a hug.

"Hi, big girl," Macy says, kissing her cheek. "I've missed you."

Lexie hugs her back in her sweet, special way.

"Hey, Macy," Thomas says. "Glad you could come."

"Thanks for inviting me," she says. "Can I help with something?"

"Think we've got it under control out here. Lila, you want to show her around?"

"Sure," I say.

Macy links her arm through mine, and we go back inside, wandering through the kitchen and then each of the bedrooms, including the master one which Thomas insisted I take with its oversize Jacuzzi and view of the lake.

Macy falls onto the bed, arms and legs splayed wide. "Wow. This is incredible."

"Yes," I say. "An incredible vacation."

"You sure it's not more than that? Y'all look like you've been together forever."

I sit down on the bed beside her. "Thomas wants to be in Lexie's life. That's what this is about."

"Um-hm. How does that explain the way he looks at you?"

"What do you mean?"

"Like he wants to devour you."

"Does not."

"Does too."

"Anyway, it doesn't matter. We've agreed that Lexie needs to be our focus. And that anything between us would just put what's best for her at risk."

"How do you figure?"

I give her a sideways look. "Macy. Be real. What's the chance of anything between us actually lasting?"

"I don't have a crystal ball, that's for sure. But I'd say you have more of a shot at it than most of us. You do have that little girl in common, after all."

"So I should snag him with the do-the-right-thing hook?"

She play-slaps me. "That's not what I'm saying."

"It sort of is."

"You do have an advantage other girls don't have with him."

I give her a sideways look. "You know I don't think like that."

"Well, maybe you should."

I shake my head. "No."

"So what's next for you two?"

"He wants us to go back to Nashville with him." I expect Macy to leap off the bed in full cheerleader mode. But she doesn't.

I lean away and look at her. She's trying hard to smile, but the tears in her eyes give her away.

"And you're going, right?" she asks. "It's what you deserve, Lila. You can't let this ship sail by you. There's nothing here for you."

"You're here."

"And what can I do for you? You've got a gift, and you've got a daughter. Both of which you need to protect. You can't do that here."

"I've been doing it."

"And it's about to wear you out. Plus, I don't think they're going to hire you back at Smart-Send."

"That's a tragedy."

We both laugh a little, even though I'm fairly sure it could still be a tragedy.

"Dinner's ready," Thomas calls from the living room.

"Coming," I answer back. I stand up and say to Macy, "Let's go eat."

She reaches for my arm and turns me to face her. "When that truck of his pulls out of here headed back to Nashville, you and Lexie need to be in it."

I slide my hand into hers and pull her up from the bed. "Anybody ever call you bossy?"

"Once or twice," she says. "But I'm okay with it."

♪

LEXIE STARTS TO cough during dinner.

At first, I think she might have breathed in pollen or dust, but it continues to deepen, and by the time we're finished eating, she sounds really congested.

Thomas looks at me with concern in his eyes. "Should I run out and get something for her?"

"I have medicine, but it's all back at the trailer. I could borrow your truck and go get it."

"You shouldn't go over there by yourself this late," he says.

"Why don't you go with her?" Macy suggests. "I'll stay here with sweet pea."

"I'll be fine by myself," I start to protest.

"If you don't mind staying, Macy, that would be great," Thomas says.

"I don't mind a bit. We'll snuggle up in front of the TV, won't we, Lex?"

Lexie looks at her and yawns, then coughs.

"Why don't we get your jammies on first?" I say, getting up to lift her in my arms and carry her to her room where I change her clothes and brush her teeth.

Back in the living room, I set her down next to Macy and kiss her on the forehead. "We'll be back in just a bit," I say.

"We're all good," Macy says, tucking Lexie under the curve of her arm and starting to flip through the channels with the TV remote.

Thomas and I head outside to the truck. We drive the first few miles without saying much. An awkwardness has settled over us when we're alone now. As if we're both aware of what we want to happen, but can't acknowledge it or admit it.

♪

Lila

Need

It's kind of a relief when we get to the trailer. I get out and pull my keys from my purse, opening the front door. I hear Brownie's tail thumping against the barrel, and I know he wants me to walk over and say hello. But Rowdy's truck is parked in the driveway, so I don't.

Inside, I find the plastic container of medicine I keep in the kitchen cabinet, and pick out the things I think we'll need. Thermometer. Meds. Measuring spoon.

Thomas waits in the living room, standing in front of the window with his hands shoved in his pockets. I know he's looking at Brownie, thinking the same things I've been thinking from the first day I saw him tied to that awful barrel.

A door slams. Brownie whimpers, and then Rowdy's harsh voice shouts something I can't make out. I run to the window where Thomas is looking out.

"What is it?" I ask, worried for Brownie.

"Somebody needs to kick the crap out of that lowlife," Thomas says, without telling me what just happened.

I squint into the darkness, making out Rowdy carrying Brownie over to the truck and dropping him into the back like he's a sack of grain. He hooks a chain to his collar, and Brownie hunkers down out of sight.

"He never takes him anywhere," I say. "What is he doing?"

"Nothing good. I'm pretty sure of that," Thomas says.

I am suddenly overwhelmed with fear for Brownie. Tears well in my eyes. "What should we do?"

"If I go out there right now, he's not going to let me have him without calling the police."

I nod, knowing he's right. "We could follow him," I say.

Thomas considers this, then says, "I'm pretty sure it won't be the smartest thing we've ever done."

I'd like to disagree, but I have a feeling he's right.

We wait inside the trailer until Rowdy's taillights disappear around the first corner. Then we run out to the truck, and Thomas guns out of the driveway, lights off to keep us from being spotted.

By the time we get to the main road, Rowdy is nowhere in sight.

"Which way did he go?" I ask, panicky now.

"We're gonna have to guess. Left or right?"

Knowing Brownie's life might depend on it, I say a silent prayer for the answer before saying, "left."

Thomas swings the truck onto the road, and within a minute, we spot Rowdy's truck up ahead. Brownie is standing with his head over the side, his ears blowing back, and I could cry for the fact that he is probably excited to be going for a ride and thinks Rowdy is doing something nice for him for the first time in his life.

I'd like to think he could be right, but I know Rowdy. He doesn't have it in him.

We hang back far enough to keep Rowdy from noticing us. I have a sick feeling in my stomach because I'm remembering all the times he threatened to let Brownie "prove his manhood" by making him fight another dog.

"Where do you think he's going?" Thomas asks.

"I don't know," I say hesitantly, afraid if I voice my fears out loud, they'll come true. And then, "He use to brag about how he could take Brownie to a dogfight and make a whole lot of money. Where else would he be taking him this late at night?"

"Damn," Thomas says. "Hold on, though. Let's not do the deep dive yet. Maybe he's taking him somewhere to leave him because he doesn't want him anymore. People do that, don't they?"

"Loser people," I say.

"I'd put him in that category."

"I'd actually be relieved to know it was that. At least he would have a chance."

"We won't let him out of our sight," Thomas says.

I hear the concern in his voice, and something in my heart melts a little. There are a lot of things a guy can do to prove himself to a girl. Shower her with material evidence of his affection. Take her out to fancy places.

But those aren't the things that do it for me. Nothing slays me faster than a guy who can show compassion and kindness. Especially when it's for a dog who's spent his whole life on the end of a chain and whose breed alone has given him a reputation he's never done anything to deserve.

"Thank you," I say, looking at him long enough to let him glance over and see the tears in my eyes. "You're a pretty amazing guy, you know that?"

He can't hide his surprise. His eyes widen. "So that's the secret then to winning your heart? Chasing around the countryside after a dog in need of saving?"

I smile. "Pretty much."

"That's how Holden won CeCe. I guess I shouldn't be too surprised."

"Are you going to explain that?"

"He helped her get her dog, Hank Junior, out of the pound one night after I let him get away. Really, no one else ever stood a chance after that."

"She sounds like an awesome girl."

"She is," Thomas says. "You remind me a lot of her. I think you two would really like each other."

"I can't imagine actually ever meeting her."

Thomas shrugs. "She's just a girl who likes dogs and music. Like you."

"I'm pretty sure that's where the comparison ends," I say.

"You might be surprised," he says. "Come with me to Nashville, and you can see for yourself."

"You're getting good at working that in," I say, trying not to smile.

He gives me a pointed look, his grin weakness-inducing. "I'm definitely getting better at it."

We drive for another fifteen minutes, mostly silent, as we wind through curvy country road after curvy country road. I'm thinking about Brownie again, and I just so do not have a good feeling about this.

"Do you think he would really make Brownie fight?" I ask, hearing the worry in my voice.

Thomas looks at me with a neutral expression, and I can tell he's trying not to let me see he's worried too.

Rowdy's signal light starts to blink, and up ahead we see him swing a left onto a gravel road. Once he's out of sight, Thomas makes the turn and flips off the headlights, pitching everything in front of us into darkness.

"Can you see?" I ask, panicking a little.

"Not much, but I don't want him to see us."

We roll slowly down the road, catching a glimpse every minute or so of the back of Rowdy's truck. It disappears over a knoll, and we slow down and wait a few moments before stopping at the top of it.

Below us, there's a small building surrounded by a couple of dozen cars. I lower my window and hear music blaring into the night with a big, heavy beat. Somewhere under the music's drone, I hear dogs barking.

"What is it?" I ask, my voice shaking out the question because I already know the answer.

"Probably what we were hoping it wasn't," he says.

"What are we going to do? We can't let him take Brownie in there."

"We'll leave the truck up here and walk down."

"And what do we do when we get there?"

"I haven't figured that part out yet."

"Are you sure this is safe?"

"No," he says. "But I think Brownie's going to need the cavalry. And we're the only one he's got."

He parks the truck on the side of the road, and we both jump out. We run the quarter mile or so to the building, stopping far enough away that we're still in the shadows if anyone looks our way.

The music is really loud with a deep bass, but I hear snarling inside the building, some cheering and clapping, followed by some booing.

"I think I'm going to be sick," I say.

"Don't think about it," Thomas says. "We're just here to get Brownie."

I spot Rowdy's empty truck parked close to the building. "Do you think he's already gone inside?"

"It looks like it. You stay here for a minute and let me get a closer look."

Fear clamps tight on my chest, for Thomas, for Brownie. "I don't think you should go inside."

"The tailgate's down on the truck, so he's already taken Brownie in. I'll be back, okay?"

But just as he starts toward the building, Rowdy opens one of the doors and drags Brownie out with a heavy link chain around his neck. Brownie is whimpering.

"You loser piece of shit," Rowdy roars at him. "Is that all you've got? Lay down on your belly and give up? I'll show you give up!"

He aims a kick at the center of Brownie's belly, knocking him to his side. Brownie cries out, trying to get up and run, just as Rowdy grabs the chain and jerks him back.

I scream at the top of my lungs. "Stop! Stop it!"

Thomas is tearing full out across the parking lot. He launches himself at Rowdy, taking him down in one crushing tackle.

Rowdy hollers like he's been stuck with a bayonet. Brownie tries to get up but falls over on his side and lies still.

I stumble to him, dropping to my knees while tears gush up and out of me, spilling down my face. "Brownie, it's me, Lila! Brownieeee!"

I smooth my hand across his side, trying to find any wounds he might have.

There's one under his belly, a rip of flesh. When I pull my hand back, my palm is full of blood.

"Thomas, he's hurt!" I yell, crying full out now.

But he's still rolling Rowdy across the gravel parking lot. I don't know if Rowdy has an ounce of muscle on him, but he's got enough fat to make it hard for Thomas to get out from under him.

I run over to them, grabbing Rowdy's oily T-shirt and yanking him backwards. The shirt rips, but he topples and flops onto his side.

Fury erupts inside me then, and I start kicking him, hard and anywhere I can land my foot. "You evil bastard!" I scream at him. "How could you do that to him?"

Thomas is up now and hauling me off Rowdy. "Lila, stop. Enough!"

I scream in frustration because I want to kick him until he's lying as still on this ground as Brownie. Behind my fury, tears pour from me, and I am suddenly sobbing so hard I can't breathe. "If he dies," I gasp, "there is going to be a special place in hell for you."

"As soon as I. . .get up from here. . .and get my gun out of the truck," he shouts, "I'm going to shoot the worthless mutt like I should've done a long time ago."

Whatever reprieve Thomas was prepared to grant him goes up in so much smoke, because he jumps him again, punching him in the face and then straddling him to hold him on the ground.

He leans in close to Rowdy's sweaty face, threatening him through clenched teeth. "We're going to leave here in thirty seconds with your dog, and if you so much as come within a mile of him or Lila ever again, I will personally kick your balls so high up your throat, they'll double as your tonsils. Are we clear?"

The heat of hatred coming out of Rowdy's eyes could melt asphalt, but he nods a small nod.

Thomas gets off him then, brushing his hands across his jeans as if he can't stand the feel of Rowdy on them. He backs away from him, then takes my hand, and we run back to Brownie.

He hasn't moved since I left him.

"I think he's in shock," I say, between sobs.

Thomas drops to his knees and lifts Brownie into his arms. "Come on, boy. Let's go get you some help."

We start back up the hill, trying to run, but Brownie is heavy and Thomas is trying not to jostle him too much. We're halfway back to the truck when

I hear a sound I almost recognize but not quite. When I realize what it is, I stop suddenly, knowing what's coming, even as I'm helpless to stop it.

"Thomas!" I cry out, just as the shot rings through the night.

I expect it to hit me, wait for the pain to ring out inside my body. Almost simultaneously, I see Brownie's body jolt once, and his scream tears open the darkness around us.

Thomas falls to his knees, and I am instantly terrified that he also has been hit. He tries to protect Brownie from the impact, landing on his left shoulder so that he takes the brunt of the fall.

And now I'm screaming, terror for them both cutting off my ability to breathe. I drop to my knees, see the gaping hole in Brownie's shoulder. Blood is pouring from it.

"Thomas! Are you okay?"

He groans and starts to get to his feet. "Yeah. You look after him. I'll be right back."

"Wait! You can't-"

He's already charging at Rowdy, who looks as if he's just been blinded by headlights. Even from here, I see the intent on Rowdy's face. He raises the gun, points it at Thomas. He fires, and I am instantly frozen with fear that it has hit him.

But the bullet misses, and Thomas keeps running. When he's almost on him, Rowdy drops the gun and turns, taking off in the opposite direction. Thomas jumps him in seconds, yanking him down. He pounds him with his fists until awareness slumps out of Rowdy, and he's lying face down in the dirt.

Thomas stumbles to the back of the truck and grabs the chain Rowdy had used on Brownie. He wraps Rowdy's wrists together with it and then links it to his ankles so that he's not going anywhere without help.

And then he's running back to us, half limping, his face stiff with pain.

He drops to the ground beside us, looking at Brownie's wound with the same fear in his eyes that I'm feeling.

"We've got to get him to a vet. Fast," he says. "Where's the closest place?"

"It's about ten miles from here," I say. "Will that be fast enough?"

"I don't know," he says, shaking his head. "We have to try."

He squats next to Brownie, sliding his arms under him and scooping him up like a baby. Brownie is motionless, and I am so scared for him that I can't force myself to move.

But Thomas is already carrying him to the truck. I run around him and open the back door. He slides him onto the seat and looks at me with this look that tells me how much he cares about what happens to Brownie.

"We can't let him die," I say, tears again streaming down my face.

"Get in," he says. "We don't have a minute to waste."

I slide in from his side, but instead of moving all the way to the other door, I stop in the middle. I want to be near Thomas. I need to feel his strength next to me. I wonder how I could ever have thought I didn't need him.

Because I do.

As he turns the truck around, gunning it down the narrow road, I slip my arm through his, and lay my head on his shoulder.

I need him.

♪

Books Six - Ten

Read the rest of the Nashville series!

About Inglath Cooper

About Inglath Cooper

RITA® Award-winning author Inglath Cooper was born in Virginia. She is a graduate of Virginia Tech with a degree in English. She fell in love with books as soon as she learned how to read. "My mom read to us before bed, and I think that's how I started to love stories. It was like a little mini-vacation we looked forward to every night before going to sleep. I think I eventually read most of the books in my elementary school library."

That love for books translated into a natural love for writing and a desire to create stories that other readers could get lost in, just as she had gotten lost in her favorite books. Her stories focus on the dynamics of relationships, those between a man and a woman, mother and daughter, sisters, friends. They most often take place in small Virginia towns very much like the one where she grew up and are peopled with characters who reflect those values and traditions.

"There's something about small-town life that's just part of who I am. I've had the desire to live in other places, wondered what it would be like to be a true Manhattanite, but the thing I know I would miss is the familiarity of faces everywhere I go. There's a lot to be said for going in the grocery store and seeing ten people you know!"

Inglath Cooper is an avid supporter of companion animal rescue and is a volunteer and donor for the Franklin County Humane Society. She and her family have fostered many dogs and cats that have gone on to be adopted by other families. "The rewards are endless. It's an eye-opening moment to realize that what one person throws away can fill another person's life with love and joy."

Follow Inglath on Facebook
at www.facebook.com/inglathcooperbooks

Nashville Books 6 - 10

More Books by Inglath Cooper

Swerve

The Heart That Breaks

My Italian Lover

Fences – Book Three – Smith Mountain Lake Series

Dragonfly Summer – Book Two – Smith Mountain Lake Series

Blue Wide Sky – Book One – Smith Mountain Lake Series

That Month in Tuscany

And Then You Loved Me

Down a Country Road

Good Guys Love Dogs

Truths and Roses

Nashville – Part Ten – Not Without You

Nashville – Book Nine – You, Me and a Palm Tree

Nashville – Book Eight – R U Serious

Nashville – Book Seven – Commit

Nashville – Book Six – Sweet Tea and Me

Nashville – Book Five – Amazed

Nashville – Book Four – Pleasure in the Rain

Nashville – Book Three – What We Feel

Nashville – Book Two – Hammer and a Song

Nashville – Book One – Ready to Reach

On Angel's Wings

A Gift of Grace

RITA® Award Winner John Riley's Girl

A Woman With Secrets

Unfinished Business

A Woman Like Annie

The Lost Daughter of Pigeon Hollow

A Year and a Day

Get in Touch With Inglath Cooper

Follow Inglath Cooper Books on Instagram.

POSTS IGTV SAVED TAGGED

Email: inglathcooper@gmail.com
Facebook – Inglath Cooper Books
Instagram – inglath.cooper.books
Pinterest – Inglath Cooper Books
Twitter – InglathCooper

Made in United States
North Haven, CT
22 March 2022

17423402R00321